# COLONYSIDE

## By Michael Mammay

COLONYSIDE
PLANETSIDE
SPACESIDE

incredible second outing from Michael Mammay, who has a truly bright future in the science fiction genre."                                        —Unseen Library

## Praise for *Planetside*

"A tough, authentic-feeling story that starts out fast and accelerates from there."
                    —Jack Campbell, author of *Ascendant*

"Not just for military SF fans—although military SF fans will love it—*Planetside* is an amazing debut novel, and I'm looking forward to what Mammay writes next."
                    —Tanya Huff, author of the Confederation and Peacekeeper series

"*Planetside* is a smart and fast-paced blend of mystery and boots-in-the-dirt military SF that reads like a high-speed collision between *Courage Under Fire* and *Heart of Darkness*."
                    —Marko Kloos, bestselling author of the Frontline series

"This was a brisk, entertaining novel . . . I was reminded a bit of some of John Scalzi's Old Man's War novels."                                    —SFFWorld

"Mammay capably writes Butler's gritty, old-school soldier's voice, and the story delivers enough intrigue and action for fans of military SF."
                                    —*Publishers Weekly*

"The book was an enjoyable read and would likely sit well with any fan of military SF looking for an action-thriller to browse while lying in the sun at the beach."
    —Chris Kluwe for *Lightspeed Magazine*

"In *Planetside,* Mammay mixes a brevity of prose with feeling of authenticity that would be remarkable in many experienced authors, let alone in a debut novel. Definitely the best military sci-fi debut I've come across in a while."
        —Gavin Smith, author of *Bastard Legion* and *Age of Scorpio*

# COLONYSIDE

## MICHAEL MAMMAY

HARPER Voyager
*An Imprint of HarperCollinsPublishers*

COLONYSIDE. Copyright © 2020 by Michael Mammay. All rights reserved. Printed in the United States of America. No part of this book may be used or reproduced in any manner whatsoever without written permission except in the case of brief quotations embodied in critical articles and reviews. For information, address Harper-Collins Publishers, 195 Broadway, New York, NY 10007.

First Harper Voyager mass market printing: January 2021

Print Edition ISBN: 978-0-06-298097-7
Digital Edition ISBN: 978-0-06-298098-4

*Cover design by Guido Caroti*
*Cover illustration by Sebastien Hue*

Harper Voyager and the Harper Voyager logo are trademarks of HarperCollins Publishers in the United States of America and other countries.

HarperCollins is a registered trademark of HarperCollins Publishers in the United States of America and other countries.

FIRST EDITION

20 21 22 23 24   QGM   10 9 8 7 6 5 4 3 2 1

*To the Readers of Planetside,*
*who made this book possible.*

# COLONYSIDE

# CHAPTER ONE

**'M NOT DEAD** yet.

That probably goes without saying, but it was definitely touch and go for a while. Omicron, the company I tussled with a couple years back . . . they don't like me much. Whatever. They can get in line with most of the rest of the galaxy. Assholes.

I spent nearly nine months in stasis. Nobody really knew what to do with a guy who had fired weapons of mass destruction for a second time, so I guess the government felt it best to keep me under sedation while they figured it out. I think what saved me is that the authorities were angrier at VPC and Omicron than they were at me. They might have revived me just to piss off those corporations. I'll take it. A win is a win, after all.

And I *did* win. The Cappans survived, and though I don't know their location now, I'm told that they're doing well. Plus, I got a giant settlement from Omicron that I'm not allowed to talk about because it came with an equally giant nondisclosure agreement. Suffice it to say that I never have to worry about money again.

So now I'm kind of into gardening. I've got almost half of a hectare planted, and I own ten, so I've got plenty of room to expand, once I clear it. Living where

I do, on Ridia Two, everyone has room to expand. The nearest city is three hundred kilometers away, which is just fine by me. It's quiet here, and quiet is good.

I'm not exactly hiding. I tried for a couple of months, but it was useless. The galaxy is too well connected, and someone always talks. The thing is, on Ridia nobody really cares. My neighbors know who I am, but they don't make a big deal about it. To them I'm just Carl. That works for me, because really, I don't want to discuss it. *Any* of it. I'm done with wars and corporations and really anything beyond the boundaries of my property. I'm not good at gardening yet, but I'm working at it. I grew way too many tomatoes and too much squash. But on the bright side, I've developed a killer vegetarian chili recipe. Like I said, a win is a win.

All I really wanted was for the galaxy to leave me alone.

It didn't.

**I WAS HEADING** back out to the garden after lunch when something tripped my perimeter alarm. Sure, I lived in the middle of nowhere, but that didn't mean I didn't take precautions. If anything, it made me *more* careful. Better safe than sorry. I slipped back into my cabin and got my rifle. That's another thing I liked about where I lived on Ridia: no laws against owning guns. I grabbed three magazines and hustled over to my security screen to check the cameras. Whoever it was, they had parked at the top of the dirt road that served as my driveway and were walking my way. It could have been one of my neighbors, but I doubted it. They didn't visit. Whoever it was, if they posed a threat, they probably wouldn't have been walking in the open when there were plenty of trees that could have masked their approach.

I couldn't get a good angle with the camera that far out—I'd need to fix that—so I took my rifle and went out to the front porch. The face still eluded me, since he was still a hundred meters out. Definitely a he, though. A big guy. I sighted through the scope of my rifle and upped the magnification.

No way.

Fucking Serata.

I laughed. I couldn't help myself. Of all the things I expected to see in my life, General Serata walking up my driveway in the middle of nowhere wasn't one of them. I lowered my rifle and waited.

When he got near enough, Serata gestured to my rifle. "Expecting company?"

"Not really." I held up the rifle to emphasize my point.

He'd traveled halfway across the galaxy to see me, and I wondered why but figured he'd get to it soon enough. I doubted it would be good news—I can't remember the last time Serata had given me good news—so I might as well put it off as long as possible.

"How'd you find me?"

"Come on, Carl. You think the powers that be would lose track of someone like you?"

"No," I said, "but the locals are pretty protective of me. They've run off reporters and corporate recruiters who wanted to find me on more than one occasion. Even law enforcement keeps an eye out."

"Yeah, well, as it turns out, you're not the only famous veteran in the galaxy."

I laughed. I had to admit, even though I knew he wouldn't have shown up without a reason—and that reason would almost certainly suck—it made me happy to see him. I'd been on the planet for around twenty months, and while I had local acquaintances, I didn't have anyone that I'd call an actual friend. That had always been hard for me. I had books, of course, and a galaxy's worth of video entertainment, but nothing compared to being around a friend.

Even when that friend tended to put my life in danger.

"Let's go inside. I could use a drink," he said.

"I don't keep liquor in the house."

"Really?" He looked at me like he didn't believe me.

"Yeah. Living alone, it seemed like a bad idea. I've actually given the stuff up."

He considered it, and I got the feeling he still didn't know if I was serious or not. "Is there some place *I* can get a drink? It's been a bitch of a trip."

"I bet. We can head up to Moop's. It's the only bar around."

"Can we talk there without being bothered?" He asked it casually, but there was clearly more behind it, lurking. I wasn't quite intrigued, but I had to admit, I wanted to know what brought him all that way. Okay, I guess that's a little intrigued.

"We can do about anything we want here without being bothered. That's what makes Ridia great," I said. "Plus, it's one in the afternoon. It will be empty."

He grunted. "It's five o'clock somewhere. Let's go."

I stowed my rifle inside, locked up, and fell in beside Serata. "It's a couple of kilometers. You driving?"

"They gave me a driver with the car."

"Fancy."

Serata and I made small talk for the short drive, avoiding the thing he'd obviously come to discuss until we reached Moop's. We entered the sturdy log building through a heavy wooden door, and I greeted the only person inside. "How's it going, Martha? Where's Moop?" Moop was Martha's husband, and they ran the establishment together. I have no idea why people called him Moop. On Ridia you didn't ask.

"He's out to get a part for one of the ovens that's been acting up. I reckon he'll be back in a bit. What'll you have?"

"Any good local whiskeys?" Serata asked.

Martha grabbed a bottle from the top shelf behind the bar. "This is the best we've got. Not much call for imports around here."

"That'll do." He looked at me. "You having anything?"

"Coffee. Thanks," I said.

We grabbed a table in the corner farthest from the bar and settled onto wooden benches across from each other.

"This is pretty good," said Serata, after taking a sip.

I didn't respond. I'd started running through possibilities in my mind. There were too many to account for, but my thoughts gravitated toward some sort of threat against me. After a minute or so it started to get awkward.

"So, I'll get to it," he said, after another sip.

"You mean you didn't spend three weeks in cryo just to come have a drink with me?" I asked.

"Two weeks," he said. "Fast ship."

"Must be important." A ship that fast wasn't cheap and probably wasn't civilian. He wouldn't have needed cryo for that length of time but would have needed it to survive the acceleration required. "I thought you were retired."

"Are any of us ever really retired?"

"I'm retired," I said.

"Are you?"

I let that sit. I didn't want to go down that path. If he wanted something, I was going to make him ask for it.

After a few seconds, he shrugged. "They called, I answered."

"Who? The military?"

"Among others," he said. "I'll get to that. Let me give you the bottom line up front. Some very important people want you to do a job."

I blew out the breath I'd been holding. He hadn't wasted much time. "Martha . . . can I get another whiskey over here? Better make it a double."

"I thought you gave it up," said Serata.

"The beauty of quitting is now I can have one, because I quit."

"So you hadn't really given it up."

"I had. I guess that's over now." That was a bit passive-aggressive of me but whatever.

"Sorry about that." He sounded like he meant it, but it wouldn't change anything about what he said next.

"Like you said, you've got a job to do." *He* had a job to do. But that didn't mean *I* did. He was going to give me a hard sell—I knew that—but I didn't have to buy. I didn't owe them anything.

"It's not bad. Have you heard of the colony Eccasis?"

"Can't say that I have," I said.

"It's new. Seven or eight years old. There hasn't been a lot of development because—"

"Because of the new laws limiting colonization. What do they call that law again? Oh yeah. The Butler Law."

"That's not important here."

"They call it the fucking Butler Law!"

Serata sat there, humoring me, waiting for my outburst to subside. "You good?"

"Why don't you start with who's behind the job? I

think that's probably a lot more important than the location."

"Officially? The request is from General Taki."

I nodded. Taki. Chief of all galactic forces. The highest-ranking soldier alive. "Unofficially?"

"The president. Though my guess is that she wasn't that involved. More like she was doing a favor for the person *really* behind it. A man named Zentas. Heard of him?"

"Rich guy? Yeah, I've heard of him."

"Reportedly the eighth richest man in the galaxy," said Serata.

"That's pretty fucking rich. What's he want with me?" What I *really* wanted to know was what it had to do with *Serata*. He didn't owe them anything. At least I didn't think he did.

"His daughter is missing."

"Sorry to hear that. But what's it got to do with *me*? I'm sure he can hire a fleet of detectives."

"Hear me out, okay?" His tone took on an edge, probably reacting to my somewhat flippant dismissal. "I wouldn't be here if it was that simple."

"No, I don't suppose you would." *And definitely not on a military ship.*

"Zentas is a bit of an odd bird. His daughter went missing on Eccasis, which, as I said, is a relatively new colony. It's just one major outpost at this point, and it has a long way to go before it's more than that."

"Any life on the planet?" I asked.

"A lot of it. Not intelligent, but complex, large, and dangerous. We've got a small military presence there."

I still wasn't sure what that had to do with me, but with the military there, I was starting to get an idea. "And that's where I come in?"

"Pretty much," said Serata. "Zentas's daughter disappeared on a mission that got violent. The military investigated it, but he's not satisfied with their work."

I started to respond but held it back. I didn't know what to say, and for some reason repeating "What the fuck does that have to do with me?" seemed like a bad idea. Serata wasn't my boss anymore, but he was still a lot bigger than me and he might not be above kicking my ass. "I'm confused," I said, finally.

Serata laughed. "I can understand that. For whatever reason, Zentas has it in his head that the military is covering something up. He knows who you are and thinks that you're the person who can cut through that and find the truth."

Martha brought my whiskey, and I took a sip while I waited for her to head back to the bar and out of earshot. The liquor burned just the right amount on the way down. "Okay."

"You're in?"

"No. Just agreeing with you that this isn't bad," I said, holding the whiskey up to the light.

"It's good," said Serata. "It's not Ferra Three, but it will definitely do."

"What is this guy thinking?" I asked. "What can I do that they haven't already done?"

"I don't know. Probably nothing. But guys like this, they're used to getting their way. He's probably got in his head that you'll stand up to the military and get the *real truth*. Nobody wants to tell him it won't help."

"I'll tell him," I said. "You have his number?"

Serata laughed again. "Or you could just go out there and look around. See what you find."

"You're serious? They really want me to do this?"

"Consider it a vacation."

"I'm *on* vacation. Permanently."

"Did I mention the part where the president herself is involved?"

"You did." *Shit.* "Who's the military commander on the ground?"

"A brigadier named Oxendine. I don't know her personally, but she's got a good reputation. A by-the-book type."

I shook my head and half laughed. "I'm sure she'd be really glad to see me."

"Look, Carl. The guy lost a daughter. Sure, his idea for you to look into it doesn't make much sense, but it's understandable, right?"

I took a sip of my drink and swirled it in my mouth. "Yeah. That part I get." It was a cheap tactic, of course. I'd lost my daughter in a military action on Cappa several years back, and Serata knew that I had a soft spot. Zentas probably knew it too. I'd forgive the president. She'd only know if someone briefed her. "You know this is a shitty thing to do, right?"

Serata had the decency to look embarrassed. He took a pull of his drink to cover it, and wisely kept quiet.

"How'd they get to you?"

"What do you mean?" He said it casually, but I detected a hint of something behind it. He knew exactly what I meant.

But I could play his game and voice it. "Why are you carrying their water?"

He took a drink and considered it. For show, mostly. He'd have thought this answer through before he got here. He'd have had to anticipate that I'd ask. "I almost didn't."

I didn't respond, giving him space to continue.

"I almost told them to get bent. But . . . I owe them.

Taki, specifically. They gave me a soft landing on my way out of the military. You know that. Well . . . maybe not soft, but they could have made it a lot worse."

I didn't have all the details on why he left, but I assumed it had to do with Cappa. It might have even been in consideration for their treatment of me after that fiasco, which had also been relatively soft. Notably, he didn't extend the "owe them" to me. If he had, I'd have probably told him to leave. But *of course* he didn't. He knew me better than that.

"What would my status be? You want me to put on a uniform again?"

"No uniform. You'd be a civilian aide to the president."

"That sounds like a made-up title."

"It probably is. There's no real definition of where it puts you, but it will open every door you need."

"Weapons?" I asked.

"Not necessary. It's a bio-dome, and the military has things under control."

I doubted that. If they did, they wouldn't need me. "I'll have to think about it."

"Really?"

*No. Not really.* I didn't want to do it, but I probably would. But fuck them. They didn't get to show up and expect me to jump at a moment's notice. They could wait for my answer. "Really."

"I can give you a couple of days," he said. "After that, we've got to look at other options."

"What's plan B?"

"There isn't one."

I didn't care, but—fuck, I did. Once Serata said *daughter*, he had me.

Manipulative bastard.

"A couple of days. Got it. Then what?"

"I brought your team with me," he said.

"I have a team?"

"You do. You've got a liaison at headquarters to report to and a team that will travel with you. Your contact at HQ is a colonel named Jack Timmons."

"No shit? They made Flak Jacket Timmons a colonel?"

"You know him?"

"A long time ago," I said. "He was a lieutenant in my unit when I was a major. Now he's a colonel. Damn, that makes me feel old."

"You *are* old. Why do they call him *Flak Jacket*?"

"No idea. I think someone just called him that one day and it stuck. I didn't really pay that much attention to the lieutenants. You know how it is."

"Sure. For your away team, the military assigned you a captain named Fader. Monique Fader."

"Haven't heard of her."

"I flew out with her. She's efficient. Smart too. She's got a bright future."

"Efficient. That's code for 'I'm not going to like her,' right?"

"You'll like her. She's very competent."

"The Mother knows I need all the competence I can get. She's here?"

"In orbit," he said. "And your personal security officer is here too. I handpicked him. McCann."

"No shit?" I broke into a smile, even though I was still pissed. Mac? I almost agreed to the mission right then.

"I figured it was the least I could do."

Right. And he also knew exactly the effect it would have on me. Say this much for Serata . . . he was good at what he did. Still a manipulative bastard, but once you commit to something, you might as well be good at it.

"Martha, let me buy the rest of that bottle and take it home." I turned back to Serata. "Two days. I'll let you know."


**I TRIED TO** talk myself out of it. I really did. I made a list of all the reasons I shouldn't do it—a list that far outnumbered the two reasons I had on the other side of the ledger.

Serata at least had the decency to act surprised when I met him at Moop's a day and a half later. "You're going to do it?"

"Do I have a choice? His daughter is missing, and if I said no, it would eat at me forever. I'm not going to find her. But at least I can say I tried. I can be ready to leave in four days."

"Four days?"

"Nonnegotiable." I had a reason, but I wasn't sharing it with Serata. I'd do the mission, but I wanted to put in some of my own fail-safes.

"Understood. You want Mac to come down, or you want to meet him on the ship?"

I smiled despite myself. "On the ship will do. I need you to do one more thing. I want a computer tech with me. If I'm investigating them from the outside, I don't want to have to rely on the military for everything."

"You have someone in mind?"

"I do. A woman named Ganos. A freelancer on Talca. I don't care what she costs. I want her."

"As it so happens, I don't care what it costs either," he said. "It's not coming out of my pocket. I'll make it happen."

Even though he was screwing me over, I still loved Serata. He spoke without any doubt that he could get Ganos. And he was probably right. After all, he convinced me. How much harder could she be? "You going to hang around here?"

Serata downed the last of his drink. "I'm not. I'll leave my ship here for you, but I'm heading back as soon as I can. I told them I'd do my best to get you on board. That's where my part in this ends."

I polished off my drink and stood up. Once Serata joined me, I shook his hand. "Wish me luck."

"You know I don't believe in luck."

"I know," I said. "I don't either. Hey, Martha?"

"What can I do for you, Carl?" the proprietress asked.

"Can you special order me two cases of Ferra Three whiskey? I need them here in three days. I don't care what it costs." I'd find a way to put it on Serata's tab.

"I can try. If they have it anywhere on the planet, I'll get it for you."

"Thanks. You're the best."

# CHAPTER TWO

**I** **HAD ONE REASON** for demanding four days from Serata. Well . . . two if you count just wanting to make them wait. The other reason was that I wanted to contact my associates, and the system I had set up let me send messages only during a specific thirty-second window each week. That sounds ridiculous, but it provided an added layer of security for both sides.

Until my appointed time, though, I had very little to do. I closed up my house, packed, and tried to give away what I could of my produce and other perishables. And picked up my whiskey of course. At home, I did some initial research on Eccasis and sent long notes to my family. We still weren't close, but my son and I were making strides. We'd become cordial enough to exchange correspondence every month or so, and I'd be in stasis for a while. I wrote to my granddaughter, too. We'd never met in person, and I didn't really know what to say to a six-year old, but I told her I was taking a trip and talked about what it was like to be in space.

On the third day, I punched a twelve-digit code into my house system and let it scan my retina. An invisible door in the floor slid open, and I climbed down a metal ladder into the hidden basement. I'd brought high-priced contractors in from off planet to build it and had them keep it off the plans. Inside the almost-sterile room, I went through three more authentications to get my computer up and functional. It didn't connect to anything in the house or any network on the planet. It got data by underground fiber connected directly to a hidden satellite dish on another part of my property. The dish itself was also underground, and the door that hid it only opened for that same thirty second window each week, always at night.

It sounds paranoid because it *was*. But I had the money, and even if it exceeded my requirements, it was *really* cool. The people at the other end of the connection didn't take chances either. Strictly speaking, I didn't know them. No names, anyway. This time I asked them for a favor. Serata had said no weapons and that the military had things under control, but I'd been enough places where they hadn't, so I preferred to have my own equipment anyway. Since half the galaxy hated me and I didn't trust the government to always have my best interests at heart, I wanted my own options available. Just in case. I had no idea how the folks on the other end would make it happen, but I'd learned not to worry about things like that. They had resources. They'd find a way.

With that accomplished, I had a driver pick me up and chauffeur me the three hundred kilometers to the nearest shuttle, and from there I caught a ride up to the orbital space station where my real ride waited. The XT-57—the fastest transport ship in the military—was still ugly. It didn't help that the last time I'd been on one I'd been headed to Cappa. Not exactly a fond memory. Captain Fader must have gotten a report of my arrival, because she timed her exit from the ship perfectly to meet me at the bottom of the stairs. She snapped a crisp salute, and I waved it away with a sloppy one of my own.

"I'm a civilian now. You don't need to do that," I said.

"Yes, sir." Her starched duty fatigues had knife-edge creases that made me wonder if she had to pry the legs and sleeves apart to get into them, and she had just a light touch of makeup on her dark skin. Everything about her screamed "professional soldier."

She probably wasn't going to like me.

"You can call me Carl."

"I'd prefer not to do that, sir." Her face didn't crack even a little bit. Dead serious. She *definitely* wasn't going to like me.

"Well, *Colonel* isn't going to work for me. What do you suggest?" I asked.

"I could call you Mr. Butler, if you preferred."

As far as I knew, nobody had ever called me Mr. Butler. Maybe an uninformed banker somewhere. "How about we just stick to *sir* then?"

"Yes, sir."

"Can I call you Monique?"

"I'd prefer if you didn't, sir."

So much for getting off on the right foot. "Okay. Captain Fader it is. Did my stuff make it?" My bags traveled separately from the passenger car that brought me over from the shuttle.

"Yes, sir. They're stowed on board. I took the liberty of securing your whiskey for travel. I didn't know your preference for the trip, so I kept out one bottle in case you wanted it."

"Thanks. I'll probably save it until we reach the other end." I appreciated that she didn't lecture me about alcohol on an official mission. I could live with her being a stickler for professionalism as long as she didn't expect me to follow all the rules too closely. She was a spy, of course. Someone high up had sent her to keep tabs on me. But that was inevitable, so it didn't bother me. Better to know up front than wonder about it. I decided to keep an open mind, despite my initial impression.

"Hey, sir!" Mac stood at the top of the stairs, a huge grin on his face. I stepped past Fader and bounded up the steps, gripping his hand and pulling him in for a half hug. I held it a little too long.

"Damn, it's good to see you," I said. It had been too long. We said we were going to keep in touch, but like with everyone else in my life, I hadn't made the effort. I meant to. I just never did.

"You too, sir."

"How'd you get suckered into this gig?"

He laughed. "Come on, sir. You know I couldn't pass this up. You should have seen my commander's face when she got a request for my service directly from the Chief of Staff's office. She wanted to know what it was about, and I played it off like I get summoned by the highest authority in the military every day. Everybody got a kick out of it."

I thought about asking him to call me Carl too, like I had with Fader, but he would have just busted my balls about it. It was different with people you knew when you were both serving. "What have you been up to?"

"Back at the desk job, sir."

"Yeah, you look like you've been slacking off." He didn't. The short man hadn't aged a day, and if anything, his arms had gotten bigger. He looked like he could punch a hole through the hull of the ship.

"You know me. Once a month at the gym, whether I need it or not."

I snorted. "Yeah. Right. You find a woman who would tolerate your ass enough to settle down?"

"I had a girl for a couple of years. We split up about

six months ago. It was mutual, mostly. Just not on the same page. How about you, sir? I heard about you and your wife splitting a few years back."

"We did. Nobody since then. Just haven't found the interest. I've mostly been a hermit."

"Ah . . . sorry to hear that, sir. You've got to get out and about."

"Well, here I am, headed to one of the great garden spots of the galaxy. You know anything about Eccasis?"

"Not much, sir. I signed on without bothering to look. Then I was busy trying to get my stuff stored and my transportation set to meet the general for the trip out here. I got the basics. Jungle, mostly. A small colony. Threat is mostly only outside the gates—a lot of indigenous flora and fauna—so we should be safe as long as we stay inside."

"I have no intention of going out in the jungle, that's for sure. But there are a couple of terrorist groups active in the colony itself, so I'm glad you're along."

Mac slapped one of his massive arms with his hand. "Point me at them."

# CHAPTER THREE

SEVEN WEEKS LATER I got my first view of Eccasis from space, all green and blue and gorgeous around the equator, brown and white and barren around the poles. I'd been over the statistics for the planet:

- Gravity: 1.04 standard
- Standard hours per day: 25.1
- Average seasonal temperature: 33°C
- Average humidity: 79%

The latter would have been miserable if we planned to be outside. Human life on Eccasis resided in protective domes and would for the foreseeable future, until microbiologists and other assorted scientists created vaccines for all the local pathogens. In the past, humans would have eliminated those things during the early stages of colonization, but the laws had changed.

Fader had all that data and more ready for me when I woke up from cryo. She'd gotten the crew to bring her out a full day before me and had used that time to update and collate information. She had loaded everything I could possibly want to know—and then some—into my device, and had my favorite post-cryo meal of biscuits and gravy ready when I zoned in. Serata was right when he called her efficient.

She waited until I was reveling in my gravy bliss before she brought up business. "Whenever you're ready, sir, I'd like to update you on the mission. Have you read the military report already?"

"I have. It seems pretty thorough." I didn't add that it seemed *so* thorough that I didn't see what I could add to it.

"Did you have any questions, sir?"

"One," I said. "The missing person is listed as Xyla Redstone, but I didn't see mention of any reason for her last name to be different from Zentas. Was she in some religious order where they name change with marriage?" There were five other missing persons as well, but Redstone . . . Zentas . . . was the mission.

"No, sir. Xyla Zentas changed her name to distance herself from her father. They had a somewhat public falling out a couple years ago."

"Was it because he named her Xyla Zentas? Who does that to a kid?"

Fader didn't crack a smile. Tough audience. "I can dig further to try to find the source of their issues if you want, sir."

"Maybe look into why, if they've had a falling out, she still works for her father's company." I gestured to the chair bolted to the floor on the opposite side of my small table. "Have a seat."

She slid neatly into the chair without breaking eye contact. "I had the same question, sir. I couldn't find any direct sources, but one gossip column quoted an unnamed acquaintance as saying that as a xenobiologist, she was focused on the science, and Eccasis was too good to pass up."

I'm not going to lie: Fader knowing that impressed me. "It's interesting that Zentas is behind us coming out here, given his estrangement from his daughter. But I get it. It's his kid, regardless of whatever might have come between them."

"Yes, sir."

I got the feeling that Fader wanted more from me, so I decided to flip it around and let her give me ideas without coming out and saying I didn't have any. "Did anything jump out at *you* in the report?"

Fader didn't hesitate. "The report seems to have focused on the mission and ignored her personal life."

"She disappeared on a mission outside the dome. That seems pretty clear. I don't know what her personal life matters in that."

"It probably doesn't, sir. But I wouldn't mind seeing her phone records, emails, and any record of what they found in her quarters. As you said before, the military report is thorough. But maybe there's something in those records that would show a potential motive, or maybe someone who knows her well and might have more information."

Interesting. Part of me thought she'd seen too many detective holos. Another part of me was even further impressed. I'd naturally focused on the military stuff—the mission—and hadn't thought to look at other aspects. Even if we didn't find anything, it would let me show that I'd gone beyond what the military did. I'd been a soldier. I didn't know the first thing about being a detective. Maybe I needed to think about that. It also confirmed Serata's assessment of Fader as efficient. "That's a good idea. Requisition those records once we land."

To her credit, she didn't let satisfaction show on her face, as if she expected to be right. "Yes, sir. If you're

open to it, sir, it would help if I knew your initial plan after debarkation so I can anticipate and get ahead of your
requirements."

I didn't usually like to tip my hand to people I didn't
know very well, but she'd earned it. "Sure. I'm going to
go talk to the military command and ask them about the
report. It's thorough, but I want to discuss it and see what
kind of vibe I get from them about it. Serata told me that
Zentas suspected a cover-up, so I have to at least look
into that. I'll talk to the investigating officer, assess their
competence, that kind of thing. It will help me know how
much to trust their work and give us an idea of how much
of it we want to check behind."

"Very good, sir. I'll let them know you're coming."
She sat there, as if waiting for more. That habit was going
to get annoying.

"Anything else?" I asked.

"Yes, sir. I have my initial report that I owe back to
headquarters ready, if you want to review it before I hit
send."

"You . . . what? You want me to *review* it?" That was
new. She might have been a spy, but she wasn't a very
good one.

"I have to report on the mission, sir. You know that.
I figure that if I don't show you, you're going to wonder
what I wrote, which could then make you question my
loyalty. It seemed best to avoid that."

"Your bosses are okay with that?" I asked.

"Sir, my orders are to assist you in any way possible
and send regular reports on our progress. All other aspects were left to my discretion."

She said *our* progress. I liked that. I liked her. I still
didn't fully trust her yet—that's normal with people I
just met—but I read people pretty well, and she'd made

a good start. Sure, it could have been a ruse on her part. She could show me one report and then send another. But probably not. "Thanks for the offer. I don't need to see it since nothing has happened other than routine space travel. But I'd like to discuss future reports when the time comes, if you're open to that."

"I am, sir. Is there anything else?"

"When will Mac be up?"

"The doctor is bringing him out of stasis now, sir. It should only be a couple of hours until he's available."

"Sounds good. Thanks for your work."

"Roger that, sir."

**DEBARKATION ON ECCASIS** didn't endear the place to me. We landed in an underground hangar and had to wait fifteen minutes for a sterile vehicle to seal to our ship, slowly traverse the three or four hundred meters to the hatch, and then wait while it sealed to that. Two receiving parties waited for us. A tall, dark-skinned male captain waited on one side of the doorway and a tan-skinned woman who would have seemed tall if not for the presence of the captain waited on the other, with a shorter man, who I marked as a subordinate, standing just back from her. Fader hurried ahead of Mac and I to talk to them. The three of them talked, hands waving and voices increasing in volume, until finally the tall captain threw his hands up and stomped off.

"What was that about?" I asked Fader, when she came back to brief me.

"Both the governor and the military sent welcome parties, sir. Sorry about the confusion."

"Don't apologize. It isn't your fault. You'd think they'd have coordinated."

"I got the feeling that they both knew the other would be there and couldn't agree on the protocol."

That seemed . . . odd. "I assume from the captain's reaction that you chose the governor?"

"Yes, sir. They clearly had the better case."

I wanted to press her on that, but I didn't see a way to do that without appearing to question her judgment. I'd have probably defaulted to the military. In the end, it didn't matter. Even though we had all the authority in the galaxy behind us, we were guests, and I'm not much for causing problems over routine things—especially when I might need to push hard later. "Lead on."

Fader checked her device. "Sir, I have an updated arrival time for Ms. Ganos. She'll be here in approximately eighteen hours."

I smiled. I hadn't seen Ganos since my time on Talca 4, and I'd been happy when Serata messaged me confirming that she'd agreed to come. Part of me hadn't been sure. I'd put her into a precarious spot on our last operation together, though I suppose Ganos would say that nobody put her anywhere she didn't want to be. Either way, I needed her. She could do things with computers that I couldn't—that most people couldn't. I didn't know yet how that would help on the mission, but it could never hurt. I hoped that she charged whoever was paying for this an exorbitant fee.

The civilian woman introduced herself as Cora Davidson, the governor's aide, and she led us to an electric cart. We rode a freight elevator up about six or eight stories and emerged into the light. It initially seemed like open air, but when I looked closely, I could make out the clear dome high overhead, but only because I expected it to be there. It didn't feel like being inside—it wasn't meant to. It helped psychologically over the long term to believe you weren't confined. The illusion was limited, of course. From my studies and the files Fader had shared, I knew the entire dome measured barely two kilometers in diameter. Underground trams connected it to four smaller residential domes as well. Beyond those, around a hundred uninhabited domes served various purposes: Power generation, food production, and all the other functions a colony of thirty thousand needed to survive. People worked shifts at those but returned to the residential domes when they weren't working.

After my eyes adjusted, I realized that it was darker than it should be, given that we'd landed at about two in the afternoon and we'd seen no clouds on the way in. The dome, again. Fader had briefed me that it could filter light to the necessary level, and I'm sure there was some optimum formula for mental well-being measured against power preservation. People bustled around us, about half in military uniform, the other half in utilitarian civvies like me. The uniformed types were heavy on ground-force uniforms, light on air and space, but I was getting a limited sample from one small slice of the base. We passed a few other passenger carts and several larger work vehicles, but most of the traffic traveled on foot. I could have walked, but I didn't mind having the ride.

Our first stop was my quarters, and Mac insisted that he go in first. He almost had to sprint to get in front of Fader, who had had her own designs. I found them both ridiculous. Did they think someone was lurking in the VIP quarters waiting to murder me?

"It's all clear, sir," said Mac. "You're not going to believe this place."

"Why? What is it?" I asked.

"Just check it out."

Fader led me into the most ostentatious room I'd ever

seen on a military installation. Everything looked brand new, right down to the marble floor and polished wood table that could seat ten.

Mac was right. I didn't believe it.

"There's more," said Mac. Again, he was right. Much more. Four full rooms, not overly large, owing to space constraints on the base, but way bigger than they needed to be. I had a bedroom; the large entry room, which doubled as a sitting room with several comfortable chairs and two sofas; a full kitchen and dining area; and an office.

"This is ludicrous," I said.

"This is the governor's guest quarters, reserved for visiting dignitaries," said Davidson.

Dignitary. Ha. Whatever they wanted to call me, I didn't need this suite. I gestured around me at the opulence. "Is there anything . . . less?"

"The governor was quite insistent," said Davidson.

I took her tone to mean that nobody wanted to question the governor, and I sighed. "Okay."

"He has a dinner scheduled for you tomorrow night," continued Davidson. "He thought you might want to rest from your trip this evening."

"Very thoughtful. Can you set up a meeting with the base commander some time before the dinner?" I didn't want to meet the civilian leaders without having a chance to talk to the military boss.

"I'm afraid I can't. I work out of the governor's office. But I'll make sure that Captain Fader has the right contact information."

That seemed a bit off. As a *dignitary*, I'd have expected her to help me, but from her tone, I took it that the two-reception-party issue might go a little deeper. But I simply said, "Thank you, Ms. Davidson," and saw her to the door.

After she left, Fader jumped into action and promised to arrange a meeting with the military commander and a half dozen other things she thought I needed to do and be back to brief me in two hours. She and Mac both had small rooms right near mine, probably designed for the staff of whoever belonged in this palace. I played the old-man card and told her that I needed some rest, which helped me negotiate her down to just sending me a schedule on my device and meeting me the next day before Ganos arrived.

**I SLEPT OKAY** for being in a new place, though my bladder thought it was in a different time zone, so I had to stumble through my mansion to find the bathroom three times during the night. It never got totally dark outside, as the dome glowed faintly at night, acting as a giant streetlight, but my apartment had blackout shades—hence the stumbling. I met Mac outside my door the next morning while Fader was off getting everything arranged for the day, and the two of us got an early breakfast at a facility that seated about two thousand. The Eccasis welcome packet on my device told me it was one of five dining halls on base. I asked another diner if anybody ate at home, and he told me that they could but that supplies were hard to come by for individuals, so most people used the communal facilities most days.

As we walked to meet Ganos, I familiarized myself with the layout of the station. One half (the half where we'd had breakfast) mostly contained living space and the other half—the half with the hangar—workspace. A few pods in the workspace looked like senior official housing, mixed in with the office buildings so they'd be close to work. I'd always appreciated the perk of location.

We linked up with Fader, who had secured a cart, and met Ganos as she reached the clean room after debarking her ship. Maria Ganos was a former soldier who had come to work with me back when I'd worked security at VPC, the corporation that employed me before they sold me out back on Talca 4. She'd helped me with my investigation into Omicron before they kidnapped me and tried to send me to my death. She was also a first-rate hacker.

She bounced into the clean room like she owned it, her hair cut finger-length short, half dyed pink, the other half green. She wore a brown leather jacket over a white tank top. "Okay, I'm here. We can start now."

"It's good to see you, Ganos," I said.

"I had them ship my stuff directly to my room," she said, ignoring my greeting.

"Where's your room?"

She waved in a random direction. "I don't know. Not far. Maybe a third of a kilometer."

"We'll get that fixed," I said. "Get you moved over by us."

She snorted. "No way. I negotiated my place when they contracted me to come out here."

"It might help with the work if we all stayed near each other," I offered.

She rolled her eyes. "Hey, sir, you remember that time where you got me chased by an interplanetary hit team? Yeah. Good times." She said it as a joke, but her words had a bite to them. She was pissed about something. It might have just been a bad flight, but it seemed like more. I'd need to talk to her, but not here in front of the others.

"We can see about getting you a room," I said, trying one more time.

"I'm good where I'm at, sir."

I hesitated briefly before speaking. I wanted her closer, but I didn't want to further anger her. "If you're sure."

"I am."

Fader stepped forward, physically putting herself into the conversation. "Sir, I can arrange—"

"I didn't ask you," said Ganos.

"I just think—"

"I don't really care," Ganos said, cutting Fader off, but the captain wasn't easily intimidated.

"You're not in charge here," said Fader. "If the colonel wants you nearby, you'll move."

Ganos smirked as she listened. "I understand that it disturbs the stick you have up your ass, but I'm not moving. I'm here to do a job, and that job has requirements that I negotiated ahead of time. I brought a lot of equipment, and I need space to set it up. More important, I need access to networks, and I put myself in the ideal spot to accommodate that."

Fader started to respond, but Ganos blew through her.

"And before you ask, no, I'm not going to explain, partly because I'm the expert and you need to trust that, but also because I don't want to. Call it plausible deniability, if that helps you swallow it."

Fader's dark skin didn't show a blush, but I'd have bet good money that she could feel the heat in her cheeks, even though the expression on her face barely changed. I should have stepped in, but I'd been at a loss for words. I needed bad blood between members of my team about as much as I needed a third foot. They were the only people on the planet I could trust. Too late, I tried to mend the fences a little. "I trust your judgment, Ganos."

Fader glared at me but quickly wiped the expression off her face.

Ganos glared at me too, and that look lingered. Yep.

Definitely pissed. I'd talk to her, but it would have to wait, since I had a ten-o'clock meeting with the military commander.

"Just let us know if you need anything."


**THE TWO-STORY MILITARY** building had only a single step up to the double doors of the first-floor entry. Wooden doors. There was a lot of wood everywhere on the base. It made sense. They'd had to clear a bunch of trees to build it, and all that wood had to go somewhere. A lieutenant met us at the door and escorted us down the hall to the corner office to meet Brigadier General Oxendine. I'd done my research on her. We'd served in some of the same places, though not at the same times. She'd done all the hard jobs and, as Serata told me, had a reputation as a straight shooter who didn't cut corners and didn't take any shit.

"Colonel Butler, it's good to meet you." She stood and came out from behind her polished wood desk when I arrived. She had dark hair, bronze skin, and was a couple centimeters shorter than me.

"Good to meet you, too, ma'am. Please, call me Carl."

"I will. Thanks, Carl. And since you're a civilian now, feel free to call me Ox." I couldn't tell if she emphasized the word civilian, or if it was just my imagination. Perhaps she wanted to show me who was in charge. I let it slide.

"Thanks, Ox." It felt weird coming off my tongue. Something in me rebelled against calling a general by a nickname. "I guess you know why I'm here."

She shook my hand with a firm grip. "I do. Have a seat. Can I get you a coffee?"

"No, thanks. I've got a dinner with the governor tonight and a lot to do before that. I don't want to take up too much of your time."

She grunted. "The governor. Have fun with that."

"I take it you won't be joining us?"

"At the governor's? Hah. Not likely. The only ceremony he'd invite me to is my own court-martial, if he could arrange it."

That settled it. The beef between the governor's office and the military went right to the top. I decided to dig a little on that. "You two don't get along?"

"We . . . see the mission differently from one another."

"How so?" I wasn't sure I approved of her attitude. As the military leader, it was her job to make it work. One could say the same for the governor, but I'd never been a governor, so I cut him more slack.

"My job is to secure the facilities and the work teams to help them clear more ground as quickly and effectively as possible. Get more infrastructure in so we can continue to expand within the bounds of the new laws. Standard colony stuff. You understand."

"Of course," I said.

"Governor Patinchak is a political appointee. No experience. Despite that, he revels in his role as the civilian oversight of the military. He likes to take every opportunity to remind us of our obligations while ignoring his own. Bluntly, he sees us as the bad guys, and looks to make everything difficult. Even routine things that should be non-confrontational."

"I suppose some of that's my fault. I didn't make the military exactly look like the good guys on Cappa."

She didn't agree with me, but she didn't *disagree*, either. "He's slow. He takes his time with every decision, and he flip-flops depending on who has been in his ear most recently. One day he's influenced by the 'greenies'—

the eco-protectionists—and drags his feet on approval
for new sites. The next day the corporations have talked
to him and he's full speed ahead."

"You don't agree with his politics?" I could sense her
frustration, but it was probably only coming out now
because she couldn't share these opinions with her subordinates. That was one of the bad parts of command—
nobody to vent to.

"I don't give a shit about his politics one way or the
other," she said. "I just want him to be predictable. I've
got a job to do, and his inconsistency makes it harder.
We don't answer to the same people, but *my* boss isn't
keen on excuses."

"I see. That's got to be tough." It was never fun working with an incompetent, especially when they had authority. I tried to keep an open mind. A lot of people
thought others had faults when both sides had their flaws.
I believed Oxendine, but I needed to wait and see. Of
course, I wasn't telling her that. Oxendine accepting me
as part of the military team could only help my mission.
"Do you know anything about his aide, Davidson?"

"She's a snake. She's more dangerous than the governor, because she's competent. She's definitely not a
'greenie,' though. If anything, she's against them."

"That's good info. Thanks. Anything else I should
know about this place before I meet the governor?"

"The eco-protectionists are a problem," she said.
"There's a good chance that they have allies on the governor's staff. That makes it hard to share information,
because the governor's office isn't exactly strict with how
they handle classified material."

"How much classified stuff *is there*? It's a colony with
no intelligent life."

"Quite a bit. For a community of thirty thousand,

we've got an awful lot of people who aren't on the same agenda. And I'm not just talking about politics. We've had attacks, bombings . . . a kidnapping of a key scientist in one case."

"They kidnapped someone?"

"Murdered, really. We found the body outside the dome without a protective suit."

"Aren't there cameras on all the exits?"

"They hacked the cameras. The one guy we did find that was connected in any way to the event didn't know anything—just a maintenance worker who took a bribe. Anyway, those are *my* problems. Let's talk about why *you're* here."

I had more questions about the murder—after all, if someone could murder one scientist, they could murder another—but Oxendine had made it clear that she was finished with the topic, so I moved on. "Right," I said. "Xyla Redstone, formerly Xyla Zentas. Changed her name to get out from the shadow of her father. Missing for about three months, presumed dead."

"She's dead," said Oxendine. "The report says missing because we haven't recovered the body. We probably won't. There's a *lot* of jungle out there, and a lot of things that will dispose of a corpse."

"What kinds of things?" I had an idea from my briefing, but an expert on the ground always knew more.

"Animals. Plants. Insects. Bacteria. Probably some other things that I don't even know about or we haven't discovered yet. If you can dream up something horrible, we've got it."

"I'm sure you debriefed everyone who was with her."

"You've seen the report. I've looked it over myself. It's accurate. Five people disappeared with her—everybody on her team. Two other teams were in the area, but by the time they realized nobody was on the other end of the comm line . . . it was too late." She spoke confidently. She knew the event, and she believed what she was telling me.

Since she was being straight with me, I decided to reciprocate. "You know why I'm here. Why I'm *really* here."

"Political games?" She seemed more resigned than angry.

"Of course. But you need to know specifically *what* game. Drake Zentas thinks that the military covered things up."

She stared at me for a few seconds, then laughed. "What the fuck would we even cover up? She went into the jungle and now nobody can find her or her team. We weren't even *there*."

"I noticed that in the report. Why didn't you secure the away team?" I kept my voice neutral. I didn't want her to read my question as an accusation.

"We secure them for government-approved missions, but the governor has allowed the development companies to make their own rules. They have their own agendas and their own security teams, and the governor basically abdicates any oversight. One of those little disagreements we have."

The lack of oversight was interesting, but I latched on to the fact that the military hadn't had anything to do with the mission. Oxendine was right. If they weren't involved, what motive could they possibly have for a cover-up? I didn't want to bias my thinking this early, but I couldn't help but think of it as a *really* good alibi. But it led to another question: "If you weren't part of the mission, why did you get tagged with the investigation?"

"Convenient, isn't it?" she said. "The governor is in

charge, right up until the point where something goes wrong and my boss wants answers."

The military hadn't been part of the mission, but Zentas suspected a cover-up. Those two things didn't jibe. Did he think the investigation itself was flawed? I could look into that. For now, I had the commander, and it seemed like a waste not to ask more questions. "Six people disappearing—I get that it's dangerous, but how common is that? I assume they were armed."

"They were. Disappearances aren't common, but they're not unprecedented. Last year we had twenty-three deaths and almost three hundred significant injuries out-side of domes. On a civilian mission with contract secu-rity, I can't speak to their training or ability." Oxendine had a cut cigar sitting on her desk, unburned, and she glanced at it, but seemed to reject the thought of picking it up, instead refocusing her gaze on me.

I could investigate that, too. Contract security teams recruited from wherever they could, which often in-cluded military washouts or people who couldn't even get in. It wouldn't take much to make me believe one of them had failed on a mission. But again, I couldn't jump to conclusions.

"This has been helpful, Ox. I won't take up any more of your time. I'll route any mundane requests through your Ops center and inform you personally if I think it's something significant. Sound good?"

"Absolutely. If I can help going forward, don't hesitate to bring me in."

"Will do."

"And enjoy your dinner with the governor." She smirked.

"Right."

# CHAPTER FOUR

WE RODE TO the governor's residence in relative style, Mac driving us in an electric cart he had procured from somewhere. I appreciated it, because it was almost a kilometer away, and my robot foot was acting up a bit. Plus, we'd probably be standing around a lot at the reception–Fader had informed me that it was heavy hors d'oeuvres, not a dinner. She expected about forty attendees, which seemed like a lot for a small colony. I didn't mind. The guest list might provide us some insight into the pecking order on Eccasis. Mac and Fader wore their dress uniforms. I opted for my best work suit from when I was back at VPC, which was a touch loose because my time on Ridia had taken a couple kilos off me. Ganos had declined my invitation, which reminded me that I needed to talk to her, and soon.

The governor's residence—mansion, really—didn't have its own dome, but it didn't exactly share a dome with the rest of the colony either. Mac drove our cart through a short, wide tunnel that created the illusion of being part of the same community while still limiting access. From a security perspective, the tunnel could be shut down in an emergency, which would be useful to those charged with protecting the governor.

A small crowd of maybe twenty-five or so protesters had gathered on the steps. Two uniformed soldiers with batons stood in front of them, possibly holding them back, though the group didn't appear to be straining to get free. It looked as if the guards and the group had a prearranged deal where they'd all stand there and pretend to be in conflict without any of the actual drama. When I pulled up, someone in the crowd shouted my name. Boos followed, then a few shouts, which escalated to cursing before I made it to the steps. They started to inch forward, pushing toward me, but the two soldiers jumped into action, holding them back with only a modicum of effort. I ignored the crowd. I'd been protested by bigger and more boisterous groups. I had standards.

Two additional guards at the top of the stairs—these ones armed—ignored the commotion and checked Fader's and my identities with a thumb pad. Mac went to park the cart and would catch up to us inside. I didn't need him for something like this, but if he had to attend, he might as well eat the governor's fancy food. Fader positioned herself half a step behind me to my left as we walked through the double doors. Heads turned throughout the large entryway, though conversations continued, perhaps a little hushed. They probably didn't get new people very often, and I'd certainly qualify as a novelty, even if people didn't know my history. Most of them probably did. The natural flow of things carried us into a large room with a polished wood floor. If I didn't know better, I'd have called it a ballroom. But nobody held balls on a colony like Eccasis. At least I hoped not.

A tall, light-skinned man with dark hair and a strong chin approached us, spreading his arms slightly at his hips in a weird but welcoming gesture. "Colonel

Butler! I'm Governor Patinchak. So good of you to join us tonight."

"Please, call me Carl." I held out my hand for him to shake it and he took it in both hands, squeezing slightly. It surprised me a little that he was younger than me—maybe forty. I'd seen a picture, but in person it became much more apparent.

"It's an honor to have you here on Eccasis. I trust that everything has been acceptable so far?"

"More than acceptable. The accommodations are first-rate. Thank you, Governor." I didn't think telling him that I found my quarters ridiculous would get us off to a good start.

"Only the best for our most important guest." From anyone else the continuous flattery would have been obsequious, but the governor sounded so sincere that somehow it worked. "I'm going to leave you for a bit so that my guests don't feel neglected, but I'd like to make time to talk privately for a few moments later in the evening."

"Of course, Governor."

Fader caught my attention as he moved away. "Sir, a few key people you should know. The woman over there in the blue." She gestured vaguely, not enough to where anyone could tell who she indicated. "That's Martha Stroud, head of the Eccasis mission for Caliber, which is—"

"The leading mining and development company in this part of the galaxy and the company for which Xyla Redstone worked," I finished.

"Yes, sir. And the short man in the next group to her left is Dante Farric, head of the EPV in the colony." Eco-Protection Volunteers. A well-funded nonprofit that tried to stop human imposition onto the ecologies of new planets. Farric was, in General Oxendine's parlance, the "head greenie."

"Seems like an odd mix, though General Oxendine mentioned that the governor was friendly with both sides." As I said it, the governor slid into the group of five around Farric and gave him a big smile as he took his hand in the same two-handed grip in which he'd taken mine just a moment prior.

"The lady in the dark green—"

"That's good, Captain Fader. Thanks." She could likely name everyone who mattered at the party and probably had a paragraph's worth of information on each of them. But I didn't need all that now—it would just distract me. "Why don't you give me some space? I'm going to visit the bar." I also had no doubt that everyone in the room who mattered knew who *I* was, and that they'd approach me if I gave them the chance, which meant getting away from Fader and her uniform. I wish I'd thought to explain that to her before we arrived, because the look on her face said I'd hurt her feelings. "I want to see who comes to talk to me. You mingle and see what you can hear."

She schooled her face to neutral. "Yes, sir."

I weaved my way through people to a temporary bar set up in the corner. Mac caught my eye on the way. He stood with his back to a wall, surveying the crowd as if someone might jump out and attack me right there, causing people to give him a wide berth. He gave me a slight nod, which I returned as I approached a short, pale woman with broad shoulders and a ponytail tending the bar. "What sort of whiskey do you have?"

"We have a Ferra Three eight-year single malt," she offered.

"Perfect," I said. It wasn't the fifteen-year that I'd brought with me, but it was an excellent pour to find in an out-of-the-way colony. The governor lived well. I wound aimlessly through the room with my drink, condensation forming on the outside of the glass from the ice. The governor had moved to Stroud's group, so I avoided that and angled toward Farric. As I approached, someone spoke a little too loudly, and I heard "ex-military asshole." I turned away, trying to look natural. I know when I'm not welcome. I was saved the embarrassment of standing alone, because no sooner had I stopped moving than a parade of men and women came up to introduce themselves. Government officials, industry executives, a few scientists, and others where I didn't catch their jobs or titles filed by and shook my hand. None spent more than a minute or two, and all seemed friendly. If they had agendas, they didn't come out during that short time. It almost felt rehearsed, like they had a planned welcoming routine.

Stroud made her way to me after the rest had cleared, and nobody queued behind her. I wondered if that timing was also planned. Up close, she had wrinkles around her eyes, and I put her age around sixty, though from the grip of her handshake, I figured she might be a match for me in the gym. "It's good to meet you, Colonel Butler. I'm glad you're here."

"Call me Carl. I wish I could say I was glad to be here." I smiled, to make sure that she got the trite joke.

"Alas. We all have our callings, and your misfortune is, hopefully, our gain."

"How so?" I asked.

"Our operations have been slowed significantly for the past three months, since the incident."

*The incident.* Interesting terminology. "How come? I was led to believe the military conducted an investigation. Things should have gone back to normal after that, right?"

"One would think," she said. "But . . . other influences

have used the situation to create delays based on false safety concerns, and with you on the way, the governor was convinced to wait for the additional investigation." *Other influences.* That tracked with what Oxendine had told me about the capriciousness of the governor's decisions.

"People *did* disappear. That hardly seems like a false concern."

"They did," she admitted. "But it's a dangerous business. We lose an average of about two a month, which is why we pay our explorers so well. They know the risks. It's unfortunate, of course, but it's also inevitable on these kinds of missions. Sometimes people die."

I understood the sentiment. Shit, I'd lived it, making the same kinds of calculations and decisions. But it still struck me as callous. "I'll work as quickly as I can."

"If there's anything we can do to speed your work, please let us know."

"There is one thing you could help with. What company—or companies—have the most to gain here on Eccasis if Caliber has problems?"

Her eyes lit up a bit at the question and her face softened, perhaps in approval, as she considered her answer. "Honestly, none. We're either in different spaces in the market or we're strategic partners. The restrictions on us hurt all the companies working here."

So much for that easy possibility. Still, it was good to rule it out. "Thanks. I'll work as fast as I can."

"The first report was very conclusive," she said, almost as if she wanted me to sign off on it right then. That seemed odd, given that Zentas himself had asked for me to come. Regardless, I couldn't promise her an outcome—any outcome—until I knew more about the situation.

Stroud left me, and a minute later Dante Farric took her place. He was several centimeters shorter than me and had a bushy, light brown beard that he groomed to look just a little unkempt. He held a half-full glass of red wine and didn't offer me his hand, so I didn't offer him mine. He carried tension in his shoulders, and his eyes darted back and forth; something about that told me we probably wouldn't get along. "Mr. Butler," he said, the words sounding almost like they caused him physical pain.

"Mr. Farric."

"You know who I am." Not a question.

"And you know who I am." I have this thing where if someone is being a dick, I naturally respond in kind. Some people would probably call that a flaw. Whatever.

"Of course I know who you are. You're the biggest mass murderer in the history of the galaxy."

That was certainly debatable, depending on which history books you read. Sadly, it takes a lot to be the biggest killer ever. But I forgave him the hyperbole. He made his point and it didn't bother me. For whatever reason, people thought pointing out something like that would draw a reaction, but it couldn't. I knew my own sins far better than they did. But I didn't feel the need to share any of that with Farric.

"Sure." I let the silence between us linger until it became awkward.

Farric broke first. "What brings you to this fine colony? Is there some species that needs murdering? Perhaps some fusion weapons that need firing?"

I started to turn away, since the conversation clearly held no value, but I stopped. Maybe I was tired from the space lag, but it pissed me off more than it should have. "You know what? Fuck you." I stared him down. I *did* understand his sentiment—I got it often enough—

but it was the governor's reception and Farric was out of line. He'd known full well that I'd be here. He could have stayed home.

He stammered, as if searching for words. Just like I thought . . . his currency was snide remarks. He couldn't deal with direct confrontation. Finally, he blew out air in an exaggerated sigh. "I'm sorry."

I hesitated. I hadn't expected an apology, and I couldn't come up with a good response. "Okay."

"I thought I had control of myself when I agreed to come, but then I saw you, and well . . . it hit me harder than I thought. I was out of line."

"It happens." I understood, but that didn't mean I felt the need to let him off the hook for being an asshole.

He started to speak, stopped, and then started again two or three times. "We're not happy that you're here."

How could I respond to that? I finished the last half of my drink in one swallow. "I'm not particularly happy about it either. But here I am. I need another drink."

"That's not what I meant." He took a step with me, effectively keeping me in the conversation. "What I meant is that we're not happy that you're here, but the situation that brought you here . . . It's tragic, and if there's anything that I or EPV can do to assist in your investigation, you shouldn't hesitate to contact me."

He was saying the right words, but I didn't hold out much hope that he'd follow through. Stroud wanted the investigation done quickly so she could get back to work, so it stood to reason that EPV would want to delay it as much as possible. I decided to test him. "I'll do that. Were those people out on the steps yours?"

"What people?"

I read his look of confusion as genuine. "There was a small protest on the way in."

He scrunched his lips up. "They might be. We're a pretty decentralized group. Some people could have organized something without me knowing about it."

I'd been mistaken. He *did* provide something useful. He didn't have complete control over his group, which changed the calculus a little when it came to their role in the colony. On the surface, their opposition to development corporations made them potential suspects. "Volunteers, right? What can you do?"

"Exactly so," he said. "It's not always convenient."

"They seemed harmless. And hey, I deserve it."

He looked at me as if trying to judge my sincerity. I think he came to the conclusion that I meant what I said, which I did. "Your law—the Butler Law—doesn't do anything."

"You know they didn't consult me when they wrote it, right?"

That got a half smile from him. "I guess not."

"But since you brought it up, why doesn't it work?"

"Enforcement. It's inconsistent at best, and nonexistent at worst. Some of it's a lack of resources locally, but even that's intentional. Corporations grease politicians back at the capital to make sure nothing too effective gets out this way."

I got the feeling that he meant the governor, but I wasn't saying that out loud in a room full of people, one of them *being* the governor. "I was told that you had people on the governor's staff."

He looked at me warily, sizing me up for a second time, perhaps trying to figure out if he could get away with a lie and deciding he couldn't. "Not directly. But sure, we have some who are friendly to our cause. We have to if we want to affect anything."

"Of course." It seemed innocuous enough. I had to

admit that Farric didn't seem like the kind of guy who would order a hit on a team of scientists, even if he hated everything they stood for. But you never know. In the holos, it's always the guy who seems like he wouldn't hurt anybody that turns out to be a whack job. Or maybe I needed to slow down on the whiskey.

A woman waved at Farric, and he acknowledged her. "I've taken up enough of your time. I'm sure we'll meet again."

"It was nice to meet you," I said. Fader caught my eye and held up a fresh drink, asking if I wanted it. I waved her over.

"That looked awkward," she said.

"It was. But I learned some interesting stuff." I filled her in on what Farric said about the protest and the enforcement of the law. "Have you heard anything?"

"Not much, sir. There's a little angst with the government workers about a semiannual report that's due next week, but that's about it."

"Find out more about that," I said. It sounded like nothing, but anything that gave us insight into the governor's operation might help, since it seemed to be a source of conflict.

I spent an hour making small talk, inserting myself into group after group while trying to steer the conversation to something useful. It felt more like four hours. I got patter about the weather, the limited entertainment options on the planet, and a few requests for stories about one mission or another I'd led but avoiding the controversial ones. Avoiding Cappa. It was as if the entire room had decided ahead of time not to speak business to me in any way. Finally, the governor rescued me and led me through double doors into a dining room that seated about thirty. It had a burgundy carpet and polished wood paneling, but the thing that caught my eye was the giant chandelier—it might have been real crystal. When he closed the door behind us, the crowd noise evaporated, and we stood alone in near silence.

"Nice place," I said.

"It's not bad for a remote outpost." He smiled.

Not bad, indeed. It made me question the priorities of the colonial administration. But that wasn't my job, and it would only serve to keep me at the party longer, so I let it go. "So, Governor, what can you tell me about the disappearance of Xyla Redstone?"

"Ah, yes. Straight to it then. Unfortunate business, that. Tragic."

I waited once he stopped speaking. Surely, he had more to say. The silence grew awkward, until finally I said, "Do you have any thoughts on what might have happened?"

"I . . . ahhh . . . yes, well, the military did an investigation. I'm sure there's a report."

*He hadn't read it.* He'd rejected the military findings and kept restrictions in place without even knowing what it said. "There is. It seems pretty open and shut."

He nodded. "Perhaps. We felt it was best to let you look at it. There are a lot of people interested."

"Like who?" He looked away and fidgeted, and I almost felt bad for pushing him. It clearly made him uncomfortable. But he *was* the governor. Sometimes when they put you in charge, you had to actually deal with things.

"Well, of course there are the authorities who sent you. They were very clear that you be given every deference. And there's interest here, of course, too. Your arrival has been one of the biggest events of the season."

*Events of the season?* I paused for a moment, trying to assess whether he was pulling my leg, but his demeanor didn't shift. He appeared to be serious. What could I do? I played along. "Well, it's an honor to be here."

He smiled and clapped me on the shoulder. "Indeed! If there is anything you need from my office, you just reach out."

"Thank you, Governor. I'll do that." By unspoken mutual agreement, we headed back out the doors and into the throng, which had fully broken down into small groups. The governor split off from me, greeting a large woman in white from across the room as if she was his long lost relative. I headed for the bar, unsure of what I'd learned or why he'd wanted to talk to me alone. It felt perfunctory—like he knew he was *supposed* to pull me aside, so he did. If I gave him more credit, I might have thought he did it for someone else's benefit. He could tell people that he laid down the law with me, and nobody could refute him. He didn't seem that shrewd, though, and I started to understand what Oxendine had said about him earlier.

I sat in a tall wooden chair and Fader took the one next to me just as my drink arrived. "I haven't been able to get much more from the room," she said.

"Tell me about it. The governor appears to be a dead end." I sipped my drink. At least they had good booze. "How long do you think we have to stay to not create a political scandal?"

She pursed her lips, thinking. "Another half hour, sir. Maybe a little more. I can suggest that we're feeling the effects of the space travel then."

"Tomorrow I want you to come back." I hadn't planned on using Fader as part of the investigation, but my conversation with the governor changed that. *Someone* in his organization would be competent, even though it might not be him. Oxendine had mentioned Davidson, but I wanted a less-biased opinion. "Talk to the people in the governor's office. Somebody here has to know what they're doing . . . I'd like to know who it is."

"Yes, sir. You want me to see what I can get from them?"

"If it's not awkward. Mostly I want to know who's calling the shots, who has influence, that sort of thing. We may not need it for the investigation, but it doesn't hurt to know the lay of the land. If they know anything about the missing person, even better."

"Yes, sir. So what do we do tonight?"

I lifted my glass. "Tonight, we drink."


WE LEFT ONCE others started to trickle out—early, but not the first to leave. I expected the night air to be cooler, but of course it wasn't, since *night* inside the bubble was artificial. No stars twinkled overhead, but I couldn't tell if the dome's canopy had gone opaque or a cloud cover in the night sky outside caused that. The crowd that had protested my arrival had mercifully dispersed, so Mac headed across the compound to get our cart.

Someone bowled into me, almost causing me to lose my balance. I whirled, ready to fight, only to find a thin older woman rubbing her knee from where she'd scraped it on the step. A chubby man rushed over to us. "I'm so sorry. Lania, are you okay?"

"I'm . . . fineth." She slurred her words. I almost laughed. I'd just had my fight-or-flight reflex triggered by a drunk woman falling on the stairs. I needed to relax.

He looked back to me. "So sorry."

"No worries." I helped him get the wobbly woman to her feet.

"Colonel Butler!" A voice called from up the stairs and I turned back to the mansion to find Cora Davidson hurrying toward us.

"What's up?" I asked.

"The governor asked me to tell you that if you need anything at all while you're here that you should let him know."

I stared at her for a second, feeling like she was putting me on. "He already told me that."

"He was very insistent that I tell you before you leave, sir."

"Okay then. Consider me informed."

"Sir . . . if I might suggest . . ."

"Spit it out, Davidson."

"If you need anything from the governor, let *me* know, and I'll make sure it happens."

Ah. Now I had it. Davidson wanted to make sure I knew it was *she* who could help, either because she knew the governor himself couldn't, or for more nefarious reasons. It felt like the latter, like she was either trying to control the currency of information within her organization or trying to curry favor with me by helping me. Maybe both. No wonder Oxendine had called her a snake. "Sure thing."

"Bomb!" Mac's distinctive voice rang out from the line of parked carts, and it took me just a split second to register him running toward me.

I reacted faster than Fader and reached for the drunk lady. "Help her up the stairs!" Her husband spun about in confusion until Fader grabbed his arm and pointed him up the stairs.

It's hard to describe an explosion—so much happens at one time. The flash, the sound, the force—academically, I know they happen sequentially, but in practice, at short range, they're so close together that they may as well be simultaneous. I'd almost made it up the stairs when the force of it threw me onto my stomach. I caught myself with my hands just before my face slammed into the stone.

Mac and Fader recovered quicker than I did and both made it to their feet. Mac had a pistol out, while Fader, unarmed, scanned the area, looking for additional threats. I turned to look for Davidson but didn't see her. The couple we'd been helping stayed down, the woman bleeding from her chin and moaning but otherwise appearing unhurt.

I scrambled to my feet and looked up, worried about the dome that protected us from the outside environs, but a quick scan showed no cracks. That made sense—it would need to be strong in this environment. I ran down the stairs toward the source of the explosion. The smoking chassis of our cart sat on the ground, only one wheel remaining, wobbling on what remained of the back axle. The vehicle next to it lay on its side, heat radiating from the flames that danced at its insides. The acrid smell of frying electronics assaulted my nose and made my eyes water as I ran to another vehicle, looking for a fire extinguisher.

Mac appeared beside me, followed closely by Fader. "Sir, let's get away from here, in case there are secondaries."

"Right," I said, a bit in shock, and I let him lead me back the way I'd come. People had started to stream out of the mansion, probably drawn by the sound. Somewhere in the distance an alarm wailed. It took four minutes and forty-five seconds for the military to arrive and only a few seconds more for them to secure the area. They forced the civilians who hadn't been there for the attack to go back inside.

It took several minutes more until someone in charge made the connection between my team and the cart, and they pulled Mac away to ask him some questions. They were a bit more hesitant to talk to me, but eventually a captain named Yolin showed up, and after consulting with the lieutenant previously in charge, made her way over. By that time, I'd recovered from my initial shock and moved on to anger at whoever had done this.

"Are you okay, sir?" Yolin stood a head shorter than me, which was pushing the limits for military service.

"My hands are scraped up a bit, but other than that, I'm fine."

"No headache?"

"Not yet. It's probably coming." I held up my hands, which were shaking. Adrenaline dump.

"Did you lose consciousness?"

"No. Are you the medical officer?" She wasn't. It was a dick question. The attack pissed me off, but Yolin wasn't responsible for that. I needed to soften my tone, but I couldn't.

"Just routine questions."

"How about we get to the important ones?" She was asking easy questions to get me used to answering her before getting to the important ones, but I didn't have the patience for that. "I'm not going to lie to you, so you can save the interrogation technique for someone else."

She transitioned without a hitch. "Do you think you were the target, sir?"

"Is there another way to see it?"

"There are always different ways to see things." She

was good, not rising to my bait, which was still me being an asshole because someone had blown up my vehicle. She also didn't call me on it, which would have made things worse. "Let's try it another way. Is there anyone who might want to do you harm?"

"Half the galaxy?" I offered.

She cracked a smile at that, despite trying not to. "Anyone specific?"

"The obvious answer—the one you probably already have—is that there was a group of people protesting my arrival a few hours back. I'm sure they're on camera. Did cameras catch anything around the vehicle while we were inside? It was parked right there with the others. There had to be coverage."

"Our team is checking that, sir. I don't have the answer yet."

"The obvious answer is EPV. They don't like me." I left unsaid that the obvious answer wasn't always the right one. She'd know that, and I was trying to dial back the asshole.

"Who knew you were here?"

"I'm pretty sure everyone did. The governor's guest list was distributed wide enough that it might as well have been public."

She made a note in her device. "I'd like to put a security team with you en route back to your quarters, sir, if that's okay."

"Absolutely." I didn't think someone would try again so soon, but I didn't need to take chances.

Four soldiers joined us and we took two military carts back to our quarters. "I'm moving in with you, sir, unless you've got any strong objections," said Mac.

"No objection. There's plenty of room."

Mac turned to the soldier in charge. "Can you have

your people move the bed from my room into the colonel's place? Just set it in the entry room."

"Can do, Sergeant," said the corporal. "But it's not necessary. My orders are to keep a two-person team on the door until further notice."

"You can do what you want on the outside," said Mac. "I still want you to move the bed."

"Roger that."

Mac left the soldiers and planted himself at my side. He didn't say anything, but he didn't have to. The pissed-off look on his face said it all. Anyone who wanted to come at me right then was going to have to go through him.

# CHAPTER FIVE

**MAC, FADER, AND** I stood inside my quarters. Even with Mac's newly delivered bed against the wall, we had more than enough space. I poured myself a drink and held up the bottle to the others as an offer. Mac shook his head, which didn't surprise me. Fader said, "Yes, sir, I could go for one," which did. To be fair, she didn't drink at the reception. I had, and I still needed one to calm down after the botched attack.

I handed her a glass with a heavy pour and a few ice cubes. "To be clear, we're all in agreement that we were the target of that attack, right?"

"I hate to rule anything out." Fader considered her drink, watching the swirls in the liquor where the ice melted. "But in this case, I think we're in the high ninetieth percentile for likelihood. There's something off, though."

"What?" I asked.

Fader swirled her liquor in its glass. "Why did the bomb go off?"

She had a point that I couldn't answer. Once Mac noticed the bomb, there was no point in detonating it unless they thought he was still close enough that it would get him. I took a sip of whiskey, savoring the taste. "I don't know. Mac, what did you see?"

"I was checking the vehicle, doing my walkaround like I always do before we use it. There was a rectangular thing below it with wires hanging out that hadn't been there before. Not hard to spot, but I didn't hang around long enough to get a look at the trigger mechanism. I ran."

"I listened in when the EOD techs were discussing what they found," said Fader. "It actually had two triggers: one GPS-activated and the other a remote."

"Interesting," I said. "I assume the GPS was the primary and that it would have detonated after a certain distance?" That wasn't uncommon. A lot of missiles and rockets worked on the same principle. That way, if you dropped them, they didn't blow up. Thinking about the attack clinically helped clear the emotion from it and relaxed me even more than the alcohol.

"It was probably tied to a specific location," she said.

I considered it. "There was only the one way out of the governor's dome that I saw. Every vehicle had to go through the tunnel. Maybe they tied the detonation to that choke point."

Mac spoke up. "That would work if they wanted to get the explosion away from the mansion and avoid collateral damage. People were walking out, and it would be hard to predict who might be around when it went off."

"That's definitely a sign of a targeted assassination attempt rather than a terrorist attack," said Fader. She was right. A terrorist would want more casualties, not fewer.

"Well, this certainly made things more interesting," I said.

"Interesting?" Fader choked a little on her drink. "Sir, we could be dead."

"And yet we're not." I noticed then that her hand holding the glass was shaking. "Sorry. I don't mean to be flippant. You do get used to it, if that helps."

"Get used to what?" she asked.

"People trying to kill you. It's like anything else. It gets easier after the first time." She probably thought I was trying to act tough, but what else could I say? You can get used to anything.

She downed her drink. "If you say so, sir. But I think maybe there's some survivorship bias in there."

"Probably. For now, let's focus on what happens next. Obviously, the stakes are higher. We don't know if whoever tried this will try again or if they'll go to ground."

"I'm planning for them to try again," said Mac.

"You definitely do that," I said. "But it will be harder for them, now that we're expecting something. There must be cameras all over the colony. Let's figure out where they are and how to access them."

"I can work that tomorrow," said Fader. "What do we think was the motive of the bomber?"

"Stop the colonel's investigation," said Mac.

"That seems most likely," I said.

"Roger, sir. I agree." Fader had stopped shaking. I didn't know if it was the liquor or, like me, she did better once she had something to do. One way to get past a tough moment was to get on to the next one.

Now if only I could do the same. I had to try to keep the investigation professional, but I didn't see how I could. I showed up to do an investigation and someone tried to kill me to keep me from it. Farric had played me.

**WE DIDN'T DO** anything the next day because they wouldn't let us leave our rooms. I raised a fuss—I even demanded to see the general—but an officer assured me that Oxendine had given the order for us to stay put while they investigated and that me running around would just make it harder. I concurred with her in theory, and probably would have made the same decision in her spot. That didn't mean I liked it. They did let Fader come to my rooms instead of having to sit alone in her own, and she used the time to go through Xyla's phone logs and emails, which she had requested the previous day. After a few hours, she gave me an update.

"She didn't seem to have any relationships," said Fader. "Not romantic ones, anyway. I didn't have access to her work email. Caliber would have that, but I didn't think to request it from them. But even her personal email is almost all business. She appears to be a loyal shopper, going with just a couple companies, but the things she ordered are all things you'd expect . . . clothes, boots, media. Nothing that gives a clue."

"Well, we didn't expect much, right?" I asked.

"Definitely a long shot, sir. The phone and text logs give us a bit more, though. There's a long text string with someone named Mae Eddleston. I'd say they were business colleagues, but also friends. It's really the only thing anywhere in the records that indicates that she even *had* a friend."

"That's something, I guess. Anything that tells you when the woman . . . what's her name? Eddleston? Anything that tells you when they last saw each other?" It was probably nothing, but we were locked in a room and didn't have any other work.

"They texted on the day of the disappearance," said Fader. "I can't say for sure from the texts, but I think that Eddleston went on the same mission."

I pulled up the official report on my device and

flipped through until I found the right information. "She did. She was a passenger on one of the other vehicles." It still didn't mean much, but it at least rose to a level where I wanted to check it out, so I made a note of it. "Did you get anything about her living quarters?"

"They were emptied out and inventoried months ago. There's nothing of interest in the inventory," said Fader.

"Well, that's not surprising," I said. "Even if there *was* a clue, if nobody approached the scene looking for it, of course they wouldn't find it." I really needed to get out of my room. It was too easy to get seduced by details that didn't matter, especially when you were left with nothing else to do but dig. The simplest solution hadn't changed: She went on a dangerous mission and died along with the rest of her team.

**THEY CLEARED US** a day later, after a major showed up to give me a briefing on the results of the investigation. They had some biometric data from the bomb. People leave traces everywhere, and an explosion doesn't necessarily get rid of everything of value, especially if it's not made by a pro. They didn't tell me the specifics, but they probably had a fingerprint, since the bomb would have destroyed most of the DNA. They had a chemical signature from the bomb as well and were tracking down the source of the explosives. The major thought they'd have that in a day or two, given the limited avenues available in a small colony like Eccasis.

One thing that didn't fit was the cameras. The governor's residence had cameras that monitored the entire area, but they'd been shut down for eighteen minutes around the time of the bombing. That kind of coordination, paired with a somewhat amateur bomb attempt, presented a bit of a dichotomy, but I could see how it happened. Oxendine had mentioned the lax security of the governor's office and that his staff was filled with partisan interests. Farric himself had even admitted it. I marked the cameras as an inside job.

A few minutes after the major left, Ganos arrived, which added tension to an already difficult situation. Being locked in her room the previous day hadn't helped her mood, and she practically stomped in and glared first at Fader and then at me. I couldn't put it off any longer. I had to talk to her and get to the bottom of her attitude before we could move forward.

I'd have rather faced another assassination attempt.

I asked Mac and Fader to take a walk, and Ganos and I stood in awkward silence while they left. When the door closed, I waited a few seconds to give her a chance to break the silence, and when she didn't, I spoke. "Clearly you're angry about something."

"You think?"

"I assume I'm part of the problem, but I don't—"

"You didn't fucking call me."

"Excuse me?" I wasn't offended. I really didn't understand.

"For this mission. I didn't hear from you. I got contacted by some random colonel who said you wanted me for a job. You want me for a job, but you can't even send me a message yourself? The level of asshole required for that is off the asshole chart."

I looked at the floor. She was right about that. I'd wanted her for the job and thought that was enough, but clearly I owed her more than that. "I'm sorry. You're right. That was poorly done."

She stared at me, seeming to want more.

"I should have messaged you myself. I got focused on my own stuff, and I didn't think about it. I'm an asshole."

"You know . . . it's . . ." She paused.

I felt like shit. I *deserved* to feel like shit. "It's okay. You can say whatever you want. I have it coming."

She shook her head. "I'm trying. It's hard, okay?"

"Sorry."

She took a deep breath and let it out. "Not all of us got to disappear from the galaxy and go hide out on a farm planet in the middle of nowhere. You know?"

I hadn't thought about that, either. I hadn't thought at all, and that was clearly the key to her hostility. "I'm sorry. I think I just assumed that you wanted to be in a more civilized place. For your work."

"Yeah. *My work.*"

"You're not working?"

"Oh, I'm working. You want to know what I'm doing, though? Freelance. Bug hunting, odd jobs, low-level black-market stuff. *Nothing* assignments."

"Why?"

"That's the question, isn't it? Corporations should have been lining up to hire me. That's how it works in my world. You get famous for doing something bad and everyone wants to pay you to make sure nobody can do it to them. But every call I made, they hung up."

"I'm sorry. I swear I didn't know. You should have told me . . . I could have pulled some strings."

"You really don't get it. I don't know if I really even *want* a job. I don't want to mess with corporate networks. I still wonder who might be out there watching me. Tracking me. I wonder who put me on the blacklist and what else they might be doing. I think about it every day. How could I work like that? So I stopped looking."

"You want to sit? I want to sit." I pulled a chair from

the table and turned it around. Ganos slumped down onto the sofa. She was right. I didn't get it. She was mad because she didn't get work, but she didn't *want* work. I'd messed her up in a big way. She always seemed so cool, and I didn't realize that some of it was a front. "So . . . why did you come? You could have said no."

"The guy didn't seem like the type of person who was going to take no for an answer."

I nodded. I could see it. They wouldn't have forced her to come, but whoever had the job to convince her wouldn't have let her know that. I really *was* above the top of the asshole chart. "Again, I'm sorry. For everything. If you want to leave, I'll make arrangements for it immediately."

"Can't," she said. "They offered me a bunch of money, and I took it. I couldn't afford not to. Parker and I are trying to buy a house. Like it or not, I'm on the job."

"I'm still sorry. But I'm really glad you're here."

"Of course you are. You'd be lost without me." Ganos smiled, and for a second it was as if nothing had happened. But, of course, it had. "And hey, it could be worse. There could be people trying to kill us."

I laughed. "Yeah. That would suck."

"Now that I'm here, where do I start? What information do we need, and who do we think has it?"

"Let me get the others back in here, and we'll dig into it."


**THE FOUR OF** us gathered around the table. I looked at Fader first. "Think big. If we could have anything—information-wise—what would you want to know?"

Fader hesitated for a moment, glanced at Ganos. I didn't know if she was thinking about my question, or worried about the younger woman's mood. "I'd like to see Xyla Redstone's work emails. And I'd like to know more about the governor's cameras. We got the military report, but I'd like to see what the outage actually looked like and the film from before the outage. The military probably checked it, but it would help me visualize things to see it."

"Yeah it would," Mac agreed. "Someone messed with our vehicle, and it should be on record. I checked *every-thing* on that cart when we first got it, so it had to have happened while we were inside."

"I can probably crack the system that controls the cameras," said Ganos.

"Do it," I said. "Fader, you go about it the straight-forward way. Go over to the governor's place and find out what they know. See if someone will talk about why the cameras didn't see anything. Even if you don't find anything specific, establish some contacts." I turned to Ganos. "What about the emails?"

"Caliber has them?" Ganos was frowning, like some-thing was wrong.

"Yes," I said. "Is that a problem?"

"I'd rather not tangle with them unless it's really im-portant. They're going to have much better security than the governor, sir." She left unsaid what she and I had discussed about corporate networks.

"It's not that important," I said. "I can request them from Caliber."

Fader continued, "I'd also like to see the details of the military's investigation into the bomb. They briefed us, but if I had the report, I'd know what they checked . . . More important, I'd know what they *didn't* check."

"I might be able to pry that loose from the com-mander. That's probably smarter than trying to hack the military." It bothered me that Oxendine might have information on the cameras and not shared it.

Ganos shrugged and kept tapping notes into her device. "Got it. Anything and everything pertaining to the bombing. What else?"

"I think that's a good priority for now," I said.

"Understood, but that's not how what I do works. I'll find what I can, but no promises it's the stuff you want. If you give me other targets, I might trip on them while I'm digging around."

"In that case, I'll take anything you can find on Dante Farric or anything that gives information on what the Eco-Protection Volunteers are up to here on Eccasis. They're the chief suspects in the bombing, in my eyes." At the last minute, I worried that Ganos might want to avoid them, too, so I added, "If the EPV looks dangerous when you start, back off them and let me know."

Ganos stashed her device in the pocket of her hoodie. "I'll be in touch."

"Do you want our contact information?" asked Fader.

"*Really?* Please. Who are you talking to? I've already got it." Ganos winked, which broke the tension. "I'm off. They're paying me an awful lot to be here, and I'd hate for whoever is shelling out for this shindig to not get their money's worth."

She left a silence in the wake of her departure, and it took a few seconds before Fader filled it. "Is what she's doing safe?"

I couldn't get rid of that thought either, especially given my private conversation with Ganos. The last time she had poked around the net on my behalf, it had almost gotten both of us killed. But she seemed to have a better handle on the risks this time. Last time she'd gone in full bore.

"The worst thing that happens is we get caught. We'd probably get in trouble, but given that someone tried to kill us the night before last, I don't think we can make it worse. What are they going to do, try to kill us harder?"

"They could succeed," suggested Mac.

"Well, sure. There's that."

"If you're heading over to army headquarters, we're going to need to take the security detail with us," said Mac. "Give me a minute to arrange something for you, ma'am."

"I'll be okay on my own." Fader pulled a pistol out from where she'd had it secured at the small of her back. "I'm not going to be caught unarmed again."

Mac looked at me with the look that non-coms give officers when they want help.

"I'd feel better if you took someone along for now," I said. "If you get into some sensitive stuff and need the freedom to move on your own, we can revisit it later."

"Yes, sir." Her face didn't register any complaint. I appreciated people who put the mission before their personal feelings. Serata had picked well.

# CHAPTER SIX

**M**AC AND I made it to headquarters amid what felt like a battalion of soldiers. In truth we only had five escorts, but they'd be a problem for my investigation going forward. I needed to talk to people, and that meant making them comfortable. An armed militia hanging around had a somewhat dampening effect on comfort. Thankfully, they let us go once we got inside the headquarters.

I should have gone straight to see Oxendine, but I decided to try another route first. I might have been subconsciously butthurt that she hadn't shared everything with me on her own. I scanned the soldiers that passed me in the hallway until I found the right target: a young sergeant with a perfect crew cut. "Excuse me, Sergeant . . ." I glanced at his name tag. "Curreris. I'm Colonel Butler and I was wondering if you could help me."

He stumbled over himself for a second before regaining his bearing. "Yes, sir! Of course!"

"I'm looking for a captain named Yolin. She had some questions for me about last night's attack." Technically it wasn't a lie, since she *had* questioned me the previous night, but I'm not trying to fool myself—I made up a story because I knew the sergeant wouldn't challenge it. "I'm not sure where she works. It might be Intel."

"Yes, sir. She's part of the Two Shop. I'll take you there." He led me through three turns until we came to a heavy door secured with a biometric pad. "This is as far as I go, sir. I don't have clearance to get in." He pressed a buzzer and a voice came across almost immediately.

"What can I do for you, Sergeant?"

"Colonel Butler is here to see Captain Yolin."

The speaker went quiet for a few seconds. "Roger. She'll be right out to escort him."

"Roger," said Sergeant Curreris. He turned to me. "You're good to go, sir."

"Thanks, Sergeant. Much appreciated." I offered him my hand, which he took, beaming. I didn't like using soldiers like that, but I had limited tools at my disposal, so I used what I had. Besides, I was only a little out of line in coming to find Yolin. Oxendine had told me to go through Ops, but I could notify them on my way out. When Curreris departed, I pulled Mac over close so I could talk without the speaker picking me up. "Head over to Ops. See if you know anybody. I'll come find you when I'm done here. I promise I won't leave the building without you."

"Roger that, sir."

A moment later Yolin came to the door. "Come in, sir. I'll lead you back to my office. Zero level on the floor!" she announced, letting everyone know that she had an uncleared person with her. Monitors snapped off and soldiers covered maps along our path.

Her office had two chairs, a desk, and a shelf bolted to the wall. Even with those sparse accoutrements, the tiny room was packed. I took the guest chair as she worked her way around the desk. "What can I do for you, sir?"

Her tone was neutral, and I couldn't read whether it bothered her that I'd showed up at her front door or not.

"I wanted to get an update on what happened last night."

"My boss told me you were briefed." Still no read on her.

"The briefer didn't have much beyond the basics. He told me you had biometrics on the bomb and nothing on the cameras."

"That's true," said Yolin.

"It's what he *didn't* say that had me wondering. *Why* didn't the cameras pick anything up, for example?"

She blew out a breath. I couldn't tell if she was frustrated with the question or that the major hadn't fully informed me. "We're still working on that, sir."

"What's to work on?" As I'd been doing a lot the last few days, I kept my voice even so that it wouldn't come across like an accusation. It seemed like a simple issue and it had me legitimately curious.

Her eyes flicked down to her hands, folded on her desk. I took it for her trying to decide what she could and couldn't tell me. I'd put her into a tricky situation. By the book, she probably shouldn't read me in, but it's tough for a captain to tell a retired colonel no. It's only a small breach. I had clearance from the highest levels for my mission, so she could extrapolate some leeway into the current situation. She met my eyes, apparently decided. "We still don't know what . . . or who . . . cut the cameras off."

"Do you think it was an inside job?"

"That's the question, sir . . . right? If we knew that, we'd have a lot better idea on the rest of the incident."

"Why didn't anybody notice at the time?"

"That part seems legit . . . well, somewhat legit,

anyway. The person who monitors the cameras has other responsibilities and only occasionally watches the feeds in real time. They're more for use after the fact."

"Surely a missing feed or two would be noticeable."

She grunted. "Sir, it's the governor's residence. Security is . . . less than ideal."

"Ah." I could believe that. "I'm assuming you looked into how they could be switched off?"

"Of course, sir. They're controlled from a small room inside the governor's mansion. The same person who watches them controls them. He said that he didn't touch them, and there's no reason to suspect that he's lying. As far as we could tell, nobody *ever* touches them."

Well, shit. I took a moment to think about my next question. I could only ask so many obvious ones before Yolin would take it as me doubting her competence. "So, what's the theory? The guard was distracted, and someone snuck in and shut them down?"

"No, sir, that doesn't seem likely. Because the same person would have had to sneak back in to turn them back on."

"That's not possible?"

"I mean, anything is possible, sir." But her tone said she didn't believe it.

"So you think someone did it remotely." Something that Oxendine had told me came to mind—the scientist who had been murdered. Someone had hacked the cameras then, too.

"I do, sir. The problem is, we haven't proven it yet."

I considered following up on that, asking why not, but decided against it. Yolin's patience was wearing thin and I had Ganos, who could probably give me a better answer. "Last question. Have you got a match on the biometric data yet?"

"We do, sir. That turned out to be easy. The man came colonyside legally, so his data was on file."

"So you've got him in custody?"

"Not yet, sir. Ops has the mission to detain the person. It should be anytime, but that's not really my lane."

"Thanks," I said. "I've taken up enough of your time. I appreciate it. I know you're busy."

"No problem at all, sir. I'll escort you out."

My mind churned with ideas, but none of them resonated. Yolin's information on the cameras was nothing more than what I already had Fader looking into at the governor's. At least they had a lead on the bomber. Once we could question him, we could extrapolate his network, which would give me more leads. *Everyone* was there. *Everyone* had at least a small motive. Everyone but the governor and General Oxendine. The attack would look bad for them; the governor because it happened at his residence and Oxendine because she was responsible for overall security. The governor didn't seem like a useful ally, since he seemed to want to please everybody, and I wasn't up for pleasing people who wanted me dead. Oxendine . . . she'd probably tell me to butt out and focus on my own mission. Easier said than done when someone tries to kill you. It's hard not to take that personally.

After Yolin left me, I headed for Ops to find Mac so we could leave. I needed to clear my head and wait for whatever Ganos could find.

"Colonel Butler?" a tall, dark-skinned lieutenant stood at a respectful distance, her uniform pressed to knife-edge creases. I marked her as Oxendine's aide.

"Brigadier General Oxendine would like to speak with you."

*Shit.* The fact that Oxendine was personally aware

that I was in her headquarters wasn't surprising, and it raised my opinion of her unit's competence. It also meant that I couldn't avoid her. "I'll head there now. If you could, Lieutenant, have someone track down Sergeant McCann and have him meet me at her office."

**OXENDINE DIDN'T STAND** when her administrative assistant showed me into her office. She barely looked up from her monitor. "Have a seat."

I took one of the two hard-backed chairs in front of her desk. "Your aide said you wanted to see me."

She looked up and held my gaze for a few seconds. "I did. I told you to run your requests through Ops or to come to me. I'd prefer that you not go directly to the captains in my headquarters." Her voice was level—not angry, but firm. The woman wanted no bullshit.

"I was—"

"I know what you were doing." She paused and picked up an unlit cigar off her desk, rolling it in her fingers for a moment. "And it's totally understandable. Someone tried to blow you up. I'd probably have done the same thing you did."

"But," I prompted.

"But that's not how we're going to do business. My people have their assignments, and we both know that you roaming around doing your own thing in my headquarters will disrupt that."

I considered bringing up my mission and how I should be able to expect her support, but she was being cordial, and I didn't want to change that. Perhaps I was getting wiser in my old age. In theory we'd agreed that I wouldn't bother her with little stuff, but she and I both knew that didn't include the type of thing I'd just done, where I'd purposely avoided the correct channels. "Understood."

"If you don't want to talk to Ops, talk to my XO. If you can't get her, come to me."

Both Ops and her XO would inform Oxendine almost immediately. I liked to play things tight, and I didn't love the prospect of a general looking over my shoulder all the time. Old habits die hard. But Oxendine didn't intend this to be a debate, so I gave in without a fight. What I *wanted* to do was to question her on why they hadn't traced the camera hack yet, but I discarded the idea. Better to maintain as much of the relationship as I could. "Roger that."

I was dismissed and left unsure of what to think. It could have gone worse with Oxendine. I *was* out of line, and she could have made things a lot harder than she did. Maybe it was a warning, or maybe she wanted to make sure I knew that she knew. She didn't *seem* like the type who had to show you that she was smarter than you, but I didn't know her that well yet, so I couldn't be sure. Either way, I'd need to play it straight with her command, which meant I had to be careful about what I shared with them. At least for a while.

**BACK AT MY** rooms Mac had his own observations. "Did you notice the people looking at us during the walk back?"

I hadn't. I'd been preoccupied, trying to figure out if I could have handled it better with Oxendine. "It didn't occur to me to check. We had a small army with us."

"It might have been nothing," he said.

"How many?"

"I noticed three different watchers. Like I said, it

really might be nothing. You're a big deal here, so it could be simple curiosity."

"It could be." It probably was, too, but the paranoia bug had bitten me. "Did you see any cameras?"

"I didn't, but that doesn't mean they didn't have them. We can watch the net feeds to see if you show up."

"I'm sure I will," I said. "The problem is, the innocent paparazzi provide perfect cover for anyone who has other motives."

Mac thought about it, as if there might be a solution. "We have to assume that our movements are known."

"We can use that," I said.

"How so, sir?" Mac had gotten comfortable enough with me in my new civilian role that he had backed off on the honorific, but he still stuck it in occasionally.

"I don't know yet. But if people are tracking us, that means they're reacting to what we're doing. That's always better than the other way around. We just have to figure out what we want to show them to get them to react the way we want."

"So . . . we use ourselves as bait."

I thought about it. "When you put it *that* way, it doesn't sound nearly as good. But yeah. Better to draw them to us when we're ready than when we're not."

The door buzzed, forestalling further conversation. Mac waved me back out of the potential line of fire, drew his pistol, and got up to check on it.

"There are still guards out front, right?" I asked.

"Supposed to be. I'm not taking it for granted." I wasn't going to, either. He went to the door and hit a button to activate the video.

A young soldier stared back at him. "Sergeant, there's a delivery here. He says the colonel is expecting him."

"We're not expecting anything," said Mac.

"Hold on," I said. I didn't specifically expect a package, but I'd reached out before I left home and asked her for help. I didn't know how it would come, and I didn't want to accidentally turn it away. We had a code. "Let me talk to the delivery person."

The soldier scrunched his face up in confusion, but he let the man up to the camera. He had brown hair and a full beard. "Delivery for Butler. Package number 55X784CT7." He had a metal case big enough to fit a human body strapped to a self-powered four-wheel cart.

"Let him in," I said. The package number matched the preset code.

Mac looked at me as if to ask, Are you sure? and I nodded. Still, he kept his pistol ready and buzzed the door open. The bearded man came in, handed me a tablet to sign, helped Mac wrestle the case off the cart, and left in under a minute.

"What is it?" Mac asked.

"Just a little help from some friends." I'd made Serata wait four days, back before I left, so that I could ask for this. Hopefully, it would be worth it. I keyed a second code into the first lock, hoping I had it right. It beeped and opened, so I followed with the other two locks. "Let's see what we've got."

The gear inside was something straight out of a radical survivalist's wet dream. Three Bikoski rifles—affectionately known as Bitches—with dozens of magazines, explosives, timers, miniature cameras and microphones, med kits—and that was just what I picked out on the first pass.

"Holy shit," said Mac. "Those are *some* friends. How did they get this stuff *in* here?"

It was all I could do to keep from laughing. I'd told them I'd needed some help, but I didn't expect *this* much.

"I don't know. Let's just say that my friends are very resourceful." It seemed like a stretch that someone could smuggle an unopened container into a colony, but I knew better than to question my contacts and their skills. The soldiers outside would have reported the package already, but if anyone wanted to see what was inside, they'd have to ask me.

The case had a programmable biometric lock.

Mac looked at me, questioning.

"What?"

"Who sent this stuff?"

"What do you mean?"

He smirked. "It was the Cappans, wasn't it?" He waited, apparently read something in my face. "It was! You got a goody box of high-tech death from the fucking Cappans!"

"Keep your voice down," I said.

"How, sir?"

"Well, you just don't speak as loud . . ."

Mac gave me a withering look. "Come on, sir. Spill it."

"We've kept in touch. You know, in case we can help each other out." In truth, it wasn't precisely the Cappans. It was Sasha and Riku, my Cappan hybrid friends. I held that back from Mac, though. Some things I couldn't share with even him.

Mac picked up one of the Bitches and started fiddling with the sight, probably adjusting it to his specs. "This is incredible . . . better than the military stuff. Look at the interface on the scope. You can't buy this kind of thing."

"Yeah?" It didn't surprise me, given my experience with my allies.

He set the weapon down and took out a box that held four tiny drones. "You know, we probably could have drawn weapons from the army if we need them."

"Probably, but then we'd have had to ask. I don't plan on humping a rifle around on a day-to-day basis, but if we need them, now we have them."

"I pity anyone who tries to break in here now," said Mac. "The only thing we're missing is grenades."

I pointed. "There are explosive charges with timed and remote fuses. You could use that as a grenade in a pinch."

I wasn't quite sure, but I thought I heard a sigh of longing. "What are we going to do with all of this?" Mac asked.

"Well, first things first, see if there are trackers. I'm going to wear one so you can track me wherever I go." I'd passed the days where I didn't think I needed security.

"Good call. I don't plan on letting you out of my sight, but accidents happen. Put it somewhere unobtrusive, in case you get abducted. Maybe a captor won't find it right away."

"I could swallow it," I joked.

Mac considered it. "I'm not sure it would survive your stomach acid. Maybe go in the other end." He had a great poker face, and I couldn't tell if he was messing with me or not.

"Pass, thanks."

Mac laughed. "Look at these drones."

"Not sure we could get away with flying them inside the dome. I have to believe they'd pick it up," I said.

"Maybe. But this is state of the art. Damned near invisible. Only one way to find out."

"We'll save it for emergencies."

"Yes, sir."

I didn't believe him for a second—he was going to try it the first time I wasn't looking.

Captain Fader entered and we both turned to look at her.

"Okay . . . you two look guilty. What did you do?"

Mac played it for effect and looked away, refusing to meet her eyes. "Nothing, ma'am."

I laughed. "We got some equipment."

Fader walked over and looked in the case. "Holy shit."

"That seems to be the going sentiment," I said.

"The army approved this?"

"The army doesn't know about it. At least they don't know everything about it."

She paused, and I imagined her debating her next words carefully. I could almost see the conflict on her face. She was a rule follower, and I was breaking them. "Are we going to tell them?"

"I wasn't going to make it a priority," I said.

"Roger, sir." Her reaction bothered me, mostly because I couldn't read it. I didn't know if she'd accepted my decision or simply concluded that I wouldn't change my mind. I had a feeling it would be in her next report either way. I could live with that. What would her boss, halfway across the galaxy, do about it anyway?

"What did you learn at the governor's?" I asked.

"Not much," she said. "I made some contacts. Everybody there seems eager to grab on to whatever they can that might give them an edge. It's an odd environment. Very . . . political, I guess. They don't much like the military, so I played the outsider, a little at odds with the unit here. That worked for a time, but Cora Davidson is a problem. I can't prove it, but I think she got to some people and told them not to talk to me. Luckily, she's not well loved, so her order had the opposite effect in some cases."

"That's good. Keep developing the relationships. See what comes out of them. Anything on the security?"

"It's a dead end, sir. They don't monitor it twenty-four

seven. My guess is that the guy was enjoying the party." That echoed what Yolin told me, but I appreciated the corroboration. I trusted Fader, and because of that, now I could trust Yolin more.

"I didn't get much from the military, either," I said. "They think it was a remote job, but I got the feeling they were hiding something—or at the least, not sharing everything. We'll see what Ganos finds."

"Why would they hold back, sir?"

"I don't know. I do know this: Whatever the motive of the person who attacked us, they sure did divert our attention. We've been totally focused on the bombing and not at all focused on our mission—finding out what happened to Xyla."

"You don't think they're related?" asked Fader.

"I did at first. And I'm still leaning that way, but I think it's dangerous to let that blind us to other possibilities. A lot of people who don't even know why I'm here wouldn't mind seeing me dead—you saw the protest. But even when we get the bomber, we'll have a tough time tying the two things together unless they confess. Even a confession might not be enough. The bomber could have been hired independent of anything else. They might not know anything. How do you see it?"

Fader thought about it. "My thought up until now was that someone tried to kill you to stop you from investigating the disappearance. But now that you put it that way, I've got no reason to think that. I'll have to watch my biases."

Good. She got it. The ability to reassess based on someone else's opinion or information wasn't as common a skill as one would hope, and Fader seemed to have it. "While we wait for Ganos, it's time to get back to Xyla."

"Where do we start?" she asked.

"I think I need to pay a visit to Caliber. It was their mission, and the missing people worked for them. Stroud played the disappearance off as the cost of doing business, but I think maybe that was an act. Even if she truly feels that way, I'm sure someone in her organization doesn't. You don't just lose six people without it having an impact. Those people had friends. I want to talk to Mae Eddleston, the woman you found in Xyla's texts."

Fader tapped her chin. "Caliber seems unlikely to be behind the bombing, so if nothing else, maybe they're the enemy of our enemy."

That made sense, though I knew better than to believe my enemy's enemy was my friend. More like we were rivals who hadn't turned to open hostility yet. But if it gave me a chance to move forward, I'd take it.

# CHAPTER SEVEN

THE NEXT MORNING Mac and my convoy of protectors escorted me to the Eccasis-colony headquarters of Caliber. The building didn't impress by normal corporate standards, but it stood out in the colony, dwarfing the other businesses around it and looking more expensive to boot. It was a two-story rectangle with a third story in the center of the long side surrounding the main entrance. The faux granite walls were of high-enough quality to seem real. Perhaps they *were* real—I didn't know if Eccasis produced granite or not. Probably not nearby, given the local terrain.

The lobby was smaller than expected—more suited to a medium-priced hotel than a corporation—but the dome had limited space, so even rich corporations avoided waste. I'd had Fader call ahead, so a delegation of three corporate stooges met me before I even made it to the receptionist. I'd have bet a lot of money that at least two of them were lawyers. Instead of suits, they wore what passed for business wear on Eccasis—khaki cargo pants and solid-color long-sleeve shirts rolled up at the cuffs. The woman in the group spruced her combo up with a pair of low heels and a white necklace, but other than that wore the same getup. I resisted the urge to make a joke about them all using the same tailor. Sometimes I don't get enough credit for my restraint.

"Mr. Butler, it's good of you to come visit us this morning." The taller of the two men greeted me. I dubbed him Lawyer One.

"Glad to be here." I gestured to his two companions. "You really didn't need to bring the entire boarding party."

He gave me a fake lawyer smile. "When the man investigating the presumed deaths of six of our employees makes an official visit, it's a significant event."

"Presumed?" I asked. If that was their attitude, this was going to go sideways quickly.

"A technicality. They found no bodies, so legally we don't have verifiable deaths."

"How does that work with potential payments to the families of the . . . *presumed* dead?"

"Perhaps we should move to a conference room for this type of discussion?" Lawyer One's inflection rose as if it were a question. But it was a clear answer to my rather innocuous question: there *was* no payout yet. As a motive, it was slim, but it did show how Caliber thought about their people.

"Lead the way," I said.

I left Mac outside the generic conference room, which barely contained the long, medium-cheap table and twelve chairs within. It had glass walls, so he could still see us, and that seemed to satisfy him. For their sakes, I hoped none of the lawyers made a quick move toward me.

Lawyer One started over, but he had the same asshole tone. "You asked about compensation for the families. Unfortunately, that's beyond our control here on Eccasis. You'd have to take that up with corporate headquarters, and even then, they might refer you to our insurer."

"It's fine. It doesn't matter." *At least not to me. Ass-hole.* "As you know, my focus is on one specific *presumed dead* person, but I don't think it's too far out of my purview to look into the others as well, since it was a single incident and it seems likely that they all *presumably died* the same way." Now *I* was being a bit of an asshole, but they deserved it.

"We're here to assist in any way we can."

I wondered if the other two would speak at all or if they had just come along for moral support. Despite his words, I didn't believe the three of them were likely to help at all, but I did expect Caliber as a whole to cooperate. After all, Zentas had been the one who asked me to come. "Great. I'd like the full personnel file on each of the missing persons, records of all their communications on company servers, and I'd like a list of the personnel who were on the simultaneous missions. Additionally, I'd like their contact information here on Eccasis so that I can talk to them. And that includes Ms. Redstone's emails and official company communications as well, please."

"I will pass the request for the emails to the IT department. The personnel records are a matter of privacy. We can't release them without the permission of the subject of the record."

Of course they couldn't. He confirmed my initial judgment that they weren't here to help. "The subjects of the records are dead."

"*Presumed* dead. Our hands are tied here. As for the other personnel, I'll have someone check to see which of them are still colonyside and find out if they are available."

He was stonewalling me, but I'd been given the brush-off by better men than him. I got the feeling that it was more a matter of habit than a legit cover-up, so I decided to call him on it. "For someone who said that he was here to help in any way possible, you're not being particularly helpful. You know who asked me to do this investigation, right?"

"I'm sorry, sir, but we have to follow the law."

Now he was being smug, and I wanted to call Mac in and let him punch the guy in the neck. Maybe he *didn't* know Zentas had requested me. If not, I wasn't going to inform him. I'd let Stroud deal with that. Let him embarrass himself. "And *I'm* sorry, but you're pissing me off, and if you keep it up, we're going to find out how malleable the law is when I report your recalcitrance to the authorities who appointed me. You've been apprised of my charter, yes?"

Lawyer One looked like he'd bitten into something sour, and he glanced at the woman with him like he was hoping for a lifeline. He'd probably planned to BS me and make me go away with as little fuss as possible. Unfortunately for him, I didn't mind fuss. Nobody would fire *me* over ruffling a few feathers. I don't think the same could be said for Lawyer One. "We will do our best," he said, finally, "to make the members of the other teams available at your convenience."

"That would be great. If they're here, of course. I don't want to put you through too much trouble." I gave him my best fake smile. I'm no lawyer, but I've had a lot of practice being a dick. "We could start, say . . . tomorrow."

Lawyer One drew his lips into a fine line but nodded once.

"Great. I'll see you then."

**I WAS HALFWAY** back to my quarters when my device buzzed. I checked it—Oxendine—and then answered. "Butler."

"It's Ox. We've got the bomber in custody."

"That's great—"

She cut me off. "There's a problem. Meet me at the governor's office as fast as you can get there."

"Roger," I said, but she'd already hung up. I turned to Mac. "You hear that?"

"Yes, sir."

"It was odd. What kind of problem?"

"Only one way to find out," said Mac. "I wish we'd taken a cart."

"I don't know. The last cart didn't fare so well."


**FIFTEEN MINUTES LATER** we reached the governor's offices, which shared the same sub-dome as his residence. The blocky two-story building had small windows and a faux-stone exterior. An aide I hadn't met before met us at the door and ushered me down the hall and into a conference room. Oxendine's aide stood outside the door, and I left Mac with her.

Inside the well-appointed conference room, Oxendine paced up and down along on the far side of a long polished-wood table with such vigor that I thought she might wear a hole in the expensive burgundy carpet.

"What's going on?" I asked.

"That motherfuc—"

The door opened and Governor Patinchak entered, forcing Oxendine to swallow the rest of her epithet. Cora Davidson followed in the governor's wake. "Please, have a seat." He took the head of the table and Davidson sat to his right, nearest the door. Oxendine and I sat across from each other, two chairs down.

Oxendine barely hit her seat before firing her opening salvo. "Governor, your people took the suspect in the bombing case into custody and won't turn him over to my security team."

Patinchak glanced at Davidson, who nodded as if giving him permission to speak or encouraging him, which was weird but told me a lot about their relationship. "It's a civilian matter. My security personnel are questioning him."

"There was a bomb," said Oxendine, sounding calmer than I thought she was. "I have the trained interrogators, and this clearly falls under the umbrella of security of the colony, which is my purview. This is a military matter."

"We don't see it that way," said Davidson, stepping in for her boss, who looked flustered.

A vein throbbed in Oxendine's temple, and she glared hot death at Davidson. She looked like she might go over the table at the woman, and I considered whether I'd try to stop her. To her credit, she regained her composure quickly. "How do you not see a bombing as a security matter?"

"It was an attack by a civilian on a civilian. That makes it a matter for civilian authorities," said Davidson. Technically, she had a point, though it seemed a pedantic one. Oxendine had better interrogators than anything the governor could possibly have on staff. Taking jurisdiction on a technicality didn't seem wise when the goal was to get information for *all* of us.

Oxendine started to speak, reconsidered, then finally did. "At least let me send over an interrogation team. We can do it at your facility."

"That won't be necessary," said the governor, apparently finding his testicles again now that his aide had made the case.

"Carl, help me out here," said Oxendine. "You've got a lot of authority with your charter."

"Colonel Butler's charter is to investigate a missing person. This has nothing to do with that," said Davidson.

"You can't know that," spat Oxendine. She was losing her tenuous grip on her temper, so I stepped in to help her out.

"Can *I* talk to the suspect?" I asked.

"We don't think that's a good idea," said Davidson. "You were probably the target, so giving you access might look like something personal. It might endanger the ability to prosecute the case down the road."

Very smooth, *and* it actually made sense. I didn't like it, but I didn't have a rational counterargument. I looked at the governor, ignoring Davidson. "Governor, if you would allow General Oxendine's interrogators access to the suspect, I would consider it a personal favor." The governor wavered. I could see it in his face. He wanted to make me happy. I had him.

Before he could speak, Davidson interjected. "I'm afraid we can't. We'll send you a full report as soon as practical. Now, if you'll excuse us, the governor has a meeting."

"This isn't over," said Oxendine, coming out of her chair. "As soon as I leave here, I'm sending a message higher to get orders to have you turn over the prisoner."

"Of course, if that happens, we'll comply," said Davidson, a little too smugly. Now I kind of *wanted* Oxendine to go over the table at her.

I thought maybe the governor would speak, but whatever flicker of courage I'd seen in his face a moment before had fled. He got up without making eye contact and left the room.

Once they left, Oxendine slumped back in her chair. "Can you believe that shit?"

"I don't get it," I said. "What do they lose by giving you jurisdiction?"

"That asshole Davidson loses a chance to stick it to me. You saw how she railroaded the governor."

"I did. But why?"

"Because she can. That's how this whole organization works. They want to show you that they're in charge, even if it's petty."

I wasn't sure I bought the idea of pure pettiness. I didn't know Davidson well, but I always found it better to assume that other people have real motives. Given that, I had no idea what Davidson gained from antagonizing Oxendine. "Do we know anything about the suspect?"

"We do," said Oxendine. "Eric Bergman. Nominally he works as a cook in one of the dining facilities, but he's full-on EPV. He participated in the protest at the governor's the night of the bombing."

"So he used that for cover to get near the cart," I said.

"Seems likely. I don't really care about him, though. We've got him dead to rights with a fingerprint on the bomb residue. I want to know who helped him. Who is still active and a threat? He didn't do this alone."

"No, you're right," I said, but I couldn't focus on it because my mind took off in another direction. EPV. They'd tried to kill me, and if they'd do that . . . I couldn't rule out that they'd attack a Caliber team as well. Certainly EPV wanted Caliber's expansion operations stopped. Maybe they wanted it badly enough to kill for it. That made the disappearance of Xyla Redstone seem a little less open and shut.

BACK AT MY quarters, Ganos was waiting, feet drawn up under her on the sofa, while Fader sat on the other side of the room, unrelaxed in an easy chair. I could almost feel the tension, and I'd have bet decent money that they'd been sitting there in silence. So much for the team getting along.

I wanted to tell them about the prisoner, but I wanted to hear what they had found, and telling them would get us started in a different direction. "What did you find?" I headed over to pour myself some coffee. "Coffee?"

"Never touch the stuff," said Ganos like I'd offered her heroin. "I got a solid answer to your first question about the cameras. As you might suspect, someone hacked them. Both the shutdown and the restart came from outside the building. There's almost no way the military doesn't know that, by the way. It wasn't hard to find."

Yolin had told me that much. "Any idea who did it?"

"That's where it gets weird. It looks to me like it came *from* the military."

I stopped with my coffee cup halfway to my mouth. "Come again?"

"I can't be sure. Someone could be trying to make it *look* like that's where it came from. And with the fact that it was so obviously a hack . . . that's not a bad play. Leave the tracks in the system so everyone can find them but make it a false trail."

Yolin—and Oxendine—had left out that part. I wondered if they didn't know or if they *did* know and didn't tell me because they didn't want to advertise their own culpability. I leaned toward Oxendine knowing, since she seemed to have a pretty good handle on her organization. I'd have to decide whether to confront her or not. "Can you get more fidelity? Like where or who in the army might have done it?"

Ganos untwisted herself and put her feet on the floor. "Not yet. The governor's security is laughable;

the military's . . . not so much. I haven't tried them
yet. It's going to take a lot of work and more time if I
need to get inside their network. And there's more of a
chance of us getting caught, which I'm trying to avoid
for now."

"No, that makes sense. This is good, Ganos. It will
give me something I can use to press the military."

"Just be careful how you push, sir," she said. "If they
know I cracked the governor's system, they'll be more
likely to watch out for me doing other things."

"Good point. I'll figure out a cover story." That did
put me in a bit of a bind as far as what I could use, but I
could always save the information and reevaluate later.
"What else have you got?"

"I didn't go after Caliber directly, but I did take a
quick look from a safe distance. It's pretty tight there.
They have a secure system that's not connected to the
public infrastructure. But some of their people do business on the unsecure side, and I got into some emails
that were safe."

"Anything good?"

Ganos shrugged. "Nothing damning. They're worried about you poking around though. A lot of talk about
controlling what you see, putting the right face forward,
et cetera."

"That might be nothing." Lawyer One had flat out
told me that they considered my arrival significant.

"Might be," said Ganos. "I've built you a virtual safe
space and dropped the files there. I gave the captain access, too. I figured you'd want that."

"Thanks." I was glad that Ganos's apparent dislike for
Fader didn't cross into professional territory. I glanced to
Fader to catch her reaction, but she didn't give any tells.
"If you'd show her how to access it, that would be great."

"Will do. The other organization—EPV, the greenie types . . . that's a bit more of a mess."

"How so?" I asked. "Because we're going to need to look at them hard after what I just learned." Both women looked at me expectantly. "The colonial government has captured the bomber, and General Oxendine says that the guy is connected directly to EPV."

"You didn't want to lead with that?" asked Ganos.

"I wanted to hear your stuff first."

Ganos rolled her eyes.

"Have they gotten anything else from him in questioning?" asked Fader.

"Not yet." I gave them a brief rundown on the battle for jurisdiction between the governor and the military.

"That's pretty stupid," said Ganos.

"It is, but we can work around it," I said. "Find me everything you can on Eric Bergman. He works— worked—in a dining facility. That's about all I know."

"On it," said Ganos. "EPV doesn't have their own network. At least if they do, I can't find it. That means they're either using the public system or they're communicating outside the network . . . face-to-face."

No surprise there. "My guess is that they'd use the net."

"Probably," said Ganos. "Unless they were doing something big. They'd be fools to plan a bombing on the public net. Base security would have those kinds of key words flagged for sure."

"Could you check anyway?" I didn't expect much, but you can't rule out the bad guys making mistakes.

"Already did. I ran a scan for on-planet traffic with certain words. Bomb stuff, your name, investigation, the governor and his reception . . . a bunch of parameters. The problem with that is that it returned a *lot* of hits, and there's not much for it other than to go through it all and see what we've got. I can do some of it by algorithm, but it's still four figures worth of documents. It would help if I knew who was part of EPV."

"I doubt they have a roster," I said.

"I could start going through some of the hits," offered Fader.

"Start with the ones that are flagged for Butler," said Ganos. "I only did a quick scan, but I can tell you this much: The greenies *hate* the colonel. I even saw some stuff about a protest."

I snorted. Hardly a surprise. "We saw the results of that. But it's still useful. Dig in a bit and see who planned it," I said to Fader.

"I looked into the Farric guy some," said Ganos. "For the record, he seems to be pretty legit. I mean, he hates you too, but he was mad about not knowing about the protest, and he was *really* mad about the bomb."

"That's good to know," I said. "Captain Fader, if you find any other names, feed them back to Ganos so she can dig deeper on them. If Farric isn't causing problems, maybe we can find out who is. Ganos, once you get names, see if you can find leverage we can use against them."

"Can do. How dirty do you want me to play?"

"Use your best judgment." I hoped I wouldn't regret saying that.

"Also," I continued, "I want everything you can find on Cora Davidson from the governor's office. Both of you. Ganos, you do it your way, Captain Fader, you head back over there and try to dig up dirt in person. She's got an inordinate amount of power, and something about it doesn't ring quite right."

"Copy all, sir," said Fader. "What are you going to do?"

"I want to talk to Dante Farric, but I want your information and the report on what the prisoner says before I do."

"I can try to get info on that when I go over to the governor's."

"Good call," I said. "Meanwhile, I'm going to work on Caliber. They're cooperating, even if it's grudgingly. Tomorrow I'll interview whoever they put in front of me and see what I find."

# CHAPTER EIGHT

BEFORE I HEADED to Caliber for my interviews, I gave Martha Stroud a call. Her lawyers hadn't been helpful, and I wanted her to address that, to let them know that her boss had put me on the case. It took a few minutes on hold, but they finally connected me.

"I just wanted to let you know as a courtesy, your lawyers were stonewalling the other day," I said.

"I'm sure they were doing their job."

"They probably thought they were. I don't think they know the real reason I'm here."

"The *real* reason? What is that?"

"They don't know that Mr. Zentas asked for me to come."

There was silence for several seconds on the other end of the line. "What are you saying?" asked Stroud.

"Mr. Zentas, the man in charge of—"

"I know who Mr. Zentas is. I'm asking what that has to do with your investigation."

Now it was my turn to pause. "He requested the investigation."

"I'm not aware of that. Why would he do that?"

"You'll have to ask him," I said. Did she really not know? I wished I'd gone to her office so I could get a better read on her.

"I will ask for guidance right away," she said.

"Great. Until then, could you tell your lawyers to be more cooperative?"

She hesitated. "I think I'll wait for clarification first."

"What? Why? Why would I lie about this?"

"Please don't take it personally, Mr. Butler. It's my job to run operations for Caliber on Eccasis. What we want here is to get back to work. We have a completed investigation that should allow us to do that. Opening a further investigation only serves to cause more delays."

I wanted to bang my head against the wall. "If you cooperate, I'll be able to finish faster."

"Once I contact the corporate office for guidance, I will let you know." She hung up.

Well, shit. That didn't help. Zentas not informing Stroud was interesting though. It didn't seem like the type of thing that would be an oversight. I wondered what it meant.

**I ARRIVED AT** Caliber to find that Stroud hadn't gotten an answer yet, or if she did, it hadn't filtered down to her staff. They did fulfill my request for interviews but put their own spin on it to keep as much control as they could. They had me set up in one of their conference rooms. I had privacy with each of my subjects, but Caliber almost certainly had listening devices in the room. I assumed that the employees knew it too, which gave me a double challenge. First, anything I learned would go straight to Caliber leadership, and second, employees, knowing that, would be unlikely to share anything that might displease their employer. It wasn't ideal, but I took what they gave me and tried to do my best with it.

After three interviews with Caliber personnel who had been on the mission when Xyla Redstone disappeared, I had confirmed my suspicion that I'd get nothing of value and was ready to give up. They'd been coached on what to say, or at least they had the same talking points. They were polite but provided nothing I didn't already have.

Thankfully, I knew something that the Caliber lawyers didn't: I already knew who I wanted to talk to, and she was my fourth interview. Mae Eddleston's file said she was in her early thirties, but her unblemished pale skin and short dark hair combined with her thin frame to make her look about twenty-two. I made sure to ask her the exact questions that I asked the others, and she gave the same answers until I got to the question about if she knew Xyla Redstone outside of work.

She hesitated, then said, "I knew her a little, but we weren't close."

I didn't push her, pretending instead to accept the brush-off the same way I had with the others, but her tone and body language confirmed what Fader had found in Redstone's text messages. They were friends. I hoped nobody at Caliber picked up on it.

I finished the rest of my interviews, trying to find anyone else who might have something to say, but none of them did. To an outside observer—like those at Caliber watching—it probably seemed like a wasted morning, and it was, to some extent. I hadn't learned anything new.

But I'd introduced myself to Eddleston, which would make it easier to talk to her again.

**LATER THAT EVENING,** after work hours, I sent my whole team to find her. I sent Ganos because she was young and might be able to relate to her. I sent Fader because she was efficient and would find a way when others couldn't. And I sent Mac because I may be slow, but I can learn a lesson. I've had too many people who might have had something to tell me turn up dead or missing in the past several years for me to take any chances. Mac had taken to openly carrying a rifle. If the authorities had a problem with that, they hadn't said anything. Hopefully he wouldn't scare Eddleston off. We weren't kidnapping her, just asking her to chat in a less monitored location.

Unfortunately, we had nowhere to bring her except to my quarters, and if anyone followed my team, they'd probably see it. At least they wouldn't hear us. I'd found a scanner in the box of hi-tech gear that detected electronic listening devices, which I used to scan my apartment. I found three, which should have pissed me off but didn't. At least I knew the playing field. My first thought was that they were the governor's equipment, since it was his guest quarters, but I couldn't rule out the military. They might not even have put them in there specifically for me. Maybe someone wanted to listen in on all the governor's guests. Either way, whoever installed them didn't have ears anymore. That itself would tip the eavesdroppers off, but there was nothing for that.

Ganos entered with Eddleston, hanging back so that the other woman could take the lead. Eddleston looked around, not trying to hide it. She wore a loose pink print shirt that hung from her petite frame and she had her short hair clipped back away from her face. "They sure took care of you."

I shrugged and tried to look guilty. "Yeah. I didn't ask for it, but I'm not complaining."

"I'd say not."

"Thanks for coming," I said.

"I felt like it was the right thing to do. For Xyla."

"You did know her, then?"

"We were friends." She paused as her face tightened. "Yeah. We were pretty close."

She'd said otherwise earlier, which told me that she understood the situation the same way I did. She couldn't talk at work, but here she could. "You want to sit down? Can I get you something to drink?"

"You have whiskey?" she asked.

"That I do." I walked to the counter and showed her the bottle, as if asking her approval. Any whiskey drinker would approve, but I didn't mind showing off. As we took seats in the living area, Fader stayed within earshot, but Mac and Ganos made themselves scarce.

"Did that come with the room? Because that's a hell of a perk."

I laughed. "No, I brought it with me."

"Still," she said.

I got two glasses and poured us each doubles. "Ice?"

"A little water would be good."

"That it would." I splashed a bit of water into each drink and brought Eddleston hers.

"So. Maria said you thought I might have more information. How did you know that?" She asked it casually and put her drink to her lips, but her eyes never left me. This was an important question.

"There was a little hitch in your voice when you men-

tioned Xyla during our interview at the Caliber facility."
I didn't feel like I should mention that I'd been through
her texts. No need to creep her out. "It made me think
that you might have had something else to say. I didn't
follow up on it there, because I didn't want everybody at
the company listening."

Her shoulders relaxed.

"Everything okay?"

"Yeah. I think we're good. I want to help."

"Has anyone questioned you before about the day she
disappeared?" I knew they had. I'd seen the transcript in
the military's report. But I wanted to give her a chance
to talk about it.

"An army officer did, pretty soon after it happened."

"Did you tell the officer the truth?"

She shrugged slightly. "Yeah, I answered what he
asked."

"But," I prompted.

"But he didn't ask the right questions."

"And you didn't volunteer information?"

She sipped her drink. "This is wonderful. No, I didn't
volunteer. He didn't seem interested. He gave me the impression of someone going through the motions. And I
didn't have anything solid anyway. Just a feeling."

I could see that happening with an investigating officer. People want to know you care before they tell you
things, and the officer would have been assigned the task
as an additional duty. Nobody liked that. "You didn't
mention it to anyone else?"

"Who would I tell? Caliber? I know this much: They
wanted to get the incident behind them as fast as possible. When the military closed the case, well . . . Caliber
definitely didn't want to hear my theory and potentially
reopen it." That corroborated what Stroud had told me.

"I want to hear it. You want to tell me about it?"

She thought about it.

"I'll do my best to make sure nothing gets back to Caliber," I said.

"It's not that," she said. "I don't really like the job anymore, anyway. If they fired me, they'd be doing me a favor. I'm just trying to figure out how to say this without coming off like a conspiracy nut."

"Would it help if I told you that I've seen enough ridiculous situations that I'm not ever going to judge someone who has an idea that's a bit out there?"

She smiled. "Okay—I'm just going to lay it out. You can make of it what you will."

"I appreciate it."

She nodded. "The first thing that drew my attention was the gunshots. A lot of them, but in a really short time period."

"About how many?"

"Fifty? Maybe more? All in about ten seconds. Then silence."

I made a note, not because I needed it but to demonstrate my interest. "Did you recognize the type of weapon?" It was a long shot, but I had nothing to lose.

She thought about it. "There were two different sounds. Most of the shots were bangs, but there were a couple of pulse shots, too. Two, I think. Maybe three? At least two."

Interesting. "Do you know if there's a standard for who carries what weapon on a team?"

"I'm not sure there's a rule, but it's pretty much the same with every team. The security guys—the non-skilled members of the groups—they always carry rifles. They look like that one there." She pointed to a Bitch.

"How many security personnel travel with a team?" I

could have looked it up, but it gave her something easy she could tell me and got her used to answering my questions.

"Four technicians, two security."

"Do the technicians carry weapons?"

"I don't. But we can, if we want. I'm just not comfortable with it. Some carry pulse pistols."

That made sense. They were light and easy to use. "Did Xyla carry?"

She shook her head. "No. She's a . . . she *was* . . . a xenobiologist, like me. None of us carry weapons. It's our job to protect the wildlife, not kill it."

"One xenobiologist per team?" I asked.

"Usually, unless there's a specific need. There are only a few of us colonyside. Wildlife protection isn't really a Caliber priority, if you know what I mean. We're mostly here to figure out ways around the protectionist rules."

"You don't sound like you approve." I wouldn't expect her to, as someone who studied living things.

She shrugged. "It's a job. Academic work doesn't pay nearly as well."

I didn't fully buy that, but I let her keep the illusion. "What happened after you heard the shots?"

"After the shooting stopped, we all kind of froze. Nothing like that had happened before—not to me, anyway. Not to most of us. All that shooting meant something must be out there. And the things that someone might shoot at . . . well they aren't good."

"Do you remember your immediate thoughts about the threat? What came to mind first?"

"My first thought was ursagrans. They're like a cross between a bear and elephant. I even remember listening, to see if I could hear one crashing through the bush. If you've ever been around one . . . it's like this rumble and you can see the lower canopy moving from a distance."

"You said that was your first thought . . ."

"Right. But when I calmed down, it didn't seem likely. Ursagrans are mostly solitary, and they generally don't mess with people unless you threaten them. Or if you go near their cubs, which are also huge, so people avoid that. That led me to hominiverts, which are pack animals that resemble extra-large green apes. They can be very territorial, and they're omnivores. Nobody found the bodies, and 'verts could conceivably haul them off to feed later."

This time I made a note for real. Eddleston was an expert in the field, and if she thought hominiverts were a potential cause, it bore another look. The military report had cited jungle fauna as the most likely cause of disappearance, but they didn't go into detail. "You came to that thought later, after nobody could find the team?"

"I don't remember," she said. "Sorry. It's been a while."

"No problem. You're doing great. Can you think of anything else natural that could have caused a similar situation?"

She pulled a coaster over and set her drink down on it. "Not really. Most of the stuff that will kill you out there . . . it's not stuff you would handle with a gun. There are insects and small reptiles . . . the variety of poisons is impressive and especially deadly to humans."

"But security carries weapons, so there must be some use."

She scrunched her face up a little in a way that showed her doubt. "I guess. But that's not what felt off to me. The thing that struck me . . . one of *our* team was missing. Schultz. One of our security guys."

If I hadn't been paying rapt attention before, that did it. "Missing how?"

"I looked around—and I remember this clearly—there were only five of us. Our other security person, a woman

named Li . . . she was there. She hustled us all into the
vehicle and we headed to the other team's location to try
to give whatever help we could."

"But Schultz wasn't in the vehicle?" I didn't know if
that was significant or not, but I had a thread and wanted
to pull it. I made a note to question Li. She'd driven
off with only five in her vehicle, which even a moder-
ately competent security person wouldn't do when she'd
started with six.

"He wasn't. But he was at the other site when we got
there, already searching."

Odd. I wished I knew the ground. That would help me
understand *how* odd. "How far apart were the two sites?"

She thought about it. "By trail? Maybe a kilometer. I
don't know. Direct line? Maybe a couple hundred meters?
I'm not great with distance and direction, but the gunfire
sounded close."

A civilian's judgment of distance regarding gunshots
was unreliable. Noise could be deceptive, distorted by
terrain or even wind direction. "Maybe Schultz could
have cut through the jungle?"

She nodded. "He had to have. And that's what he said
when I asked him about it. That he heard the shots and
reacted on instinct."

"You asked him? How did he look when he answered?"
I wish I could have asked him that myself. I would, now,
if he'd been on my list from Caliber. I checked. He was
one of two people out of the twelve who'd survived the
mission and weren't available.

Of course he wasn't.

She scrunched her face up a bit again. "I don't know. I
was kind of freaked out at the time. I didn't really think
it through until later."

I kept my voice steady and deliberate. I didn't want to

show any disapproval that might stop her from talking. "Do you remember how long it took you to reach the site of the incident?"

"Maybe ten minutes? I'm not sure. It took a while to get our team loaded up. I remember Ivan didn't want to leave his equipment, and Li was yelling at him to hurry up."

That answer didn't help much. Too many variables. It could have been five or fifteen minutes, given her estimate. "Do you remember anything about the site when you arrived? What happened?"

"We all wanted to get out, but Li told us to stay in the vehicle. But someone went out—I don't remember who—and the rest of us followed. Security started yelling at us and people were yelling back. I think I yelled. It was chaotic."

"Did anyone look for the bodies?"

"I don't think so. They wanted to get out of there, I know that. Then it started pouring. One of those jungle rains where it goes from zero to blinding in about three seconds. Once that happened, everyone jumped back in the vehicles. It's hard to see in our suits because the face-screens get wet. They're treated so the water slicks off, but it still causes problems."

I sipped my drink to give myself time to think. The timing of the shots could have meant a lot of things. Security firing first with their rifles followed by a few pistol shots when the technicians realized the danger— that could apply to any situation. The speed of the incident—that's what struck me. It happened fast. Fast usually meant planned. And if this was a planned operation, that changed everything. But I didn't see any way that EPV could get a team out into the jungle that could disable a group of six and make them disappear as fast as it happened.

That made me think about Schultz. I hadn't thought much about him not being available to interview at the time, but with Eddleston's information about his role on the mission, it became more significant. Maybe Schultz was working for more than one organization. After all, the bomber had worked another job. "Hold on, I need to check something." I looked at my list of interviewees and compared it to the list in the official report to find the name of the second person who hadn't been available for an interview.

"Who is Ortega?" I asked.

"He used to work security," said Eddleston. "I think he transferred out maybe a month ago."

"He was on the mission."

She considered it. "I guess. He wasn't on my team. You think he's important?"

"He worked on the third team. To answer your question, I don't know what I think," I said. "I'm just collecting fragments of ideas in hopes that I can piece them together later." It was thin. Two missing people out of twelve didn't seem unreasonable. People moved on from jobs. The fact that both were security on the mission might be coincidence.

But I didn't believe in coincidence.

"Can you think of any reason why someone would want to harm that specific team?" I asked.

"Do you think there was foul play?" Her face lit up a bit, as if that idea excited her.

"Do *you*?" I asked.

"I . . . well . . . that's the conspiracy part I mentioned. I think Schultz knows more than he told the military. He has to."

I pulled up the report on my device and found Schultz's statement. It only took me thirty seconds to read. He didn't mention being first on the scene of the disappearance. All he said was that when he arrived, everybody was already gone. "Did you ever question him about that?" I asked.

"No way. I'm not accusing a guy who carries a gun for a living of lying."

"Right. Of course not. Let's go back to my original question. Was there anything special about that particular team?"

"Xyla's team? I'm not sure. She was working on something with the hominiverts. She'd mentioned that it would help us move them out of areas we wanted to develop."

"What can you tell me about that?"

She frowned. "Not much. It was hush-hush, and it's not my area of expertise, so I wasn't involved. She told me it was big, but that's about it."

"Was she working on that the day she disappeared?"

"I can't say for sure," she said. "Hey, you can't tell anybody about the research, okay? They'll know it came from me."

I mimed zipping my lips. "I won't say a word."

"Okay, good." She paused, as if debating what to say. "You think this was intentional. I can tell by your questions."

"Not necessarily—"

"You *do*. Who? Who would do this?"

I had to regain control of the interview. "Who do *you* think would do it?"

She didn't hesitate. "The eco-protectionists. They'd do anything to keep us from developing the planet, and if Xyla had a breakthrough that would move us in that direction, well . . . it would make sense that they'd want to stop her."

That she'd come to the same potential conclusion as I did wasn't surprising. EPV clearly had the motive. What

I couldn't see was the means. Schultz might have been on their payroll, but one guy taking on a team of six and making them disappear didn't make a great theory. Regardless, Eddleston couldn't help anymore with that, and I didn't want to drag her in any deeper than I already had. "I really appreciate you sharing your honest thoughts. I have some questions about EPV myself, and I promise I'm going to give them a hard look."

"Thanks." She finished her drink, and I downed mine as well. We shared contact information and I had Mac and Ganos escort her back to her quarters. I poured another drink and offered one to Fader, who refused.

"What do you think, sir?"

"EPV was already a suspect, so not much changes there. I want to talk to Li again and ask her about Schultz. That will piss off Caliber, but that's a good thing. The more I can pressure them, the more they'll have to react. They're hiding something, and I want to know why."

"Roger, sir. You want me to set that up?"

"No, I'll handle that. The Caliber lawyers are going to be obstinate, so I might as well get involved right away. Besides, I have something else I want you to work."

"Yes, sir." Fader opened a screen on her device to take notes.

I took a deep swig. "You're not going to like it."

"Why's that, sir?"

"I think we need to go see the site where Redstone disappeared."

To her credit, Fader didn't overreact, though her face and shoulders tensed. "Mac's going to be the one who doesn't like it." She wasn't wrong about Mac. "What's your purpose, sir?"

"As I was talking to Eddleston, I found that I couldn't put the picture together in my head."

"There's video of the entire location, sir. And for what there isn't, we can task a drone to get some. Since the information is available from easier means, my recommendation is that we do not need to leave the dome."

I had to admit, having Fader around as a sounding board and voice of reason was starting to grow on me. She had a point, and I honestly had to consider it. I had to be sure I wasn't acting out of frustration or from some hidden desire to get back into the field. I wouldn't be the first person to fall prey to that kind of seduction. More to Fader's credit, she didn't interrupt me as I thought about it. She'd made her case and stopped pushing.

"That's a good point. I'll ask the military for a drone recon first. I don't know if it will be enough though— Eddleston mentioned a guy cutting through the jungle, and that they didn't search immediately for bodies. I don't know if a drone will give me an appreciation for that, but it won't hurt to try."

"I'll let Mac know a mission outside is a possibility so he can start planning."

I laughed. "And so he can have time to swear about it and calm down before we actually go."

"That too. I'll call the military in the morning to set up the drone flight. If they push back, I'll let you know."

"Great."

I shook my head once she left. I kept doing it. All I had to do was accept the military report and let it go. I'd officially questioned people at Caliber. I'd talked to the military and I didn't suspect a cover-up. I could write up that I hadn't found anything new, pretend that the bomb was unrelated, get on a ship and go home. Nobody would even question it. Instead I was going to keep digging. Apparently, I'd never learn.

# CHAPTER NINE

I CALLED ON CALIBER'S lawyers again, this time with a specific question: What had happened to Schultz and Ortega? Lawyer One got back to me quickly, which made me think that word had come from higher to help me, but when I asked him, he still hadn't heard anything. Schultz and Ortega had both been sent away. The lawyer insinuated that it was for misconduct about a month ago, but he refused to tell me what the misconduct was because it wasn't germane to my investigation and there were privacy issues. I didn't buy it, but I didn't have leverage at the moment, so moved on to another angle.

It took me almost ten minutes to get Lawyer One to set me up with another meeting with the security guard, Li. I refused to meet at their office, citing my schedule and a subsequent meeting. I'm sure he didn't believe me, but it kept me from having to mention being monitored out loud, which let everybody save face. I needed to have her on my own turf. Letting someone hear my questions to Li would give away too much about my suspicion regarding Schultz.

Li was my height, with an athletic build, and she stood in the door to my suite almost at the position of attention. Mac sat at the end of the table, to my right, and I asked Li to sit across from me. I'd asked Mac to stay because Fader was out trying to coordinate drone surveillance.

"You're ex-military, aren't you?" I asked, trying to make her more comfortable.

"Yes, sir. Eight years."

"You miss it?"

"I miss the people, sir." She spoke in short, clipped syllables, and I got the impression that she just wanted this over with, so I decided to curtail the small talk.

"Yeah, me too." I really did. When I missed it at all, it was always the people. "I just had a couple of follow-up questions from our meeting the other day, if that's okay."

"Yes, sir."

"You were paired with another security person on the mission, right?"

"Yes, sir."

"Do you remember who that was?"

"Schultz, sir."

"Was he with you the whole time?"

"Yes, sir."

That didn't match Eddleston's story, but it could have been an oversight. I gave her another chance. "When you first heard the shots, I assume you loaded your team up in the vehicle. Schultz was with you then?"

"Oh. No, sir. He went on foot."

"How did you know that he was doing that?"

"He told me over the headset, sir. Security personnel have our own net."

"Did you find anything odd about that?"

"No, sir."

I waited for her to add something to that, letting it hang until the silence got awkward, but she seemed determined not to give me anything. "What kind of guy was Schultz?" I asked, finally giving up. "Did he know his stuff?"

"I don't know, sir. He seemed fine."

"He didn't have any issues with the company?"

"We weren't close, sir."

I tried several other versions of the same questions, but no matter what I asked, I got the same clipped answers. I couldn't say for sure that someone had rehearsed her, but I'd have bet a lot of money that she'd been directed not to say anything. It seemed pointless to continue, so I ended the interview.

"Well, that was useful," I said to Mac, once she left.

**FADER GAVE ME** more bad news when she returned, informing me that we wouldn't get a drone flight. It took me a minute to understand that it wasn't about us—the law banned *all* drone flights on Eccasis. Which seemed ridiculous. Fader researched it and found it was tied to an environmental protest—courtesy of our good friends at EPV—regarding some sort of moth. Apparently, drones impacted their migration or something. Fader gave me the reference document, but life is too short to read forty pages of bureaucratic nonsense.

What made it more bullshit was that I'd seen someone launch a small drone with my own eyes. I sent Oxendine a message about that, and she acknowledged that corporations routinely violated the rules, but she didn't. I'd asked her why, if she knew that, she didn't do anything to stop them. After she told me to do something anatomically impossible to myself, she explained that enforcement of that law fell on a civilian agency that reported to the governor, not the military. It wasn't security.

With no drone flight and with satellite video obscured by the jungle, we made plans to do it the old-fashioned way. It took a full day to set up the mission.

The military didn't exactly try to stop us, but they didn't go out of their way to make things happen, either. I think Oxendine might have been hoping that I'd come to my senses and drop the idea, but she couldn't really tell me no unless she had a strong reason, so I pushed on.

My team made use of the time. Ganos kept digging into systems to see what she could find. I specifically had her look for real-time communication regarding my outside mission. Once we'd told the military, it was no longer a secret, so I wanted to see what sort of changes it might cause in local patterns. Because the camera hack during the bombing came from the military, I had to believe that somebody inside the headquarters might have reason to leak information. If EPV had done something to sabotage Redstone's mission—though I still couldn't figure out how they could have—and EPV had also been behind the bombing, it stood to reason that they might come after *my* mission as well.

Ganos informed me that EPV's communications security was "a total joke" and that she could read anything Dante Farric put on the net. None of it even mentioned our mission, which I took as a good sign. She was still hesitant to go after Caliber, which I understood. At some point I was probably going to have to tell her to do it anyway, but for now I asked her to dig up whatever she could on Schultz, his background, why he'd left, and any potential ties he might have had to EPV.

**THE MORNING OF** the mission, Mac, Fader, and I joined three soldiers at their vehicle, which was a six-wheeled version of a GOAT—a personnel carrier. A tall, dark-skinned master sergeant named Williams greeted me with a crisp salute when I arrived. I returned it but told him he didn't need to do that.

"Roger that, sir," he said, without a trace of emotion in it.

"It's just us?" I asked.

"Yes, sir. We're good. Minimum out-the-gate mission is three soldiers, which we've got. Plus, your man there looks like he knows how to use that Bitch he's carrying. But we won't need it."

"Got it." Mac also carried a black duffel bag with two more rifles as well as a few other goodies. I had him keep everything hidden until we left the dome—let anyone who saw us leaving see just the four weapons. Unlike Williams, I didn't hold any illusions. I wanted to see the terrain, but I was also setting us out as bait. If I was going to go fishing, I wanted to have some surprises planned. "You know the mission?"

"We've got the coordinates, sir, and we got some general parameters. But as far as I'm concerned, the mission's whatever you tell me it is." He was the kind of no-bullshit noncom that I'd always loved when I served. Guys like him made me miss it.

"Should be simple," I said. "I just need to see the ground. Get a feel for things out there. I'll probably want to visit the two secondary locations too." I wanted to see where the attack happened, but I also wanted to see where Eddleston's team—especially Schultz—had been in relation. I'd seen it on a map but being there might show me something different.

"Roger that, sir. We've got your suits. My soldiers will help you get them on properly."

"How are they? The suits?" I asked.

"Not bad. Way better than the older model, which was stiff. These are super flexible, but they won't tear. They *will* puncture though, so be careful of that. A suit breach won't kill you immediately—a human can survive about twelve hours out there—but with all the meds they pump into you if you get exposed, you'll almost wish you were dead."

That sounded horrible. "Good to know."

He picked up a helmet and rotated it as he spoke. "The helmets are pretty low tech. They've got great sight lines, but no heads-up. This version was designed for exploring, not combat. The military versions are modified with a tracking system that allows us to use guided bullets, so at least there's that."

"How much does the lack of tech in the helmet hold you back?" I asked. It seemed like a strange place to cut back on tech.

"Not at all. The stuff that's dangerous out here wouldn't show up on a heads-up display anyway."

That jibed with what Eddleston had told me, so I took it as truth. We suited up, which took a few minutes, making sure of our seals and that we all had the right mix of oxygen. I tried a few stretches to get a feel for the suit and found that I could move naturally, almost like walking around in street clothes and a helmet. The wide bubble of the faceplate allowed full vision, and while it wouldn't stop a bullet, it felt like it would take a pretty good thump without cracking.

Williams checked the entire team a second time and we loaded up. The master sergeant rode next to the driver, which left the three of us in the back with the third member of his team. The vehicle had a gunner's hatch up top, but nobody occupied it. Each side of the vehicle had three long, rectangular windows, and when I tapped on one I estimated it as about two centimeters of armo-glass. *That* would stop a bullet, but still allowed us to get a decent view. A flat screen at the front of the crew compartment showed a forward view, and the soldier with us showed me how to use the joystick to rotate it. I hadn't seen that feature in a military vehicle before. Usually in the back, you were just a passenger. You went where the vehicle took you and you got out when ordered.

"Why do we have this?" I asked.

"We carry scientists sometimes," said the soldier. "They always want to see what's going on, and this keeps us from having to dismount every twenty meters. It's got a zoom function, too."

"That's convenient. I wish I'd had one of these on every mission."

"It's a pain in the ass, sir. People in back start thinking they're in charge and trying to drive."

I laughed at the not-so-subtle hint. Soldiers had a universal distaste for being told what to do by people looking at a screen, unless that person really knew what they were doing. "I won't do that."

We moved out slowly, maintaining the fifteen-kilometer-per-hour rate allowed inside the dome, and then stopped for several minutes when we reached the gate until someone came over, opened Williams's door, and took his tablet that had our authentication on it. They returned it several minutes later.

I keyed my comm. "Is it always this secure on the way out of the dome?"

"It is when you take the military gate, sir. It's always staffed, and if your digital pass doesn't check out when they call Ops, you don't leave."

"So theoretically we know everybody who is outside the gate at all times."

"Not even close, sir. The corporations run the commercial gates. Basically, anyone can have their own exit if they're willing to pay for it and keep it up to code. It's not cheap, since the rules for the airlocks are one thing that everybody takes seriously, but the companies control their own access in and out."

That seemed like a poor way to do business. "So it's a free-for-all."

"Yes, sir. But in truth, we'd need a lot more manpower to operate all the gates that this place needs, and we don't have it. We do random inspections to make sure that people aren't bringing in stuff that they shouldn't, but that's about it."

That confirmed Oxendine's reported lack of resources, but it sounded like a recipe for smuggling. Suddenly, it didn't seem so outlandish that a bomb got through. That reminded me—certainly the military had tracked down the source of the explosives by now. I sent a message to Fader's device asking her to check up on it once we got back.

Outside the dome we drove about a hundred meters down a paved road before it turned to dirt. Bright green grass grew to the sides, but only a few centimeters tall, probably trimmed to keep the heavy vegetation away from the dome. After about four hundred meters we reached the jungle where the vegetation grew so thick along and over the road that it resembled a multihued green tunnel. The video feed adjusted to accommodate the lower light coming through the triple canopy, and I was immediately glad that we came. Pictures didn't do the jungle justice. In most places dense growth came right to the side of the road, if not actually encroaching on it. In other places it opened a bit with clearings large enough to park a vehicle or two. Small trails led off the main one at random intervals, and we passed one full-size track that branched from ours in a vee.

We had about forty kilometers to travel, so I settled

in for what I expected would be almost an hour's ride. The mission on which Redstone disappeared had been to assess the soil, vegetation, and animal activity in sector 376R as an early step toward development there. The mission log hadn't mentioned mining, but given Caliber's business, they probably always assessed that. Expansion wouldn't reach sector 376R for at least four years, based on current rates for development of Eccasis. Maybe Caliber was that far ahead of the game, but it seemed more likely that they had some other purpose. Eddleston had mentioned research, and they'd want to keep that as far away from the main dome as possible, given that it might not be legal.

"Look at that, sir," said Fader, interrupting my thought. A swarm of pink moths, each the size of a human hand engulfed the right side of the vehicle. Some of the insects seemed to bounce off the glass, almost like they wanted to get in.

"They're beautiful," I said.

"Deadly, too," said Fader. "Just one of them is poisonous enough to rot a limb off a human. And they travel in swarms of thousands."

"I'll keep my distance," I said.

"Our suits are proofed against them," she said. "But there are plenty of other things out here that can kill you even in your suit."

Williams's voice broke in over the comm. "There are a lot of things that can kill you, but we've got scanners that track significant life-forms in the area. I can port it back to your screen if you'd rather have that than the visual-spectrum view."

"Visual is good for now," I said. "I want to get a feel for the terrain. I trust you to watch the scans."

"Roger that, sir."

"Do the civilian teams that come out have those sensors, too?" I asked. I hadn't seen it in the report.

"I'm not sure, sir. I've never been in one of their vehicles."

I made a note to check that when we got back. We slowed a few times to work our way around parts of the road that had developed holes and gullies, probably from the regular rains, but otherwise we made good progress. I directed Williams to the spot where Eddleston's team had been. "Are we safe?"

"Scans show no major life-forms, and they've got a two-kilometer range in this terrain," he said. "Keep your eyes out for snakes, though. Sometimes the scans miss them."

"Roger."

Mac handed Fader and me rifles, and I checked my load to make sure I had guided bullets. The rear door dropped, and Mac led our team down the ramp into a small clearing. He paused after a couple of steps and scanned, though a wall of green vegetation blocked everything past twenty meters. A low-growing plant with almost-round leaves the size of a kitchen table proved especially challenging to visibility.

"Holy crap." I'd had doubts when Eddleston told me that they hadn't looked for bodies, but now I got it. If someone went fifty meters from where I was standing, I might never find them. It took me a minute to locate a small path into the jungle, and I walked toward it. I'd have to crouch, but it would allow me to push past the first wall of jungle. "Pull up a map," I said. "Tell me what's in that direction. Is it toward the spot where the team disappeared?"

The net stayed silent for a moment before a female voice that I assumed was one of the soldiers answered. "It's close, sir. About twenty degrees off, give or take."

"Thanks." So that part of the story checked out, at least initially. If Schultz had heard firing, he might have seen the hole in the foliage and moved that way. I started to push my way into the jungle, but Mac hustled to get in front of me. Williams and one of his soldiers hung back, weapons ready, keeping watch while I followed Mac in. Vines grabbed at my feet, which reminded me of the low-level pain in my robot foot that I usually ignored. After a few steps I figured out that if I stepped deliberately high, I could move easier. After maybe twenty meters we hit another clear area. I looked back, and I couldn't see anyone from our team until Williams—identifiable by his size—broke through into the clearing.

"Are we okay out here?" I asked.

"We're fine, sir. Darby will warn us if there's anything headed our way. We'll have plenty of time to make it back to the vehicle if that happens."

"How far could we go and still be safe?" I asked. "It's only a couple hundred meters to the site of the disappearance. Could we make it on foot?"

"It'd be risky, sir. The sensors would cover you, but if they did show a threat, you'd have a two-hundred-meter sprint through shitty terrain to get back to safety."

"But in an emergency, you could do it, right? Especially if there was another team at the other end. Let's go a little farther. I won't push it." I needed to know if Schultz could have made the trek, if only to rule some things out.

"We're good, sir." Williams held up a half-meter-long knife, which started to vibrate when he thumbed a switch. "If we've got to, we can cut our way out."

I wondered if Schultz had had a vibro-machete. Eddleston hadn't mentioned it. "Don't use that for now," I said. "I want to see how far we can get without it."

"Roger that, sir." Williams flipped the switch and the blade went silent.

I gestured to an opening on the far side of the clearing. "Lead on, Mac."

We had to wind our way through a couple tough spots before we finally came into another, smaller clearing. I called a halt and looked around before we headed back. Schultz *could* have made it through. But how would he have known that in the heat of the moment? Maybe the sound of the guns had motivated him to take a risk, but the openings and paths weren't obvious.

We worked our way back to the vehicle and loaded up for the trip to the spot where Redstone had disappeared. I timed the drive at eight minutes, forty-six seconds, which confirmed the estimate that Eddleston had given me.

"Where to, sir?" Williams asked, after we dismounted. "Looks like we'll have to cut our way in if you want to move beyond here."

"Let's give it a shot," I said. "Take a heading that would bring us to our previous location on a direct line. I want to press into the jungle for about forty or fifty meters and see what we see." Not seeing an opening here didn't mean someone couldn't get through from the other direction, especially if they'd had gunfire to lead them.

"Roger that, sir." The vegetation fell quickly to the practiced vibro-machete swings of Williams and one of his soldiers. Fader stayed with the third soldier, who remained with the vehicle again, in the top hatch, weapon at the ready, providing overwatch and keeping an eye on the sensors.

It took us several minutes to hit a clearing, only managing about five meters per minute, waiting for our guides to clear the way. Unfortunately, that didn't tell me anything. Schultz could have found a clearer path from the other end. To know for sure, we'd have to re-create the event or search an entire arc around one side of the vehicle.

A burst of automatic fire jumped my heart into over-drive, and I whipped around. "What was that?" No re-sponse. I took a split second to check the settings on my comm before I realized the problem. Nobody else had spoken on the net, either. My comm was dead. Mac was banging the side of his helmet, probably dead too. An-other burst of fire. I'd figure out the comm later. I started running.

Williams reached our recently cut path first, followed by Mac, and I chased them with the other soldier hot on my tail.

More shots. Two distinct weapons. Bitches. Probably the soldier with the vehicle and Fader. I tried my comm again. Dead. Except for the gunshots, nothing registered over us crashing through the jungle.

We tumbled out into the clearing with the vehicle and I swung around, looking for the reason for gunfire. A huge figure burst from the other side of the clearing, its green fur making it almost invisible against the jungle back-ground. It had to be three meters tall. I raised my rifle to my shoulder and fired four quick shots. With guided rounds, I couldn't miss from forty meters, and they all slammed into the ape's chest.

It roared in pain and stopped, arms raised, angry. It didn't fall, instead focusing in on me as if appraising an annoying pest. Shots popped around me, but none hit it. Movement caught my eye. They had their own targets.

Shit.

I dropped my magazine, letting it fall to the ground, grabbed a mag of explosive from my thigh pocket, and slammed it home.

The monster—the hominivert—charged. I manually

flipped my weapon to automatic and fired a long burst. The exploding rounds drowned out the gunfire. Blood and chunks of fur flew. The ape-thing screamed, took a staggering step toward me, and finally fell five meters away, thudding against the ground so hard that the vibration reached my boots.

I scanned for more targets and found two by the vehicle, pounding on it. One was on top while the other shook it from the side, rocking it on its wheels. I fired a burst of three into the back of the one on the ground and resighted on the one on top. It looked at me for a split second before I fired and leaped off the rear of the vehicle just as I pulled the trigger.

I missed.

I scanned for more targets but couldn't find any.

"They're running." Williams's voice in my headset startled me. "We have comms back."

"Fader, are you in the vehicle?" I said over the comm.

"Roger, sir. Two of us in here. I'm hurt but not bad." I assessed the rest of our force quickly, all four up and moving. Only the one dead hominivert remained. What was left of it. The one I'd wounded must have made it back to the jungle.

"Let's move before they regroup and come back," said Williams.

"No argument here. Load up explosive bullets, just in case."

"We don't have them, sir. It's not part of the basic load."

"There are more magazines in the vehicle," said Mac, and Williams quickly moved to get them.

No explosive rounds? That made no sense, but I didn't have time to dig into it now. I hustled to the vehicle, only then realizing how out of breath I was. I fell into my seat and we lurched forward, moving before I got belted in.

Fader was already in her seat, and though it was hard to tell with her suit and helmet on, she seemed to be breathing deeply. "You okay?" I asked.

"Bruised, I think, sir. One of the creatures hit me from behind just as I reached the vehicle. Luckily the force of the blow threw me forward into the vehicle. But I banged my shoulder pretty hard."

Shit. If it had grabbed her instead . . . we got lucky. I ran through the action in my head, trying to piece it together. If nothing else, we'd learned for sure that it was hominivert territory. That still didn't explain something though.

"What the fuck happened to our comms?"

"Not sure, sir," said Williams. "If I didn't know better, I'd say it was jamming."

I got a chill despite the sweat dripping down my face. It *did* remind me of jamming. I hadn't thought to try an alternate channel in the moment, which is the first thing I'd have done in combat. The thing was, we didn't even *have* an established alternate frequency set. I hadn't even considered it for our type of mission. You don't expect green apes to be able to jam your comms. What the actual fuck? The apes couldn't have jammed us. Could they? That was absurd. The timing was so perfect, though. We lost comms right as they attacked, and I didn't know of anything else out here that could interfere like that. "I'm going out on a limb, but hominiverts don't jam comms, right?"

"They don't, sir," said Williams. "At least they never have before."

*That we know of.* "I'm going to want the techs to go through the electronics when we get back and see what they can figure out."

"You and me both, sir," said Williams. "Darby, did you try the vehicle's comm, or just your suit?"

"Both, Sergeant," the driver responded.

"Just to us, or back to base?"

"Just to you, Sergeant."

I could forgive Darby for not trying base. Headquarters couldn't have done anything for us anyway.

"Did we have sensor warning?" Williams asked.

"We did, Sergeant, but it came late. The alarm flashed and I tried to call you and then they were on us. It all happened in just a couple seconds. I fired a burst in the air so you'd hear it."

"That was smart thinking," I said. She'd probably saved us. If we'd been caught in the jungle instead of in the clearing . . . I didn't want to think about it. Instead, I focused on the hominiverts. From what I knew from Eddleston, they were territorial. If what had just happened to us happened to an unprepared team of civilians, I could close my case.

Again, though, this made everything almost *too* neat and clean. Something in the back of my mind rebelled against it. Redstone was a xenobiologist. It was her job to know these animals. Had their sensors failed, too? And why weren't people carrying explosive ammunition, when the job clearly required it? I had too many questions to answer to even begin to think of putting a bow on the mission.

On a positive note, I had some ways to move forward now. We survived the attack only because we had weapons that nobody else knew about. We could have died. Almost kill me once, and that's just business. But twice? That was getting personal. That's where my mind went. My gut said that this attack wasn't random, and I usually trusted my gut. Farric, Oxendine, Caliber, the governor . . .

Yeah. I had questions.

# CHAPTER TEN

**A**FTER SENDING FADER—against her will—off to get a med scan, I headed over to Oxendine's headquarters. Mac practically stormed in front of me, slamming his feet down with every step. I felt very safe. Seeing him like that, nobody would dream of coming at us. The three soldiers scrambling to keep up helped too. Already informed of the events of our patrol, Oxendine was waiting for me in her outer office.

"How come your soldiers don't carry explosive rounds?" I asked, before she could even get the door closed to her inner office.

"Slow down, Carl. I've got information you're going to want."

I paced over to a chair without waiting for her to offer it. "Okay. But I'm coming back to that question. You're putting soldiers at risk."

"Noted. There were some anomalies with the technology in the vehicle that took you on mission."

"Anomalies?" I put a sneer into the word. No *shit* there were anomalies, and I was still pissed about the explosive rounds.

"The cameras that should have captured the attack didn't."

"They didn't work?"

"They *did*," she said, "Except for the time during the attack."

"Same as the comms."

"We're still working on that." She picked up her unlit cigar but didn't look at it. "It's not unreasonable to think that the same thing that blanked the comms also got the cameras," she said.

"The sensors too."

She sighed. "Yeah. A lot went wrong."

*You think?* "Too much. Too often."

"Too much," she agreed. "I've forbidden single vehicle movements for the time being until we get to the bottom of this. It's never been an issue before. The 'verts . . . they don't bother vehicle patrols."

"I disagree."

"This is the first time," she said.

"Unless it's the second."

She paused. "You think that's what got the Caliber team?"

I still didn't know for sure, and I didn't want to blind her—or myself—to other possibilities. I also didn't want to piss her off with a blatant lie. Frustrated as I was, I still needed her help. "Your investigation suggested natural causes. Hominiverts are territorial, and we were in the same area, so they're definitely a possibility. Now, about the explosive ammo."

"I'm under a lot of pressure from the governor to keep down the damage to the local ecology. When you give soldiers weapons, they tend to use them. You know that. The last thing I need is a patrol lighting up the wildlife for fun or because they get nervous. Patinchak would shut me down over that."

"So, you put soldiers at risk, instead."

"Oh, fuck off, Carl. Until today it hasn't been an is-sue. There hasn't been an injury to a soldier by a large mammal in the entire year I've been in command here."

I felt my face flush a little. I deserved that. Oxendine had to do her job, and I was second-guessing her decisions after the fact. "Might want to revisit that policy. If I hadn't had my explosive rounds, we'd have been in deep shit."

"I'll take it under consideration." She said it like she meant it, so I let it drop. I couldn't force her, regardless. After a moment she spoke again. "We've got other prob-lems, though."

Her tone put me on edge. "What problems?"

"Eric Bergman, our suspected bomber, is no longer on the planet."

"He escaped?"

"The governor moved him. The story he's feeding me is that a high-powered lawyer got a change of jurisdic-tion from a judge on Talca, and he had no choice."

"But you don't buy that." I didn't buy it either.

"*Of course* I don't buy it. I did what I said at the meeting—I sent a request higher for them to turn the prisoner over to me. I got approval, which the governor knew I would, so he moved him before I could enforce the order."

"Why would he do that?" I asked.

"You mean beyond the fact that he's a vindictive little asshole?"

"It's got to be more than that."

"Maybe," she said. "My guess is that Davidson is responsible. He wouldn't have the balls to do it on his own."

"I'll look into it."

"Don't bother. It's not like we can get the ship back. It's done. I'm pissed, but I'm not spending energy on it."

I didn't agree with that decision but kept it to myself. Whoever transferred the bomber interfered with an investigation into a person who tried to kill me, and I took that personally. But I had my own channels, and could look into it without Oxendine's help, so I dropped it. "Sure."

"So what's your move now?"

"There are too many things going on here that don't add up. I'm going to shake up EPV and see what falls out and pressure Caliber to see why they're hiding things."

"Watch yourself," said Oxendine. "Rumor is that someone's trying to kill you."

I held it in for a couple seconds before I burst out laughing. "Yeah. Fuckers."

"Indeed," she said.

"If anything happens to me, avenge me."

"Really?"

"No, not really. I just always wanted to say that."

It was her turn to laugh. "Just watch yourself."

**DESPITE WHAT I** told Oxendine, I headed first to the governor's office to ask about the prisoner transfer. He wasn't available when I arrived—at least that's what they told me. I didn't believe it, but I couldn't do anything about it either. Instead, after making me wait longer than necessary, a staffer ushered me into an office to meet with Cora Davidson. The interior pissed me off, boasting a polished wood floor, small conference table, original art on the walls, and a desk so big that if Davidson were a man, I'd have accused her of overcompensating for having a small penis. As it stood, I still suspected she was overcompensating for *something*.

"Colonel Butler. I'm glad to see you." Her face said she wasn't, but she gestured to a chair and I took it.

"I'm sure you know why I'm here."

"They told me you wanted to see the governor." She smiled, a thin, bitter thing, like she'd eaten a bite of bad food at a fancy dinner and had to pretend she liked it.

I could have played along and kept things fake and polite, but that would be playing her game. Instead I decided to change the rules. "I wanted to ask him why he lied to us about the prisoner, Eric Bergman, and shipped him off planet in order to keep him from military questioning."

She stopped smiling. I don't think she expected me to be so direct, but I find that sometimes that's the best time to *be* direct. It puts people off balance. "I don't think *lied* is the term I'd use."

"Of course you wouldn't. But I would, and I will in my next report to the person who assigned me the job. The president. Maybe you've heard of her. You think maybe the governor will see me after that?"

Davidson's lips thinned even more as she sucked at her teeth. She took several seconds to respond, probably deciding on a course. She didn't crack. I'll give her that. "The governor had nothing to do with the decision. The change in jurisdiction for Mr. Bergman was ordered by a judge on Talca."

I assumed that was bullshit, but I didn't say so. She had more information than I did. "How did a judge on Talca even see this case?"

"I have no idea. I assume that attorneys for Mr. Bergman brought it to court." Her smile came back, just teasing the corner of her mouth.

"Attorneys. A colonyside dining-facility worker has attorneys on Talca."

"I doubt he hired them himself," said Davidson, treating my sarcastic response as a legit question. "He works for EPV. Perhaps they hired them."

I wanted to say bullshit to that too, but I paused and thought about it. It *could* be true. I hated to admit that. It was easier to blame the politicians. But if Bergman really was working on behalf of EPV, it would be in their best interest to get him off the planet before he could talk and compromise the rest of their network. The governor should have at least given me—or Oxendine—a heads-up, but we both knew that, and I wasn't going to give Davidson the satisfaction of me saying it. Besides, I wasn't sure I bought Davidson's excuse. The speed with which they moved still seemed suspicious. "Who were the attorneys?"

"I'll find out and send it to you. Anything else I can help you with?" asked Davidson. Her tone had changed now that she had me on my back foot.

I wanted to rub the smug look off her face, but I know when it's time to retreat. "Just one last thing. I need to know what Bergman said—please forward me a copy of the interrogation report."

"Absolutely," she said. She'd won. She could afford to be gracious. "But I can tell you what it says now. Bergman claims he didn't do it. He was at the demonstration, and after that he left. He claims he's never touched or even seen a bomb in his life. If you wanted to know that, all you had to do was ask."

I ignored the shot at the end, because what she said was interesting. "The interrogators believed him?"

"I'll forward you the report."

"Right." I stood and headed for the door. "Thanks."

GANOS HAD SHOVED all the furniture in her modest-sized room to one side and set up a long table along the other side with a bunch of equipment and four monitors.

Despite the transformation, the room was spotless and smelled of bleach. Ganos wore pajama bottoms and a gray sweatshirt.

"You brought the whole setup," I said.

"Never leave home without it."

"What do you have for me?" I asked.

"First off, your bomber—Bergman—has got no record. Not even a parking ticket. He failed out of university, got disowned by his parents, and worked a series of menial jobs, never staying in one too long. He's an active member of EPV but isn't on any of the radical threads. He's kind of a normal guy who overshares on social media. His life is an open book."

"Interesting. Davidson told me he said he didn't do it." Ganos's information didn't corroborate it, but it did fit with the same profile.

"Maybe he didn't," said Ganos. "But I'm not sure I'd take Davidson's word for anything."

"You found something on her?"

"Take one guess at what her job was before she started working for the governor."

"What?"

"Mining company executive."

I wish I could say that surprised me. At least it clarified which side she supported. "That's really useful. Was it for Caliber?"

"Not directly. How is something like this legal?" asked Ganos.

"I don't know. It happens quite a bit though. Any idea how she got the job? Maybe she's got some unique qualifications?"

"Political appointee," said Ganos.

"Okay, maybe not."

"It's funny. People say what I do is wrong, that I have

access I shouldn't, but with this kind of thing, nobody bats an eye. I'm in the wrong line of work. I should have gone into politics."

"But you're really good at what you do," I said.

"Yeah, yeah, I know." Ganos blushed a little, which I didn't think was possible. I'd have to remember to tell her more often how much I appreciated her.

"Seriously, you're the best."

"Of course I am."

IT TOOK A lot of cajoling to get Dante Farric to agree to a meeting. I had no leverage over him and in our initial call, he told me that I had nothing to offer him. He had a point, but I didn't tell *him* that. Armed with Ganos's information, I called him again and offered him a piece of the truth: Maybe Bergman didn't do it.

Farric told me I was full of shit, but even over the comm I could sense the doubt in his voice. It still took me another fifteen minutes to talk him into meeting, and then he would only agree to meet me in a public place. I'm not sure why he insisted on that, but I agreed in a hurry. I'd have preferred to bring him to my apartment for privacy, but a public place seemed like the next best option.

We settled on a restaurant with outdoor seating—outdoor being somewhat of a misnomer inside of the dome. Mac hated the idea because the place always drew a crowd. The few restaurants that did exist on Eccasis did good business. Probably because they gave a sense of normalcy—a feeling like you weren't on a colony in the middle of nowhere. But that crowd gave me comfort. The attack on my cart seemed designed to specifically avoid collateral damage, so staying around people added some potential safety. Mac grumbled but made himself scarce, probably somewhere trying to watch everyone at once. At least no protesters showed up.

I tried to act normal as I talked to the waitress, despite Farric glaring at me from the other side of our small wooden table. They didn't have real whiskey, so I ordered a beer, even though it was a couple hours before dinner. I'm pretty sure the five-p.m. rule doesn't count colonyside. Besides, I thought that my having a drink might put Farric at ease.

The waitress turned to Farric, smiling. "For you, sir?"

"Water." He barked the word. So much for putting him at ease. I consoled myself with the thought that the waitress would probably spit in his drink. When she left, he turned his disdain on me. "Let's get to the point. What's going on with Bergman?"

"Slow down, now," I said. "It's not like I've got a signed affidavit that I can whip out right here in the restaurant."

"You don't have anything, do you?"

I kept my face neutral as I continued to stretch the truth. "Let's just say that I'm no longer convinced that he was the bomber."

His face lit up at that. As mad as he was at me, he wanted to believe. "My source says they have his fingerprint on a bomb fragment."

I jerked back in my chair slightly. He shouldn't have had that information, and it caught me off guard. I guess it shouldn't have, given all the leaks and interbreeding of organizations. Thankfully, the waitress came back with our drinks, which gave me time to recover. I didn't confirm his source, just in case he threw it out there without knowing for sure. "Look, I just have some questions."

"We've all got questions."

"Here's what I can tell you," I said. "Bergman got moved off planet because some high-priced lawyers back on Talca got to a judge."

Farric leaned in. "Really? You're sure?"

"Yes. Any idea where a dining-facility worker gets that kind of representation? More specifically, did your organization provide them?"

He snorted. "Organization. You're giving us a little too much credit."

"How so?" He'd made a similar remark at the governor's reception, and this time I wanted to follow up on it.

"To answer your question, no, there's no way that EPV provided lawyers for a criminal case. When we spend money for lawyers, it's environmental law."

"So . . . who provided them?" I asked.

He thought about it. "When I say we're not an organization . . . we're more like a loose conglomeration of entities that have goals that might be somewhat aligned. But not all the time."

In other words, EPV existed as a nonhomogeneous entity. I often had that blind spot in my thinking. I needed to work on that. For now, I wanted to keep him talking. "So . . . you're not in charge."

"Right. No. Sometimes." He sighed again. "I'm in charge here on Eccasis, except when I'm not. It's complicated."

"It would help me a lot if I understood." I left unsaid that if I understood, I could find the cracks and pull it apart.

He sipped his water. "I don't think this is really a secret. For the most part, we don't pay people. *I* get a check, and so do a few others. But mostly, the V in our name is accurate. There are a lot of volunteers. We help them get jobs in the colony."

"Sure." I took a pull from my beer. As long as he kept talking, I wouldn't interrupt.

"Not everyone who claims association with EPV has the same agenda." He paused, looking at me like he thought I'd understand something meaningful from that.

"I think I understand." I did. But I also wanted him to elucidate.

"I, and the leadership, believe in non-violent means. The protest at the governor's mansion? That was us . . . not me, but people I know and trust. We're not above confrontation. We'll block access to a destructive work site; we'll chain ourselves to trees . . . we'll do whatever it takes. But we won't *kill* someone. At most, we might try to scare someone. Even that's rare though."

"How rare? And what do you mean by *scare someone*?"

He covered his delay with another sip of water. He was horrible at this. "*Scare* is probably a bad word. *Intimidate* is more accurate. If you're worried about us and what we might do and that makes you take more care with the ecology of the planet, I'm okay with that."

"*Bombs* are intimidating."

"They are. And that's the problem. There are elements that associate themselves with us—might even call themselves by our name—that see violence as a legitimate tool."

I stared him down for a couple seconds. "But not Bergman."

"Nothing I know about the guy suggests that he'd be involved with this."

"But you know who would," I said.

Farric paused with his glass halfway to his face. I had him. "I told you, we don't encourage that kind of thing."

"So you don't encourage it, but you don't *discourage* it either."

His face reddened. "We *do* discourage it, when we can. But it's not like we have board meetings. We don't have a mailing list. I don't even *know* Eric Bergman. I had to look him up just to find out what he looked like. So what can I do? I can make a statement, go on the news to condemn the attack. But does anyone even believe that?"

"Probably not," I admitted.

"Exactly. You'd listen to my public statement denying involvement while tacitly thinking that I'm just saying it to save face."

I was in a bit of a bind. Bergman said he didn't do it, but I couldn't prove that, so I couldn't get him off the hook. But maybe Farric could. He seemed like he truly cared, and I could exploit that. "You want to help Bergman? Give me some names."

"Didn't you hear me? I don't *have* names. We don't deal with the radicals. We don't even acknowledge them publicly . . . for obvious reasons."

"Surely you have *some* idea. Even if you don't have contact directly, you've got to have ideas. This asshole tried to kill me, and I want to nail them."

Farric had inched forward on his seat. I almost had him. Just one more little push.

"And if you cooperate, I'll do my best to make sure that it's not associated with EPV." I took a pull of my beer, letting that statement hang out there as I observed his reaction. His face lit up a bit, but he didn't speak for a moment. I let him have the time. I'd put out the bait, and I had to be patient while he took it.

"I can probably get you a name. I don't have it now, but some of my legit associates probably have some ideas of someone who *might* involve himself—or herself—on the radical side of things."

"Thanks," I said. "How long until I can expect to hear from you?"

"Give me a day or two."

"Sounds good." I didn't know what I'd do with the name once I got it or how I'd convince anyone else that we had another suspect. I'd deal with that once I got the information.

# CHAPTER ELEVEN

I WAS FEELING CONFIDENT after what I thought was a success with Farric, so I decided to press my luck and head over to Caliber, hoping to catch some people still there, even though we were approaching the end of the workday. Mac materialized out of nowhere and we moved out.

Since I hadn't called ahead, there was no delegation of lawyers to meet me, so I walked up to what was either a receptionist or a guard ensconced behind a black polymer standing desk.

She met my gaze. "Can I help you, sir?"

"I'm here to see Ms. Stroud."

The red-headed woman looked at her screen, and the way the light hit her face cast a green tint on her pale skin. "You don't have an appointment."

"I don't." We stared at each other for a few seconds, me trying to project confidence, she trying to get me to go away without explicitly telling me to.

She broke eye contact first, noticing Mac. "He can't be in here with that."

I didn't have to look to see what she meant. Mac had his assault rifle. "He's my protection."

"I don't care. *He* can be in here, but the weapon stays outside."

"Is there somewhere he can sign it in?"

"No," she said. "And even if there was, you don't have an appointment."

"Humor me. Call up and see if Stroud's available."

She gave me a "you're an asshole" look for several seconds. I didn't back down. I'm used to it. I *am* an asshole.

Finally, she asked, "Name?"

"Butler. Carl Butler."

"You can have a seat over there, Mr. Butler." She gestured to a set of three wooden chairs along the far wall of the small, low-ceilinged reception area. She turned to Mac. "*You* can get out. You've got five seconds until I call base security."

Mac looked to me and I nodded. He backed toward the door. "I'll be waiting right outside, sir."

"Roger." I admired the receptionist's guts. Not everybody could face down a man with a gun and come out on top.

She waited until Mac closed the door before she made the call. She spoke too softly for me to make out what she said. And I tried. I wouldn't have put it past her to make a fake call to get rid of me. She stopped speaking but kept the device to her ear, looking intent, as if she might be getting instructions.

"Mr. Butler," she called me over once she put her phone down. "Someone will be down to get you in a moment."

"Thanks." Great. The lawyers were coming.

I am sure my surprise showed on my face a minute later when Stroud herself entered. She walked up to me and offered her hand, shaking with a powerful grip.

"Mr. Butler. We meet again."

"Please, call me Carl."

"Carl. What can I do for you?"

"Is there some place we can talk?" I noticed that she didn't offer me *her* first name.

She considered it. "Sure. You mind if we take the stairs? It's only two floors up."

"No problem." My robot foot wasn't bothering me too much.

We walked to her office in silence, passing a thin man at a desk whom I took for her assistant. She didn't speak to him, and while his eyes followed us, he didn't speak either. Her inner office was small for a boss, though large enough to hold a desk and a small conference table with six chairs around it. The furniture reflected the lights in its polish, and while none of it was ornate, it wasn't cheap, either. If I had to describe the place in one word, it would be functional. I noted that, because I feel like an office can give a window into a personality, though there's a chance I was reading too much into it.

"You caught me at a good time." She gestured to a chair.

"I've been lucky like that today."

"Not all day, I heard. A bit of a rough trip this morning . . . no?"

I took my seat to buy some time to think. Why did she know that? "You heard?"

"I make it a point to hear." She took the chair directly across from me. "Everything that happens outside the dome has an impact on my bottom line."

"Where's your source?"

"Come on, Carl. I'm not giving you that. But there's more than one. It's not like I'm getting classified information. It was a scheduled mission."

I needed to find my balance, needed to put her on the defensive instead of me. "Your lawyers are continuing to stonewall me and cause delays. I thought you were going to talk to them."

"I haven't heard from Mr. Zentas. He's been out of communication."

"Seems like it's been long enough where someone could find him," I said.

"I expect to hear from him soon."

Since that was a dead end but she seemed willing to talk, I changed directions. "Why do you employ xeno-biologists?"

She chuckled. "I wish I didn't. They cost too much and don't add anything to the bottom line. But the rules are the rules. If we want to develop this planet, we have to work around the existing wildlife. That means we need to understand it. So, either we study it ourselves, or we're stuck with the somewhat whimsical nature of public science. Their timelines don't really work for me."

"Plus, you want your own results."

"I'd prefer to say we want a balance to the opinions that might be slanted against development."

"Sure. Two sides of the same coin." I didn't buy her rationale, but I understood it, and I didn't want to shut her down. At least I had her reacting to my questions instead of the other way around. "Do you know an employee named Schultz? Or Ortega?"

"The names don't ring a bell. But if you tell me they work here, I believe you. We've got a lot of employees I don't know personally."

"They were on the mission the day that Xyla Redstone and her team disappeared. I've talked to most of the people involved, but those two aren't here anymore."

She turned her palms up. "What do you want me to say? People leave all the time."

"I feel like these two might know something."

"Just a feeling?" she asked. "Sounds like you don't have much if you're grasping at this."

"Let me put it this way," I said. "If this was something other than a straightforward disappearance—"

"It wasn't," said Stroud, cutting me off. It struck me how adamant she seemed about that.

"Humor me," I said.

Stroud relaxed a bit and sank back into her chair. "Sure."

"*If* there was foul play, who on Eccasis has the strongest motive?"

"EPV," Stroud answered immediately.

"Right. What if somebody—Schultz for example—worked for both them and you?"

Now she stopped to think. "You think EPV had an agent working for Caliber?"

"You think they don't?" I asked.

She considered it some more. "Sure, I guess they probably do. But it doesn't matter."

"It matters if Schultz was one of them."

She shook her head. "It really doesn't."

I paused. I didn't understand her attitude. "It's in Caliber's best interest to help me get to the bottom of this."

"And that's where we disagree. It's in *our* best interest for you to sign off on the report that's already there so we can get back to work. This whole thing has set us back, and I have to answer for it. Soon. Corporate has already dispatched a VIP to come observe." Her expression said she wasn't excited about that prospect. I didn't blame her. Nobody wants her boss looking over her shoulder.

"If I could talk to Schultz, it might help me wrap it up faster." She wouldn't buy that. Shit, I didn't even buy it. But it was the best lead I had into what really happened on that mission.

She thought about it for a few seconds. "Okay. I'll see what I can do."

"Thanks. And you might want to avoid sending anyone to sector 376R. I'm pretty sure there's a pissed-off pack of hominiverts that see it as their territory."

"I'll take a look at it," she said. "But we don't usually avoid sectors. Our scientists are more focused on moving the wildlife to places where they have less impact on us."

"Bring bigger guns then."

"Oh, we would if we were allowed. We most definitely would. I'd arm my teams with laser cannons and rocket launchers if I could get away with it. Alas . . . rules. You know the fine for killing a large mammal?"

"I didn't know there was one. I guess I'll find out after this morning."

"I'm sure you're okay," she said. "The military doesn't have the same penalties as we do. You probably fall under their regulations."

I fake-smiled. "I hope so."

"Anything else? I do have that VIP to prepare for. Busy busy."

Something she said stuck with me—the idea of moving animals out of a location—but I didn't know why. I wanted to follow up, but I couldn't think of a smart question immediately. As I worked through it, her assistant popped his head through the door.

"Ms. Stroud, you have a call. It's about the VIP."

Stroud looked at me. "I've got to take this."

"Of course," I said. "I really appreciate your time."

**MAC MET ME** right outside the building. "Sir, you've got to see this."

"What's up?" A group of about fifteen people stood across the street, chanting and waving signs.

"It's that same group who protested against you when you went to the governor's. At least a lot of them."

"Are they here for us?" It seemed suspicious that they'd be here right after I met with Farric.

"No, sir. As far as I can tell they're protesting Caliber. But that's not the good part."

"There's a good part?"

"Yes, sir. A few minutes ago, there was a group of about five or six counterprotestors. They had a sign that said 'Humans First' and they were yelling at this group. I thought it might turn violent." The smile on Mac's face said he wouldn't have been at all opposed to that.

"But they're gone."

"For now. Unless I miss my guess, they went to get more of their friends, and they'll be back."

"You think we should call the authorities?" I asked.

"We *could*. *Or,* we could stand here out of the way and watch a bunch of nerds fight."

I laughed. "I don't think we want to get caught in the middle."

Mac patted his rifle. "Something tells me they'll give us a wide berth. Anyway, it's too late." Mac pointed down the street where about an equal number of people to the protest group had appeared. "Here they come."

"Let's get pictures of everyone on both sides." I took

out my device. "Maybe Ganos can run them through a search and figure out who they are."

Mac took his device out as well. "Roger that, sir. I'll get video."

"You just want a fight video you can post on the net," I said.

"You caught me, sir. What can I say?"

Voyeurism aside, we couldn't do much about it. None of my authority extended to breaking up public disturbances. I wanted to visit the governor, but I felt safer knowing I could retreat into the safety of the Caliber building if necessary.

A huge light-skinned guy led the new arrivals—maybe two meters tall and weighing a couple hundred kilograms. He was carrying a short metal telescoping baton. A couple others had weapons as well, but no firearms and no knives, as far as I could see. The protestors didn't seem to be armed, but several of them had signs on wooden poles, and those looked pretty solid. The new group headed straight for the protest fanned out behind their leader like migrating geese. It started with shouting, then pushing. Then someone swung a sign and suddenly everyone was in it, men and women, throwing punches, kicking, cursing. A man screamed. I feared for anyone who fell. They might be kicked or trampled, even by their own people.

A siren rang out, but from a long way away. I considered firing Mac's rifle into the air to break things up but remembered the dome. I didn't know what high velocity bullets might do to it. It was probably safe, but without knowing for sure, I couldn't risk it. Someone stumbled from the crowd—from which side, I don't know—and started across the street toward us, blood streaming from his nose down over his lips and chin. Mac stepped in front of me, rifle held professionally across his chest, and shook his head. The man seemed to take his meaning, because he changed direction and headed away down the street.

A minute later a military vehicle arrived, stopping thirty or so meters away. Six armed security guards dismounted, formed up, and headed for the melee. People ran in every direction other than toward the soldiers. One woman couldn't run, limping instead, and one man lay on the ground, apparently unconscious or unable to get up. Two guards ran to him, one going down on a knee to evaluate the casualty while the other five took up defensive positions.

"Wait here," I told Mac, and I started across the street. I didn't want Mac with me since he was armed, and I didn't want a soldier who might be on edge already to get the wrong idea. I called out to the leader before I got within ten paces, my hands visible at my sides so they could see I wasn't a threat. "Sergeant, we saw the whole thing, if you need information for your report."

The sergeant in charge looked at me before turning her gaze back to her watch. "Thanks, sir, but we've got it on camera. That's what triggered us to show up in the first place."

"This happen a lot?"

"More often than it should."

"Any idea why?" I checked her nametag: Benevidez.

"These folks just don't like each other."

"What's the penalty?"

"For those we catch, like this guy?" She gestured to the unconscious man. "Usually a fine the first time. Second offense can be expulsion from the colony, assuming the governor is in a mood to sign the paperwork. Usually they get slapped on the wrist and sent back out into the population."

"Really?" I asked.

"Everyone knows someone, sir. It's all politics."

"What do you think about that?"

"I think it's above my pay grade, sir."

It *was*. "Sounds frustrating."

"Not really. They aren't dangerous to us, just to each other. So it's no big deal. Can we get a quick statement from you, sir? Get your info in case we need it for some reason?"

"Of course." I gave my card to a freckled corporal who looked like he was too young to be serving, collected Mac, and headed out the way that the soldiers had arrived. None of the combatants had run that way, so there was less risk we'd run into them.

Mac seemed disappointed.


**FADER AND GANOS** were both waiting for me when I got back to my apartment. I guess it was a good sign that they were tolerating each other. After I filled them in about my recent meetings and the fight we saw, Fader even glanced at Ganos before she briefed me. Ganos gestured for her to speak first. I cut in before she got the chance.

"How was your X-ray?"

"Negative, sir. Just a bruise. A little news from the governor's office though, beyond what you already know about the prisoner transfer. First, the governor is upset about what happened to us today out on the mission. A couple staffers say he's considering closing all exploratory traffic until the military can confirm that it's safe. Those same staffers say that will never happen, because Caliber and some of the other companies will put too much pressure on him if he does."

"What do you think will happen?" I asked.

"Bets seem to be that he'll either back off and leave things as they are or cancel all but mission-critical traffic for a day or two, as a gesture."

"Any chance that he'd ask Oxendine for her opinion?" I thought I knew the answer, but Fader had been closer to it.

"I think that's unlikely, sir."

"Me too."

"Okay. What else do you have?"

"There was a lot of talk about a VIP showing up in the next day or two."

"I heard that too, over at Caliber. I thought it was company internal, but if the governor is interested, it might be something different."

"Or the Caliber person has political ties."

I stifled a laugh. My being here was proof that Caliber executives had political ties. "Let's see if we can find out who it is. When something comes up in two places on the same day, it makes me wonder."

"Roger, sir," said Fader.

"Any info come in from the military regarding the potential cause of the comms malfunction?" I asked.

"I got a message, sir. You're copied on it too. The short version: They found nothing in the hardware. The mission recordings don't show anything either. As far as the systems go—both helmets and vehicle—nothing happened."

I went over to the counter and poured myself a whiskey. "Anyone else?"

Fader and Ganos shook their heads. Mac didn't respond, but he rarely drank, and if he wanted one, he'd have fixed it himself.

"I think we have to consider the possibility that the

comms outage was an attack," I said. "If it was, who has the capability?"

"To white out military comms?" Fader considered it. "I could ask an expert for a better answer, but off the top of my head, there *are* some commercial solutions. The military system hops frequencies, so you have to jam across a pretty wide spectrum. That means a lot of power, or a close distance, or some combination of the two."

"It doesn't account for the other vehicle systems that went down beyond just the comms, though," I said. "We lost sensors, too."

"True," said Fader.

"EMP?" asked Mac.

"The vehicle is almost certainly shielded," I said. "Plus, we didn't lose function in our suits, and the comms came back on line."

"How about a hack?" offered Ganos.

"A hack of what? The vehicle?" I asked.

"Why not? You said to consider that it might have been an attack. If you were close enough to a power source that was strong enough to jam your comms, it could have attacked the vehicle systems as well. It would be an order of magnitude more sophisticated, but it's doable."

I didn't understand how that could work, but I believed her. You don't have to be the smartest person in the room, but it does help to recognize who is. "Is there any way to tell if it was a hack after the fact?"

"There should be signs," said Ganos. "But you'd need access to the systems involved, and you'd have to know what you were looking for. If the hacker was competent, it wouldn't be obvious unless you were specifically trying to find it."

"Does the military here have people who could figure it out?" I asked.

"Of course," said Ganos. "But I'd bet good money that they didn't bring those people in on it. Not unless a smart leader somewhere got involved and forced it, and let's face it . . . officers never think of that kind of thing. No offense. People think hacking, they think computers. The thing is, *everything* is a computer."

"So, I need to get you access to the vehicle."

"Yes, sir. Or at least get them to agree to look at it and get me access to the people doing the looking. I can make sure they know their stuff. But if they put me on their system to check the vehicle hack . . . that would give me an *in* to their network. I could maybe get to the bottom of the camera hack from the bombing at the governor's as well. I'm still dead-ended on that."

"I'll work on getting you access tomorrow. Meanwhile, Mac and I got some pictures of the fight between EPV and Humans First. Can you run them through a search and see what you can find out about the people involved? We might find some kind of connection."

"Sure thing. In other news, your boy Farric lit up his comms maybe an hour ago. Just before I came over here. He contacted pretty much everybody."

"That would have been right after I talked to him. Any specifics?"

"He talked some people into a protest. Told them it was important, and that it had to happen right away. I didn't get it all—I didn't access his voice comms, just his email. But I got the impression that he was calling people too."

"I'm guessing that was the protest we just saw," I said. "I wonder why he ordered it."

"I didn't find anything on that," said Ganos. "But

there was something else. Not as obvious . . . kind of
hidden behind the protest noise."

"Let me guess. He was looking for a name."

Ganos stared for a second. "The last time you knew
what I was going to tell you before I told you, we were
in deep shit. Please tell me this is different. Because I've
got chills, and not in a good way."

"I think we're okay." I meant it. This was a different
situation than when she and I had been hacking a major
defense contractor. We'd been doing something totally
illegal back then, and we didn't know the significance
of what we found. This time it was only slightly illegal, I had a pretty good idea what Farric was up to, and
EPV didn't have nearly the capability of a company like
Omicron. Although I had to watch out on that last one.
*Somebody* had gotten Bergman off the planet. I *did* have
Mac, though, which made it different from last time. He
helped balance the scales.

Ganos hesitated. "I'm going to need more than that,
sir. Sorry. I went in blind last time and it almost cost me.
Almost cost *us*. I'm not doing that again."

Fader started to speak, but I cut her off. Ganos was
right. I owed her—and the other two— the truth. "That's
fair. In this case, I had a good idea of what he might be
looking for because I met with him and I put him up to
it. Farric has conflict with radical elements in his own
organization, and he was willing to give me a name of
someone who might have had something to do with the
bombing. When he does, *if* he does, I'll pass it on to you.
But that person—if the name is valid—might be dangerous. They tried to bomb us. And if they also hacked
the military or routed their network attack through the
military . . . well, that might mean they're a threat to you
as well."

Ganos thought about it for a minute. "Okay. I can deal with that. Terrorists . . . that's a known quantity. Terrorist hacker . . . yep. That's a worry. But that's a worry I'm happy to face. Because fuck them. Faceless, multibillion-mark corporations? No thanks."

"Well there's still Caliber."

"And I'm being careful as shit around them," she said. "Fool me once."

I had to admit, the new Ganos—the cautious, calculating Ganos—I liked her. She'd grown up. And I felt like an asshole for liking this new version, because she wouldn't have had to grow up if I hadn't put her in danger a couple years back. "I'll keep you as fully in the loop as I can. And you do the same, okay? No taking big risks without talking them through with us, first."

"Deal," she said. "Now about that drink."

**AFTER EVERYONE LEFT,** I couldn't sleep. I had too many loose ends and no way to tie up most of them. I needed help. I didn't hold out much hope, but Serata *had* given me a liaison, and he was worth a try. I sent him a message.

*Flak Jacket,*
*It's been a while. Do they still call you that? Probably not. Congrats on making colonel. The mission is going well, but I've hit a couple of dead ends and I thought maybe you could help. I'm sure you got the report on the bombing, but did you hear that the suspect got moved off planet to another jurisdiction? I've attached his information. Thing is, this guy is small time, and apparently some*

high-priced attorneys got involved. I want to know why. Can you look into that back there on Talca?

One other thing. A guy named Schultz (File attached) disappeared from here about a month ago. I need to talk to him in order to get this thing done, but nobody knows where he went. Can you have someone track him down and make him available to talk? I don't have to talk to him personally, but I'd like to feed some questions to a trained interrogator. There's a chance he was involved in the incident that led to Xyla Redstone's death.

Thanks,
Butler

# CHAPTER TWELVE

**I** **WENT EARLY TO** talk to Oxendine about getting Ganos access to the vehicle. I worried a little about what Ganos would try to do once she got inside the military system, but if we'd been hacked, I wanted to know. I'd had Fader call ahead, so Oxendine was expecting me.

"You here to wrap this up?" she asked.

That caught me a bit off guard, and I waited while an aide brought us coffee, which gave me time to mask my confusion. Was she being sarcastic? I decided to answer it straight. "Still have a way to go."

"You've got your answer: It was a territorial incursion, and the alpha predators didn't like it. Write it up and send it in with a bow on it."

I paused, unsure where her attitude came from. "I'm not sure it's that simple."

"Sending in the report?"

"What goes *in* the report."

"*Of course* it's not that simple," said Oxendine. "But it can be. If you say that's what happened, that's what happened. The government can close it out and tell the rich man that you did your due diligence and that's that. Everybody's happy."

"Except the dead people."

"Maybe," she said. "But even for them, the situation gets closure. This is about Zentas, and he already got what he wanted. Carl Fucking Butler looked into his daughter's disappearance. He can brag about it at cocktail parties. It's over."

"There was an assassination attempt and the chief subject got shipped off planet. I'd think you'd want to get to the bottom of that." I couldn't separate the bombing from my case, even though I couldn't prove any connection.

"I do. But that's my job, not yours. And it's not even mine anymore now that the governor gave away the suspect. They'll have to figure it out back on Talca once the guy gets there in a month or two."

The sudden change in Oxendine's attitude didn't make sense, and the only reason I could surmise was that she got orders from somewhere to let it go. "Who got to you?"

She looked away for a split second. "It doesn't matter."

I almost said something mean, but I caught myself. Oxendine was an honorable officer, and she wouldn't have backed off if she had any other choice. In the end, if she didn't do what her bosses told her to, they'd find someone who would. Some officers would say that out loud, but she was too professional. "I just want to finish—"

She cut me off. "Look, Carl. I know you can do more. You know you can do more. But is there anything you can do that ends with that girl coming back alive? No. Whatever you do, whatever you find, that doesn't change. She's dead, and that's not in question."

Except . . . what if she wasn't?

Five years ago, on Cappa, everyone believed that Mallot was dead. And I found him. Then I killed him.

But that's not the point. When I *found him,* he was alive. Oxendine wouldn't know that, of course. We buried that deep, and it was supposed to stay that way. I needed her help, though, and in my mind, that constituted a need to know. "I'm going to tell you something, but it's so classified that if anyone finds out I told you, I'm probably going to jail, and you might be there with me."

"Hold on." She reached under her desk and flipped a switch, and the telltale hum of an electronic disrupter filled the room, feeling almost like it increased the air pressure slightly. Nothing could eavesdrop through that.

"You know why I was on Cappa."

"Of course. Everyone knows that."

"You also know that it started as a missing-person mission. That's why I was there."

"Right. And the body never turned up."

"Except it did."

She paused. Good to know I could surprise her, even if it took a galactic conspiracy to do it. "You found him?"

"I did. *Alive.*"

She stared at me.

"Then he died under circumstances that couldn't get out. I covered it up." Even with my swearing her to secrecy, I couldn't tell her any more than that.

Oxendine considered my story for a moment. "Okay. That explains your reluctance to close this one. But it doesn't make you right. The two missions are unrelated. You need to take the win here and move on."

"You're getting pressure," I said. She didn't respond, which told me what I needed to know. She'd have denied it if she could have done it honestly. "I can't quit." I wanted to—I really did—but I couldn't. I'm not wired that way.

She pursed her lips. "Okay. Understand, though, that

I'm not putting people in undue danger. I'll meet my requirements to the letter of the order, but that's it."

I held back a chuckle. "About that. I need a favor. It doesn't put anyone in even the slightest danger."

"I'm listening."

"I need access to the vehicle for one of my associates. She thinks the vehicle might have been hacked, causing the sensor outage. With access to the system, she can track it."

Oxendine crossed her arms. "Absolutely not."

I started to respond but hesitated. I hadn't expected her to answer so quickly and without at least thinking about it. Even if she wanted me out of her hair, she'd been reasonable to that point. If I'd been her subordinate, I'd have had to accept the answer without explanation. But while I respected her rank, I didn't work for her. "Why not?"

"Two reasons. First, you were in the middle of the jungle. Who hacked you? The hominiverts? I'm not an anthropologist, or whatever the scientist is who studies these things, but I'm certain that they don't have that capability. Second—and more important—in what world is it a good idea for a commander to give access to military networks to a known hacker?"

Of *course* she knew about Ganos. Oxendine had done her homework. I should have seen that coming. "Fair point. How about instead of access to the system she explains her suspicion and how she'd go about investigating it to someone from your team?"

"I have people who can do that," she said. "After all, where do you think Ganos got *her* training?"

I didn't know the answer to that for sure, but I suspected that she'd learned a lot of what she knew *outside* the military. "Can I get a copy of the report when they've checked?"

"If there's anything that applies to you, I will ensure that you are informed." Her tone said that she was done being questioned. It also made me doubt that I'd ever hear anything. She'd left herself a wide path out by saying I'd be informed of things that *apply to me*, since she could define that criteria.

"Thanks. I appreciate it." I didn't, but she'd clearly made up her mind, and uncooperative beat openly hostile. I'd have to find another way.

**I'D MESSAGED GANOS** to meet me at my apartment, but she hadn't made it yet. Fader was waiting though, pacing. Not a good sign.

"We've been evicted, sir."

I stood there, confused, for several seconds. Even then, all I managed was, "Huh?"

"The governor's people want us out today. They need the rooms. They're moving us to a different location. I've lodged a protest. I'm sure the governor doesn't know that his people are doing this."

"Withdraw the protest. We'll move." I didn't need the room. Didn't really want it.

"Sir, it's not appropriate for them to make you move."

"Sure it is. If someone outranks you, you give up your spot. I'm sure whatever they have for me will be fine. If there's a toilet and a way to get coffee, I'm happy." I *did* wonder a little bit if I'd done something to cause the action. It could be Davidson getting even.

"Roger, sir." Fader's tone said she didn't agree, but she let it go.

"When you call to tell them it's fine, ask who the new VIP is. They can at least give us that."

"Roger, sir." She already had her device out as she

moved away. Just then, Ganos buzzed, and Mac let her in. I hated that she traveled alone. We needed to do something about that, but when I'd mentioned a security detail to her before, she gave me a death glare, and I was still sensitive about our previous conversation, so I didn't want to push it.

She bounced into the room. "Tell me something good."

"Wish I could," I said. "The general knew who you were and when I asked to get you access, she didn't say no, she said hell no."

"Smart woman." Ganos smiled. "I think I'm going to break in."

"I thought yesterday you told me you didn't want to get involved with things that might be dangerous or where you could get caught."

"No . . . I said that I didn't want *you* putting me in those situations without me knowing about it. *This* I'm doing myself. That's different. Eyes wide open and all that."

I understood. And for selfish reasons, I was happy to have the cocky Ganos back. "I thought you had to be inside their network to do what you need to do."

"Probably," said Ganos. "It would definitely be easier. But don't worry about it. I'll find a way. In more pressing news, I ran those pictures that Mac sent me from yesterday to see if I could find matches for the faces. I'm not done yet, but I already got some interesting hits."

"Excellent." I meant it. We needed a win.

"At least three of the people from the Humans First side—the counterprotestors—work for Caliber."

"That's . . . interesting. That means the counterprotest to the protest that happened outside Caliber was by Caliber employees." I was being repetitive, but I needed to say it out loud. "I don't suppose the big guy who led the counterprotestors was an employee?"

"He wasn't. But I ran him first. His name is Jan Karlsson. Ex-military. Infantry. Put out of the army for insubordination and assault. He took a plea bargain to avoid jail time. Spent some time in the contract-security business, mostly in bad places that smart people avoid. He appears to be unemployed now, which shouldn't be possible on a colony like this. There's more, if you want it."

"More on Karlsson? Yes, please. He may be a guy I can lean on a little."

"Just remember he can snap you in half like a twig," Mac said from across the room.

"He's a big boy, that's for sure," I said. "I'll try not to make him mad."

Mac laughed. "Not sure that's your strong suit, sir."

"What else do you have on him, Ganos?" I said, ignoring the dig.

"The guy has no job, but he spends money like he's got it to spare. Food, liquor, high-tech toys, streaming entertainment. He's also got some weird tastes in porn, but that's not really important."

"Okay—I definitely need to talk to Mr. Karlsson. Any hints on where he hangs out?"

"Not from memory, but I can pull up where he's spent money when I get back on my system."

"We could try the gym," said Mac.

"Good call. Maybe if you meet him there, you can set something up," I said.

Mac nodded. "An excuse to go to the gym? I'm on it. But that means you can't go out, sir. I don't need to remind you what happened on Cappa when you decided to ditch me, do I?"

"No, I remember that ass kicking as if it were yesterday. I can stay put for a couple hours. After that we need to move to our new quarters."

"Hold on, Mac," Fader was still on her device, and by the look on her face, she'd heard something important. "Okay, thanks," she said, and disconnected. "The VIP . . . it's Drake Zentas. I trust we've all heard of him."

"Fuuuuck."

My first thought after the expletive was incongruent—I wondered if Oxendine knew. When she told me I should close the case and leave, I wonder if she knew *he'd* be arriving. It seemed unlikely that she *wouldn't* know. She made it a point to know things, even if the governor didn't share. Maybe that was why she got orders to have me shut things down.

My second thought was about the mission. How did it change with the father of the missing person and the guy who sent me here showing up colonyside? If nothing else, it would clear up the hurdles I'd had with Stroud. She'd wanted to talk to the man before helping me—looked like she'd get her chance. Zentas would have the governor's ear, for sure. Me being evicted showed that. If the others had thoughts, they held them, waiting for mine. Before I could share them, my device buzzed.

It was Farric. Well shit. When things start to happen, they all happen at once. I answered. "Butler."

"Marko Hubic." He hung up.

Just a name. But that's all I'd asked of him. "Let's regroup," I told the team. In the span of a few minutes, I'd gone from having almost no leads to having too many. "That was Dante Farric. He just gave me a name. Marko Hubic. The implication is that he's someone from the more radical wing of EPV who might have connections to the bombing." I paused to let the others absorb the information. "Let's do this: Mac, you escort Ganos back to her place, then go to the gym and see if you can find Karlsson. Try to get him to agree to meet. Ganos, if you would, get me everything you can on Hubic as quickly as you can. After that, if Mac hasn't found Karlsson, see if you can track him down through the network. Captain Fader, let's you and I go over to the governor's and see what we can find out about Zentas. We should at least be able to get an itinerary."

Mac looked at me like he was about to object. They'd released the protection detail the previous evening when Oxendine's Intel shop determined that there were no continuing threats that warranted it.

"I will stay with Fader and we'll both carry weapons. We'll be okay." Mac couldn't stop a bomb any better than I could, though I didn't know if he'd agree with that.

"Sir—" Mac began.

"Okay, you win. Captain Fader, call up Ops and tell them we need part of the detail back. Ask them to send two soldiers over to escort me." I looked to Mac. "Okay?"

"Yes, sir."

He was right, but the delay still frustrated me. Things were finally happening, and it was time to get shit done.


**THE ARMY DIDN'T** give much pushback on sending the soldiers we needed, but we had to wait on them. Fader was flipping through the news feeds on her device when something passed over her face that I hadn't seen before. She usually kept her emotions in check, but not this time. I couldn't read it, though. Was it sadness? Fear? Anger? Maybe some combination. I don't think she trusted herself to speak.

"What happened?" I asked.

She showed me her device, where she had frozen a

live feed. A dark-skinned local newscaster sat at a generic desk in a generic studio, but that wasn't what mattered. The words framed at the bottom of the screen told the whole story.

*Dante Farric found dead.*

I sat down hard on the sofa. I'd done it again. I'd gotten another person—presumably an innocent one—killed. I'd pressed him for a name, and he'd got it for me, and thirty minutes later he was dead. Wherever I went, people died. *That* was what I saw on Fader's face. Revulsion. Shit, I'd probably get her killed too. Maybe it was fear I saw in her eyes.

"Call ops. Cancel the soldiers," I said. While Fader did that, I got the bottle and filled a glass, not even bothering with ice. Things got a little blurry after that, but I think Fader drank too. By the time Mac got back, I was barely functional and drinking out of the bottle. I think maybe he got it away from me and got me to bed, but I couldn't say for sure. I woke up there in the middle of the night, and the first thing I thought of through my splitting headache was that we were supposed to have been evicted. Fader had probably taken care of that. She was efficient.

# CHAPTER THIRTEEN

**M**AC HAD FOUND Karlsson the previous day, not at the gym but at a bar that Ganos tracked him to. Mac had bought him a drink and convinced him to talk to me the next day for a hundred marks. Smart. I hadn't considered straight-up bribery. At least when I got him killed, this guy would die with a hundred marks in his pocket.

We had to move out of my quarters first, and we did so with little fanfare; Fader had indeed gotten us an extension, but only until the morning. Two soldiers showed up to provide security and a driver and an assistant came with a big cart from the protocol department to help us shuffle our stuff. My new suite was sufficient, and I would have called it luxurious if I hadn't been living in the palace first. Its two rooms didn't have a door between them, but there was a wall with an opening at the end, so you couldn't see the bed from the sitting area. Mac relented on living with me in the smaller place, but arranged for security outside at night. He didn't say it, but I think Farric's death had him on edge as much as it did me, though for different reasons.

Mac and I headed out to meet Karlsson for lunch and I decided to broach the topic of Farric's death on the way. I needed to talk about it. I probably needed to talk about it to a therapist, but Mac would have to do. "What do you think happened with Farric?"

"You mean cause of death? You saw what the news said. You think it's something else?"

The news had called it an apparent suicide, but I didn't believe that for a minute. Unfortunately, I couldn't look into it because Oxendine was already on my case for working on things outside my purview. If she caught me around this, she'd have more reason to shut me down. Regardless, I couldn't help but think it was connected. "You think it's because he gave me a name?"

"Maybe," said Mac. "Does it matter? I mean . . . it does matter. If the killer—or killers—know that he gave you a name, then they know you *have* a name. That's what matters. If someone is willing to kill once . . ."

"Right. I'll take whatever precautions you recommend."

I liked Mac's view. He wasn't worrying about what happened, he was worrying about what he could do about it now. He was controlling what he could control. I usually tried to think that way, but I couldn't at the moment. I kept thinking about Gylika back on Talca and how he'd died for meeting with me a couple years ago, and how I put Ganos at risk, and even Elliot back on Cappa, which wasn't my fault, but maybe if I'd done something different, she wouldn't have taken her own life. "Do you feel bad about it? Him being dead?"

"We didn't kill him, sir."

"We . . . *I* put him in the situation. I pressured him to give me the information."

Mac considered it. "Nah. I don't buy it. He was a big boy. He knew the risks. He should have, anyway. If he didn't, that's on him. If we let something happen to us, that's on us. I get the feeling that you're blaming yourself for this, though."

"Little bit. Yeah."

"What's the first rule of facing the enemy, sir? If it's them or you . . ."

"It's them." I always told my soldiers that, especially in complex situations. When there were civilians around, you wanted to protect the innocent. You didn't want to shoot the wrong person. The problem is, when you think about that too much, you get slow. When you get slow, you get dead. The enemy doesn't hesitate. To get eighteen-year-old kids to appreciate that—to not shoot when they shouldn't but still shoot fast when they should—you had to simplify it. To keep them alive, we tell them that if they're in doubt, protect themselves. We have to. Anything else would be irresponsible. Was Farric an inevitable casualty, beyond our control as we tried to get at the actual enemy? Did a pat phrase equal absolution?

"Does that apply here?"

"I don't know," said Mac. "I just know that if you get bogged down thinking about people who died, you join them."

"I'll try to make sure you don't."

"If I go into it face-first, weapon up, I'll have no complaints. Let them come. That's my job. The enemy, whoever it is, they've got a job too. It's not personal. I don't hold it against them. But I *do* want to fucking bury them."

I wasn't sure the talk had helped. I felt a bit better about Farric, but now I feared that I'd let Mac down. If I got him killed . . . I couldn't take that. And that meant I should hang it up. Once you started getting risk averse, you made it more likely that something bad *would* happen. You can be cautious as a leader, but you can't be overcautious. It was as bad as being overaggressive and just as likely to get someone killed. "Fuck, Mac. I'm getting too soft for this."

"Bullshit. Why do you think I'm here? I had a choice. You know that. I'm here because I followed *you*. I figure you're going to do the right thing most of the time. You'll screw up. But you won't screw up because you don't care. You'll screw up trying to get it right."

"Same result."

"You don't even believe that," he said. "You've promoted guys who screwed up if they were doing the right thing when they did it. Sometimes you lose a fight. As they say, the enemy gets a vote in what happens."

I walked in silence for a minute, thinking it through. "Damn, Mac. When did you get so wise?"

"Don't tell anyone, sir. They might try to make me an officer or something stupid like that."

We came in sight of the restaurant—really more of a bar that served food—just as Karlsson went in. "One thing's for sure. If someone tries to kill this guy for talking to me, they better bring more than one person. He's a big bastard."

"I hope he tries something," said Mac.

I laughed. "Come on."

"No lie, sir. I'll give him a go, as long as there are no guns and knives. I'd feel a lot better if I got to kick someone's ass."

I looked at him.

He smiled. "What? You called me wise. Doesn't mean I don't want to take my frustration out on someone."

The building had no windows, and I stood inside, letting my eyes adjust, but even that didn't help, as if they kept it dark on purpose. I could make out the shapes of people, but faces were mostly shadows. The dark wood furniture and walls seemed to absorb light. I had to move through the room before I saw Karlsson at a back booth. I left Mac at the bar and headed over.

"You Butler?"

"Yeah."

The big, bald man gestured to the seat across from him. "You're buying."

"Sure."

"I'm drinking."

"They have real whiskey here, or just synthanol?" I asked.

"They distill their own. It's real. Expensive, but it's not bad."

"Then I'm drinking too." I didn't need to go down the path I'd taken last night, but one or two wouldn't hurt.

"Fuckin' A."

I waited for the drinks to come before I questioned Karlsson. He didn't strike me as being open, but maybe the liquor would help that. He drank half of his in a gulp, and I tried mine. He was right. Not bad.

"So," he said. "I'm here. You're that army guy, right?"

"I was."

"No, I mean, you're the one that fucked up all those aliens."

"Yeah."

"Fuckin' honor to meet you. You aren't serving anymore?"

"Nope. That was the end of the line."

"Political bullshit," he said. "Your man said you wanted to talk."

"I saw you and the protestors."

"Yeah?"

"What was that all about?"

"What'd it look like? A bunch of animal lovers that needed their asses kicked."

I didn't buy it. "Just for fun?"

"Yeah." He polished off his drink and signaled for another. I nodded when the woman behind the bar looked at me asking if I wanted a second one as well. "Nah . . . not just for fun. These green bastards . . . they're holding up progress. Putting people out of jobs."

That sounded a lot like a rehearsed answer. "What do you do for work?" I knew, but he didn't know I knew.

"I work construction, when there's work."

"There's no work now?"

"Not for me."

"So how do you stay on the colony? I thought there was a one-hundred-percent employment rule."

"Guess they haven't gotten around to me."

"So . . . you just hang out and beat up protestors?"

"Somethin' like that."

The bartender brought our drinks, and I let her go before I spoke again. "Just one more question, and I'll let you get back to your day. Did you decide to fight the protestors on your own, or did someone put you up to it?"

He smirked, and I knew he was going to lie before he even spoke. "I don't know nothin' about that kind of thing." He was a horrible liar, but he didn't care. He wanted me to know he was lying and that I couldn't do anything about it.

I considered threatening him. I could report his unemployment. The thing was, I didn't know if anyone would act on it. Karlsson probably did. I try not to bluff when the other person has more information than I do.

"Let me give you my contact information. In case you remember something."

He snorted. "Sure."


**OUTSIDE THE BAR,** Mac and I paused for a moment to let our eyes adjust to the light. The meeting had been mostly a waste of time, and I needed to get food. The liquor on an empty stomach hadn't been a great idea. Before we got fifty meters, two soldiers approached. Before they even spoke, I marked them as military police. They walked differently from other soldiers. I couldn't explain it, but I think Mac sensed it too, as he took his hands off his weapon and let it dangle from his shoulder when they got close.

The leader was a pale-skinned staff sergeant with light hair pulled back into a tight bun. Her partner was shorter, a dark-skinned sergeant with a small mustache that fit perfectly within regulations. The staff sergeant spoke. "Colonel Butler." Not a question.

"How did you know where to find me?" I figured it was best to ask my questions before she got to whatever hers were.

"Cameras. They're everywhere."

"Sure. When they work."

They looked at me, unsure what I meant by that. Finally, the staff sergeant said, "I need to ask you a few questions relating to the death of Dante Farric."

I'd had contact with him, so of course they'd want to talk to me about his death. I should have seen that coming. "How come you're handling this and not the civilians?"

"Our captain says it's related to the bombing, so it's a security issue."

I wasn't sure the governor—or more likely Davidson—would agree, but I wasn't getting in the middle of that. "Fair enough. You want to do it here, or somewhere else?"

"Here should be fine initially. If we need to do more extensive questioning, we'll move somewhere else." She left unsaid that the somewhere else in question would be in a detention facility. I didn't think they'd do that. It would have to go all the way up to Oxendine, and I didn't see her as that type. If she wanted to put me in jail, she'd call me in and do it herself.

"Okay. I saw on the news that they were calling it a suicide. Was it?"

She ignored my question like a good investigator. "You were the last call in his device, sir. Care to tell us what that was about?"

"He called me. We'd met the day prior and he'd promised to follow up." I was walking a thin line. I didn't want to lie to them, but I wasn't sure I wanted to share the name that Farric gave me either. I wasn't sure I *didn't* want to share—I needed to think about it. But if I told them now, I couldn't untell them later. If I didn't tell them now, I could always volunteer it in the future. But it left a hole in my story that even a low-level investigator would spot.

The staff sergeant didn't disappoint. "What was he following up about?"

"He had promised to get me a point of contact . . . someone I could talk to as part of my investigation. He called to tell me he couldn't get it."

And there it was. I'd blatantly lied to an investigator in a murder case. Even if I *didn't* kill the guy, I had just broken the law. I didn't glance at Mac to see his reaction. Nothing says *I'm lying* like looking around as if you're scared. I had to hope they didn't have a recording of my conversation with Farric. But if they did, the only reason they'd be talking to me was to trap me, and again, I didn't think Oxendine would send someone else to do that.

The investigator continued without missing a beat. "What was the meeting about the day prior?"

"I questioned him about EPV's involvement in the bombing attack at the governor's." *That* was the truth. Maybe it balanced the scales a little.

"Is that part of your official investigation, sir?" As she spoke, her partner tapped notes into his device.

"It is not. Or it is—I'm not quite sure. They may be related, since the attack was intended for me. Truthfully, I'm pissed that someone tried to kill me, and I'm not the kind of guy who lets things go."

"Roger, sir. Thank you for your time. We'll be in touch if we need anything else."

"That's it?"

"For now, sir. We're just running down initial leads."

"Right. Thanks." This was trouble. I hadn't killed Farric—not directly, at least—but from an investigator's point of view, I'd look like a pretty good suspect. I'd need to get in front of that, and soon.

# CHAPTER FOURTEEN

FADER MET US at the door to my new quarters. She had to have been watching, which made me suspect that she intentionally got herself a room where she could see mine. That was a smart thing I wouldn't have come up with on my own. It made me appreciate once again that Serata had picked Fader for the mission—or someone had, at his suggestion. She and I would never see things the same way—we had different styles—but as he'd told me, she *was* efficient. I needed to send him a note. Not just about that—I needed to let him know about Zentas arriving, see what he knew that might be useful. Get his advice on how to handle it. He was much better with things like that than I was.

Once inside, Mac made himself scarce and Fader didn't wait for me to sit down before speaking. "I've got two updates, sir. Ganos found some stuff on Marko Hubic, and I found some stuff about the Zentas visit. Which would you like first?"

"Zentas." He was already on my mind, and I probably had to lie low on Hubic with the military investigation into Farric's death happening.

"Yes, sir. His arrival is this morning. The exact time is classified. The governor's reception for him is this evening. You're invited if you want, plus one. Same sort of thing that they threw for you."

"I wonder if EPV will protest him the same way they did me," I said. He was, after all, the head of Caliber's parent company. "Probably. If I go, they can get two for the price of one."

"Maybe not, with Farric dead," said Fader. "I'm not sure if there's a clear succession plan in EPV. Losing their colonyside leader might throw them off their game for a while."

"Good point. We need to know who's next up in charge of EPV. Make a note of that, please." I waited while she did. "What else do you have?"

"Zentas came on his own business, not government. The official reason for the visit is oversight of his company assets here. Big boss checks things in the field— that kind of thing. Unofficially, nobody in the governor's office buys that for a second. *Everyone* thinks it's because of your investigation. But since that's not official, nobody has asked to schedule a meeting with you. The staffers believe that invite will happen through Caliber, not the governor. The governor himself—while I didn't talk to him—is reportedly put out that nobody asked him to facilitate your meeting. Regardless of the official purpose of the visit, *he* sees Zentas as his official guest."

"Do you know if they have a past relationship?"

"Nothing I could find on that publicly. And I looked. But everyone knows that Governor Patinchak will kiss the ass of anyone who can help him get ahead. Pardon the expression, sir."

I laughed. I don't know what was funnier, Fader slipping into more of my style, or her apologizing for it. "You're not wrong."

"Finishing up on Zentas, sir: He's scheduled to be

here for a week, but the ship that's bringing him isn't leaving, so the staffers consider that flexible."

"Roger." He didn't need a week to check on a relatively small operation like what Caliber had on Eccasis. They had maybe two thousand people working a dozen or so different job sites. But there were a lot of reasons he might want to stay. Maybe he just didn't want to jump straight back into cryo. "Go ahead and tell me about our friend Marko Hubic. I'll give guidance on both once I hear it."

"Yes, sir. He's got quite a history. This next bit is Ganos's exact wording—she made me promise to repeat them exactly before she'd give me a briefing. 'Sir, he's a fucking thug.'"

I laughed. "Okay. I assume there's more."

"Yes, sir. Arrested twice, once for assault, once for robbery. He did jail time for the robbery. Three years on a planet called Favia."

"How'd he get *here*?" I asked.

"I've got that, but there's more, sir. Ganos dug up some other cases where he was suspected but never charged. Arson, another robbery, two assaults. I'm not sure how she found that stuff—it's not in any public search that I can find."

"Best not to ask. Best to believe her, though."

"She did seem very sure of her information," said Fader. "I asked the same question you did. How he got here. Bottom line, it was EPV. Not officially, of course, but they got him hired using their connections with a company that builds solar power plants."

"A company that makes its money by developing colonized planets hired a member of EPV? I guess they didn't do much of a background check."

"Probably not, sir. Apparently, they hired him for

his official skill set. He's a demolition expert. I guess when you've got an in-demand skill and you're willing to travel to the end of the galaxy, people might overlook some things."

She had a point, but I couldn't dismiss more sinister possibilities. "Or EPV has someone inside the company that they either control or can bribe."

"We can look into that, sir, if you want."

"Let me think for a moment." Obviously Hubic was a suspect. Almost too good of a suspect—a flashing red light on his forehead, open-and-shut lock of a suspect. There were three possibilities. "I'm going to talk this out to you, Captain Fader. I want your honest opinion after I do, but mostly it's an exercise in making myself think. Here are my three thoughts. One: the obvious solution. Hubic is a radical EPV agent with a skill for explosives. He helped or directed whoever planted the bomb, or he planted it himself. Two: the obvious counter solution. Farric needed to give me a name, saw Hubic as an obvious suspect, and fed me his name to get me off his case, and then someone found out and killed him. And three: the conspiracy theory. Someone else fed Farric the name so that he'd give it to me, then killed Farric to confuse the trail."

Fader didn't answer immediately, thinking. "What's Farric's motivation in number two, sir? He gets you off his back, but if you investigate Hubic and find that there's nothing there, you go back to Farric. You didn't believe Farric was part of the plot, so he's not on the hook. Unless he intended for you to find enough on Hubic to get him out of here. But if that's the case, it seems more likely that Farric's motive might have been to eliminate a problem. That doesn't mean Hubic helped the bomber. But it doesn't exonerate him either."

"Good point." I appreciated Fader's consideration of the problem. Having someone to talk things out with helped me process information. I needed that. "What are your thoughts on the other? Is number three too far-fetched?"

"That would be a significant conspiracy." She said it softly, almost drifting off. "Although . . . it wouldn't take much to get there. If I was the bomber, or involved in any way, I'd want you looking anywhere but at me. If I knew Hubic's record, all I'd need was a way to feed it to you. Farric is the obvious choice, if I knew he'd met with you."

"We met in a public place," I said. "Anyone following either of us would have seen that."

"Yes, sir. That could be the connection. *Or* . . . it could have fallen into the bomber's lap. Ganos said that Farric was making calls. Maybe he called the bomber, or maybe he called someone who told them. Maybe he asked them to give him someone else to throw under the truck. And so they did. But then, if I'm the bomber, I see Farric as a liability. If he's willing to give up a name, maybe it's only a matter of time until he gives up mine."

"Huh. I posed it as a conspiracy, but when you put it like that, it sounds plausible." I considered it for a minute. "There's a lot of conjecture there though. Right? I mean, that's a lot of things that would have to be true. Though if we simplify: Farric wants a scapegoat because I promised to take the focus off of EPV if I could. He asks around, he gets a name of someone to frame from someone who works with the bomber. They kill Farric to erase the trail."

"They could have planted the stuff Ganos found," said Fader. "It might not be real."

"I trust Ganos to catch that sort of thing, but we can ask her."

"Occam's razor still says it's number one though, right, sir? Hubic being the bomber is the simplest solution."

"It is. But if, as you suggested, we rule out option two, there's an easy test to see if it's straightforward or conspiracy."

"What's that, sir?"

"If Hubic is alive, then it's not a conspiracy. Because if I'm framing him, the last thing I want is for an investigator to talk to him."

"So if we find him alive, he's probably guilty. Farric probably told the truth and got killed for it."

"You want to take bets?"

"That's a bit morbid, sir."

It was. And earlier, I felt like shit for getting Farric killed. The difference here, though, was that I didn't cause Hubic's death if it had happened. Maybe tangentially, but even my guilt-ridden conscience didn't dig that deep. If Hubic was dead, someone else killed him. Maybe my being here caused that, but even then, I didn't send *myself* here. I had a weird sense of justice. "Probably. But I'm going to bet that he's dead."

"Betting on conspiracy, sir?"

"That's just how my life works."

IF I'D BEEN hoping for an immediate answer, I would have been disappointed. I had Ganos run a search for Hubic the way she had for Karlsson, checking expenditures or other evidence of his location, and nothing came up. She even used a picture she found on the net and searched all the cameras she could access to try to find him that way.

Still nothing.

He was either dead or hiding, but we had no way to know which. I considered turning over the name to the military as part of their investigation into Farric's death, but that thought got interrupted by an invitation from Martha Stroud to have lunch the next day at their corporate dining facility in the executive room. She didn't specify who would be there, but it didn't take a genius to figure it out. I decided to skip the governor's reception. I had questions for Zentas, and I wanted to ask them one-on-one instead of having the governor around.

I did send Mac and Fader out to observe the reception from the outside. I wanted to know if there was a protest, which there was, though it was smaller than the one that had welcomed me. Oddly, I got a little ego boost from that. I really needed to get back to my therapist. Ganos had disappeared, working on her own things, which left me alone and with time on my hands. Never a great combination, so I logged on to my machine securely, with the stuff that Ganos had put on it since she didn't trust what came with the room, to send a message to Serata, but I had a message waiting from Flak Jacket Timmons.

*Good to hear from you, Butler.*

The opening made me smile. He couldn't call me sir, since he'd made colonel, but he didn't feel comfortable enough to call me Carl because of our history, where I'd outranked him.

*Sorry it took me so long to get back to you, but your requests took some work. Bad news first: I couldn't find Schultz. And I tried. I put some good people on it, but the guy's a ghost. There's no record of him landing anywhere.*

That gave me a chill. I could think of a place he could have ended up. There was a lot of jungle on Eccasis.

*Bergman was a little more interesting. When I looked at it, something felt off. The lawyers were retained by an anonymous benefactor and there was no record beyond that in the court. So I started digging. Turns out, the benefactor was a company, but that company didn't exist. I put a data specialist on it, and she tracked it back through three shell companies to Recort Systems, which is a sister company to Caliber.*
*So that's weird.*

Weird didn't begin to describe my thoughts on it. Caliber's sister company paid for the lawyers for an EPV bomber. Stroud had mentioned wanting things over and back to normal, and I suppose this could have been part of that. But I doubted it. Either way, it certainly put a different spin on the Zentas visit.

*Unfortunately, I can't do anything about it. The man has a right to lawyers and someone else hiring them isn't a crime. Maybe you can do something on your end with the investigation.*
*Speaking of that, you might want to wrap it up. I was directly told NOT to give you an order to end it, but trust me, there's talk about it, and that's definitely what the brass*

*wants. I get the feeling that they only sent you to pacify Zentas, and the boss figures you've done that. Again, I'm not telling you what to do. I just want you to have all the information.*

*Let me know if you need anything else.*

*Jack*

I appreciated the information and the straight talk. I'd have to sit on it for a bit to parse out what it meant. The brass being anxious for me to finish helped me understand Oxendine's position, but it didn't change my immediate plans. I'd still meet with Zentas, so I continued on with my note to Serata.

*Sir, I know I don't owe you an update, but I still wanted to check in and let you know what was going on with the investigation. The missing person appears to be truly dead. She and her whole team are gone, and while there are a couple of missing witnesses I'd like to talk to, it looks open and shut. There are some ancillary issues—someone tried to blow us up—and it might be related. But it might not. I'm going to hang around for a few more days until that resolves.*

*An interesting VIP arrived this morning. Drake Zentas. Did you know about that? If so, what can you tell me? Regardless of the official reason for the visit, I'm sure the real reason is about his daughter. I have lunch with him tomorrow and I'm not sure how to play it. Could use your advice.*

*Fader is doing well. Good call on putting*

*her on my team. I trust that she's keeping her superiors informed, but if you hear any rumblings that they're not happy, let me know. The commander here—Oxendine—isn't happy about my presence, but she's not being an asshole about it.*

*Give my best to Lizzie.*

*Butler*

I held back the stuff that Timmons told me. I trusted Serata, but only so far. That was sad, but he'd burned me before.

# CHAPTER FIFTEEN

SERATA'S MESSAGE WAS waiting when I woke up.

*Carl,*
*Trust your own judgment on the mission. If you think there's more, there probably is. If you say it's done, it's done. Nobody is going to push back on your findings. They'd just as soon it was over. But they won't push you to close it, either. They can't be seen doing that.*
*I didn't know about Zentas. I've never met the guy. People who know him say that he's straightforward, no bullshit. He's going to tell you what he thinks and won't give a shit about your feelings. Sounds like our kind of guy.*
*If you need anything, don't hesitate.*
*Serata*

I didn't know what to make of it. He said he hadn't known that Zentas was coming, and I guess I believed him. Maybe. It did cross my mind that he'd set me up before. I should have asked who *did* know. Someone should have told me. But then, no matter how fast his ship was, Zentas had left to get here before I ever arrived. It was always his plan. At this point, it didn't matter. He was here, and we were having lunch.

**MAC ESCORTED ME** to lunch at the Caliber dining facility, a low, flat-roofed building right behind their headquarters. He waited outside while I entered the facility to meet Zentas. It had seating for maybe 750, but an employee ushered me past the main area to the executive dining room, which seated twenty and held exactly two. Drake Zentas stood at the head of a long polished-wood table with Martha Stroud standing at his shoulder. Both faced me, giving me the feeling I was late, even though I'd shown up five minutes early. The dimly lit room had a plush carpet, and the whole place oozed of quality, much more so than the offices I'd seen. I wondered for a second if they had redone it just for Zentas.

Stroud spoke, looking at her boss, not me. "Mr. Zentas, this is Colonel Carl Butler. Carl, this is Mr. Zentas." No title needed, apparently.

"Nice to meet you, Mr. Zentas."

He gave me a big, genuine-looking smile. "Colonel Butler. So good to finally meet the man I've read so much about. Please. Call me Drake."

"And I'd appreciate it if you called me Carl." I got the feeling he was sizing me up, like we were going to fight or something. Maybe that's what super-rich guys did when they met someone new. Maybe that's why they were rich. I sized him up too. I could take him. He was a bit older than me, with a tanned, lined face that said he spent time outdoors, but he had slender shoulders and soft-looking hands, which said he probably didn't do much physical work when he was out there. We weren't going to wrestle, of course, so it didn't matter. But years of habit die hard.

"Come. Take a seat." He gestured to the chair beside him. It would have been more interesting if he sat me at the opposite end, where we'd have had to shout across ten meters of table. The thought made me smile. "Ms. Stroud was just leaving us."

"Before you go," I said, "did you find anything out about those two employees I asked about? Schultz and Ortega?" It was a dick move, calling her out in front of the big boss, but I didn't blow up the meeting from the start by asking about Bergman's lawyers, so at least I showed *some* restraint. I didn't want to get too confrontational until I had a chance to hear from Zentas.

Stroud didn't miss a beat. "Unfortunately, both gentlemen no longer work for our company in any capacity, and we have no way of knowing where they are. My assistant was supposed to message your captain. Did he not?" Her plastered-on smile might as well have said *fuck you*.

She'd won the round, and I should have let it go. But of course I didn't. "I'm going to need their complete records, including full name, employee number, and last known location. I'll have them rounded up, wherever they are." Not even a bluff. If they had the information, I thought Flak Jacket would work with me.

"That information is—"

"Please don't say that it's protected by privacy issues. If it matters, I'll have a formal request from higher up sent to you an hour after I walk out of this lunch." This one probably *was* a bluff, made better because her boss was present.

"I'm sure that won't be necessary," said Zentas. "Carl is here under the highest authority, and he has our full cooperation."

"Yes, sir." To Stroud's credit, her smile didn't waver.

"What was that about?" Zentas asked, once the door closed behind her.

"The company hasn't exactly been cooperative in my investigation." I could have said Stroud, but I thought that referring to the organization made it less personal. I wasn't out to ruin her. I just wanted answers.

"Ah. Unfortunate. And probably my fault."

"Your fault?"

He sucked in a breath through his teeth. "Yes. I asked for a favor to get you here at a very high level. That's not something I like to publicize." Before I could think about it and respond, he moved on. "I took the liberty of ordering for both of us." As if on cue, a tall, pale-skinned, extremely attractive waitress entered with a tray that held two glasses of whiskey with double pours and light ice. She wore a skintight gold dress about half a size too small, but my eyes locked on to the tray. "Ferra Three. The twenty-year," announced Zentas.

"Excellent choice. Hard to get that kind of thing out here." I had the fifteen-year in my quarters. The twenty-year cost about twelve times as much. It wasn't only hard to get out here, it was hard to get anywhere.

"I brought it with me. The food too."

I smiled. I didn't know what to say. He could certainly afford it, and if nothing else, I'd eat well. It made me wonder if he'd brought the waitress with him too. Either way, I got the feeling we were done discussing his disconnect with Stroud.

"I'm sure you know why I'm here."

My intel from Serata was right. No bullshit. "I assume so."

"It's my daughter. The official version—the one the

governor approved—it's a front. Obviously." He sipped his whiskey, taking time to savor it. Whatever else happened, we had *that* in common.

"I'd have done the same job whether you came or not. I'm not a man who requires much oversight."

"Of course you're not. But I'm sure you can forgive a father in this situation. She's my only child, and even though she'd distanced herself from the family . . . it's hard to let go."

"I understand. I lost my daughter at a much too early age."

"The governor suggested that you might be ready to close the investigation."

Had he? I certainly hadn't reported that to the governor. I'd had barely five minutes of conversation with him my entire time colonyside. I wondered how he had come to that conclusion. Wondered who told him. "I'm still considering some of the information, including the two missing people I mentioned to Ms. Stroud."

"What's your gut tell you?" He met my eyes firmly, and it was oddly compelling. He was a man used to getting his way, and I could see why.

"The facts so far suggest that it was an incursion by her team into an area inhabited by very territorial primates."

His eyes hardened and his lips drew into a line so thin they almost disappeared. "That's such bullshit."

I didn't speak. I didn't understand why he would immediately question my premise, and it put me off balance.

He continued. "We let animals dictate what we do. We put so many protections in place for them, but none for us. It's ridiculous."

I still didn't interrupt. He didn't want to hear from me on the subject, and the man *had* lost a daughter. Some righteous anger was justified.

"Colonel Butler—Carl—when you finish your investigation, you should come work for me."

*Say what?* I started to take a drink to mask my surprise, but the waitress had perfect timing and bailed me out when she entered with a tray carrying two covered plates. It took Zentas's attention off me momentarily, allowing me to recover.

"The steaks are Vanilorian beef. I trust you'll find it to your liking."

The waitress set my plate in front of me and removed the polished lid, displaying what had to be at least a five-hundred-gram cut of the most expensive beef in the galaxy, set off by a side of yellow root vegetables. The myth said that a specialized veterinarian certified each cow prior to slaughter. That Zentas was serving it here, two-thirds of the way across the galaxy from its origin, blew my mind. He was looking at me expectantly, so I picked up my knife and cut into it. It had a perfect sear on each side with a lot of pink and just a touch of red at the middle. "It's perfect." I tried not to think about how he knew how I like my steak.

"I take care of people who work for me," said Zentas.

He'd offered me a job and I didn't understand why. It could have been to buy influence into the outcome of my investigation, but that wasn't likely. What was there to influence? He didn't know that I knew about his lawyers helping Bergman, so it had to be something other than that. I took a bit of steak and lost my train of thought for a moment. It was a chewy cut, and the flavor . . . I now believed the hype. In the end, I went with the most basic question. "What's the job?"

"The job . . . is whatever I need you to do. There would be travel, of course. I have interests in many places. Sometimes being on the ground at a key spot provides a lot of benefit."

"So I'd go places as your proxy?"

"That, yes. Sometimes. And places I wouldn't necessarily go. Places with problems. As my fixer."

Fixer. I had to admit, if I had any intention of taking another corporate job in my lifetime, it did sound good. It fit my skill set too. But as much as I could get used to this lifestyle, I didn't want anything to do with it. Still, it didn't seem prudent to tell Zentas that at the moment. He didn't seem like the kind of man who would take no well, and I still wanted to figure out Caliber's game. "I trust you don't need an immediate answer. I'd like to think about it."

He looked at me for what felt like a minute but was probably four seconds. "What's to think about?"

"It's a great opportunity, and a job that I think I'd like. But I was enjoying retirement. I need to weigh those things."

"I usually don't wait for things I want." He paused, letting it sink in. "For anyone else, I'd say take it or leave it. But for you . . . I think you've earned a couple of days. The offer stands until I leave the planet."

Something in his manner felt just the slightest bit off to me. I couldn't explain it, but it made me decide to dig in a little. He claimed he came here because of his daughter, and though the meeting wasn't over, he hadn't made it a priority topic. He'd transitioned right into the job offer. "Just out of curiosity, what types of things would I be fixing?"

He considered the question, perhaps deciding how much to share in his answer. "Things like this place."

Despite my minor issue with Stroud, I didn't take the bait. "Your team here seems capable. What would I fix with them?"

"The team here is fine. Stroud is unimaginative, but competent and motivated. She's sufficient. The problems here are beyond the control of my team."

"Such as? Forgive me, I'm not trying to be obtuse. I just want to see what I'm getting myself into."

"Such as the delay in expanding our operations. Ever since your actions on Cappa, there's been a political shift that's gone in a decidedly un-business-friendly direction. Anti-development candidates have made gains at both the galactic level and at the local planetary level in a lot of systems. Not all, of course. But enough to cause problems."

"I don't have any experience with elections."

"But you do. You've already influenced them. Politicians have exploited your action to create sympathy for anti-exploration and anti-development policies. Some have run entire campaigns on that as their lead issue."

"I don't see how that has anything to do with me now. I did what I did, but that's over."

Zentas looked at me like a man who might be regretting having offered me a job. "They've rallied one side of the political battlefield, but nobody has rallied the other side. Specifically, *you've* been silent. If you spoke up—"

"I have a nondisclosure agreement."

He waved his hand as if shooing away an insect. "I have very good lawyers. Things like that are a temporary roadblock at most."

I didn't want to tell him that for the most part, I didn't agree with the side he wanted me to rally. Instead, I went back to my excellent steak.

After another moment he spoke again. "Carl, your

silence on the issue has been a problem for me. When I have a problem, I usually buy the solution."

Serata *had* said he was direct. That he wanted to buy me didn't bother me as much as what he wanted to buy me *for*. "So, the fixer thing . . . that's just a cover?"

He smiled. Maybe he thought he had me. "Absolutely not. That would be your primary focus. For the other stuff . . . I have people for that. They'll craft a marketing campaign, roll you out slowly. They'll know which races you can help. Meanwhile, you fix places like this. You'll have a team. You can pick most of it."

That caught my interest. The chance to bring in some of my own people and take care of them was a big incentive. I didn't need the money, but some of them could probably use it. People like Mac. "It's an enticing offer. That said, I'm not clear on how I'd *fix* a place like Eccasis."

"You'd find a way. That's what you do, right? You find a way to do things when other people can't. Now you'd just be finding a way for me instead of the government. You influence the governor. You get the local environmentalist types to get out of the way. You get expansion moving faster. Whatever it takes."

I'll admit, I gave it serious thought. The task held some appeal as an academic exercise if nothing else. "I'd need to do something about the hominiverts. As long as they're out there, it would be tough to make progress. We'd need to map their territories and work around them."

"We've got xenobiologists and anthropologists and whatever else you might need in order to craft your story."

"It's not about a story," I said. "It's about figuring out where they go and how to get them there."

He smiled, but it was flat and cold. "You're looking at it wrong. It's *all* about the story. Those things have killed humans. They've killed *my daughter*. They're a threat, but nobody sees it that way. Not yet. But if *Carl Butler* says they're a threat . . . well, then people will listen. They'll see the data our team develops, and if you do your job right, they'll act. Or they'll let *us* act. Either way."

My device buzzed, saving me for a moment from responding. I glanced at it. A message from Oxendine. She wouldn't send something that wasn't urgent. "Excuse me. I have to check this." I thumbed it open.

*I've detained your hacker. Oxendine.*

Shit.

She had to mean Ganos, which probably meant that they'd caught her doing something she shouldn't. That could have been any one of several things.

I cleared it and looked at Zentas. I didn't really want to leave. I had a lot more questions, and Zentas seemed ready to talk, but this couldn't wait. "I'm really sorry, but it's General Oxendine. It's an emergency."

"By all means."

"You'll hear from me soon, Drake. I promise."

"I look forward to it."

"Thanks for the meal. It was outstanding."

I just hoped I could keep it down while I figured out what happened to Ganos.

# CHAPTER SIXTEEN

**M**AC AND I headed to my quarters instead of going directly to see Oxendine. Whatever had happened there, I needed as much information as I could get before I went. Fader was at my quarters waiting.

"What happened?" I asked.

"Ganos came running into my place, threw a pair of earrings at me, then three MPs showed up a few seconds later and took her away."

"Did they say what for?"

"I asked. I even tried to pull rank. They said they had orders not to speak to anybody about it, and that included you. All they would say was that you should come to headquarters and see the general about it."

"Why did she throw her earrings at you?"

"That was my question too, sir. Turns out they've both got computer chips in them."

"She was passing information."

"She was. There was even a short video file . . . it almost seems like she knew she'd get caught and wanted to make sure we got the information."

"The video—"

"Her explaining the rest of the data, sir. Here, best if you just watch it."

Ganos's face appeared on Fader's device. She spoke in a whisper, leaning into whatever she used to make the recording.

*Sir. If you're watching this, that means I probably got caught. I'm sorry for any inconvenience that causes you, but there was no other way. Whatever they tell you I did, I probably did. I probably did more than that. The data on this chip will confirm everything I'm saying here if a professional reads it, but since I'm your professional and you might not have access to me, the bottom line is that the hack of your vehicle came from inside the military. It wasn't routed through the military—someone inside did it. From the data on the chips, any competent cyber tech can trace the terminal and the time, which should lead them to the culprit. A military insider hacked the cameras at the governor's and your vehicle. It was a good hack—hard to find—so there's a chance that the good guys looked for it and missed it, but if that's the case, they need some better techs.*

She glanced to the side.

*Shit. Gotta go. You owe me big for this one.*

"That's all there is, sir," said Fader.

"You think she's okay?" asked Mac.

"The message I got from Brigadier General Oxendine said that she'd detained Ganos. I think she's probably okay. Whether we can get her out or not is a different question."

"When the general sees the data, she'll have to let her go," said Fader.

I snorted. "Because commanders are always happy

when someone points out that their organization is tied to illegal activity? Besides, I might not be able to show her the information."

"Why not, sir?"

"I don't know what she has on Ganos and what she can prove. If I give her the data, it might be the evidence she needs for a conviction."

"What are you going to do, sir?"

"I'm going to go meet with Oxendine and wing it."


**I FOUND OXENDINE** in her office. At least she didn't pretend to be busy and keep me waiting. Her XO joined us, a tall, dark-skinned colonel with short, curly hair. She hadn't been present for any of our other meetings, and I'd only met her in passing. Oxendine wasn't afraid of me, so that only left one other reason.

"You figure you need a witness?" I asked.

"I might. While I don't suspect you of a crime right now, that could change."

She was sending a message that we both understood. She didn't want to read me my rights, but that didn't mean she couldn't still use something against me. As soon as I said something incriminating, she'd stop me and read them then. It might not apply since I'd retired from the military and wasn't subject to their jurisdiction, but I *was* here on military orders. The lawyers would have to figure it out later, if it became an issue. I didn't think it would. Ganos had done a fine job of keeping me out of it. I truly hadn't known her plans. I could have guessed, but I didn't know.

That made a difference. "I took it from your message that you have Ganos."

"We do. She's fine. She's not in a cell. That's a courtesy."

"What's the charge?"

"Officially? At the moment, it's unauthorized access. Depending on what we find, it could go as high as espionage."

"Espionage? Come on." That was bullshit. They'd have to prove she was trying to do harm at a galactic level.

"The final charge will probably be somewhere in between. She did more than just unlawfully access."

"Can I see her?" I asked.

"Maybe in a bit. First I need you to tell me what you knew about this."

"Not a thing." It was only a small lie. I intended to stick as much to the truth as I could without making things worse, but I wasn't ready to give up anything just yet. "I knew Ganos was running down a lead, but I didn't know what it involved."

"You didn't tell her to get specific information?"

"I might have. What information did she get?"

Oxendine smiled, but it wasn't a happy smile. "Nice try. You think you're clever, but you really aren't. Tell me what you had her looking for, or we're done talking and we'll let the lawyers figure it out after I ship Ms. Ganos off world."

It was a bluff, but the only way I could call it was to shove everything into the pot. I couldn't. There was too much at risk. If I called out the inside job from Oxendine's organization, I'd be admitting that I knew what Ganos found. "She was working on several things for me. Most recently, she mentioned the possibility that our vehicle had been hacked. You'll recall I asked you for access and you turned me down. I told her that you turned me down, and I did not give her further instruction."

"You didn't tell her *not* to try to access it on her own?"

"I didn't."

"Why not?"

"I didn't tell her not to shoot anybody, either. I just assumed she wouldn't." Oxendine had asked a stupid question, so she deserved the flippant answer.

"Those are hardly the same, Carl."

"I did not tell her to break the law. That's what you're asking, right?"

"I believe that you didn't. What I'm asking is if you specifically told her *not* to break the law."

"Not specifically." I didn't add that that wasn't a crime because Oxendine knew that. She just wanted to make me *feel* guilty. Probably so I'd give her other information. But it went beyond that. It was a basic interrogation technique, and Oxendine would know that I knew that, which meant she had a different purpose. She might have been covering her ass, in case someone asked later, or it might have been performative for her subordinates. That would explain the presence of her XO, who could leak that the general had really grilled that Butler asshole.

"Did Ms. Ganos communicate with you after her actions?"

"I'm not sure I want to answer that." I didn't have to play her game.

Oxendine's jaw tightened for a split second before she schooled her face back to neutral. That one had pissed her off. "You realize that if she passed you classified information, then you're party to a crime."

"My orders make it pretty clear that I have a clearance that gives me access at the highest level, and that I define my own need-to-know as it relates to my investigation."

"This isn't part of your investigation."

"I have a lot of leeway in determining that, too."

She started to speak but stopped. Judging by the

narrowing of her eyes and the hard breath she blew out, she was frustrated. Good. We'd finished the game and it was time to negotiate. She knew it too. She had Ganos on a legit charge, but I was right about my access to information. "How does this end, Carl?"

"You give me Ganos. You drop all charges and agree not to reinstate them and not to bring new charges. In return, she will turn over to you everything she found."

Oxendine considered it. No way would she accept the offer, but I'd given her something to counter and she had to at least pretend to think about it. I appreciated her in that moment. She didn't take it personally. Just business. I could always work with that, even through a conflict. "I give you Ganos, I drop the charges, and you ship her out of here on the next thing moving. She doesn't touch a computer of any kind on this planet ever again, and you wrap up your investigation in the next twenty-four hours and get out of here as well."

I kept my face neutral. Her demands were unreasonable, but mine had been too, so I deserved it. We had a starting point. "For any of that to happen—and I'm not agreeing—you'd have to throw in that you'll look at what Ganos found and track the lead—"

"I'm doing that regardless," she said, cutting me off.

"*And* share the results with me."

"Why? That's internal to the military and outside your investigation."

I took that to mean that Oxendine already knew the basics of what Ganos's information showed. Of course Oxendine would want to keep the fact that she had a leak quiet. "Because whoever did those hacks was involved in not one, but two different attempts to kill me. Even if it *is* outside my investigation—and I'm not convinced it is—I want to know who is behind it."

"Do you see why I'm reticent?" she asked. She was good. She wanted me to put it out there instead of her having to voice it.

"I do. It seems likely at this point that someone *inside* your organization was part of a crime *outside* your organization. Someone is compromised. That's not something you want getting out."

"Go on," she said, still unwilling to say it, but acknowledging it with her tone.

"I'd like to promise you that I won't put it in my report, but I can't—"

"Then I'm not likely to share the information—"

"Hear me out," I said. "I can't promise it won't go in my report, because if it's linked to other issues I'm investigating, I might have to include it. What I *will* do is this: If it doesn't matter, I won't put it in, and if I *do* have to include it, I'll add the caveat that it was your team that found the compromised agent."

She thought about it for several seconds. "So you'll lie."

"Who said anything about lying? We haven't found the person responsible yet. It's going to be your people who do that. That's the truth."

"A half-truth," she said.

"I can live with that."

She thought some more, glancing to her XO, who didn't give any sign. I couldn't read their communication—couldn't tell if no sign meant okay or no sign meant no. I wished I'd done a little more research on the XO now, to find out if she was a by-the-book type or was more flexible. Oxendine would know, and that third person in the room might make a difference. On the other hand, Oxendine probably wouldn't have had her in the room unless they were working on the same wavelength. "We have a deal on the information. I'll share whatever we find with you.

But the jurisdiction for the potential perpetrator remains with me."

"Happy for you to have it." I meant it. She could have that nightmare. If the governor didn't try to take it from her again.

"That still leaves us with the issue of Ms. Ganos," said Oxendine.

"Ganos was never here," I said.

Oxendine looked perplexed.

"Or she was, and she helped you solve the issue. You write the story whichever way you want." I had to push this. It forced Oxendine to take ownership of part of the half-truth. It tied us together in it, and it gave her incentive not to flip on me later.

Oxendine looked at her XO again. "What do you think?"

"If we do it, ma'am, the story has to be that we brought her in. Too many people know about her to hide it."

"How do we explain her detention?"

The taller woman considered it. "She's not detained. She's currently in a briefing room. I leave here and go talk to her alone. The information she found is so important, she needed to brief a senior officer directly."

I almost smiled. Brilliant. A good XO was worth her weight in silver, and it seemed like Oxendine had a good one. The corners of Oxendine's mouth turned up a little. She knew it too.

"That will work. Make it happen, XO." Now that the threat of potentially charging me had passed, we didn't need a witness anymore.

"Yes, ma'am."

Oxendine turned back to me, smile gone. "You seem to have gotten exactly what you wanted. But we're not done. I still want Ganos gone and you hot on her tail."

"I need her. But I'll agree to keep her off any military network. If she has something that you need to look into, I'll bring it to you directly."

She didn't speak, so before she could make another counter, I decided to sweeten the deal.

"To add something to the table, I'll provide you with information that I found in the course of my investigation that might help you with another matter."

"What matter?"

"The death of Dante Farric. If I don't miss my guess, the governor is probably interested in the outcome of that one."

She narrowed her eyes. "Do I need to get a witness in here again?" She implied that I might have done something illegal, which, the more I thought about it, I probably did. But neither of us was going to take it in that direction at this point.

"Your call."

"What have you got?"

I had her. "The day before he died, Dante Farric promised me a name of someone from the more radical side of EPV. Someone who might know something about the bombing. His implication was that the person might have been *involved* in the bombing."

"And you think he was looking into that when he got killed."

"More than that. The next day—the day he died—he gave me a name. Marko Hubic."

"We have the bomber. Or we did, before he got shipped off planet."

"I don't think Bergman did it."

"You know this how?"

"The governor's aide wasn't lying about lawyers on Talca. Expensive ones. Want to know who paid for them?"

She thought for a minute, but declined to guess. "Who?"

"A sister company to Caliber. Another Zentas business."

"Why would—" She let it trail off, making the connection herself. "Why didn't you tell this to the investigators when they questioned you?"

"Don't make me lie to you," I said. We both knew the answer to that question. I hadn't wanted to.

"You know, Carl, I'm tempted to let Ganos stay and throw *you* off the planet."

"I do have that effect on people."

She laughed. "Any other bombs you want to drop while you're here?"

"Drake Zentas offered me a job."

"No shit? Doing what?"

"Whatever he needs me to do."

"What's his angle?"

I shook my head. "I don't know." The truth. I had ideas, but I didn't feel like giving *everything* away. Oxendine and I weren't friends, even though we'd come to a mutual understanding.

"You taking it?"

"I'm not sure. There may be a conflict of interest, right?"

"Maybe. But you're not in the military anymore, so maybe not. Do you want me to run with the Hubic thing or do you want to keep it?"

"You take it. If it's related to my case, it's tangential." I also had no leads and nowhere to go with it. "I'd love to talk to the guy if you catch him though."

"That might be tricky, legally, but I'll see what we can do."

"Thanks." I stood and shook hands with her. She could have made this a lot harder than she did. It's nice when things go the easy way for a change.

# CHAPTER SEVENTEEN

GOT BACK TO my quarters and it was only a few minutes until Ganos arrived, escorted by Mac. He'd only let me go after I got a security detail from Oxendine, which I agreed to because I didn't want Ganos walking around alone, and she'd have bullied anyone but Mac into letting her do it. For a small community, bad things seemed to happen to a lot of people.

I greeted her when she arrived. "Hey, remember that time when I saved your ass from rotting in a military cell?"

She rolled her eyes at me. "You don't do it right, sir."

"No?"

"No. Here, I'll show you. Hey, sir, remember that time you were totally dead-ended on your investigation and I found the information that cracked open—"

"Yeah, yeah," I said.

"You didn't let me finish, sir. In the second verse, I become the hero, probably to the entire galaxy. I'm still working on that part."

"I'm glad to see your time in detention hasn't dimmed your spirit."

"Are you kidding, sir? It all went according to plan. I found the hacks and forced the military to do something about them."

I laughed. "That was the plan?"

"As far as you know."

"Well, keep it quiet. General Oxendine is telling a slightly different story, and as part of securing your release I agreed to let her."

"Roger that. What am I on next?"

"Why don't you take a day off? I want to let things cool down a bit, and I gave the search for Hubic over to the army."

"I *could* use a nap. I was working all night on that stuff. Can I get my earrings back? A girl needs to accessorize."

"I'm pretty sure those will turn up someday and be called *government exhibit one*," I said. "Seriously, though . . . don't we need to give that data to the military?"

"I already shared it with them face-to-face. The tech I talked to didn't have the same dim look in his eyes as everyone else, so I think he's got it."

"Great. You go take your nap. And try to stay out of trouble."

"Don't I always?"

After she left, I poured myself a well-deserved drink, and before I finished it, Fader showed up. I'd messaged her as soon as I finished up with Oxendine and asked her to find Mae Eddleston. I had no idea how Fader had accomplished it so quickly, but she brought the young-looking woman in with her. Something that Zentas had said struck me the wrong way, and I wanted to look into it.

"Thanks for coming," I said.

She looked around. "You downsized since the last time I saw you."

"Yeah, they moved Mr. Zentas into my old place."

"They can do that?"

"Apparently," I said. "I wanted to ask you a few more questions, if that's okay. Mostly about xenobiology."

"Sure."

"You've studied hominiverts, right?"

"Absolutely. It's been one of our top priorities."

"Something in a conversation struck me earlier today. Would you say that you're trying to understand them better, so that we can cohabitate?" I didn't think so, but I wanted to confirm.

She snorted. "I'd say we were trying to understand them better so we could find a way to get them to move. I'm a scientist, but I work for Caliber. I know who hits send on my pay transfers."

"I understand. No judgment. Could you elaborate on how you get them to move? That would seem to be—"

"Morally questionable?" she offered.

"I was going to say borderline illegal, but sure. No offense."

"None taken. We work within the parameters of the law. Recently we were studying the effects of low-frequency noise and its ability to drive the hominiverts out of an area. There were some promising tests that indicated that we might be able to shift their territory via sound."

"You could move them with sound?"

"That was the theory, yes. There are still tests to do—it's not complete, but it's promising. We would insert sonic devices in areas we wanted the hominiverts to leave."

"Would humans be able to hear it?"

"Absolutely not. It's below our natural hearing range. Under perfect circumstances, you *might* feel it as a slight vibration."

I paused. If they had the ability to move them out of

an area, what would stop them from moving them *into* an area? I got a chill, and it had nothing to do with the air circulator. Suddenly the attack on my patrol—and possibly Xyla's—took on a different hue. I didn't share it with Eddleston, because I didn't want to scare her and make her shut down. Plus, the less she knew, the better. "Do you have hominivert territories marked out?"

"We have a rough map of part of the terrain, yes. We've been able to tag a few animals with radio trackers."

Whoa. That also changed things. If they could track them . . . I was pretty sure the military didn't know that. But then, the military wasn't even carrying the right ammunition . . . because someone had told them they couldn't. There were too many coincidences. I hate coincidences. They have this ugly way of not being coincidences. "You don't happen to have the map on your device, do you?"

"Sorry, no. But I can go back into work and get it for you."

I considered it for a second before rejecting it. No way. Not this time. I wasn't getting someone else killed. And if my theory was correct, Caliber wouldn't want anyone sharing that information with me. Best to keep Eddleston out of it and find another way to get what I needed. "No, that's okay. I can get it."

"If you're sure," said Eddleston.

"Zentas offered me a job. This will be a good chance for me to look around the place."

"Sure. Send me a note if I can help."

"Will do," I said.


**WHEN SHE LEFT,** I picked up the remainder of the drink I'd forgotten when Eddleston arrived.

"What just happened?" asked Fader. "You were going down a path with her, then all of a sudden you broke off."

"I wanted to keep Eddleston out of it."

"Out of what, sir?"

"If they can move 'verts out of an area, why couldn't they move them into one?"

Fader caught my meaning immediately, but when she spoke, her tone indicated doubt. "You think it's possible, sir? You think someone targeted the 'verts against the patrol?"

Fader had a lot of positive qualities, so it was easy to forget how little experience she had. "I've learned to believe that everything is possible. That's not the question."

"What's the question, sir?"

"The question is who would do that to a Caliber patrol?"

She considered it. "The easy answer is EPV, but I don't think you're looking for the easy answer."

"The easy answer doesn't make sense. The technology belongs to Caliber. EPV is opposed to Caliber. So why would Caliber help EPV attack their own patrol? If it had just been *my* patrol that got attacked, I could maybe see it. Common enemy, or something. Assuming Caliber sees me as an enemy, which is . . . I was going to say hard to see, but really I don't know. Something is going on there. Regardless, though, the attack against Xyla's patrol hurt Caliber."

"Maybe there's a blurring of the lines between EPV and Humans First."

"Maybe. But they have almost diametrically opposed purposes."

"They do, sir—on the surface. But on the radical ends of both, they might dip into an element that's more about the violence than the agenda."

"Interesting. That could make somebody like Hubic a potential player on both sides."

"Yes, sir. What if he's just a contractor? Have bomb, will travel."

I thought about it. Once a guy made a bomb, it wasn't a big step to working for the highest bidder. Not everybody working for a cause is a true believer. "It certainly makes more sense that way. But I have a hard time seeing Hubic involved in this latest thing. The hominivert attacks use technology that's a lot different from a bombing."

"But the camera hack and the vehicle hack were a bit more sophisticated."

"Good point. If you're right—if the lines are blurred with the people—we have to follow the weapons. Caliber has the sonic tech."

"I also got an answer from the Intel shop that they tracked the source of the explosives used in the bomb to a Caliber work site."

"Individually, I wouldn't think too much about that, but when we combine the hacks and the bomb material? It might be more than a coincidence, and it's worth checking out."

"It's not like we can walk into Caliber and ask them about their tech," said Fader.

"I mean . . . we *could*. *I* could." I had a plan. Well . . . part of a plan. The first kernel. But I'd gone into things with less.

"Sir, please. You're hardly going to fly under the radar."

"No. Not under it. Right through it. Drake Zentas offered me a job."

Fader's eyes went wide. "Really, sir? Doing what?"

"We didn't really get that far." I trusted her, but the look she had given me made me not want to share everything. It almost looked like fear, as if I'd actually take it. "But even without that detail, I could pretend to be considering it and ask to see their facilities. While I'm there, I look around and ask questions." I was talking myself into it even as I said it. I needed a voice of reason. Caliber was a sophisticated company, and I should have learned by now that a simple ruse wouldn't fool them. Fortunately, I had Fader, who had quickly recovered from her shock.

"Sir, I think you showing up there would immediately be suspicious, job offer or not. Everything you do is going to be scrutinized, filmed, and scrutinized again. Plus, the idea that Caliber gave tech to radicals to use on their own patrol leaves out one critical factor: Xyla Redstone. More significant, Xyla *Zentas* Redstone."

"Who would name their kid Xyla Zentas?" I asked, not for the first time. What can I say? It bothered me. "Initials X Z. That's just ridiculous." Once more, Fader stayed stone-faced during my nonsense as I stalled to let my mind work. She was right, of course. How deep a conspiracy would I have to imagine for Caliber to be a part of the death of their CEO's daughter . . . ?

"Unless that's why he's here," I said.

"You lost me, sir."

"Pure conjecture, but what if he—Zentas—came because it *was* part of the plan, but he didn't plan for it to involve his daughter. He's got a lot of holdings. He wouldn't be managing day-to-day operations. What if he came here to deal with that?"

She frowned. "Not buying it, sir. First, he was the one who sent you here. Why send you and then come himself?"

"I don't know. But he *did* send me and then come himself, so that's a matter of record, regardless of why."

"Yes, sir. But if you're right, why does Stroud still have a job?"

Huh. I hadn't thought of that. If she was responsible for the death of Zentas's daughter, she'd be done. Zentas himself had called her competent. "Maybe she didn't have anything to do with it."

"She's in charge. She's responsible."

"But by that logic, she's in charge and Zentas's daughter is dead, regardless of the cause. In my meeting with her about the disappearance of the patrol, she said it was part of the cost of doing business." I thought about it. The attitude fit with what I knew about Zentas as well. I just didn't know what it all meant. There were too many permutations. "Maybe he'll just fire her later, after I deliver the results of my report. It gives him cover."

"Does he seem like a man who needs cover?"

"He doesn't. Which brings us back to the same spot. Why is he here? If we solve that, I think we solve everything. He doesn't do things by accident."

"Are we off of EPV as a suspect, sir?"

"I don't know. What I do know is that Caliber isn't playing straight. Zentas didn't even tell his own people that he asked for me to come here. They're hiding something."

"Okay, sir. If you're right, how do we figure that out?"

"Zentas has an ego. We get him to tell us."

# CHAPTER EIGHTEEN

**DESPITE THE SIMPLE** solution I'd presented to Fader, I didn't move forward with it immediately because I didn't know how to actually *do* it. Zentas would talk about himself. Of course he would. But I had to come up with a reason for him to do it publicly. And it hit me. The press. If Eccasis had press beyond the local news feed, I didn't know about it, but a quick search would turn it up. I put Fader on that while I went to my go-to source for all press matters, Karen Plazz. She was big-time now, so no way would she work a story in a distant colony, but Zentas was news, so she might at least be able to put me in touch with someone who would. Either way, it didn't cost anything to ask, so I sent her a message.

> Karen,
>     I need a favor. Imagine that! I'm on a job out on Eccasis—I was supposed to be looking for the daughter of a rich guy named Zentas. Thing is, Zentas himself showed up here in the ass end of the galaxy, and I can't figure out why. His story is that he's checking on his holdings here, but he's admitted to me that

*that's BS. There might be a story in the real
reason that he's here.*

*I know it sounds like a lot of work, but
I'm not sure it would take much prodding.
Zentas likes to talk, especially about himself,
and if a reporter gave him a forum, he might
take it.*

*Thanks, and remember all those great sto-
ries I gave you that helped make your career.*

*Carl*

The last part was a joke. Mostly. I *had* given her some
huge stories in our time working together, but she'd done
just as much for me, which she'd probably remind me of
in her response. Having finished that, I lay down to take
a nap, and when I woke it was in that disoriented state
where I might have been asleep twenty minutes or two
hours. A quick check of my device told me it was closer to
the latter. Mac and Ganos were in my room. It had been
he who woke me, but Ganos immediately took the lead.

"Sir, I found him. Your guy. Hubic. Okay, maybe I
didn't find him, but I found something, and he could definitely be there."

"Slow down, Ganos. I thought I told you to take the
day off."

"Turns out, I don't really listen to you that much, sir."

"Tell me about it." I looked at Mac.

"Don't look at *me*, sir. You told me to make sure nothing happened to her. Nothing happened. Besides that
though, I can't control her."

"Damn straight," said Ganos. "But forget that. This is
so cool. Someone's hiding in the jungle."

"What? That's impossible. People can't live outside
the domes."

"But they can live in domes that aren't supposed to have people in them. Look." She pushed some buttons and a map came up on my wall monitor.

"What am I looking at? It's a map of Eccasis—I can tell that much."

"This is a map of all the communications traffic on the planet. I got to thinking that if someone was hiding, they'd still have to communicate. And since I didn't have a way to find that communication directly, I decided to hack into the central comms hub for the planet and find all the activity. It's a heat map. The more red you see on the screen, the more activity is coming from that spot."

"Please tell me it wasn't a military system," I said. *Please.*

"It wasn't, sir. It's a planetary asset. Civilian. You told me not to hack any military systems until tomorrow."

"That was not at all what I said."

"Agree to disagree."

She was screwing with me. I hope.

"Anyway," Ganos continued, "it's not military. I really didn't know what I'd find or how it would help me find Hubic, but sometimes it works that way, you know?"

"I do." I really did. That's how things happened for me a lot.

"And see what I found? This supposedly abandoned dome out here. It used to be a research station, but they shut it down over a year ago."

"Except they didn't?" I asked.

"Apparently not. There's not much, but it represents somewhere between fifty and sixty communication hits over the last month."

Her excitement about her find was infectious. I had to admit . . . she had me hooked. I stood and went closer.

"There are no active domes anywhere near there. What kind of comms are they using?"

"Satellite. Same as the rest of us. When I first looked, no dome registered there at all. But the governor's office has records that go back until the start of the colony—don't ask me how I know—and I found this one out there by itself, nothing within thirty kilometers."

"Whose dome was it?" I asked.

"It was registered to a company called Garrabond Solutions, which is a sub-company of a little organization called Caliber. You've probably heard of them."

"Shit. Wow. No chance that other missions in the area are just using it as a stopover?"

"Super unlikely, sir. This sector got pretty much abandoned once rules tightened up, and even if someone *did* supersede their parameters, it wouldn't be every day."

"Every day?"

"Every day at exactly the same times, sir."

That set off my not-a-coincidence radar. "That's something."

"Right? You want the bad news?"

"Do I?" I asked.

"Probably not. But here it is: I can't trace it."

"Can anybody?"

Ganos paused for the first time since she arrived. "Maybe. Someone who had full access to the comm system and didn't have to hack in. But it would still be hard. Whoever is using the comms there is doing their best not to be found."

"I don't know how we get official help on this without admitting that you hacked in in the first place."

"That *is* a quandary." Ganos smirked. She seemed to put me in a lot of those, but it was worth it for the information she gained. "Sure glad that's not my department."

"I need time to think." I had angles, now, but it had almost gone beyond what I could manage. I had *too many* angles. In theory, it was a good problem to have. In practice, it meant I had to pick an option. I had the military looking for both their internal hack and Hubic, and now Ganos had a lead on what might be Hubic. But I couldn't immediately tell Oxendine, because then I'd have to admit that Ganos had been back at work, and I *really* didn't want to do that. I'd have to let things cool first. I also had the link to the Caliber tech. "Ganos, if I ask you to not push any further today, would you actually listen?"

"Probably. I'm kind of at a dead end. Even I'm not dumb enough to go back after the military, and I still don't really want to tangle with Caliber. What are you going to do, sir?"

"I'm going to go back to sleep and attack this stuff with a fresh mind in the morning."


I WOKE IN the dark, soaked in sweat, my heart hammering in my chest. The sheets clung to me like another skin, and I kicked at them to free myself. It was probably a good thing that I couldn't remember the details of the dream. I hadn't had an anxiety-fueled nightmare in a couple of years, and I didn't welcome this one. Someone had been chasing me—I remembered that much—some combination of people and animals. The setting had shifted throughout, from the mountains of Cappa to the jungle to an abandoned warehouse complex where the floors didn't appear to match up, creating some sort of impossible maze. I checked my device for the time. Just after three. I considered trying to go back to sleep—I even closed my eyes for a few minutes—but it wasn't going to happen. I got up and padded over to my terminal.

I had a message from Plazz.

> Butler,
>    You're welcome. You owe me.
>
>                                    Plazz

Along with the note she sent a link, which I opened. Drake Zentas's face appeared in a split screen with a reporter, a pretty thirty-something woman with copper skin and perfect teeth. The location bar under her said Talca 4, while Zentas's said Eccasis. They couldn't have done the bit in real time with the space lag, so they must have recorded the questions and answers separately and then edited them together. That they did it all while I slept impressed me, though Zentas had often bragged in the media about only sleeping three to four hours a night, so I guess he had the free time. I turned up the volume and hit play.

The first few questions didn't matter to me—some things about the health of his company, projected earnings, and other business stuff. At the 1:47 mark I got what I wanted. The anchor asked him about his trip to Eccasis. She framed it by saying that it was a move not many CEOs would make, implying that it might be something that gave him an advantage over the competition. A total softball, but it did play to his ego. Something in Zentas's demeanor shifted—a minute change—as if this question changed the tenor of the interview.

"I *do* like to check on my holdings. I feel like the idea that the boss can show up anywhere in the galaxy makes everything work just a little better. And I did have that purpose for this trip. But there was another reason. My daughter, Xyla—we've been estranged for some time, but I was hoping to change that—she disappeared here on Eccasis." He took a deep breath, paused, let his eyes shift, before reengaging with the camera. "I hoped . . . I . . . I really hoped it wasn't true. That there'd been a mistake." He looked away again and blinked several times, fighting tears. "I'm sorry. It's hit me hard."

I paused it. As he said it on the screen, he came across as sincere, but it wasn't the same vibe I'd gotten from him in person. Either the entirety of the situation had finally hit him, or he was playing to the audience. My gut said performance. He'd have received the questions ahead of time and been able to prepare. He'd have rehearsed and then gone on the news and used his daughter's death intentionally to gain sympathy. I pressed play.

"Since I've been here—since I've come face-to-face with this hard reality—I've found another purpose. Not just here . . . galaxy-wide. But starting here. We've tried to coexist with the different species on our colonies. Recent laws have pushed us more and more in that direction. I'm here to say that it has gone too far. These *animals* . . . they're dangerous to humans. They *kill* humans—they killed my daughter! And we just stand by and let them. No more. No. Not when I have something to say about it."

The news anchor didn't react . . . she'd have only seen his diatribe after the fact. I pictured the people back on Talca filming a new question for her to fit the direction that Zentas took the interview. "Mr. Zentas, what are you proposing?"

"I'm not proposing anything." He looked at the camera now, locked in, as if staring someone down in a business meeting. "I'm *doing* something. I'm taking action. If you're a politician—local, galactic, I don't care—if you're not on board with putting humans first, I'm going to fund your opposition and we're going to put someone in power who is. We need people who believe in the supremacy of human life in this galaxy. I urge everyone—my fellow humans—to join me in this. Demand that your representatives put us first."

It wound down from there with the required pleasantries from the host, but I let it slip by me. I'd heard enough. He'd used his daughter's death for political gain. It also didn't escape my notice that he used the term "humans first." That could have been a coincidence, but he employed members of the group through Caliber, so I doubted it. Though he hadn't said anything illegal, the interview ended any chance that I'd go work for him. It did another thing too.

It told me that my next stop needed to be at Caliber.

# CHAPTER NINETEEN

**I** MET MARTHA STROUD the next morning before most people had eaten breakfast. I'd guessed that she'd be in—her boss was on planet, and that tends to get people out of bed early. I'd called ahead to make sure, though. I'd spent the previous hours thinking through my moves. Stroud herself was the first play. I didn't know what information she had, but I figured that with Xyla's death and her boss leaving her out of the loop about me, she might not feel super secure about her job. I wanted to use that.

"Thanks for meeting with me so early."

"What can I do for you, Carl? I thought your investigation was pretty much finished."

"It is," I lied. "I'm looking into something new. Mr. Zentas offered me a job. I'm exploring that option." Her face tightened slightly at my words, but I didn't know if it meant she didn't know and I'd caught her by surprise, or if she *did* know and didn't like it.

She controlled her expression. "If that's the case, I'm sure he'd want us to do what we can to help you out."

"Is he here?" I made a show of looking past her.

"He's not. He left early for a tour of some of our outer facilities."

"Is that wise, with the attacks?"

"He's well protected. If you don't mind, what job?"

So he hadn't told her. Either that or he had, but she was playing dumb. I doubted that. "He didn't say, exactly. 'Fixer' was the role he mentioned. I'm sure you know he's not happy with how fast things have moved here."

Her hands clenched and her eyes narrowed slightly, but again she regained control quickly. "I look forward to your help."

I pretended to ignore her discomfort. "That's if I can help. That's why I'm here. Mr. Zentas proposed a task, but in order to accomplish it, I need to know what tools I have at my disposal."

"Of course. What are you looking for?"

"I don't know. While I think Mr. Zentas would like a broad-sweeping solution . . . Did you see his interview last night?"

"Of course."

"What did you think?" I asked. This wasn't part of pushing her . . . I really wanted her opinion. Plus, it served the purpose of changing the subject without alleviating her stress.

"Mr. Zentas is a visionary. He's looking beyond the scope of a single problem. What about you?" This was the risky part. I wanted to create a gap between Stroud and Zentas, but in doing so I might drive them closer together.

I shrugged. "Seemed to me like a guy using the death of his daughter for political purposes."

She froze for a second. "Then why are you here about a job?"

"Oh, you got me wrong," I lied. "That *is* why I'm here. Any man who could do that—that's a man who

gets things done at any cost. That's a guy I could work for." More risk. I was intentionally making myself look like an asshole, and I didn't know how she'd react to that.

This time her face didn't even give a hint of her thoughts. "What can I do for you specifically?"

"Tech. Can I see anything we've got that we can use to affect the hominiverts? And anything that might help us with the ursagrans, too, while we're at it. Though I see them as less of a problem." I used the word *we* intentionally.

"Sure. Follow me." We walked, but we took our time. "Don't dismiss the ursagrans too soon though. They can be more troublesome than you'd think. They're not a dangerous, but they're hard to move, and they don't sti to one spot. They follow the food. If one moves into area where you're working, you can lose a full day even two, trying to get them out of there."

"Interesting. How *do* you get them to leave?"

"Right now? Giant electric prods. They don't real damage. Ideally? We'd defoliate areas we i develop. No food, no ursagrans."

"Makes sense." Maybe Stroud and Zentas v together on their thinking than I thought. I' uncomfortable, but I hadn't gotten anything "But the laws protecting the vegetation pr

"Correct. Which ends up being less animals. There's plenty of food for the lation. Clearing some would have al on them. Let me ask you something were no laws—if Mr. Zentas gets you deal with the hominiverts?"

"Explosive ammo seemed to didn't flinch, I followed up. "B approval for that right away. H

legislation, it won't be fast enough for what we're doing here."

"I agree. Which is why we've been using sonic technology to move them where we want them."

Pay dirt. I'd wanted to know more about that since Eddleston mentioned it. "Interesting. Some sort of sound weapon?"

"Not a weapon so much. Low-frequency emitters that bother them enough to make them move."

"Mr. Zentas didn't mention those. Does he know about them?"

"Of course. He's the one who approved their development and ordered their use."

I almost stopped walking. Zentas had ordered their use. But my theory was that those devices had been deployed to force hominiverts onto the Caliber research team. If my theory held, and if I believed Stroud, that would mean that Zentas had ordered the policy that killed his own daughter. Did he know that? I couldn't ask Stroud about it. But if his daughter accidentally got caught up in the fallout of his plans, *that* would be a reason for him to come to Eccasis. But an accident like that, and nobody important had been fired—at least not publicly. So I had to wonder if he knew. "How long have you been working here on Eccasis?"

If my radical shift in topic bothered her, Stroud didn't show it. "About eighteen months."

"How long does someone usually lead a mission like this?"

"The understanding I had when I took the assignment—I volunteered for it—was that I'd be here three years and then we'd talk about an extension if it made sense for both of us."

"And that's still the plan?"

"Nobody has said it wasn't. Until you did, that is. Your report that Mr. Zentas isn't happy . . . well, if he's not happy, he's always got the option of replacing me. For a minute I thought that might mean you were here for my job, but given what you've said, I get the idea that he's got something else in mind for you."

"I wouldn't be taking over here. He specifically mentioned travel. And even if he had wanted me here, I wouldn't take your job. Not really my strong suit, running day-to-day operations. No offense." I'd put her on edge with my earlier comments about Zentas, so now I'd reassured her, trying to turn her to my side. It was a shitty way to manipulate somebody, but I had a shitty job to do.

"None taken. But I'll certainly try to work around to my status with Mr. Zentas the next time I have him alone. If he's got a lack of confidence in me, I have other opportunities. It's just a job. I took it because it gave me the most autonomy—the biggest chance to make a name for myself as someone who gets things done. I don't plan to grow old here. If Caliber wants to make a change, a dozen other companies would hire me in a day."

Her confidence made me trust her more. If she felt like this was her only option, maybe she'd do something desperate. But if she spoke the truth—and I believed she did—then I doubted she'd intentionally have been part of any order that led to people dying. That would make her less employable by other companies. I'd seen a callous attitude from her earlier, but that didn't make her a murderer. To cross that line, a person needed suitable motivation, and she didn't appear to have it. That didn't make her my ally—she'd never be that—but she didn't feel like an enemy either.

"And here we are." Stroud put her hand against a

biometric pad and a metallic *thunk* announced a bolt releasing. "After you."

The door opened easily, and I entered a laboratory—or more a collaboration between a laboratory and a workshop, combining areas that looked semi-sterile in proximity with areas that looked like they might be more appropriate in a mechanic's shop. Glass dividers broke up what would have otherwise been one open room and probably helped those semi-sterile areas stay that way. Pillars rose at regular intervals to bear the load of the roof, and the architecture didn't incorporate them very well, leaving some of them in odd places. Six or seven people worked at different stations, but the space would accommodate twenty-five or thirty during peak hours. The place had a distinct smell that reminded me of mild astringent mixed with lubricating oil.

"There's a second room beyond this one with some more sophisticated machine tools and the 3D printers. If we need something, somebody here can make it. It's much more efficient than shipping things in from off planet."

I wanted information on higher-tech stuff, so I drifted toward one of the clean compartments. I had no idea what a sonic device might look like, especially disassembled, but it didn't have an electric engine, so I could rule out a lot. "I'd love to poke around. I don't always know what I'm looking for. Sometimes I see something, and it sparks an idea." That was true, but in this case, I also wanted Stroud to offer to leave me on my own so I could question a tech without her hearing.

"Go right ahead. I've got some time." She either suspected my motives or wanted to be a good host.

I didn't push it. If she *wasn't* suspicious, me trying to get rid of her would change that. Since she wouldn't leave and I'd already mentioned the sonic tech, I could at least use her help. "The first thing I'd like to see is the sonic devices you talked about. That idea has some promise."

"Sure, follow me." She bypassed the first clean room and wound her way through a couple of open workshops to another one. The fact that she knew her way around the tech lab said a lot for her as a leader. A lot of bosses wouldn't even know where their tech lab *was*, let alone know the stations inside of it. Stroud was comfortable here. I didn't know if that helped me or hurt me.

The door to the clean area—and I use that term loosely, as we walked in wearing our street clothes—opened without a biometric check. Once inside the lab, we had access to everything. "Is there a sterile area, too? Somewhere to fabricate chips and more sensitive items?"

"There is. It's all automated, though, with very limited access. Engineers here input what they need through their systems and it's delivered complete."

"Pretty sophisticated for a colony company," I said.

"We go into new colonies focusing on the long term. That's a company-wide attitude."

"Can I talk to the technician?" A medium-height woman in a white lab coat and wearing electronic magnifying glasses was hunched over a small device, working with both hands.

"Sure. Valeria, if you have a minute?" said Stroud, in the tone that a boss uses when it's not really optional.

"Yes, ma'am." The woman took off her glasses, blinking a few times, then walked the ten steps over to us. "What can I do for you?"

"This is Colonel Butler. Carl, this is Valeria Rosario, one of our best techs. Colonel Butler is a special guest." Rosario wasn't wearing a name tag. Knowing her name was another point for Stroud and her leadership. She'd claimed not to know Schultz or Ortega, but they likely didn't work in this building, since they secured away missions. She could have been telling the truth about that. Or not. I couldn't rule out her lying to me.

"It's nice to meet you," said the tech.

"I had a question about the sonic disruption that you're using to move the large primates."

"I can help you with the technical specs, Colonel, but most of the work on that came from the people on the ground. The tech is basic—a transmitter on a telescoping pole. The only tricky part of it was the power source. Since it's for use under the jungle canopy, we couldn't use solar power. But that's a factor in most of what we're doing out here."

"Is the frequency adjustable or fixed?"

"Good question." The tech smiled. "The original versions—the test versions—had adjustable frequencies. This allowed the field operatives to experiment to find what frequency range worked. When we got that, we started making them with fixed frequencies. Fewer moving parts means less chance for catastrophic failure."

"How did you get the frequency range narrowed down?"

"That was all field techs and xenobiologists. We gave them the tools and they figured it out. I assume they tried different frequencies until they got the reaction they wanted, but I couldn't say for sure."

"They did it in the jungle?" I asked.

"They'd have had to. They can't exactly bring a hominivert in here." She snorted when she laughed, which made me smile, despite the chills that her answer gave me. *Of course* they couldn't bring a large ape into the main dome. It was illegal and even hacking cameras, you couldn't do something that blatant without someone seeing it. At the same time, doing it in the jungle would have been slow and produced hard-to-quantify results. But if someone had a secret facility in a location where they could go unobserved by the authorities, they'd have an ideal place to take a test subject. Ganos's discovery now made a lot more sense. When she'd told me about Hubic hiding in an abandoned dome, I hadn't ruled it out, but it hadn't struck me as likely. But Caliber skirting the rules of ecological exploitation? Zentas had basically told me he'd do exactly that.

And it seemed like he already was.

"Thanks. I don't want to take up too much of your time, but I did have a couple more questions." This was the one I didn't want to ask in front of Stroud, but she didn't give me much choice. I thought I knew the answer, but I had to verify. It's why I visited in the first place. "They can move the animals out of an area—is it possible to use the devices to move the animals *into* an area?"

She thought about it. "I don't know from a field perspective, but as I understand it, the hominiverts move away from the source of the noise. If you used multiple transmitters—like made a wall of them—they should move away from that wall. We specifically talked about that to protect a crew working on a new dome."

And if you could keep them out of a dome, you could keep them in one. Or you could open one side of it and force the primates in that direction. "Last question. What's the range?"

"The production model has a planning range of two hundred fifty meters. It's omnidirectional, so it would be two fifty in any direction, so you'd need to put your devices every five hundred meters to make a wall. We could increase the range, but it takes more power and you have to deal with dampening from the terrain, so it gets more complicated. I can run down the specifics on frequency, amplitude, and power if you want."

"That won't be necessary," I said. I wouldn't have understood it anyway. "Thanks for your help." Having what I needed, we moved to different areas, and I wasted the next hour looking over technology and construction of products that had nothing to do with my investigation, hoping to make the sonic device disappear into the background of other things in Stroud's mind . . . just one stop on a tour. I glanced at her from time to time, trying to read her, but I couldn't. She stayed focused on me the whole time, never even stopping to check her device.

Afterward I thanked her for her time, met Mac, and headed back to my quarters. As we walked, my mind danced through what I'd learned. I wanted to know Zentas's role in everything that had happened on Eccasis, and I thought that I might find answers hidden at the not-so-abandoned dome.

Ganos had pegged it as a hideout for Hubic. My mind drifted into more conspiracy-filled waters. If they'd used the dome for illegal research on hominiverts, they'd need a xenobiologist to run it. Someone like Xyla Redstone.

# CHAPTER TWENTY

**'D LOST A** bit of my grip on reality. Somewhere, deep down, I knew that. But on the surface, I kept coming back to the idea that she was alive. What better way to hide the head of illegal research than to fake her death? Everything fit. Suddenly Zentas having ordered the use of the sonic tech made sense. He hadn't killed his daughter, he'd hidden her. From there, it only took me a short leap to get to Zentas and Redstone faking their estrangement.

Now I just had to convince Oxendine to let me take a mission out to examine the signal Ganos had found. I sure as hell couldn't tell the commanding general that I expected to find the subject of my investigation alive. Authority or not, she'd have me committed. The problem was, to talk about the signal itself, I had to tell Oxendine how we got it, and Ganos's endeavors were already a sore subject.

Surprisingly, Oxendine agreed without much coaxing. She got more caught up in her own failure of intelligence and that she didn't know about the location until I told her. On top of that, she'd failed to catch her internal traitor, and that bothered her more than she would say. They'd traced the hack to a contractor named Alexandra

Trine, but not until Trine had apparently been tipped off and disappeared. That someone could disappear in such a small, well-monitored area belied belief, and it hung a stain on the fabric of Oxendine's command. Part of me wondered if we'd find the hacker on our mission to what we now called *the facility*.

What Oxendine *didn't* agree to was Mac and I going along on the mission. She flat out refused when I first brought it up, rightfully claiming that it was a mission for soldiers and that I wasn't one anymore. When I pulled rank via my orders, she then shifted to the argument that it should be a contiguous unit, not something cobbled together with out-of-practice old men, which was again, a legitimate argument, even if it was a little bit of a personal shot. But I didn't give in. I wanted into that dome, and I couldn't have stayed away from it if my life depended on it. Chalk up another issue for my therapist at a later date.

After Oxendine finally relented, I had to deal with Fader. She insisted on going along with us, and this time it was my turn to flat out refuse. She was a very competent officer, but there are outdoor cats and indoor cats, and she was the latter. She's not a combat soldier. It seems like an arbitrary distinction, but it's not. She'd had the basic training, the same as any officer, but her assignments had been on staff, mostly because she excelled at it. I put my foot down . . . until she made me move it. She played dirty. She told me that the only reason why she'd agreed to the mission in the first place was to learn from me, and what better way to learn? And then she said that if I held her back in this, I was breaking the unwritten contract between us—the one where she did whatever she could to help me be successful and I helped her develop into a better officer.

As well as I'd done negotiating with Oxendine, with Fader, I never had a chance.

Ganos was easier. When Mac told her what we were doing, her exact response was, "You assholes have fun with that." I did have a job for her though. We'd been hacked the last time we ventured forth from the relative safety of the dome, and I wanted her to prevent that from happening again. The army would be more aware of it, and Trine had fled, but having Ganos monitor it in real time—and counter it if needed—would make me feel a lot better. She couldn't defend us—apparently that's not how it works—but she could look for someone breaking in and go after them. Convincing Oxendine to let Ganos on the net took another half hour, and I only won the concession that she could patch into a single vehicle—the one I rode in—and even then, only from an outside system. But Ganos said she could make it work, and when it came to computers, I trusted her over anybody.

Then the governor got involved.

*How* he got involved, I didn't know. Oxendine didn't clear missions through him, or even report them. But he called Oxendine directly and told her to shut the mission down. According to her, he'd never contacted her directly before. Once he did, she had no real choice. She was pissed—she made that clear enough, slamming around her office and cursing—but the current environment gave him that authority. She could push back by sending it up channels, but that would have to go off planet, and neither of us thought we'd get a quick response.

I considered going to the governor's office. I could have bullied him into the mission by threatening to message the president's office and say that the governor was hindering my mission. He'd have folded like a T-shirt on laundry day.

But I couldn't. Not with Davidson and all the other leaks in his organization there. Caliber would know my mission before I even got out the door, and anything I hoped to find in the not-so-abandoned dome would be gone before I got there.

So I pulled rank.

Oxendine drafted an order on my authority from the president's office telling her to ignore the governor's protest. A pure cover-your-ass job, but whatever worked. Meanwhile, Oxendine loudly and publicly ordered the mission delayed and continued to hound the governor to approve it, knowing he wouldn't. If we didn't push back, he—or more likely Davidson—would get suspicious. Meanwhile, we secretly moved the mission timeline up. While the governor basked in his victory, we'd already be on target.

It did beg another question though. Why had he said no? It could have been his natural opposition to anything Oxendine wanted, but I doubted it. Davidson had worked in mining, and mining meant Caliber. In my mind, Caliber wanted our mission stopped.

I really wanted to see what was in that dome.


**OXENDINE'S TEAM FITTED** us with gear. We'd brought our own, but they had body armor integrated with modifications for the environment that we didn't. The chest and back plates nestled into a carrier with a wide strap that slung across each shoulder, and the molded arm and leg protectors fit into Velcro-sealed pockets in the environmental suit itself. They offered weapons too, but Mac, Fader, and I still carried our civilian versions of the Bitch. They were just as good—if not better—and we had them sighted the way we wanted them. I did check the platoon's basic loads of ammunition—they had explosive rounds this time.

We loaded into ten vehicles, which was probably overkill for the mission, but sometimes overkill is good business. We split into two platoons of five vehicles each—thirty dismounted soldiers per platoon, along with three for each vehicle crew. We'd approach the objective from two directions. My team had the front, under the command of a lieutenant named Yoon, who came with Oxendine's personal assurance that he was one of her best. The other platoon, under the command of Lieutenant Peretz, would circle around to prevent people from leaking out the back side. We'd flush people out, and Peretz and her platoon would round them up.

I had by far the most experience on the mission, but I'd agreed to defer to the traditional leadership. I could always take charge on the scene, depending on what we found inside the facility if I found it necessary. I'd envisioned all sorts of things we might find in the dome and had a mental list of how I'd approach each one, right down to what I might say if we came across certain people.

The other platoon had the longer route, so they departed first. The vegetation kept us bound to the roads and trails for the most part, which wasn't ideal. But we had no choice—we couldn't walk that distance. We made up for it with firepower. Each of the five vehicles had a heavy mounted weapon on top—three pulse and two projectile in our platoon. The big vehicle-mounted pulse weapons beat their handheld counterparts, mostly because they could draw on the power plant of the vehicle. They'd blow human-sized holes in a cinderblock wall. Or melt a hole in a dome.

Fader loaded into the third vehicle in our convoy

while Mac and I rode in the fourth, sitting across from each other with four other soldiers. We didn't talk. We didn't need to. He and I had been down similar roads before together, and we both had different objectives on our minds. I fingered the card that I carried in my pocket. I hadn't done that in a long time. It had the names of every soldier who'd died under my command and each one since I'd left command that I held myself responsible for. Gutierrez was the most recent on the list. She'd died back on Cappa when a bomb went off that someone meant for me. I didn't take responsibility for the bullshit that went down more recently on Zeta Four. Somebody else owned that. Farric I still had to process fully.

The thrum of the vehicle relaxed me, and I found myself almost dozing. We had the video feed from outside piped into the back with us, so I could follow along, but it showed a wall of green. We had about an hour drive to the drop point, and for the first forty minutes or so we traveled roads and paths that the soldiers had traveled before.

The vehicle jostled and my belts dug into my body as we hit a stretch of rough road about five kilometers from our release point. We slowed almost to walking speed as we transitioned onto a half-kilometer stretch that resembled a dry stream bed more than a road. The bad road made sense. They couldn't have a new road leading to an abandoned facility without painting an *open for business* sign on their foreheads.

An explosion rocked the vehicle and jolted me fully awake.

"Holy shit," someone said on the intercom. "That was big."

Big and close, judging from the sound and pressure wave. I started to key my mic to ask what happened when the radio burst to life with chatter.

"Vehicle one is hit!"

"Fuck!"

"It's gone. I can't see it."

In their excitement they dropped call signs, and the transmissions came too fast for me to identify the speakers, but the message came through clear enough. A few seconds later a commanding voice took charge and brought order.

"This is Alpha Seven. Clear the net. Alpha Two, report." The platoon sergeant. Realizing that the platoon leader had been in vehicle one, he'd stepped in and called for a report from vehicle two.

"This is Alpha Two," a female voice answered. "Something exploded. A mine or something, but bigger. Estimate five hundred kilograms." Wow. That *was* big, if accurate. Enough to split one of our vehicles in two.

"What's your status?" asked Seven.

"We're stationary. Operational. It shook us, but no significant damage. The smoke and dust is clearing around One. I don't know how anyone could have survived that, but we need to get in there and see if there are wounded."

"Roger. Two, Three, and Four, put your dismounts out. Watch for secondary devices. Three, get forward to far-side security and give cover to Two's people. Two, establish near security and search the wreck. Four, you've got rear security."

Nine soldiers. That's how many each vehicle carried between crew and dismounts. If we'd lost that many . . . part of me didn't believe it. This wasn't a war zone. Even *in* a war zone, we didn't see anti-vehicle mines that big. Not often. Despite the setback, it made it even more imperative that we reach the facility. That sounds callous. I know that. But if someone would go to that length to protect it, there had to be a reason, and we couldn't turn back and try later. Nothing would be there.

Mac and I dismounted with our team but didn't immediately take up security to the rear with the others. Four of them could handle it. We'd passed through the area already and had seen no enemy. I walked to vehicle five, which held the platoon sergeant. He had his door open but still sat in the seat. I stood by him as we waited for the initial report. He had the video replay from vehicle two up on his screen, showing the incident. The explosion initiated directly beneath the vehicle, which was good news. There might be survivors. The v-shaped undercarriage would have shunted some of the force away from the crew compartment. If only the explosion hadn't been so big. Seeing it, five hundred kilograms seemed like an overestimation, but not by much.

"We have survivors," came an excited voice over the net.

"This is Seven. Roger. How many."

"Working it. At least three alive. Stand by."

The platoon sergeant flipped his feed to live, and the camera from vehicle two showed the team at work. Two soldiers were inside, and the four outside already had two soldiers evacuated. Neither was moving, but neither had visible wounds. They wouldn't, necessarily. The overpressure and concussion from a blast that size could be enough to kill them. I found myself holding my breath, waiting for the next report.

"Casualty report, three KIA, six WIA. All need immediate evac. Major concussions in all cases, broken bones in most. Medic is treating for shock and says all are stable and can await transport."

"Wow," I said.

"Yes, sir." The platoon sergeant, Sergeant First Class Ahwed, opened a direct channel to me. "We got lucky." It seemed odd to say when we had three dead, but he was right. "What now, sir?"

"It's your call. I'm along for the ride," I said.

"We both know that's bullshit, sir. Call it. I reported it to HQ and they're not sending anybody else. We go with what we've got or we head home. You think we still have enough ass to complete the mission after we get these evacs done?"

I took a few seconds before responding, trying to get the emotion out of my decision. Of course Oxendine wouldn't send more troops. She couldn't, with the governor watching. "We have enough. I don't think they've got anything that's going to stop us. Then again, I didn't expect a deep-buried bomb."

"Nobody did."

"We'll have to go dismount, watching for more traps. They obviously know we're coming."

"Maybe not, sir. This thing could have been there for a long time."

"They probably heard it, though," I said. "How's the other platoon doing?"

"No contact. On schedule."

"Good." The enemy might not be expecting someone to come from the back side. "It's five klicks. We can walk it. Have the other platoon hold up to get in synch with us. I'm afraid that if we back off now, they'll evacuate the place before we arrive and we'll miss any value that we're going to get."

"Roger that, sir." Ahwed's voice stayed neutral. Just another day at the office for him. "There's a clearing about four hundred meters ahead. We should be able to get a dust off for the casualties there. I'll get that set, then we'll regroup and move out. I'm coming on the dismount."

"Roger," I said. "You take charge. I'll advise you as you see fit."

"Yes, sir. Would the colonel like to change the rules of engagement, given what just happened?"

I thought about it. We had set the engagement criteria tight because we didn't want a firefight unless it was absolutely necessary. The mine changed things, but while it seemed likely, we didn't know for sure the people at the facility had planted the bomb. "Let's keep them the same for now. If nobody else dies today, that's our best outcome. So, keep weapons tight . . . but have a plan to kill everyone we meet if it comes to it. And if it's you or them—"

"It's them. Got it, sir."

Mac and I backed off, letting Ahwed do his job. I checked in with Fader, who probably hadn't experienced live casualties before. When she had made her argument to go on the mission, she hadn't mentioned any combat action, and she would have. Now I wanted to look her in the eyes. You never knew how something like this might affect someone until it happened.

"How are you doing?" I asked over a private channel. Mac had faded back to give us a little space.

"I'm pissed, sir." Pissed was good. Pissed kept you moving forward. The only problem with pissed was that sometimes someone did something dumb, trying to retaliate. Fader didn't seem like that type.

"The mission's still a go. We can't let them evacuate the place. We're staying dismounted. You still good?"

"I'm good, sir."

I believed her. I might have been fooled by false bravado once or twice back in the day, but I didn't suspect it here. "Okay. Hang toward the middle of the formation when we move out."

**WE COMPLETED THE** air medevac and moved out, walking either side of the road, sensors attuned to other possible booby traps. We didn't hit any, and we covered most of the distance to the facility in about fifty minutes. When we got to about five hundred meters, we left the trail and moved into a wedge formation in the jungle. We picked our way through the growth without much trouble, though in spots we did get canalized into one or two paths.

The first shot took the point soldier in the chest, dropping her.

I dropped too, but not before I saw the soldier roll away. Her body armor did its job. We didn't have time to celebrate, as the entire jungle lit up. A pulse weapon scorched a tree next to me, and I had to scramble away as part of it came tumbling down with a thud. I tried to count the enemy weapons, but I lost track when our side opened fire. Red icons started to populate my heads-up as others identified targets.

We had the numbers, but they had a defensive position, and for a moment we were stalemated. We didn't have rockets and our vehicles couldn't support us from their position, so we had two choices. We could try to pin them in place and flank them, or we could keep them tied up while our other force closed in from behind. Ahwed quickly made the call over the radio. "Two and Three, provide base of fire. Four and Five, flank right. Lift and shift fires on the call of Four, green flare for backup." A simple plan, swiftly communicated. I appreciated the professionalism.

I moved with the rest of my team around to the right, keeping low and moving in short bursts so that the enemy couldn't get a bead on me. As we got clear of our troops returning fire, the sounds distinguished themselves. Even with just two teams of six firing for us, we had them outgunned. My heads-up showed four, then five red dots for the enemy, but the sounds indicated more like six or eight. We just couldn't get a clean fix on them in the jungle. Other fire sounded in the distance. Our other platoon had hit resistance too. Good thing Ahwed hadn't counted on them supporting us.

My heads-up went dark. One minute it had showed a map with both blue and red icons, the next . . . gone. I didn't hesitate this time—my mind went directly to our systems being hacked.

A burst of fire tore through the vegetation in front of me, shredding a giant leafy plant, and that snapped me back to the more immediate problem. I didn't know if the enemy had detected our flanking force or if the burst had been random, but I stayed down for a few extra seconds, just in case. I made eye contact with Mac, who had grabbed the ground about a meter away, before springing back to my feet and sprinting a few steps. A distinctive *thwunk* came from the enemy position, followed quickly by several more.

Fucking mortars.

I keyed my system to announce incoming, but nothing happened. Dead.

Shit.

An explosion burst overhead—*way* overhead—up in the treetops. The thick canopy had intercepted the mortar. We caught a break with that.

No sooner had I thought it than a second mortar round riffled through the vegetation to my right. I dove left, but too late. The crunch of the explosion shook me as I hit the soft ground. I lay there for a few seconds, waiting for a burst of pain. When none came, I pulled myself to my knees to look around. The round had hit maybe twelve meters away, but the soft soil and thick undergrowth it landed in muffled the blast.

Someone from our side lobbed a few smoke grenades between us and the enemy, giving us even better cover, the gray smoke swirling through the vegetation and giving the whole area a look right out of a horror holo. I scrambled back to my feet and ran. Anywhere beat where they were shooting mortars. The next explosion came well behind me. Somebody screamed. I whipped my head around, looking for Mac, who burst through another one of those large, leafy plants.

"Let's go, sir!" I could barely hear him through his helmet, but I got the point.

We sprinted for more than a few seconds, which is not a good idea, but we had enough vegetation between us and the enemy that they didn't zero in on us. We hit the ground again near the rest of our team. We'd gone far enough to begin our flanking move. Hand signals flashed, and three soldiers rushed forward while three of us waited and watched, ready to suppress any enemy fire. None came. When the first group set, Mac and I joined the other soldier and leapfrogged past them, staying to the right so we didn't block their line of fire. Still no response. The continuing enemy fire must have been focused on the other squads. Good. That was how we planned it.

After four rushes, we reached our position. The jungle obscured any chance of seeing the enemy, but the sounds of gunfire came from our left. Six or seven projectile weapons and one pulse, based on the volume. The pulse fired sporadically, probably running out of charge. We had six in our squad and fifth squad had four remaining. I could make out part of the dome through an opening in the vegetation, still a hundred meters away. I'd expected it to be bigger. It was maybe forty meters in diameter and low, possibly recessed into the ground. We turned and put it on our right, orienting on the enemy.

The squad leader gave the hand signal for attack, then he stood and fired a green flare forward at a forty-five-degree angle upward. The bright-green projectile blazed over the enemy position, signaling the rest of our platoon to lift and shift fire. I said a silent thanks for troops who trained in backup plans, just in case they lost comms. Lift and shift meant our support force would keep shooting to make the enemy keep their heads down, but that they'd redirect the fire, to the left or over the enemy's heads. That way, as we ran forward to clear the position, we wouldn't get shot by our own troops.

I tripped and almost fell, jamming my wrist as I caught myself. I shook it off and kept moving, blocking out the pain. The adrenaline helped.

I found my first enemy by accident, when I broke free from some thick undergrowth. He had snugged down in a depression, which gave him cover from the other direction. He looked up and froze for a second, then tried to swing his weapon around to shoot me, hindered by his fighting position.

I fumbled my weapon, too slow, so I ran forward and kicked him hard in the face. His head snapped back, and his faceplate cracked. The top of my foot throbbed from the impact. My good foot, not my robot foot. I leveled my weapon at him. He groaned and twisted, trying to get up, and I went for my trigger. If I'd had my finger on it, I'd have shot him, but I thought better of it and instead stepped on his rifle, driving it down into the soft ground before clubbing him in the helmet with the butt of my weapon. This time he didn't rise.

I took some plastic zip ties from a Velcro pocket and knelt on his back while I fastened his hands together. Shots to the front caught my attention, but nothing came near me. A pulse weapon fired wildly, burning a hole through the canopy above.

Everything went quiet in what felt like an instant. One minute the jungle echoed with gunfire and yelling, the next, nothing. Voices gradually replaced the gunfire, one person crying out in pain, another swearing.

The comm came back to life, and fourth squad leader called for reports from his soldiers. Mac called in to announce his status, and I took that as my signal to do the same. "This is Butler. Uninjured. I've got one prisoner with a cracked faceplate." The outside air wouldn't kill him right away. We had about twelve hours to get him to quarantine and treatment. Plenty of time, now that the shooting had stopped.

I flipped to the company net to hear the other platoon's traffic and heard Ahwed calling in his report. With our platoon leader down, the other lieutenant had overall command now with Ahwed in charge of our unit.

"This is Red Seven. We've got six enemy KIA, two prisoners, one is WIA. Friendly forces, one KIA, three WIA."

"This is White Six. Roger. Continue mission. Secure the facility. Watch for additional shooters inside."

"Roger."

Our platoon consolidated on the objective and got all the wounded to one place. Ahwed called his squad leaders together. He could have done it over the comm, but he probably wanted to see them and get an assessment of their mental state. He took less than a minute, and our squad leader came over the comm. "We've got the airlock. The other squads will cover us."

Good. I wanted inside in the worst way. Ahwed probably knew that when he gave the assignments. The defense we'd just fought through made me believe even more that we'd find answers in there. We moved in a squad wedge, the other squads in the same formation, one to our left and one to our right with the final one securing the prisoners and the wounded. The flank squads would drop and return fire at the first hint of resistance. I didn't think we'd see any more on the out-side. Someone might take a shot at us after we entered. There had to be people still inside. Not everyone they had would have handled a rifle. Not if it was a facility where Caliber conducted experiments.

We were about fifty meters from the airlock when the world flashed and then went dark, as my faceplate blacked out. My helmet muted sound as I flew back-ward. My feet hit, then my ass, then the back of my head. White flashed in my eyes and I tasted blood. My face-plate cleared, but smoke and dust hazed the air, making it hard to see. I lay there, stunned. I wiggled my fingers and toes. Everything worked, even my robot foot.

"Sir, I'm hit," said Mac over a private channel.

I pushed myself up and the world swam for a moment. I put a hand on the soft ground to steady myself. "How bad?"

"I'll live. It fucking hurts, though. Suit's compromised."

Shit.

I got to my feet, still wobbling, checked the status of my suit in my heads-up and found it intact, then squinted into the haze. I found Mac, sitting, his hand over his left side, just beside the chest plate.

"Shrapnel," he grunted, and I could tell it was worse than he was letting on.

I grabbed the med pack from the pouch on his left arm. "Okay. On three, take your hand away. One, two, three."

He pulled his hand away and I replaced it with a coagulating bandage. Mac jerked at the pressure, but I held firm, keeping the dressing in place with my gloved hand, putting pressure on it. We'd worry about getting it cleaned up later. For now, we needed to stop the bleeding. Blood had already soaked through his inner shirt, and some leaked down his armor.

"What happened?" I asked.

"The dome," said Mac. "It blew. The whole thing must have been rigged."

"That had to be a hell of an explosion. How are we alive?"

"I don't think it was targeting us." He winced. "I think a lot of the blast focused inward. There was a lot of flame, too. Like an incendiary."

That explained my blacked-out faceplate—my helmet had done it automatically, saving me from being blinded. "Someone didn't want us to find whatever was in there."

"Nope."

The medic showed up, a short woman. "This looks stable. We'll get you an evac. You want a shot for the pain?"

"I'm good," said Mac. "The colonel's going to want to search the wreckage. I'm not going anywhere until that's done."

The medic looked at me and shook her head.

I turned to Mac. "We need to get you back. It's not just the wound. It's the bacteria in the environment. The faster they start treatment, the faster you'll be back on the job."

"Sir, you need—"

"I've got him." Fader walked up. Her chest plate had a hand-sized piece of shrapnel embedded in it.

"Lucky," I said, pointing at it.

"Didn't feel like it at the time. I'm going to have a hell of a bruise. But yes, sir. It could have been a lot worse."

"Let me get Mac to the evac point to make sure he actually goes, then we'll get a team and see if there's anything left up there."

I wasn't optimistic.

# CHAPTER TWENTY-ONE

WE PICKED THROUGH the wreckage but found mostly slag. Mac's take had been correct—they'd used some serious incendiaries. The residual heat had kept us away for three hours before finally cooling enough where we could approach. Not everything burned. It never does. But sifting through melted polymers and twisted metal would take time and better equipment. Entire rooms had been jumbled together in the explosion, and I couldn't work out even a general idea of the facility's purpose. There were computers—nothing left to those now—and some stuff that looked like lab equipment, but that might have been me projecting my bias.

Fader took a lot of pictures while also fiddling with the program that Mac had given her to track my movements, which seemed to amuse her. A couple of industrious soldiers used a beam to lever some of the larger pieces of junk up, hoping to find some undamaged stuff underneath, but just found more charred ruins. Whoever had rigged it to blow—possibly Hubic—had known their business. Still, I hoped that something here, paired with what we got from the prisoners and potentially the enemy casualties, would provide a link.

Ahwed gave me an initial list of the prisoners and enemy casualties. They hadn't identified all of them, but they got a hit off Hubic's fingerprints. Unfortunately, he was among the dead, so the burning questions I had for him would go unanswered. I wanted to talk to the prisoners, but Oxendine would play that by the book and keep it with her interrogators. Instead, I discussed the way forward with Fader. We'd backed away from the wreckage but stayed inside the perimeter the military established. They'd sent another company of soldiers out from the dome once the situation became clear, and small groups of people milled about. They'd trampled down a lot of the jungle, making it easier to traverse.

"They're not going to let me anywhere near the prisoners, but I'm going to want a full copy of the interrogation sessions. I don't want the summarized version—I want a transcript."

"Yes, sir," said Fader. "Did you know that with this thing I can tell what direction you're moving? This could come in handy. It would be nice to know your boss could never sneak up on you."

"I think Ganos is rubbing off on you," I said.

"Sorry, sir."

"Don't be."

"Why won't you get access to the prisoners, sir?"

"This was a military op, especially once people started shooting. Oxendine bent the rules to let me go on the mission, but I used up that card. I can't press her again the same way. Especially when she has the professionals on staff. I like to consider myself a good interrogator, but I don't have any credentials to back that up."

"We might be able to get the interrogators to ask some of your questions if we feed them through the right channels."

"Good idea," I said. "First, I want to know who they work for. Any connections we can draw between these people and Humans First, EPV, or Caliber would be critical. Especially if we can connect them to more than one."

"Roger, sir." Fader made a note in her device.

"I also want to specifically ask them about Hubic. I want to know each prisoner's connection to him, but more important, I want to know his story. He's dead, so they don't have to worry about protecting him. That might work in our favor."

"You know, sir . . . there might be a way around Brigadier General Oxendine on this."

"I'm listening."

"The one guy is going to be in quarantine for a while. I don't know if the military will supervise that or if it's strictly medical, but either way—"

"Mac will be there, which gives me a perfect excuse to be there as well. Brilliant. I should have thought of that." Nobody would tell me I couldn't check on my own man. Even Oxendine would let that one slide. "That's good. The faster I get something from the prisoners, the faster I can confront the people who are really behind this."

"Doesn't the military take over now, sir? There's a clear violation of the law. There was a *firefight*. They have to act."

"I'm not sure they can. Ecological law isn't the military's purview. It's the governor's. So to enforce it, Oxendine would have to go to the governor."

Realization dawned on Fader's face. "After we snuck out to do the mission without telling him."

"Yep."

"What do you think he'll do?"

"I'm not sure. Probably not what we want him to."

"You still think it's Caliber, sir?"

"I don't know. It's going to be hard to prove. The hack . . ." I needed to think about that. The military had been hacked again, and I doubted it came from inside this time. In theory, that shouldn't happen, but we spent a lot of time fighting enemies with fewer capabilities than our own. The ability for a technological peer—or superior—to breach our systems might be a systemic issue that we hadn't discovered because of a lack of competition. But I couldn't do much about that at the moment. I'd need to see if Ganos saw anything. "I want to confront Zentas and get him to talk, but I need proof before I try that. He'll be a tough mark. He won't be in- timidated, and I won't be able to bluff him into thinking I know something if I don't."

Fader scrolled through something on her device. "They aren't kept at the military base. The hospital has a specific quarantine area. Apparently, exposure is a common-enough problem."

"Let's go, then. You can pass the questions to the in- terrogators for the other prisoner after." The blown facil- ity would change things for the military, and I'd need to talk to Oxendine about that, but anything she did would take time. I'd get only one shot at the prisoner.

**THE HOSPITAL SMELLED** like every other hospital I'd ever been in, and there had been more than a few. It looked the same too. Some things never changed, no matter where you went. I stopped at the information desk and asked about Mac. Fader had already pulled up the schematic and knew where we'd find him, but I wanted to be on record as asking about my soldier in case some-

one checked. Oxendine seemed like the type who might
do that. Receiving directions, we headed to the quarantine area, which resembled the rest of the hospital, except the room doors on either side of the hallway had
seals reminiscent of airlocks. Two armed soldiers stood
outside one of the rooms, marking the prisoner's location
like a flashing sign. The prisoner's name was Mbabe,
and he had no prior arrests in any system we could find.
We'd called that in to Ganos to check, so I trusted the information. His local record listed him as a construction
worker, certified for outside-the-dome work, who was
employed by a small subcontractor called External Solutions. They worked for another company called Dynan
Enterprises, who did most of their work colonyside for a
larger company called—of course—Caliber.

I looked in the window of the unguarded door on the
opposite side of the corridor to get an idea of the setup. A
hallway lay behind it, connecting three separate rooms, all
with see-through walls, all empty. What great luck. That
meant that Mac was on the other side—the same side as
the prisoner. I glanced over at the soldiers, two women,
one tall and dark, the other short and light skinned. Both
tried to pretend they weren't watching me. I didn't blame
them. It wasn't like the prisoner would try to make a break
for it from quarantine, making their role largely a formal-
ity. That worked in my favor, so I leaned into it.

"Is Sergeant McCann in there?"

"Yes, sir," said the tall soldier. She had an extra stripe,
which put her in charge. "But our orders are that nobody
goes in or out."

I put on my best confused face, trying to project it to
the soldiers without saying anything. Kind of a "Wait, I
can't go in?" expression. I didn't like to lie to soldiers,
but I would if I had to. I'd try honesty first though. I

didn't ask if they knew who I was. I could see on their faces that they did. That helped. "Sergeant Mac got hit while protecting me on a mission. I've got to check on him. I couldn't live with myself if I didn't." That much was the truth. More, it was the perfect story. Soldiers all wanted leaders who would check on them if they got hurt. Many of them had those leaders and would expect them to be let through.

I was counting on these soldiers to feel the same way.

The tall soldier glanced at the short one, who nodded. "You need to put on a mask, sir. The hallway in there is supposed to be clean, but better safe than sorry. And you can't enter his room without full bio gear."

"Can he hear me through the glass? If so, I don't need to go into his room."

"Yes, sir. There's a speaker." That presented a small problem. If I had to use a speaker to talk to Mac, I'd also have to use one to talk to the prisoner. The soldiers might not see if they faced out, but they might look through the window to check on me. I'd have to play it by ear. Fader had disappeared but now showed up with a mask in her hand.

"Thanks," I said.

"I'll wait out here, sir." She inclined her head slightly toward the two soldiers. She'd try to keep them busy while I went inside. The more I worked with her, the more I liked her.

The soldier keyed a code into the door pad and pulled it open for me. I went to Mac's room first, both because it was the right thing to do and it fit my story. "How are you feeling?"

"Not bad, sir." His voice sounded a little mechanical through the speaker, but even with that I could sense his good spirits. "They gave me the good drugs."

I laughed. "Feeling no pain, huh?"

"Nope. Good thing too, given all the places they've jammed tubes."

"I don't even want to know. They give you a time-line?"

"Two days, sir."

"Could be worse."

"Could definitely be worse. They're treating the wound at the same time as they're doing the cleanup of the contamination, so I should be close to a hundred per-cent when I get cleared."

"Sounds good. But you take your time. I'll be careful, I promise."

"Sure you will, sir."

"Can the guy in the other room hear us?"

"Hey, asshole!" Mac looked at the guy in the next room as he said it, and the guy turned toward him. "He can hear me, at least. You need me to pass him a message?"

"Can he hear me? I need to ask him some questions, and it will go quicker if we don't have to relay."

"I can hear you," Mbabe said. "Is this where you threaten to come in and unplug my tubes if I don't coop-erate?" I could barely hear him through the glass and the speaker, but it worked.

"Of course not. If I wanted to threaten you, I'd tell you that Mac here is going to wait until nobody is around, come over there, and beat your ass."

"He's tied up to a machine, same as me."

Mac held up his arm and pulled out one of his IVs. "Huh. Look at that. It slipped."

"You know you probably need that," I said.

Mac shrugged. "They'll give me a new one once you leave."

"This is some bullshit," said Mbabe.

"Look, I just want to ask you some questions. No threats. Mac was just screwing around."

Mac glared at the guy. He wasn't helping. Or maybe he was.

"I want full immunity."

"You got it. Everything I'm authorized to give." That was nothing, but I didn't feel the need to include that detail. The guy had been shooting at me a few hours back. Unlike with the soldiers, I felt fine about lying to *him*.

"What can you give?" Smart guy, I'll give him that.

"You know who I am?" I asked.

"Yeah."

"So, figure it out."

He thought about it. "Yeah. All right."

"Did you work at the dome out in the bush?"

"Yeah."

"How long has it been operating?"

"Maybe six, seven months."

"What did you do out there?"

He stared up at the ceiling, and for a second, I wished I *could* send Mac in there.

"Who pays you?"

Nothing.

"You're not doing much to earn your immunity."

"I'm not doing much to incriminate myself, either."

"Your job status is incriminating?"

"It might be. How the fuck should I know? Somebody torches a multimillion-mark facility, you have to believe they're hidin' somethin', right?"

"A few hours ago, you were holding a weapon, shooting at galactic soldiers. I think who burned what is kind of a moot point when it comes to incrimination. You're on my helmet camera with a rifle in your hand."

"So there's no way out for me."

"Sure there is. Give me a bigger fish." Normally I'd have left and let him stew, but I wouldn't be allowed back in here once Oxendine found out, so I had to press.

He thought about it. "I didn't want to fight you."

"Could have fooled me."

"They didn't give me much fuckin' choice."

"I saw a gun in your hand, not one to your head."

"You weren't there half an hour before the fight."

I started to snap something back at him but held off. Mbabe wanted to tell me something, and I needed to let him instead of pissing him off further. "What did they do?"

"You saw the facility blow. We couldn't stay there."

"Right. But you didn't have to fight."

"The fuck we didn't. If we didn't delay you, there was no evacuation."

Well that changed things. "They told you that?"

"Yeah. And after some of the shit I saw them do, I believed them. They'd have left us to die in the jungle."

I fired my next question quickly. Now that I had him talking, I wanted to keep the momentum. "What went on in that building?"

"Research. That's all I know. No shit. I don't know what kind, nothin' like that."

"You must have some idea. What did you see? Did you ever see animals brought in there?"

"Yeah, sometimes. The big ape-looking ones. I figured they was puttin' trackers in them or somethin'."

My heart sped up a little and my mouth dried. It was confirmation, or at least something close to it. I wanted to follow up, but if I did, he might sense how important it was to me. I didn't want to give him that edge, so I changed directions. "Did you ever meet a guy named Hubic?"

"Yeah. I know him. What about him?"

"He's dead."

"That supposed to matter to me?"

"Not specifically. I just wanted you to know." Really I wanted him to know he had no reason to try to protect the guy, but I couldn't say that.

"Okay. Now I know."

"You have any idea what he did?" In my head, I sensed I was running out of time. The soldiers outside would get suspicious at some point.

"Not really. He was pretty close to the boss though. Always talking to her."

"Who was the boss?"

Mbabe grunted. "I'll tell you that the minute I'm walking free."

"That's not how it works," I said.

"It is now. You think I'm stupid?"

*I'd hoped.* "Tell me this, then. The boss—was she a scientist?"

"Dunno." He looked at me. "Really. I don't. She over-saw everything."

"Was she there today?" If she was, we had her body, unless it burned up in the facility.

"Nah. I haven't seen her for a while."

That caught my attention, and I pulled a picture of Xyla Redstone up on my device. It was small, so it would be hard for him to see, but she had a distinctive look—pale skin, short and stocky, dark hair, flared on top. Like a soldier's cut, but with style. "Ever seen this woman?"

Mbabe squinted, and hesitated. "Nah." He was ly-ing. I don't know what made me sure, but I was. Why would he lie? It wouldn't be to protect Xyla. He'd said he hadn't seen her in a while. But if she'd been the boss—he wouldn't want to give that away, because he'd want to protect his immunity deal. I debated the best way to press him on it, but a knock on the door broke my thoughts. One of the soldiers stared in through the window. She yelled, but I could barely make out what she said.

"Time to go, sir."

I gave her a thumbs-up, then turned back to Mac. "You get well soon. I've got a feeling I'm going to need you before this is over."

"Roger that, sir."

"You want me to send someone in to fix that IV?"

"I've got a buzzer. I'll call them once you're clear."

"Mbabe," I said. "Not a word of this to anybody, or the deal's off. Got me?"

"Yeah, I got you. Have a nice day."

He might as well have said, "Fuck off."

# CHAPTER TWENTY-TWO

I WANTED TO CONFRONT Zentas about the facility and his daughter's role associated with it, but I still didn't have enough information. I could accuse him of involvement, because his employees were there, but he'd deny it, and I would have spent my ammunition for no result. The thing that irked me was that he knew. No way did a hands-on boss like Zentas not know about a Caliber facility where his daughter worked. Even if he didn't know about it before her disappearance, he'd have learned after. So then why send me here? It couldn't be just to offer me a job. Could it? There had to be an easier way to do that.

There was too much I didn't know, and it made me start doubting my own theory. Maybe she worked there and it had no relation to her disappearance. One illegal action could be unrelated to the other—assuming the Caliber technology was used to kill Xyla, as I believed. But if Xyla truly ran the facility, that would have put her in charge of developing that tech. Even though Mbabe hadn't seen her lately, she could still be alive, hiding out somewhere else. I wished that I could have gotten an exact timeline from Mbabe on her last appearance.

It was an interesting thought. Xyla didn't kill herself . . .

or maybe she did, accidentally. There were too many variables, so I focused on the one thing I believed to be most likely: That Caliber's sonic technology caused Xyla's death or disappearance. If I stuck to that one assumption and treated it like fact, there were only two possibilities relating to Zentas. Either he knew about it ahead of time or he didn't. If he didn't know ahead of time, then why he brought me in became easy: He wanted me to find and expose the culprit. But he couldn't come out and say that without acknowledging the illegal facility and probably a host of other things he'd rather not cop to. If he *did* know ahead of time, it became more muddled. Unless he wanted to use me to make it *look* like he didn't know ahead of time. In that scenario, I became his alibi. Like the murderer who calls the police to report the dead victim.

Regardless of what Zentas knew, Caliber held at least some of the blame because the technology was 100-percent theirs. And regardless of what *I* knew, I couldn't prove anything. So Caliber would need to wait. I went to see Oxendine. I didn't hold out much hope that she'd be helpful, but Mbabe had the last piece of the puzzle, and I needed it. On the way, I called Ganos to see what she'd seen when we lost communications on the mission. Unfortunately, she hadn't seen anything. She spouted off some technical stuff about how hard it is to observe something like that in real time, but I didn't understand the specifics. She couldn't even say for sure that we'd been hacked, though she suspected that we had. At least with what Ganos told me, I could ask Oxendine more about it.

I found her in her office. As usual, she was expecting me. "What can I do for you this time, Carl? I'm a bit busy."

"What's going on?"

Oxendine looked at me like I'd just taken a dump on her rug. "Well, let's see. I circumvented the governor to send out a mission. A dome blew up, which alerted the governor to that, and now he's up in my shit. Did I mention the part about the dome blowing up? Turns out, I've got stuff out in the jungle that I'm not aware of, and I want to do something about it, but the same governor has curtailed all activity outside the dome."

"He can do that?"

"It's debatable," said Oxendine. "For now, I'm acquiescing, because I don't have the intel or the forces to act anyway, and I'm trying to get him to look past that whole thing where I ignored his order."

"I authorized that."

"I'm well aware, and trust me, I've made him aware too. I'm sure you'll be hearing from him soon. But in the meantime, please, Carl, what can I do for *you*?"

"I need a favor."

"And I need you to go fuck yourself. The last time I did you a favor, it turned into a full-on firefight."

"But we found the illegal facility, which we didn't know about. If you think about it, I did *you* a favor in exposing that."

She glared at me. "Not funny. In addition to the mess with the governor, we lost four soldiers and have several more wounded, including your man. Forgive me if I don't celebrate. And we have no proof that it was illegal."

"It wasn't supposed to be active. That's got to be illegal."

"Okay. It was illegal the way that parking in a no-parking zone is illegal. Sure."

"Come on. It was more than that. They were doing illegal research on primates."

"And you know this . . . how?"

I hadn't slipped. I intended to tell her. "One of the men who was there told me."

"Which man?"

"A guy named Mbabe."

"You went and questioned a prisoner who was under medical treatment. Speaking of illegal . . ."

"I went to talk to Mac. Mbabe just happened to be there."

"You think a court would see it that way?"

"You think something like this would ever see a courtroom?"

"For you? No. For Mbabe? It's more likely. And anything you learned is probably excluded as evidence now."

"You've got film of him with a gun shooting at your soldiers. I hardly think me asking him who he worked for is an issue in his guilt or innocence."

"Doesn't matter. You had no right. And I'm getting tired of it. I'm done cutting corners for you."

"So . . . no favor?"

"What do you want?" She crossed her arms and gave me as close to an angry look as I'd seen from her.

"I need you to let Mbabe walk free when he leaves the hospital—"

"No way I—"

"Hear me out," I said, cutting her off before she could finish her protest. "He doesn't actually have to *be* free. He just needs to *think* he's free for a few minutes."

She considered it. "Okay . . . I'm not saying I'm going to do it, but I'm curious, because that sounds ridiculous. Why?"

"I need him to tell me who his boss was at the secret facility." She didn't respond, so I continued, trying to prompt her. "That would be useful information for you, too. So you'd know who to charge."

"I wouldn't turn that information down if it came to me, but it's the governor who has to file charges."

"But you could use the information to force his hand. Make him act."

"Even if I *could* do that, it's not a criminal charge, Carl. It's a fine. Maybe it's a big fine, if we can prove significant damage—something I don't have the assets to prove, by the way. Corporations can deploy an army of lawyers. Me? Not so much. Even if the fine is big to you and me, do you think it hurts Caliber? And all that's if the governor's office doesn't push it under the rug. Which they will."

"They're breaking the law. There has to be more to it than that."

Oxendine sighed. "Don't be naïve, Carl. It's only a law if you've got the resources to enforce it. We don't."

I wanted to pound my fists against something. "So you don't report it?"

"*Of course* I report it. I flag the report and make it high priority. Maybe someone will act on it, but prior experience says probably not. I'll get a response. Maybe a promise for more assets that will never materialize, or if they do, they'll be so far down the road that they don't matter." She paused. "I've laid out my issues. Now you answer one for me. Why do *you* want to know the facility boss so bad?"

I should have seen that question coming. As much as it put me on the defensive, I appreciated Oxendine's ability. "It's important to my investigation."

"To your missing-person investigation." Her tone said I was full of shit.

"That's right."

"You're going to have to draw that picture for me, Carl."

I sighed. I didn't want to, but I didn't see another way to get her on board. "My theory is that Xyla Redstone—my missing person—worked at that facility."

"But she didn't disappear from there. We know her mission's origin point."

"We do. But I believe that the work she did at the facility had a direct impact on the reason she disappeared."

"Primate research," said Oxendine.

"Among other things, yes."

"It's thin."

"It's not." I could hear a tinge of whine in my own voice, and I didn't like it. I didn't want to, but I was going to have to pressure Oxendine another way. "I can prove it if you let Mbabe walk free."

She considered it for a time—longer than she needed, probably for effect. "No."

"Really? You're refusing to help me with my mission?"

"I'm refusing to con a prisoner."

"This will have to go in my report," I said.

She considered that for a shorter time. "Like I said: Go fuck yourself. And then do what you've got to do, Carl."


I WAS PISSED when I left, but more at myself than at Oxendine. Her response didn't surprise me once I thought it through. I'd approached her wrong. When

I threatened to put it in my report—that was chicken-shit. It made her dig in deeper. I'd threatened her career, which would have worked with a lot of officers, but not her. Oxendine would put doing the right thing over serving her own self-interest. We needed officers like her, so I couldn't be mad, even though I didn't like her decision. I liked to think that we needed guys like me, too. Guys who would bend the rules to get things done. That might have been arrogance. It might have been what led to some of my big mistakes in the past. But it was the only way I worked. People knew that. People in charge. People like Serata.

Once that thought hit me, I couldn't shake it. Serata had set me up back during the Cappa mission. He knew my nature and sent me into a situation because he could predict how I'd act. At the time, I'd thought it was because they needed a rule breaker to fix the problem. In retrospect, I'd done exactly what he planned for me to do. Maybe here, on Eccasis, I was asking myself the wrong question. I had fixated on why Zentas wanted me here. Maybe I should have focused on why the military leadership said yes. They knew Oxendine and the governor. They'd know that neither of those two would do anything to curb Zentas and Caliber. But why would the military want to do that? Military leaders didn't tend to be supporters of green laws. Some would be, of course—there are as many different opinions as there are officers—but as a group, they'd lean toward pro-expansion. So why put me here?

Fader had given me quiet to think, but as we neared my quarters she spoke. "I take it that it didn't go well with the commander." She did well to keep any hint of *I could have told you that* out of her voice.

"I screwed it up."

Fader accepted that without comment instead of trying to reassure me, which I appreciated. "I gave the questions to the interrogators, including asking about who ran the facility."

"How'd that go?" I asked.

"They made me fill out a formal RFI."

RFI—request for information. "So they'll send it through channels and somebody will reject it, but we'll never find out who, and it will be too late even if we do."

"Seems likely, yes, sir."

"Okay."

After another minute she spoke again. "So what do we do now, sir?"

I knew what I wanted to do. I wanted to go confront Zentas and get him to spill his guts. But I'd rushed into the meeting with Oxendine, and I wouldn't make that mistake again. I needed to sleep on it. Plan. I needed more information, but barring Ganos stumbling into Xyla's online diary of incriminating facts, that seemed unlikely. "Now, we go get drunk. Or, at least I do. It's optional for you."

"Is that the best plan, sir?"

"Right now, it's the only one I've got."

I COULDN'T FIND my rifle. Somehow, I knew I'd left it in the shower facility, but I couldn't find the right shower because they all looked alike in the prefabricated landscape of the camp. But I kept looking. It was ridiculous, of course. I'd stayed in camps like that, but it had been years ago. This one was in a desert, somewhere, with an orangish sun, though that color may have been due to the hour. I knew I was dreaming, but I couldn't wake myself.

The scene shifted. I still didn't have my weapon, but now the terrain had changed. Now I needed it. Enemies approached. Soldiers ran everywhere, lacking leadership, in no sort of order. I needed to get them focused, but I couldn't get past not having my weapon. The terrain started out rugged and mountainous, then jungle, then some combination of the two. We had a mission, but I'd forgotten the brief. I'd forgotten where to go to get the brief, or if it was even my job to know it. Maybe I was supposed to have prepared it. And still, no rifle.

**I WOKE, UNCOMFORTABLE,** but not as bad as I've been at other times. I didn't read too much into the dream, other than it meant I hadn't consumed enough whiskey to shut it out. I checked my device for the time: 0320. Too late to have another drink to help me get back to sleep. I didn't want to sleep anyway. That's not exactly right. I wanted more sleep, but I didn't want to dream anymore, and I feared that I would. It hadn't been bad, but something told me if it continued, it would have worsened. I lay there for a while debating it, but eventually I got up and made coffee. Since nobody else would be up for a couple hours, I logged into my terminal and sent a message to Serata. The thought that he sent me here for a reason hadn't left with a few drinks and a few hours of sleep. I needed to get it into the open. I'd retired, so some of the customs no longer applied. People sometimes *acted* like they did, but that was more a matter of comfort than regulation. Screw comfort.

Sir,
    Need to know why you (or they) wanted me specifically on this mission. I know Zentas

*asked. But why was the answer yes? Who*
*thought this was a good idea?*

                                        *Carl*

I'd kept the language neutral but made the message
direct. I knew Serata better than I knew anyone in the
galaxy when it came to things like this. He'd understand.
He'd take it exactly how I intended it: as a personal attack. Regardless of who put him up to it, he took responsibility the minute he agreed to recruit me. He'd
understand that part, too. What I didn't know was when
he'd respond. Figuring out lag times and then figuring
out the time on a specific planet took work, and I didn't
care enough to look it up. I'd said what I had to say and
hit send. It was out of my hands now.

To pass the time until the rest of the planet woke, I
took care of personal stuff that I'd neglected. I sent a
note to my son, and another one to my granddaughter for
the first time since we arrived. I sometimes forgot about
the time I spent in cryo, but to them, those days passed
like any other.

I got another coffee and started in on the information
I had about the dead and captured enemy from the previous day's mission. Eight names, a couple fake. The military had determined that much but little more. Ganos
had done better. Based on the time stamps on her information, she had gone to bed right around the time I woke
up, and her effort showed. I had real names, criminal
records, and most important, a trace of how each person
came to be here on Eccasis. Those got interesting.

Only one of the eight—one of the six dead—had a job
directly with Caliber. Four others worked for contractors or subcontractors with Caliber affiliations. But that
meant that three didn't. It didn't prove anything. Most of

the people involved had arrived under false pretenses, and Caliber, with its subcontractors, was the biggest employer on the planet other than the government. They'd be the obvious target for fake credentials. But the one employee who did work for them made a big difference. Schultz. The same man who had been on patrol the day Xyla disappeared. The man that Stroud said had left the planet and no longer worked for them. Except he didn't, and he might.

Somewhere during my second cup of coffee, I decided to confront Zentas with no evidence. I didn't love the idea any more than I had the previous night, but I had a ticking clock. Without a doubt, Oxendine had reported to her superiors yesterday and asked them to pull me off the case. They might not do it, but I knew from Flak Jacket that they were already leaning that way. Knowing that, I wasn't leaving without taking a shot at getting answers. From the outside, taking a foolish risk might look like capitulation. I mentally prepared myself for Fader to express exactly that. She probably wouldn't—she was too professional to say it out loud. But she'd think it. I worked out in my head how I'd explain it, but that was probably more to convince myself than her.

The trouble was, in my hypothetical argument with Fader, she was right: I couldn't prove anything, and I held out little hope that Zentas would self-incriminate. I'm good at manipulating people, but he resided on an entirely different level in that regard. I know my limits. But he still had an ego. He'd asked for me to come here for a reason. I still didn't know that reason, but it hadn't been an accident. I meant something to him. It stood to follow that what I thought meant something to him as well. If nothing else, I'd make sure that he knew that

I knew what he was up to. And I did know. I couldn't
prove it, but I knew. When I told him that, he'd react. He
still wouldn't incriminate himself or his company without proof, but he'd do something. I had no idea what. I'd
wait for his move, and I'd figure out my next action from
there. It ceded him the initiative, which I disliked, but I
wanted to nail him and I had to force him to act. It wasn't
about his daughter any longer. It was about him existing
outside the law. At one point in my life, I'd been okay
with that. Not anymore. Maybe I'd learned something
from the Cappans.

A wiser man might have seen his own hypocrisy in
all of that. At 0445 hours, I wasn't very wise.

Once people arrived at work, I contacted Caliber and
set an appointment with Zentas. I refused to divulge the
subject. He'd assume I wanted to give him an answer
about the job, and his people would assume it wasn't any
of their business. He had a busy morning, but they set me
up to meet him that afternoon. Plenty of time to rethink
things and back out.

It also gave me plenty of time to get things done. I
visited Mac again, getting mildly surprised when they
allowed me in until I realized they'd moved him to a
room on the other side, away from the prisoner. I had to
give Oxendine points for thinking that one through. Mac
continued to heal, and promised he'd be good to go the
next morning. I sent Fader on a mission to find out the
next in line in charge of EPV. I also got a message back
from Serata.

*Carl,*
   *At the time I got the job to recruit you, it*
*appeared to me to be on the level. But if you*
*think it's not, I trust your judgment. I'll look*

*into it. It will take some time. The players in-*
*volved are significant.*

*Serata*

That settled it for me. He hadn't equivocated. Saying it appeared that way to him—that was Serata's way
of admitting he may have made a mistake. That alone
made me trust him on this one. His offer to look into it
probably wouldn't matter. This would be over before he
could learn anything.

I MET ZENTAS in an office that he'd appropriated from
someone and had redecorated. At least I assumed he
had it redecorated, since I didn't think a random office
on Eccasis would have exquisite carpet, polished wood
furniture, and art on the walls that probably cost seven
figures. A tall male assistant dressed in an expensive suit
escorted me in and then quickly left us alone.

"Drinks?" asked Zentas, and then apparently read
something from my face or body language. "Ah . . . I
see not."

"I'm fine, thank you."

"So, this is a bad news visit. You're not going to take
the job."

"I'm not here about the job." I'd already let him take
control of the conversation, which wouldn't help. Not
that I had much choice.

"But you're not going to take it. If you were, you'd
have said so. Don't tell me you haven't decided. Give me
a little respect."

"I'm not here about the job," I repeated.

"Fine." He exaggerated a sigh, then gestured to a
chair. "What are you here for?"

"I want to give you a report on the situation I came to investigate."

"My daughter."

"Right."

He quieted himself. Not just his voice, but his whole body seemed to shrink into itself. It was a good act. "Okay. I'm ready. This is very important to me."

I was prepared for that and undeterred. "I'm going to tell you the same thing you told me."

"What's that?"

"Give me a little respect."

"Excuse me?" He almost came up out of his chair. I didn't react. The *I'm going to kick your ass* thing might work in the business world, but he'd have to do better than that if he wanted to intimidate me. I'd had my ass kicked by better men.

"I watched you on the news—"

"Where I expressed my feelings about the tragedy—"

"Where you exploited her death to make a political point."

He started to snap back at me then held it and relaxed in his chair. He shrugged. "Sure. That's fair."

That caught me by surprise a little. I hadn't expected him to concede that point. Especially not so quickly. "So—"

"That doesn't mean I don't care about her," he said, cutting me off. "What's done is done. How I use it after the fact is a completely different issue."

I nodded once. I couldn't disagree. "That's fair too. I'm going to tell you up front, I don't have a lot of proof for my findings. But you requested my presence on this mission for a reason. I'm pretty good at this sort of thing." I wanted to admit the lack of proof up front so he wouldn't jump right to that after I told him my findings.

"Sure," he said.

"Understand, I haven't filed this yet. I'm giving it to you first as a courtesy."

"I appreciate that."

And so, with that, I jumped in with both feet. I had decided prior to arriving to state it as fact. Not *I think,* or *I believe.* Fact. "There was a supposedly abandoned facility that we found yesterday that subsequently blew up. Your daughter, Xyla Redstone, was the leader, or one of the leaders of that facility, which conducted potentially illegal research on local animals, specifically hominiverts." Zentas didn't jump in and I didn't want him to, so I continued. "Part of her research involved audio sensitivity of indigenous primates. Whether it was her initial goal or not, she, or others working with her, discovered that hominiverts are sensitive at certain frequencies that humans can't hear, and that broadcasting those frequencies causes them to move out of an area."

"Okay. I'm not agreeing with you, but I understand what you're saying."

"There's more."

He gestured for me to continue, giving me the rope to hang myself. And I was going to oblige him. The next part—I wasn't even sure I believed it myself. But the clock was running out and I was losing, so I took the desperation shot. "Your daughter was killed—either intentionally or unintentionally—by people from your own company. Personnel from Caliber, or in the employ of Caliber, used low-frequency broadcasts to intentionally drive a group of hominiverts into her research team. Guards from two other teams moved to the site to ensure the job was complete, driving the hominiverts off in the process, thus confusing the initial investigation."

Zentas sat silently for several seconds—long enough

for it to become uncomfortable, like maybe he expected me to continue. "This!" He paused again. "This is why I wanted to hire you!" He laughed loudly, but it didn't seem forced. "The balls! The absolute stones that you have to come in here and tell me this to my face. Who else could do that? Nobody. That's who. Absolutely nobody." He fell silent again.

I didn't know what to say at that. He hadn't refuted anything, which is what I expected, but he hadn't confirmed anything either.

Zentas smiled. "Of course, it's all bullshit."

"Excuse me?"

He'd said it with perfect confidence. Absolutely nothing to indicate that he didn't believe what he was saying. He was either telling the truth as far as he knew it, or he could lie like a sociopath.

"Well, not all of it. There *was* an unauthorized dome. We know that from your excursion to it. But there's no evidence linking it to Caliber, and certainly none linking it to Xyla."

"There's some."

"Really? What?"

I walked into that one. The prisoner had recognized Xyla, but he hadn't said so, and even if he had, I wouldn't have shared that with Zentas. Mbabe was too vulnerable, in more ways than one. He could be paid off, or more likely, disappear. I had to say something, though. Schultz was dead, which made him invulnerable. "A man named Schultz was on security, working for Caliber, on the excursion where Xyla died. He was first on the scene with no witnesses."

"So?"

"The same man died in the firefight at the unauthorized facility yesterday."

"A little suspicious, I'll give you that. But still not even close to solid evidence."

"When I questioned Martha Stroud about the man, she said that he no longer worked for you—"

"I'm sure he doesn't," he interjected.

I took that to mean that if he did, I wouldn't find him on the books. "And that he left the planet and couldn't be found."

He started to speak again—he wanted to brush that off as an oversight—but he restrained himself. He probably realized that an instant denial made him look guilty. He didn't have to speak. We both knew I couldn't prove it. "Let me sum up to make sure I've got this right. Your findings are that my own company killed my daughter."

"That's correct."

"That's what you're going with?"

I looked him straight in the eye, my expression flat. I didn't respond verbally, but he got the message.

"You'll find this doesn't end well for you. I've got a lot of friends in the government. They'll bury whatever nonsense you make up as you try to smear me, and then they'll bury *you*."

"There are pluses and minuses to bringing in an outsider who doesn't give a shit. On the plus side, I'll do what's right, regardless of what the government thinks. On the minus side . . . I really *don't* give a shit."

He smiled again, but this time it wasn't real. "You'll find I'm much better as a friend than an enemy. You think you're untouchable. You're not."

*I could say the same for you.* I really wanted to say it, but I didn't. I'd done what I came to do. I'd served notice. I told him what happened, and while he called it total bullshit, something in his reaction told me he knew it wasn't. My accusations almost certainly hadn't hit the mark with 100-percent accuracy, but I only needed to be close to force him to act. He *did* have friends in the government, but he had enemies too. They'd jump on any excuse to bring him down. I also had enemies, of course, but what else could they do to me? "Like I said. This was a courtesy briefing, before I send it in. I didn't want to blindside you."

"Consider me briefed." He turned away and pretended to busy himself with other work. I sat there for a couple of seconds before showing myself out. I'd probably blown the job offer.

# CHAPTER TWENTY-THREE

FADER GAVE ME some bad news the next morning. She'd tracked down the new colonyside head of EPV, Tatiana Garabaldi, but Ms. Garabaldi declined to meet with me. I think her exact words were, "Tell him I'd rather walk naked through the jungle." According to Fader, it hadn't been lost on Garabaldi that Farric had died in sketchy circumstances, and she had booked passage off planet on the next thing moving.

On a positive note, Mac rejoined us, and that made me feel better. I'd goaded Zentas into some sort of action, and I needed all the help I could get for when that happened. I didn't think he'd stoop to a direct attack, but if he did, Mac provided a good insurance policy. I'd convinced myself that Caliber had something to do with Xyla Redstone's death, and that Zentas probably knew about that before I told him. If he'd allow that to happen to his own daughter—even one who was estranged—then there was no limit to what he might do to me.

Unfortunately, he had all the initiative. I had two moves left. First, I could send in a report, and once I played that card, I couldn't take it back. As soon as I did, Zentas would find out through his sources and then he'd have even more control over what happened next. I did prepare it. I wrote up everything I knew, listed every witness and every piece of conjecture I'd made to come to my conclusion, complete with how strong I felt about each piece of it. I didn't oversell it. I acknowledged that I had a margin for error in my work. I had to. I had to present as dispassionate a case as possible if I wanted anyone to buy it. I encrypted the whole thing and got it ready to send, but I didn't intend to push the button. I wanted to see Zentas's move first and hear back from Serata as well. Back on Talca, in a similar situation, I'd set the file to send automatically, only to have it hacked by my captors. I wouldn't make that mistake again. This time I went old school. I gave Mac access to it, just in case something happened to me. If it did, he was to send it as soon as safely possible. I considered giving access to Fader or Ganos as well but decided against it. Fader might see it as her moral obligation to forward whatever I gave her to her higher headquarters. And—again, while I trusted her—I didn't trust her boss, whoever that was. If Ganos wanted access to my information, she'd already have it.

My second option was to visit the governor. He'd opposed my mission to the facility, and it was his job to enforce the laws against places like that. Oxendine couldn't confront him about it, but I could. If I could get him to press charges against Caliber, it would put even more pressure on Zentas to make a move. To do that, however, I had to get past Davidson.

I tried to simply skip her, but someone must have alerted her when I entered the building because she caught me well before I could reach the governor's office. "Colonel Butler. So good to see you." She didn't even pretend to mean it.

"I need to see your boss."

"I'm afraid he's busy."

"I'll wait," I said.

"He'll be busy all day."

She pissed me off, but I'd prepared for that. "Of course he will. Do me a favor. Tell him that I'm filing my report in an hour, and I'm specifically mentioning his failure to execute his responsibilities as one of the causes for the disappearance of Xyla Redstone. I just wanted to let him know ahead of time as a courtesy." It was a bluff, but a strong one. I figured the only thing that would get the governor to act was self-preservation. I also guessed that if the governor went down, he'd take Davidson with him. I turned and left.

Davidson caught me before I got out of the building, which meant I'd probably guessed right. "You can't do that."

"Of course I can. I have independent authority."

"It would be a lie," she said.

"First, that's rich given your position and where your true allegiances lie—"

"That has no bearing on—"

"Second, *is* it a lie? The facility we found was in use doing illegal research on animals. It's his responsibility to prevent that."

"You had no authorization to go to that facility."

"And yet I did. What are they going to do to me? Revoke my authority and send me home? Oh, no. Please. Not that. Tell you what—you go ahead and argue that your failure to oversee the illegal actions of corporations here colonyside is because I took some leeway with my authority and went out and found one *big* illegal action. Let me know how that works out."

"We don't have the resources to monitor everything going on here."

"And I'm sure you've got all the requisitions asking for more assets to back that up." Her face tightened. "No, I didn't think so."

She started to snap back at me but paused. After a few seconds, she sagged in on herself. "What do you want?"

Part of me wanted to press her, ask her what she had to offer. Part of me wanted to know what kind of bribe she could come up with from her corporate masters. But more of me wanted to go after Zentas, and Davidson would never do that. She couldn't. "I want to talk to the governor."

"Fine."

"Alone."

She didn't respond for a moment, then sighed. "Fine."


IT TOOK FIFTEEN minutes in the governor's office sitting in a wooden chair as various people traipsed in, each with something that would *just take a second*. I assumed that Davidson sent them to frustrate me or try to catch some snippet of our conversation.

"Colonel Butler," he said, finally. "How is the investigation going?"

"We're stalled right now."

"That's a shame. What's holding you up?"

I couldn't go right at the governor the way I had with Davidson. I had to build into it and let him trap himself. After that, I could offer him a way out. "As you know, we went on a mission outside the dome and found an illegal facility."

"Yes, I'm very perturbed about that." His demeanor didn't change at all, which seemed odd if he was truly perturbed. Someone probably had told him to be mad about it, but he didn't understand why.

"I'm really sorry about that. I forced Oxendine into it. As you know, my charter gives me the authority to take any action I deem necessary to find out what happened to Xyla Redstone." It wasn't that clear-cut, but he didn't know that.

"Yes, of course."

"I really thought we were going to find the answer there. I mean . . . an illegal facility . . . they had to be hiding something."

"Did you find anything?"

"We didn't. They destroyed it before we could get there."

"That's too bad." He sounded like he actually meant it.

"It leaves me with a problem though. I've got to put it in my report."

"Well, no help for that."

He didn't get it. I was going to have to spell it out for him. "I'll have to mention the illegal facility, which leads to the question of why nobody knew about it. Something like that falls—"

"Under my authority." His face fell as he finally realized the significance.

"Your people really let you down on this." I'd reached a delicate spot. I couldn't accuse him directly, so I needed to give him an out. This wasn't it though. First I had to get him on my side. "I'm sure everyone will see it that way."

He thought about it. "No, they'll blame me. It's my post, and it happened on my watch."

"But it's not your fault," I said.

"That's not how they'll see it—they never do for people in my position."

"You're probably right," I said, trying to put hesitation into my voice, as if he'd just convinced me.

"What am I going to do?"

I pretended to think about it, even though I had the answer prepared. "Well, since I haven't sent it yet, you could get in front of it."

He looked at me with the eyes of a drowning man who'd just been thrown a lifeline. "How would I do that?"

"I could delay the report a bit. No harm in that."

"You'd do that?"

"Look, Governor, this really isn't on you. I'd hate to see my work make it seem that way."

"So . . . how would I . . . how—"

"Well, you're under-resourced. You could put in a requisition for more assets so this thing never happens again."

He nodded. "Yes, I can do that."

"You could fire someone beneath you and shift the blame." I stopped short of giving him a name. He'd come up with Davidson on his own. I hadn't set out to wreck her, but I didn't mind if she got caught in the collateral damage. With her here, companies like Caliber would continue to run roughshod.

He seemed less sure this time. "Okay. I might be able to do that."

"And you could file charges against Caliber for having an illegal facility and conducting illegal experiments on hominiverts."

His eyes went wide. "I can't do that," he whispered.

"I'm afraid I have to insist on that." I dropped the conciliatory tone for a flat, matter-of-fact one.

"Insist? No. You can't report that. There's no evidence. You said so yourself."

"Okay, so instead I'll say that I had a lead on finding what I needed to know about Redstone but was forbidden from continuing the investigation by local authorities."

"But that's not true!"

"Isn't it?"

"You can't know what was out there, so you don't know that it would complete your investigation." Gone was whatever façade of cool he had. He gestured now with his hands as he talked.

"Maybe you want to tell me?"

"Tell you what?"

"What I would have found out there."

"How would I know?"

"I assume you do. Why else would you be protecting an illegal facility?"

"I'm not—" He stopped himself. Perhaps he realized that I was purposely trying to wind him up, and he took a few seconds to gather himself. "That's ridiculous. Pure conjecture. You can't put that in a report without substantiation."

"I *can't*? Governor . . . I nuked a planet from orbit. Twice. You heard about that, right?"

"Of course."

"So . . . *can't?* . . . That's something that might not apply to me. You know?"

He stayed silent for an uncomfortable amount of time, probably weighing the damage to him from what I might do against what Caliber would do if he filed the charges I'd demanded. Since I didn't know which way he'd go, I had to make it easy for him.

"You can blame it on me," I said.

"How can I do that?" He sounded like a sullen teenager, mad because his dad took away his device.

"File the charges publicly. Privately, tell your staff that I made you do it." I figured it would take ten minutes at best before that news made its way to Zentas. I didn't care. I *wanted* him to think it was me. Zentas wasn't a fool. In a battle between the governor and me, he'd know the likely winner. He'd have to act.

"I'll need some time to think about it." He saw me frown, and hastily added, "An hour. I need an hour."

"Of course," I said. I'd made my play. I could give him that much.


**BACK AT MY** quarters, I tried to predict Zentas's next move by working through what I'd do in his place. I didn't worry about the governor. What I'd done there was blatant, and he'd take it for exactly what I intended: an attack. Things internal to Caliber didn't sit nearly as well. He'd tear the company apart to figure out where I got my information about the hominiverts. That would lead to my visit to the tech department, but more important, it would lead to Mae Eddleston. I hadn't considered that when I confronted Zentas, and now it seemed like a glaring error. I needed to warn her, so I asked Fader to call.

Eddleston didn't answer.

"Get an escort and go to her place. If you don't find her, get Ganos to track her down. I want a rundown in an hour."

"Yes, sir."

I give myself some credit for not yelling or throwing anything, but in truth, I couldn't move.

Fuck.

I sat there and waited. I tried to think of Zentas's other actions, but I couldn't make myself concentrate.

When Fader returned, she launched into her briefing. "She wasn't at her place. When nobody answered, I had the MPs open it. Nobody home. The room appeared normal, though it looks like she may have packed and left. Her toiletries were gone, and there was no bag in her apartment."

On the surface, that didn't mean anything; she could have gone anywhere. But I had a bad feeling about it. "What did Ganos—"

"I had Ganos check the cameras that should have picked up any time Eddleston came or left her quarters. She found Eddleston entering last evening but couldn't find her leaving."

"Someone hacked the cameras," I said.

"Yes, sir."

"Fuck."

Fader didn't respond to that, waiting for me to say something else. What could I say? I'd made a mistake and someone else had paid for it. Again. I glanced at the bottle on the counter. If I started down that path, it wouldn't end. I needed to think. After a moment, an idea came to me. "Since she obviously left—either alone or under duress—there would be more cameras. Let's expand the search in rings around her quarters. If we check the feeds to see which cameras went out, we should be able to determine the path she took."

"Ganos had the same thought, sir."

"Did she find anything?"

"Multiple cameras went out in several directions. They could have gone a dozen different ways. She's still running it down, but as each camera failed, the possibilities went up exponentially."

"How does nobody notice all these cameras going down?"

"Apparently cameras fail briefly all the time. They reboot themselves, and they only trigger a maintenance warning if they're out for more than three minutes," said Fader.

"Which is more than enough time to move through an area and on to the next camera." Shit.

I thought about how this new information changed things. Even with Eddleston out of the picture, it was still Zentas's move. He just potentially had another piece. In my mind, I connected my confrontation with him and Eddleston's disappearance, but I had nothing to prove that. Even if he *did* have her, she'd confirm where I learned about the sonic technology. But I'd told him I knew about it, so it didn't affect me. What it did was put Eddleston in danger. I couldn't predict how he'd respond to her providing information.

To cover my bases, I called Oxendine's direct line and reported the missing person and my suspicion.

**ZENTAS USED HIS** new pawn in a way I didn't predict. So much so that at first I questioned whether it was Zentas's move at all. The call didn't even come to me. It came to Fader, who came to my suite to brief me and Mac. She brought Ganos with her, so we had the entire team.

"Mae Eddleston called," began Fader.

A wave of relief hit me, since I'd assumed the worst. "She's okay?"

"She says she is," said Fader. "I asked her about her disappearance, and she said she freaked out and left her quarters because she realized someone was watching her."

"Where is she now?" I asked.

"Staying with a friend. One who doesn't work for Caliber. She's scared."

"This feels off," I said. "The cameras."

"I think so too," agreed Fader. "If she left on her own, who hacked the cameras?"

"What did she want?"

"She wanted to meet, sir."

"Is she coming here? When?" I asked.

"She wouldn't come here," said Fader. "She said they're watching your place, too."

"Who? Caliber?" They probably were.

"She didn't say so, sir, but that was the implication, yes. She wants to meet somewhere nobody will be watching. She wouldn't say anything else over the comm, because she doesn't trust that someone isn't listening."

I looked at Mac. "This *really* doesn't make sense. If someone is listening, they now know that she wants to meet me. It could be a rookie mistake by Eddleston, but I don't really believe that. What are the odds that this is a trap?"

Mac shrugged. "I don't know. Pretty high. What do you think, sir?"

"Ninety percent?"

Mac thought about it. "Maybe. It sounds like they got to her and now they're using her as bait."

"I agree," I said. "I think they're coercing her into something to get to me. But for what?"

"Well, the least harmful thing I can think of is that they want to plant false information, maybe give you something that sends you off in another direction—back toward EPV, or something. But if she wanted to do that, why wouldn't she just come here?"

"Right. What's the worst case?"

"Kidnapping," said Mac, without hesitation.

"Kidnapping? Not murder?" asked Fader.

"If they wanted to kill him, they wouldn't need a meeting. A meeting just puts us on guard. They'd be much better hitting us at a random time when we didn't suspect it," said Mac.

I thought about it for over a minute. I had to give Zentas credit. He definitely knew how to set the bait. Even suspecting the trap, I was always going to bite. Even without the promise of information, I'd put Eddleston into this situation, and I had to get her out. But at the back of my mind, as small as the chance was, I also held out hope that she'd give me the thing I needed to break this open. "So how do we flip this?"

"What do you mean, sir?" asked Fader.

"I have to meet her. It's almost certainly staged, probably by Caliber. They want something. How do I use that against them?"

"I don't suppose there's any point in telling you this is a shitty idea," said Mac.

"We'll take precautions."

"The only precaution I'd settle for willingly was us meeting her on a different planet. Or better yet, a ship in space in the middle of nowhere." But as much as he protested, Mac would support me.

"Before we jump into this with both feet, can we discuss options, sir?" asked Fader.

"What options are there?"

"The job's done," said Fader. "Pass your suspicions about Eddleston's safety to the military, report that Xyla's patrol was attacked by hominiverts, say what you can and can't prove about the technology and how it may have had a part in the attack, and we ship out. Xyla's dead. We're sure of that. Everything else is another job."

"Are we sure?" I asked. "Isn't it possible that Xyla Redstone is still alive? What if they faked the disappearance of the patrol?"

"To what end, sir?"

"So that Zentas could exploit his daughter's fake death for political gain," I said. "So Xyla would have cover to continue experimenting on hominiverts."

Her face tightened. She didn't buy it. "There are a lot of holes in that, sir. First, there are the other five members of the team."

"They could have—"

"And even if they were *all* in on it, they can never show their faces again," she said, anticipating my argument.

She made a good case, but still I couldn't leave it alone. "If I walk away, Caliber continues to get away with what they're doing," I said, changing the point.

"Like I said, sir, report it. The government can shut them down."

"But they won't." Talking to the governor had confirmed that, and I couldn't get past that part.

"And you can?" she raised her voice, then caught herself. "Sorry, sir."

"No, don't be. Speak your mind."

"Is this about Eddleston or Caliber, sir?"

I had to think about that. I wanted to get Eddleston out of the jam I'd put her in, but if I was being honest with myself, I wanted to go after Caliber more. If I proved what Caliber was doing and put it in my report—got it to the highest levels of government . . . What if I did that, and they *still* didn't do anything? Was the lack of resources and oversight on Eccasis truly an oversight or part of the plan? I could always leak it to the press. That was, after all, my go-to move. No. Maybe I was being naïve, but I had to believe that if I got it to the right person in the government, someone would take action. "It's Caliber. They shouldn't be allowed to violate the law at will."

Fader glanced to the others, clearly uncomfortable. "This is going to sound callous, sir, but that's not your mission."

I glanced at Mac, who shrugged. "I'm kind of with the captain on this one."

"How about you?" I asked, looking to Ganos.

"Me? You don't want my opinion on this."

"Go ahead," I prodded.

She looked at each of us. "Okay, sure. I don't think we should be here at all." Apparently seeing confusion on our faces, she clarified. "I don't mean the four of us. I mean humans shouldn't be here at all. What right do we have to take over a planet that has complex life on it? Sure, Caliber is exploiting the planet. But so is everybody else."

Nobody answered. I'd considered it before, of course. It's not like hers was a fringe opinion. After my actions on Cappa, more people held it than ever. As Zentas had mentioned, politicians even ran campaigns on that stance. However, her posing the question right then helped me clarify it in my own mind. I didn't agree with her, but I didn't *disagree* with her either. What I knew was this: I was a government man. I'd spent a lifetime supporting the will of elected officials, whether I agreed with them or not. Caliber was violating that will in the form of subverting the Butler Law. The fact that Oxendine and the governor didn't have the resources or will to stop them didn't change that.

Ten years ago I would have taken Fader's advice. I'd have *given* Fader's advice. I would have completed the mission assigned to me and that would have been that. I couldn't say exactly when I changed. I still didn't care that much about Eccasis, and I didn't care that much about hominiverts either. But I was tired of corporations making their own rules. It had pissed me off when Omicron did it by trying to exploit the Cappans, and it pissed me off now. Zentas made me angry—the way he used his daughter's death—the way he'd use anything he wanted and didn't care about consequences because he didn't think there *were* any. It *wasn't* my job to stop him. But somebody had to do it.

"Thank you all for your honest opinions." I looked at each of them, but longest at Ganos. "Let's be clear: I believe that Caliber is involved with this overture by Eddleston, and we're going to come into direct conflict. I need to know before I make a decision: Are you with me?"

"Of course, sir," said Fader. I believed her. She had her orders, and they said to help me in any way possible. She'd follow them.

"Do you need to ask?" said Mac. I didn't.

Ganos was the one I was worried about, but she didn't hesitate. "I'm in. But before we do anything, if Caliber is behind this and we're going after them, you need to know that I'm going into their system."

Now it was my turn to pump the brakes. "Hold on . . . I thought—can we talk for a minute?" I gestured toward the far side of the room, and Ganos headed there while Mac and Fader moved away.

"What?" asked Ganos, once I joined her. As if she didn't know.

I waited for her to meet my eyes. "I thought the rule was don't hack giant, evil corporations."

"It was."

"What's changed?"

"You're going into this meeting. You think you're the only one who gets to take risks?"

"I'm going to meet an informant. Once I'm out, I'm

out. I can go hide away again. For you—Caliber has a long reach and a longer memory."

"Yeah, they do. But you know what? I'm tired of living scared. I'm tired of being bullied. I *want* to do this. I *am* doing this, sir. End of debate."

I didn't like it, but I'd be a hypocrite to say so. Plus, she'd do what she wanted the minute she left my sight anyway. "Promise me you'll be careful."

Ganos grinned. "Of course, sir. You know me."

And there it was. I *did* know her, and she was ready. Her involvement upped the stakes, but it only made me more determined to win. "Okay, then," I announced to the room. "That brings us back to the original question. How do we flip this thing?"

Mac came over. "If we're doing this, sir, we're doing it my way. I set the location, I set the terms."

"Roger that," I said. "Set it up."


I PULLED FADER aside once Mac left. "If things go wrong, I want you to get Mac and Ganos and get out of here. You'll have to force Mac. He won't want to go."

"What are you talking about, sir?"

"Mac's in charge of plan A. I'm giving you plan B. The other side isn't stupid. They're going to have a plan too, and there's always a chance that theirs will work better. If something goes wrong and you can't track me, or if *anything* else goes wrong, you get everyone on a ship. Tell Oxendine what you know and let her deal with it, but get the team to safety."

"They're not going to like it, sir."

"Of course they aren't. That's why I'm telling you."

"*I* don't like it, sir."

"And that's fine. I need you to promise me you'll do it anyway."

"Can you help me understand, sir?"

I paused. I could do that much. "Sure. If something happens to me, if I know everybody is safe, I can make whatever decision gives me the best chance. If there's a threat to others, especially when I can't be sure what that threat may be, it adds variables. It gives the enemy leverage."

"It also gives you a source of help."

"Given the two options, I like the clarity of going it alone." It had taken me a long time to get to that point. I'd always fought as part of a team when I was in the military. As a civilian, I'd come to appreciate the independence of only having to worry about myself. It would help to know my team was out of reach off planet. I'd gotten enough people killed. "I don't expect you to understand."

"You're right, sir. I don't understand."

"One day you might. Tell me you'll do it anyway." I wouldn't trust Mac if he told me—he'd tell me whatever I wanted to hear. But this was Fader. Her word was titanium. Once given, she wouldn't dream of breaking it.

"Okay, sir. I'll do it anyway."

# CHAPTER TWENTY-FOUR

MAC SCHEDULED THE meeting with Eddleston in an open area—the only park inside the main dome. It allowed good observation and didn't allow anyone to approach unobserved. It had trees and grass and even a fountain, all meant to give people some sense of normalcy on an otherwise alien planet. So much of space exploration involved being able to fool the mind into thinking things were the same. Researchers put a ton of effort and money into ways to change that need, but it always came back to the human brain. We understood it, but only enough to appease it, not enough to adapt it.

Eddleston sat on a park bench made of painted wooden slats, the whole scene so rustic it seemed fake, like someone's idea of home, except lifted from a sales catalog instead of reality.

"I've got eyes on her, on the bench by the fountain." The sub-cochlear implant made it seem like Mac spoke directly into my brain. I didn't respond. I had a subvocal mic, so I could communicate back to him, and a backup mic in my belt. Mac had made great use of the gear, seeding the area with almost invisible cameras and whatever else he could find. We planned to conduct the meeting and hear what Eddleston had to say, but if things changed, we'd spring the trap and then capture whoever we could.

Mac had also brought backup. We didn't tell the military about our plan due to potential leaks, so Mac had requested an escort, much like we'd had on several other occasions. Once they arrived, he repurposed the soldiers to help us and convinced them not to call it in to headquarters. Bored garrison soldiers are usually up for anything that gets them out of the daily routine, so it didn't take much for them to agree.

The pulse pistol I had tucked into the back of my pants, hidden by my untucked shirttail, dug in, and I fought the urge to adjust it as I approached her. Someone would be watching. Eddleston must have heard me coming, because she turned on the bench to watch me. She glanced in other directions as well, clearly nervous. Once I got within a few paces, she spoke. "I don't know if they're watching."

"They probably are. That's okay. Once we talk, we'll get you into protective custody. Have you talked to anyone from Caliber recently?"

"Yes," she said. "I'm sorry. I didn't tell you, because I thought you wouldn't meet. They made me call you."

I was hurrying around the bench to reach her when Mac spoke into my brain. "Something's happening. Ganos is seeing a spike in activity."

"We need to get out of here. Fast." It was part of the plan. If anything happened, my only job was to grab Eddleston and move to a new spot that would give our team an advantage over someone who planned to take us from the bench.

"What's going on?" Eddleston stood as she spoke, probably hearing the urgency in my tone.

"I'm not sure," I said. "Let's go."

"It's—" Mac's voice cut out.

An electric vehicle appeared, driving off road, into the park. I turned to run, trusting Eddleston to follow. I didn't know why I'd lost comms with Mac, but it didn't matter. A sharp pain blossomed in my right butt cheek. I turned back to Eddleston, who held an auto-injector.

"I really am sorry," she said.

"Mac, Eddleston's in on it . . ." Maybe I could still transmit.

But Eddleston shook her head and pulled a gray disc out of her pocket. "Pocket EMP. Knocks out all the electronics in about a ten-meter radius. He can't hear you."

When I spoke again, my tongue lagged, heavy in my mouth, and I had to force the words. "Mac will come."

"No, he won't." Her face started to fade as whatever she'd drugged me with really took hold.

The last thing I saw was Jan Karlsson's face in the windshield of the car as it arrived.


I WOKE ON a medical bed, adjusted to a reclined position. I'd been in enough of them to know that much without opening my eyes. Even coming out of unconsciousness, I knew I was in trouble, so I tried to assess my situation before tipping off whoever might be around that I'd awoken. Nobody spoke, so I got no clues there. The recirculated air was fresh but odorless, lacking the astringent smell of a hospital. I had an IV in my arm and a pulse monitor on my finger. I shifted a bit, but I didn't appear to be restrained, which struck me as odd. Perhaps I was alone in a locked room.

Someone moved. Not alone, then.

I opened my eyes.

"Good. You're awake." I followed the voice to a tall, bronze-skinned woman with black hair wearing a lab coat. "The sedative usually has no ill effects, but we monitored you just to be safe. Everything is normal."

"Where am I?"

"That's not my question to answer. Someone will be with you soon. I've notified them that you're awake."

The automatic blood pressure cuff on my arm inflated, and I used the time to consider my options. We were in a small room—like a medic's office or something—with only one door. It was closed and looked solid, made of white-painted metal, almost like what one would find on a spaceship. Shit. Had they taken me into space? *Why?*

The woman didn't have a weapon. I could probably overpower her, take her hostage. But without knowing what lay outside the door, that plan had too many variables. I assumed that I was under the control of people . . . I'll just call them *bad guys*. The bad guys had me, but I didn't know where, why, or even when. A rash action on my part might negate another advantage I could find later by cooperating. "Can you tell me how long I was out?"

"No, I can't. Sorry."

"What can you tell me?"

"I'm happy to talk about your medical condition. It's fine, by the way. You could afford to cut out sodium."

"I'll work on it. Can you tell me where my clothes went?" I had on a hospital gown, though at least I had shorts underneath it.

"They were taken as part of the search. We also removed a device from your gum."

"Thanks," I said. It was valuable information. The EMP had probably fried everything anyway, but now I knew for sure I had no outside communicators and that nobody could track me. That meant that Fader should be triggering plan B and getting the team off Eccasis. Once I knew how long I'd been unconscious, I could estimate when they'd be safe. Once they got to safety, Mac would send my report. Not that I expected it would do any good.

More than anything, I wanted to know who would walk through that door.

I didn't have to wait long. A metallic *thunk* shook the room, then a hiss, as if the room depressurized slightly, but not enough to feel it in my ears. Two men came in, dressed in black jumpsuits. They even *looked* like bad guys. Someone had to be messing with me. "Hello, gentlemen."

"He good to go, Doc?" asked one of them. In my head I named him Guard One. He had dark hair and pale skin. Guard Two had darker skin and no hair. He stood back by the door, holding a canvas bag.

"As soon as I take out his IV."

I considered ripping it out like Mac had done with his, but I wasn't that much of a badass. I held my arm still. "Can I have my clothes? It's a little chilly."

Guard One nodded to Guard Two, who brought the bag forward. "The belt is gone," said Guard Two.

"Fair enough." Like I was going to use my belt as a weapon or something. The EMP had surely fried the mic hidden in it, so I didn't care about that. I swung my feet off the bed and got dressed while still sitting, taking stock of my body as I did. My ass hurt a bit from where Eddleston had stabbed me with the injector, and I had a little pain in my robot foot, but otherwise I felt fine. I found dressing a bit awkward with an audience, but I had bigger worries. "Can you fellows tell me where we are?"

"I'm sure someone will," said Guard One.

"Have we met before? You look familiar." He didn't, but it seemed like a way to keep him talking. Anything he said might give me information.

"Don't think so."

"You're prior military, right?" He had the look. They both did.

"Let's go, s . . ." He almost said *sir*. Yep. Prior military. It probably didn't matter, but without my team coming to the rescue, I couldn't know what might help me. Every piece of intel counted.

We walked down a corridor with walls the same as the door in the office—white-painted metal. It looked like a spaceship, but didn't feel like one—or, if it was, it was docked. It didn't give that slight sense of movement that happens in space. However, it didn't have any windows, so that didn't help. Guard One walked in front of me, Guard Two behind. Neither had visible weapons, and again, I contemplated resistance. Obviously they didn't see me as a threat. Better to keep it that way for now. We passed another hatch and proceeded to one farther down the hall, which led to a wider corridor— big enough for maybe ten people to walk abreast. We followed that for maybe forty meters before we reached a set of four oversized empty cells with huge doors. Given the dimensions, they'd probably been designed for something much bigger than a person. They'd still work, though.

Guard One ushered me through the open door of the second cell, which differed from the others in that it had a toilet in one corner and a padded bench against the back wall that probably doubled as a bed. The door closed behind me, powered by some unseen electric motor that had seen better days based on the grinding sound. He checked its security, then both guards disappeared back the way they came, leaving me alone. I didn't have to wait long for the welcoming committee, as Eddleston entered the area via a door right across from the cells.

"You got me," I said. I could admit it. She'd totally fooled me. I expected Zentas to try something, but I hadn't suspected Eddleston would actively take part. I probably should have. "What did I miss? Was it a setup from the start?" I'd think back through it and figure out how she fooled me, but if she told me, it would shorten the process.

"Forgive me if I don't give you all the answers. My ego doesn't require explaining myself. But yes, we set you up from the start. We planted the texts you undoubtedly found in Xyla's device."

I shook my head. What an idiot I was. "Is Redstone dead? Was that part true?"

"She is. It happened as reported. A mistake. She wasn't supposed to be part of that team. She changed things at the last minute. Obviously I left that part out when I talked to you. But the rest of it . . . all true. Sometimes it's easier to manipulate someone with the truth than with lies. You know?"

*Asshole.* "Most of the truth. Except for your own involvement."

"Well, sure, except for that."

"Here's what I don't get. What if I didn't bite? You planted the text messages, but I almost didn't look at them." I caught myself before I mentioned that Fader found them. The less they thought about Fader right now, the better.

"There were backup plans," she said.

"You wanted me to know about the sonic manipulation of the primates."

"Yes."

"And you wanted me to find the not-so-abandoned facility."

"That was actually all you, but it worked out." That was good to know. At least we forced them to react there, though it didn't help me much now.

"And Zentas wanted me to come accuse him."

"I don't presume to speak for Mr. Zentas."

"Is he here?"

"Do you see him?" She was good, not letting me make her answer questions she didn't want to.

"I mean watching. There are cameras in here. Microphones."

"Of course there are."

"And he's watching?" I flipped both middle fingers into the air and waved them around violently, in case he was.

"I really don't know. I'm in here with you, and while they can see us, I can't see them."

"Where are we?"

"Outside of Dome One. That's all you need to know. We're underground. So even if you escape, there's nothing but jungle."

Another valuable piece of information. Whatever I could gather would help in my eventual attempt to escape. "How does this place even exist?"

She chuckled. "Easy. Politicians make laws, but nobody actually comes to the frontier and *enforces* them. Or, when they do, they're ineffectual. Or bribable. We're not the only company with secret facilities on this planet. Not even close."

"They'll have seen us leaving Dome One." I didn't believe that, but I wanted to see if she'd respond.

"They never have before. But enough of the interrogation. Let me answer the rest of the questions I'm going to answer so we can be done with it without you thinking you're being clever. It's been six hours since you left the park. Your people are looking for you, but they're nowhere close. Captain Fader is working on passage off the planet. Ganos is talented, but out of her league."

"Let them go." Letting Eddleston know that my team meant that much to me gave her leverage, but I couldn't help it. They probably knew anyway.

"We might. We don't need them. In fact, them leaving the planet fits our story."

"What story is that?"

"The story of the rogue ex-colonel. You've probably heard it."

"Refresh my memory."

She sighed dramatically. "There was this rogue ex-colonel. You know the type. Full of himself. Plays by his own rules. Makes things happen and doesn't let anything stand in his way. All that macho bullshit."

"I'm under your control. You don't have to be an asshole." Just because *I* was didn't mean I liked it when *other people* were. Yeah, yeah. I'm a hypocrite.

She smiled. "You asked. Now . . . ask the question you really want the answer to."

I considered it. She wanted me to ask what they wanted me for. I didn't feel the need to give her that satisfaction. "So you're saying Zentas didn't authorize the death of his own daughter?"

Her face twisted slightly, and her hands came together in front of her for a second. The question made her uncomfortable. Good. It wasn't much, but it was a start. "I've told you; I'm not going to speak for Mr. Zentas."

"Then let me talk to someone who can. Until then, you're just wasting my time."

"Now who's being an asshole?"

"I always have been. It's part of the rogue ex-colonel story. Or did you miss that chapter? Can we stop playing games? What do you want?"

She glared at me, but if she thought she was going to stare me down . . . nope. Eventually she turned and left, calling over her shoulder "I'll see you soon, Colonel Butler."

**SOON DIDN'T COME** soon enough. I couldn't track the time, but it felt like maybe a day. They brought meals twice, and the second one looked enough like breakfast to make me think it was the next day. I'd slept a little, but as I'd been sedated for several hours, I wasn't really that tired. It was part of their plan, I'm sure, to make me wait, to let me sit with nothing to do and think about all the bad things that could happen. I didn't like being alone with my own thoughts, but in this case, I accepted it gladly. Every hour gave Fader more time to get the team off the planet.

Two guards came for me—Guard One and a woman I hadn't seen before. I considered calling her Guard Two-Point-One but decided I'd need a different naming convention.

They led me in silence down a wide corridor and around a corner, and then we stopped outside of a biometrically locked door on what I thought was the wall toward the interior of the facility. That led to another hallway and quickly to another door and another biometric lock. This one opened into a small lab with a couple of stand-up workstations and a desk tucked into a corner. Shelves were built into every wall, and the whole setup felt designed to maximize space.

Mae Eddleston stood alone in the room wearing a

light blue lab coat over cargo pants, which made her look older, but still probably younger than her actual age. She waited for the guards to leave before she acknowledged me. "I'd like your opinion on a military matter."

"I'm out of that line of work."

"Call it an advisory role. Whatever helps you sleep." She pushed a button on her device and a three-dimensional map of Dome One and the surrounding area popped to life from a projector in one of her tables.

"Where are we on this?" I asked.

"Nice try. But I *will* share the plan, so you'll want to pay attention."

"Why would you do—"

She cut me off. "They're going to incite the hominiverts to attack human outposts."

"That's ridiculous." I responded without thinking. Of all the things I'd considered, that hadn't even crossed my mind. "And what's that got to do with me?"

"How would the military react to that?" she asked. "Would they be able to stop it?"

That was a good question. The military wasn't prepared, didn't have enough resources, but they could still fight in an emergency. Oxendine was deliberate, which probably meant she'd be slow to act. She'd want to gather intelligence first and build her case. The governor might interfere. I paused my thought. Something Eddleston said caught me. She'd said *they're*. Not *we're*. I wondered what that meant. More important, I wondered if I could use it. It couldn't hurt to fish for more information. "I'd need more detail on the attacks to answer that."

"In the near future, hominiverts from these locations"—a couple dozen red dots appeared on the map in different places. None of them were adjacent to Dome One, but, based on the scale, they all lay within two or three hundred kilometers—"will start moving in this general direction. We can't predict their exact path, but we expect them to overrun support domes here, here, and here." She indicated three small domes that lit up with blue dots. "This one here"—another dot lit up—"might be in the path as well. It's not an exact science."

"You'll be moving them using the sonic technology."

"It's crude, but it's all we have. The primates will continue in the direction of Dome One. We're not certain what they'll do as larger groups meet up, given their territorial nature. They may stop until one group establishes dominance over the others. But we think they'll keep moving."

"Because of the sonic torture."

"Right." That she didn't deny my term said a lot. "If you were the military commander and you found this threat, how would you react?"

"You brought me here to answer *that*? There are hundreds of ex-colonels you could have hired who would willingly answer this question for the price of a paycheck. And don't give me any shit about me somehow being better qualified. Because it's not true, and anybody who knows anything about the business would have told you that it's not true."

"It's in your best interest to be useful." She let the threat hang for a few seconds before continuing. "You have a combination of attributes that fits what we need. This . . . this is just because you're here."

The last bit didn't ring true. The slight hesitation— she was hiding something. It hit me then. They probably *did* have other retired colonels, but Eddleston wasn't part of the team. She'd said *they're*, but she wanted in. And she wanted me to help her. The colonels probably didn't work for her at all. Maybe they worked for Zentas, and she wanted to be able to contribute. As a civilian—and a young-looking one at that—military officers would ignore her. That's why she needed me. I could use that to my advantage, but to make it work, I'd need to gain her trust. "Okay. I'd find the cause of the changed behavior and attack the sonic broadcasters."

"Let's say you didn't know about them, and your first indication of the attack was at the overrun of the outer domes. The animals are within thirty kilometers of Dome One when you learn of it, and it's probably longer before you understand the extent of the threat."

"We're outside of the general here and into specifics. I don't really feel the need to help you." I *did* need to help her for a time, but I didn't want to make it too easy. She'd get suspicious.

"Let's be clear. Your team—Fader and crew—they're not off Eccasis yet. It would be easy to stop them."

I read it for a bluff, but I let it pass. It gave me a suitable reason to give in to Eddleston's demands. Once I did—once she came to rely on me—I'd figure out how to make her pay. On top of that, it didn't hurt to buy more time for Fader. I tried to look suitably cowed and hesitated before I spoke. "Okay. The primates are within thirty kilometers. Maybe closer. So it's an immediate problem. I'd need to know the threat to the dome itself—structurally—to assess exactly how much danger we're in by standing pat. The dome is solid, but I'm not sure about the integrity of the airlocks and gates. I'd put my engineers on that, first thing. Because standing pat and waiting it out is my best option."

"Your engineers suggest there is a risk of a breach . . . between five and ten percent, but reports come in of much more substantial damage to outer domes."

I thought about it, then answered the straightforward

part first. "Even five to ten percent is beyond tolerance because a breach would be catastrophic." That said, I shifted to her implication. There were two possibilities for receiving reports about substantial damage. Either they'd ensure the damage through some means or fake the reports. I wanted to know which. "How will the outer domes be different?"

Eddleston hesitated, probably trying to decide how much to share. If she was leaking stuff she shouldn't, that was another weapon for me to use later. "We'll make sure the damage happens. That's all I'm going to say about that."

So sabotage. That would change Oxendine's battle calculus. Now it was my turn to decide how much to give away. It didn't take me long. I had to give her something so she'd seem smart when she went back into a room with experts. That would build the trust I wanted to abuse later. "I'd need to know what assets they have to give you a specific answer, but in general, they're going to want to engage as far away from the dome as possible, so they will push out and try to divert them or, if they can't do that, stall them and buy time to figure out why they're coming. Deciphering that signal or finding its source isn't impossible. Especially since I can establish martial law and drag in experts for questioning."

Eddleston made a note in her device. I'd given her something useful, and she'd caught it. The martial law. Caliber employed the experts. They'd now make sure they were somewhere that the military couldn't get to them. That would give her something she could add to the planning that others may have overlooked.

"Can you stop the attack with the soldiers you have?" she asked.

"Maybe. It comes down to a decision for the commander as to whether she's going to try to delay, stop, or destroy. Given what you say about the destruction at the outer domes, I'd personally err on the side of destruction. But it's going to be a bit of trial and error, as I don't think anybody knows what it would take to stop an attack like that, since it's never happened. Explosive bullets and shoulder-fired rockets will work, but that puts soldiers at risk."

"But you'd use them?"

"If I had to. In a perfect world, I'd want more weapons. Armed drones if she has them. Bombers would be best, but I don't think there are any on the planet, and getting them from orbit, if they're there, would take time . . . that's possible, but I don't think they're there."

"If you had access to even bigger weapons, would you use them?"

"The big hunter-killer bots from a decade ago would be ideal, but she definitely doesn't have those. They're designed for stuff like this. They'd be almost invulnerable to attack from the 'verts, and they have the right weapons. The jungle would be tough terrain for them, but a smart commander could make them work."

"So you're saying that the military could defeat the threat if they had the right weapons."

"Obviously. Yes. You didn't need a colonel to tell you that. Any officer with three years in service could have come up with the same thing."

"But officers with three years in grade aren't going to be making decisions about whether people live or die. Tell me, what do you think *Brigadier General Oxendine* will do? After all . . . knowing people . . . isn't *that* your specialty?"

I smiled. I'd given her enough to hook her. I needed to end the discussion and let her sit with it for a while.

"I'm done playing games. Get Zentas out here and let's cut to the chase."

"It's a simple question. What will she do?"

"You already know."

"Not as well as you do."

I didn't need the flattery, but in this case, it was justified. I *did* know how Oxendine would react. Giving it to Eddleston would give her something that anyone else they had working for them might not have. It was what she wanted and, I hoped, the thing that would bring her back for more. "She'll follow her orders. If they don't fit, she'll try to get new orders."

"To the detriment of the colony."

"What? No. That's not how she'd see it."

"I don't understand."

I did my best to keep a neutral tone and avoid condescension. She needed to feel like I was treating her like an equal. "She'll see the long-term survival of the colony as more than the dome. There are political implications. She'll be aware of them, take them into consideration."

"What would *you* do in her place?"

"It's irrelevant. I'm not the commander, and there's no situation where I would be." Frankly, I didn't know what I'd do, but if I said that, it would undermine her confidence in me.

"She's going to delay," Eddleston said. "You know that. When she does make a decision, it will be too late."

"Still her decision to make. And if it's not hers, there are a hundred other people before it would even possibly get to me. Which it won't. Look, I've told you all I'm going to tell you. Now I want something in return."

"However I respond, you're not going to believe me."

"I want to talk to Zentas."

"He's not available."

She was right. I didn't believe her. "Fine. Then I want to go for a walk."

"You . . . what?"

"A walk. I live in a small cell, and I want exercise. You can put guards with me. I don't care. I'm an old man with a robot foot that acts up. I just want thirty minutes a day to stretch my legs."

She hesitated, probably trying to find my angle. I had one, but I doubted she'd find it in my reasonable request. "I'll see what I can do."

Which meant she didn't have the authority to make it happen. Another useful piece of information.

# CHAPTER TWENTY-FIVE

**I** **GOT MY WALK.** Two guards showed up to take me for a walk after dinner—one man and one woman, different from before, both wearing black jumpsuits and appearing to be unarmed. They probably had telescoping batons, or something similar, that I couldn't see. They wouldn't need them. I had no designs on escape. I'd be the perfect prisoner for now. I wouldn't even speak to them. Not the first time I went out. People would be watching. I had to establish a routine first and bore everyone to sleep. But I could gather information.

We walked a hallway that ran around the circumference of the base, which took approximately seventy seconds. Estimating 1.8 meters per second—it's just one of those things you know about yourself when you've been in the military as long as I have—that meant it was 125 meters. That made the base about forty meters in diameter, making the area about twelve or thirteen hundred square meters. We passed a staircase down, indicating at least one more level. On the opposite side of the base we passed a passage up, but that appeared to end in an airlock, so I assumed it led outside.

We also passed seven different narrow hallways and five doors, all on one side of the hall, and all of which had bio-encrypted locks. One of those—the biggest of them, probably to allow for the transport of large animals— led back to the block of four cells that had become my home as of late. We walked for about forty minutes, so I passed each door dozens of times, and I had the chance to study each without looking obvious about it. I tried to get a view of the airlock, but the slope of the tunnel didn't allow for it. Would they have environmental suits up there? Did it require a bio-authentication to work the door? For safety reasons, it shouldn't. But for legal reasons, this *place* shouldn't exist. So I probably couldn't count on them worrying about worker safety. I filed the information away for later.

EDDLESTON HAD ME escorted back to what I now believed was her office the next morning. I had no way to directly assess how the information I'd given her had helped her, but the fact that she'd brought me back gave some indication that she wanted more.

She didn't wait long to tell me what. "If you had to stop the hominivert advance and you had access to assets that the military didn't, what would you want?"

She was implying that there were on-planet military assets that Oxendine didn't control. I should have seen that coming. Caliber had a production shop, and Stroud had told me they could build what they needed. I'd seen enough of corporate-sponsored war to understand the situation, but that didn't make it right. I decided to play dumb for a minute. "Hello to you, too."

"I trust that you had a nice walk?" Subtlety wasn't her strong suit. What she gave, she could take away.

"Lovely, thank you. What are my choices? For assets." What I meant was, *What do you have?*

"Everything you need. Hunter-killer bots. Surface-to-surface missiles. Space-to-surface missiles, if necessary."

Everything *I* need. That's what she said. I had a bad feeling I knew their intent for me, but I needed to play it out to see for sure. "No way. They'd see any weapons you had on a space-based platform."

"They might. If they were looking. They're not. They're under-resourced, and we most definitely aren't."

I could believe that, and her body language suggested she wasn't bluffing. They had weapons, and they wanted *me* to use them. They wanted to kill a bunch of 'verts, and they wanted to blame me for it. Of course they did. Who better to blame than the galaxy's best-known mass killer of alien life? I needed her to say it. "Why am I here?"

"To make the decision to use the other assets."

"I told you. Not my call."

"You see a disaster coming that's going to cost human lives. Are you telling me that if you had the power, you wouldn't step in?"

"*You* have the power. You can simply turn off the sonic devices."

"Which we're not going to do."

"And you're not going to let *me* do that either."

"No."

"Because you want conflict. You want me to kill the hominiverts. Because you want them out of the way so that the planet can expand faster."

The door opened, and Drake Zentas walked in. His salt-and-pepper hair was perfect, and he wore the same cargo pants and pressed white shirt he'd met me in previously. How did you keep a shirt pressed under an environmental suit? That didn't matter. A huge figure in cargo pants and maroon workout shirt squeezed in behind him, muscles bulging. Jan Karlsson. Apparently I could get close to Eddleston without a guard, but not Zentas.

"Ms. Eddleston. You've been keeping our guest all to yourself. I went by his cell to see him, but . . ." Zentas let it trail off.

Eddleston's face reddened slightly, and she took an inadvertent step back away from the new arrivals. She and Zentas weren't on the same script—good news for me if I could figure out how to exploit that. "Yes, sir. Just trying to get ahead on the next phase of the plan."

"Of course." Zentas smiled and waved it away as if it didn't matter. But it did. The tension hung between them like a wet towel on a slack rope.

"You've been here all along and you're just now coming to see me. Why are we playing games?" I bailed Eddleston out of the immediate situation and threatened her at the same time. It drew Zentas's attention from her to me, but she and I both knew that she'd told me he wasn't here. A quick glance her way—she was holding her breath—and I knew I had her. If I told, she was in trouble.

"I'm a busy man, Carl. Please, no offense intended."

I did take offense, but felt it best not to share that. "Is this because I didn't take the job working for you? Kidnapping is supposed to convince me?"

He turned his palms up, as if it was that simple. A shrug. Asshole. "I wanted another meeting."

"My line was open. I could have stopped by."

"It was pretty clear that I needed a home-field advantage."

"Just cut to the chase. Why am I here?"

"You want me to say you're the only man in the galaxy who can pull this off? Is that what your ego needs?"

I let it sink in for a minute. Zentas had touched on it in our first meeting—people would listen to me about this sort of thing. They'd named the law after me. *Did he need me?* Either way, he'd worked to get me here, so he had a reason. I decided to provoke him, see if I could get him to make a mistake. "You killed your own daughter to get me here."

"That's a strong accusation, Carl. Once again, I do admire your stones. Though this time, I think you're just desperate."

"Tell me I'm wrong. It was the only way I'd agree to the mission. Serata played on my sympathy, because I'd lost a daughter." My mind jumped to Serata and his complicity. I didn't ask Zentas, because I wouldn't believe his answer either way.

"I'm not going to tell you anything," he said.

"Then let me tell *you* something: Your plan is ridiculous. There's no motivation for me to go along with your farce."

"Obviously I disagree. You asked me to cut to the chase, and I will. I offered you a job once, and you turned me down. I'm offering one more time, albeit with slightly revised terms. You work for me, you live and become a rich man. If not, we do the mission anyway, and your body turns up. You see, tragically, we had no idea what you were up to, and we had to stop you to protect the colony. Meanwhile, we clear the immediate area so we can expand a little quicker. It's not ideal, but it's still progress. And we highlight for the galaxy one more example of alien life being a threat to humanity."

I considered his plan. If he succeeded—if we lost settlements . . . if we lost soldiers . . . the galaxy *would* react. Polls would change overnight, and they'd change enough to make politicians switch their positions. Some of them, anyway. The true believers would hold, but the moderates—those who cared about public opinion more than right or wrong—would cave. Especially with someone like Zentas helping to stoke the pressure. He'd make sure it stayed in the news. But it would take time. More than he thought.

"Killing the hominiverts won't get you what you want. There are more dangerous animals here, and bombs and bots won't work on them. There are poisonous moths here that will rot off a limb. Don't even get me started on the bacteria. This planet isn't compatible with human life."

"Thank you for that lesson in terraforming. Of course it will take time. Years. But there's no way to finish if you don't start."

"You'll be dead before it's completed."

He gave me the deliberate palms up shrug again. "The burden of being a visionary. I'll be dead before a lot of my ventures come to fruition."

"Why are we having this conversation? I'm dead no matter what." He'd offered me riches, but that was because he had to give me hope. Without it, I had no motivation to help.

"There are worse things than death. You have family . . . a son, a granddaughter. I can make sure the news hits hard where they live," he said.

I froze.

"Thought that might matter," he said. "Besides, maybe you *do* live. I told you when I offered you the job the first time; you have value to me beyond this colony . . . *if* we can find assurances that you won't spoil the story."

They'd have assurances built in—I had no doubt. "Someone's going to spill even if you kill me. You know that, right? The story always gets out."

"It will. The key is to tell a louder story. We can do that. You can help. We'll have video of you in action. You'll make statements about how you assessed the situation, how you came to have the equipment . . . how you just *had* to act to save human lives. You'll be convincing. If not, there's always another take. We're obviously not putting you on live."

He had me. I believed him when he said that if I didn't cooperate, I'd end up dead. I didn't have to think too hard to decide between dying and living when dying didn't accomplish anything. As long as I lived, I could keep trying to find a way to screw Zentas over. I couldn't make it too easy, though. I put all the disdain I could muster into my voice. "You're going to kill humans to expand your business."

"It's not all about business. We need new planets. The shortsighted laws preventing expansion will cost millions of lives over time. Billions, perhaps. Sure, it will take fifty or a hundred years before that's realized, but it's coming. How many of our current planets are overcrowded?"

"You're talking to a guy who lives on Ridia Two. The idea of overpopulation is going to be a tough sell."

"*Pfft*. Ridia Two is in the middle of nowhere. It's useless. It's uncrowded because nobody wants to be there. This place though . . . half a billion people could live on this continent alone, and it's close to the trade routes."

"And you'd be happy to sell to them."

"Yes, I would. Doing something important for the galaxy and turning a profit aren't mutually exclusive. The population growth in the galaxy is expanding at an unsustainable rate for the livable planets we have. Smart people can see that. We've got a hundred, maybe a hundred and twenty years before it's a real problem. And that's *including* putting a billion new people on Ridia Two. Poor bastards."

"Someone will stop you." Even I knew that sounded weak.

"Who? Politicians? I doubt it. Nobody running for office looks more than a few years into the future, and they don't look more than a month into the past."

There was a hole in his plan . . . There always is. But I needed time to find it, and to do that, it was time to make him work to get me on board. "So what do you need from me? Just murder a bunch of hominiverts?"

"They're animals. It's not murder."

I shook my head, hesitated for a few seconds, looking down, pretending to be conflicted. In truth, I had nothing to lose. If people learned of my involvement, it would tarnish my reputation, but they couldn't really tarnish something I'd already blown to pieces years ago. I glanced at Zentas, who smiled. He knew he held a winning hand. He could afford to be gracious. "Can I have some time to think about it?"

"I told you before I'm not used to waiting. But for some reason, I feel magnanimous around you. So, yes. Absolutely. Take a day. I'm on a twenty-year timeline. I'm not going to worry over a question of what day of the week we start."

That worked for me. It gave Fader and the team time to get off the planet, and it gave me time to think about how to best position myself to ruin his plans. I gestured at Karlsson. "Am I a prisoner, or a guest?"

"As much as I'd like to say that you're a guest, I'm not letting you have free run of the place. So, I'm afraid it's the cell for now."

"I understand." I did. He wasn't an idiot. "Can a guy at least get a drink?"

"Of course." He turned to Karlsson. "Get Colonel Butler some whiskey. Something good." Turning back to me, he asked, "Is there anything else we can do for you while you make your decision?"

"I really hate being alone. I think I'd be more comfortable if Ms. Eddleston was in the cell next to me." Of course that wouldn't happen, but I got to watch Eddleston's face as she debated whether her boss would do that to her or not.

Zentas smiled, taking it for the joke I mostly intended. "I think I'll keep her out here and working."

"It was worth a shot." She'd set me up. I'd let them think I was over it.

I wasn't.

# CHAPTER TWENTY-SIX

AFTER A FEW drinks and a night of thinking about it, I had to admit that Zentas had played me perfectly. He'd appealed to my weaknesses to get me to the planet, and he'd shown me a false trail once I got here to drag me in deeper. I jumped right into the trap, and now he had me in a tough spot. He didn't need me. People knew I'd come to Eccasis, and if something happened to me, nobody would refute his story that I was involved with his twisted plan. Someone like Fader could protest, say that I wouldn't have gone down that path, but my history and the power of Zentas's propaganda machine would wash over that like the tide on a multi-moon planet. To be sure, he'd manipulated politicians and military leaders as well. They might be mad about it, but his money and their potential complicity made it unlikely that they'd make public waves.

All in all, it didn't look good for me, but in a weird way, that helped. Zentas wouldn't trust me—of course he wouldn't—but I *needed* him to be confident. If he didn't believe he had me under control, he wouldn't take risks. The only way to beat someone in a big pot is for them to think that they're going to win it. I didn't know if I could exploit that, but I would sure as shit try.

I started with the man who brought me breakfast. He

wasn't dressed like a guard, but he didn't have a badge with his job title, so I couldn't be sure. The tray he carried was loaded with too much food—bacon and eggs and biscuits and potatoes. No gravy, but it didn't seem like the right time to complain about the menu. I tried a different line. "Is there any word on whether my team made it off of the planet or not?"

"I'm not sure, sir." He met my eyes, and while I didn't know him, I'd have bet on him honestly not knowing.

"Any way you can ask someone for me? I understand it's probably above your authority level to find out and tell me yourself—I'm not trying to get you in trouble here."

"I'll pass the message. Yes, sir."

"Thanks. What's your name?"

"Hanson."

"Thanks, Hanson." Hanson probably wasn't the right guy, but I didn't care. I'd try everybody I met until I found someone I could use. Yes, that probably makes me a bad person. Whatever. It's what I do. I manipulate people. And this time I was pretty sure I was doing it for the right cause. I'd been manipulated too. But unlike last time, I knew it and could try to do something about it.

**MAYBE A COUPLE** hours later, Eddleston came to see me. I say *maybe* because I still didn't have any real way to tell time. They'd turned the lights off for me to sleep, then turned them back on at what I assumed was morning. I also assumed they would bring me lunch, which hadn't happened yet.

"Hanson relayed your question."

"And?"

"They've shuttled up to a larger ship, but it hasn't departed yet."

"Good." I could let them know my feelings about that. If they'd wanted to make a play for my team as hostages, they'd have never allowed them to get on that shuttle. Mac wouldn't have sent the report yet, but he'd do it before he went into cryo. Soon. But I doubted that would bring a swarm of soldiers to save me. I certainly couldn't rely on it. If I wanted to stop this, I'd have to do it myself. "You can tell your boss that I've made my decision, and I'll share it once they are safely on their way." I was playing dumb on purpose. Whether they left or not didn't matter. They could be seized just as easily at the opposite end of the trip, where they'd be in cryo and nearly helpless. But maybe someone on the other side would see me tying my already made decision to their departure as a mistake. I didn't know what that might accomplish, but any misinformation I could seed was good.

"I'll pass that on to him. And I'll be back for your decision once I have confirmation of the ship leaving orbit."


**LUNCH CAME AND** went, and Eddleston hadn't returned. Hanson didn't bring my meal, and the woman who did wouldn't respond to me in any way. I didn't know if my captors had made a deliberate change or if she just happened to be antisocial. Maybe she just hated me personally. I did have that effect sometimes.

Eddleston finally showed around dinnertime. I was lying on my bed and didn't get up. I didn't want to look too eager. "The ship has left orbit, headed for Talca Four."

"Thanks. I appreciate the information."

"Care to share your decision?"

"I'd be happy to. Is Mr. Zentas available?"

"He's not presently on the base, no. You can share it with me. I assure you that I'll relay it."

I pretended to consider it, lying there without looking at her. Unlike Hanson, whom I'd wanted to befriend, I wanted Eddleston to question our relationship. I thought her more likely to help me if she thought it would advance her standing with Zentas. She didn't care about me. She cared about her next promotion. I had to position myself in a way that made that promotion more likely if she helped me. I had some leverage. If I forced Zentas to come and take my statement personally, it would show Eddleston as unable to get the job done and she'd lose face. She'd lose the power of being my go-between. The question was, what would she be willing to do to avoid that? I let the silence hang for maybe fifteen seconds. "Sure, I can tell you. As long as you agree to deliver the context as well as the answer. Plus, I want you to answer a question."

"Of course." If my delay or conditions perturbed her, it didn't come across in her voice.

I levered myself to a sitting position and flipped my legs over the side of the bed. I wanted to watch her as we spoke. I'd come up with the seed of an idea that might screw up the mission, and I had to see her reaction. "I'll agree to help with the mission, but only as a means to minimizing casualties—both human and hominivert. And I want to be directly involved in how we do that. It's not that I don't trust you . . . well, yeah, actually, it's exactly that."

She remained businesslike and didn't give me anything I could use as she made a note in her device. "That's it? No demand to be allowed to roam free? To see the plan?"

"I'm not naïve. I know that's off the table. But the casualties . . . I feel like we can work together on that. Zentas and I." I threw the last bit in as a dig. She didn't react, but hopefully it hit her on the inside.

"Any specifics on that?"

I smiled, tipping off my joke. "Well, I'll need to see the plan."

She laughed. Good.

"Seriously, though, I think that we can choose the outer domes that get hit and save a lot of lives without losing the effect Zentas is looking for." I gave her that one for free. I expected her to take it to her boss as her own idea and to try to get credit for it.

She made her note. "In case he follows up, what are some of the things we might look for?"

I answered without hesitating, pretending her question was innocuous, so she might think she got something out of me. "We can look which ones have the lowest staffing. We can time the attacks to off-shift hours and reduce casualties that way."

Her face lit, a slight crack in her previously unreadable demeanor. She covered it quickly, but it had happened. "I'll pass along your decision, as well as your suggestion. We'll see what the boss thinks. Now, you said you had a question?"

"I did. I'm just curious, really. The hacker working from inside the military—Alexandra Trine—I assume she was yours?"

"Honestly, I don't know. We had someone working undercover, but they didn't read me in on that. I didn't have need-to-know."

"Is she working here?"

"I don't think so. I think they got her off planet once she finished her mission."

"Thanks. I appreciate your honesty."


**I HATED WAITING.** I'd played my hand with Eddleston, but I had no way to see the result until she returned. I ended up dozing off after dinner, which proved to be a bad idea because I woke with the lights out and then couldn't go back to sleep. Alone in a cell at night, my mind couldn't help but wander to all the ways this could go wrong or how I could be misreading the situation. Tonight's special angst included a continuous thought that a politician or someone like Serata was working with Zentas. Eddleston had fooled me. Who else had? Oxendine? My rational side doubted it, but my rational side didn't have control. I still had part of the bottle Zentas's man had provided, but I'd been trying to stay mostly sober. I had no idea when Eddleston would return, and I wanted a clear head. After a couple of hours—or what felt like a couple of hours—I gave in and poured myself a heavy double.

**EDDLESTON RETURNED THE** next morning while I was eating my breakfast. Hanson had brought it, but I'd given up on him as a target. Eddleston jumped straight to the point. "Mr. Zentas appreciated that you saw reason. He was less receptive to your suggestions on the bases. He believes that a certain number of casualties are necessary to put—and this is a quote—'a human face on the tragedy.'"

I hadn't expected he'd acquiesce immediately. I'd keep working at it. My first goal was to stop the entire plan, but if I couldn't do that, I at least wanted casualties as low as possible. "Hmmm. And what do you think?"

"I think he's the boss, and if that's his plan, we don't have a lot of room to work. Your help was predicated on limiting casualties. I can no longer promise that."

I appreciated her candor, and her implication that we had a deal and she'd stick to her side of it. "There's still room to work together on this. He says we need *some* casualties. Unless he's got a specific number, we're still negotiating. I'd argue that fewer could be better, as long as you got the right people."

"What do you mean by that?"

"As you said, he's the boss, so it's important that we acknowledge his goal and show that we're working toward it. He wants a human face on things, and I agree that casualties would do that. But what's more human than a survivor?"

She nodded, though I'm not sure she meant to. "Survivors. That could work."

"We'd need somebody with a good story. Somebody photogenic, but not too slick. Somebody with kids. Maybe a combination. Someone they can plaster all over the news."

"We plant an actor?" She sounded eager.

"No way. That might work well at the beginning, but when the truth about it came out, it would undermine the entire effort. We do our research, find the person—or better yet, people, so there are multiple options—and time the attacks so they are on duty. Then we make sure they survive. The press handles the rest."

"I'll tell you right now, Mr. Zentas won't want to leave it up to chance, and he'll reject any solution that does."

"He's got influence with the press. It's hardly chance if you control all the variables."

She made a note. "Just so we're clear, I don't trust you. You're not going to make me believe that you're on board with this."

"I'm on board with minimizing casualties." She couldn't possibly detect a lie in that, because I spoke truth. If I lied, she'd shut down on me. But I kept my real reason to myself.

To make sure that Zentas went down.

# CHAPTER TWENTY-SEVEN

EDDLESTON AND I kept going like that through-out the day and into the next. Zentas seemed genuine in his statement that we weren't in a rush, and while I didn't see him, Eddleston assured me every time she came that our planning pleased him. That Zentas didn't seem to be on base seemed odd. He wouldn't be in the main dome during the attack. Or maybe he would. That would give him the ultimate alibi, after all. Did he have the guts to put himself at risk like that? I suppose foreknowledge and preparation lessened the danger. I wanted to know his planned location during the mission, and to learn that, I needed to communicate outside of my little prison.

That became my objective when Eddleston showed up after breakfast.

She had a canvas bag with her, much like she'd had the previous day, when she'd brought me new clothes. "More clothes," she said.

"Thanks," I said. "How did it go with the boss?"

"I think we've got the bases selected, and we're work-ing on the timing. It's a lot of work, sifting through all the schedules to select the ones with minimal staffing." She opened the door with her palm and a seven-digit code and handed me the bag. That she felt safe enough to do that meant that she still didn't see me as a threat. That gave me a last-ditch option if I couldn't change Zentas's plan into something I could stomach. I could probably disable Eddleston and mess some stuff up around the base before they got me.

"Sure. There are—what, thirty thousand people colonyside? It's not like you can put this into a public search engine. How are we doing on casualties?" I asked.

"We're projecting between nine and fourteen right now. One of the most logical targets never has fewer than six, even on the shortest shift."

"That's still too many," I said.

"What am I supposed to do about it?"

"Look, I'm working for *you*. You get in there and work for *me*. Get that base taken off the list."

"There's no way. It's right in the path, and a diversion around it would take too much work."

"So don't sabotage that one."

"What do you mean?" she asked.

"The domes aren't at much risk unless we give the 'verts a way in, right? So don't give them a way into that one. Let them flow around it."

"I'm not sure he'll buy that."

"*Try*," I said.

She sighed. "Fine. But right now, we've got another issue to work through. We're trying to figure out how to stop this whole thing once it's going full bore. Mr. Zentas wants the horde to get within five hundred meters of one of the heavily staffed domes. The problem is, once we get them that close, we lose the ability to destroy them without risking blowing up the dome too."

"Yeah. There's a reason we don't turn missiles and bots loose on colonized planets." *Imagine that.*

"He's not going to back off of that requirement, so if we don't figure something out and the 'verts do breach that dome, we could be looking at a tenfold increase in casualties." She stared me down, and I began to wonder who was manipulating whom. I hoped my attempts weren't quite so ham fisted as hers.

"I'm sure Zentas has former officers on his staff who can figure this out."

"I'm sure he does. But are they as good as you?"

*Probably.* "I don't know."

"More accurately, are they as motivated as you to save lives?" She had me there. But it also gave me an opportunity.

"What weapons do we have in the inventory? There are at least seventy variations of war-bots. I'll need the specs." Murder aside, it posed an interesting problem. The bots weren't built to do close defense of a settlement, but a lot of military gear did stuff the designers hadn't planned for once you put it in the hands of innovative soldiers. I'd once watched a soldier heat her soup on the engine of a ground-support aircraft.

Eddleston thought about it a moment. "I'll get you a briefing on the arsenal."

"We've also got to figure out how we deploy it. We can't position the bots ahead of time. It would spoil the story. I'll need to know ships and other delivery assets. Plus, platforms that fire missiles. Everything we use will have to be mobile if we want to make it look like we reacted after the threat materialized."

She sighed. "I'll try to figure out how to get you all of that."

"Just put me on a targeting terminal. I'll make it happen."

She smiled. "Nice try."

"I'm not trying anything. You want me to lead this counterattack? Then I need to know. *Someone* is going to have to synch the assets and get them tasked. At a minimum, I'm going to need to talk to the person doing that and make sure they know their business. This isn't rookie-level shit." If she took that as an insult, I could live with that.

"You will definitely be in the room during execution."

Of course I would. They'd want video of that. "I need to be in there for planning before that."

"I'll take it under advisement."

"Thank you. And don't forget my walk."


**IT WAS THE** third time I went on a walk, and I got the same two guards—a man and a woman. On about lap fifteen, I decided to engage them.

"How long you been here?" I asked.

Neither responded.

I didn't change my tone. "Not here, specifically, if you can't talk about that. How long have you been colonyside?"

The man glanced at the woman, who shrugged slightly. *That's right. There's no harm in answering a simple question.* "About a year," he said.

"Same," said the woman.

"Pay good?"

"Better than the military," said the woman.

"Usually is," I said with a chuckle. "Same kind of duty?"

"Easier," said the man. "But they don't tolerate fuckups as much. They expect us to do our jobs without being told all the time. And there's no manual for simple stuff, like how to sweep a hangar."

I fully laughed this time. "That must be nice. I wonder how much they'd pay a guy like me."

"You're not getting paid?" asked the woman.

"You *did* see that they're keeping me in a cell, right?"

"Guess I didn't think about it. Doesn't seem right, you being a war hero, and all that."

I didn't agree with her assessment of my hero status, but I wasn't going to disabuse her of the notion when it worked to my advantage. I might have found the break I needed. "They don't want me leaving, I guess. I'm working on the plan for the attack."

"No shit?" said the guy.

"No shit." I stopped talking for a lap or two. Cameras monitored us all along the hall, and I didn't want to look too chummy. The silence worked to my favor, because it made them more curious.

"Can you tell us what we're going to be doing?" the woman asked.

They kept their soldiers in the dark. Not uncommon, but it made troops nervous. I'd use that too, but I couldn't seem too eager. "I really shouldn't. If the bosses wanted you to know, I'm sure they'd have briefed you."

"What they don't know won't hurt them," suggested the man.

"Cameras." I nodded to one as we passed.

"They don't have sound," said the woman. "They'll see us talking, but they won't know what we're saying. If someone asks, we'll make up some bullshit."

I stayed silent for half a lap, pretending to think about it. "They're expecting something to happen with the hominiverts. The green apes. But you didn't hear it from me."

"Oh, shit," said the woman.

"About time," said the man. "We'll blow the shit out of 'em."

I hadn't considered sowing discontent until that moment, but when life presents an opportunity, I don't pass. I tried to come up with the most damaging possible rumor. "If they let you."

"What do you mean?" they asked, almost simultaneously.

"Relax," I said, indicating a camera. "Hey, what's down there?" We passed the stairway down.

"Living space and the mess hall," said the guy. "Come on. What did you mean, *if they let us*?"

I pretended to think about it. "The boss is scared. He's a civilian, you know?"

"Fuuuck," said the woman.

"You get the pay, but you also get the civilians," I said. "What can you do?"

I knew what *I'd* done. I'd planted a seed that would spread among the soldiers and make them question their leadership. It wasn't much, but it was the first time in a long time I felt like I'd accomplished *something*.

# CHAPTER TWENTY-EIGHT

WHEN I GOT back to my cell, someone had brought in a portable table and chair, along with a tablet. I picked it up and opened the interface. Of course it didn't have a connection to a network. It did have a series of files, but it looked like someone had dropped them without any sort of a searchable database. Eddleston came in a few minutes later.

"Seriously?" I said. "Dump files?"

"You wanted access to our material, but we couldn't have you on the network. It was a compromise."

I shook my head. "Okay. I'll get to work on this. It won't be as easy as if I had access to the whole system."

She fake-smiled. "We all sacrifice for the cause."

That line stayed with me after she left. Did they? What portion of Zentas's empire was actually in on this? The soldiers I'd walked with hadn't known. They probably kept it to as small a crew as possible. Even after the fact, they'd want as few witnesses as they could manage. That led me to a darker place. If I could kill Eddleston and Zentas, would that end the plan? Not that I could pull that off. One, maybe. I doubt I'd get the opportunity for both. Eddleston had let her guard down enough to get close to me without an escort, but I doubted her death would stop anything. And Zentas wouldn't be so lax. On top of that, I didn't have any weapons, unless I wanted to hit someone with the tablet they gave me.

I'd call that Plan C.

Plan A was on a ship on its way out of the system, and Plan B was more pressing. I flipped through the files, concentrating first on the bots. There was a reason that the military rarely used them—they had flaws— and maybe I could exploit that. It was tricky, because I needed two different sets of parameters. I needed a bot that would serve the purpose that Zentas thought I wanted—saving people without collateral damage— which at the same time would also allow me to thwart their plan. I broke the second part into two pieces: First, stop the attack, and second, get them caught. If I could only manage one of those, I'd probably still take it.

I had to be careful of the biases in my own thinking. From the start, I'd thought about taking out the low-frequency broadcasters, but I had to put that out of my head because it ran the risk of blinding me to better answers. That's always a tough thing to do. It's like when someone tells you not to think about bugs in your sleeping bag, but then you can't help it.

After an hour I focused in on the Mark XI. It had originally been developed (by one of Zentas's companies, I learned) to hunt a specific animal on Tau 4, two decades ago. Someone on the design team had thought ahead and allowed variable parameters. We could program it to target a specific species and only that species. It also came with a high-velocity 14-millimeter weapon, which could function as a seriously overpowered hunting rifle. The round would penetrate just about anything, including the wall of a dome, so it presented risks. But it didn't explode, so that helped.

The bot itself wasn't ideal for jungle warfare, with four legs and standing almost three meters high. It looked a little like a giant headless dog, if the dog were made of metal composites and had rifles in its shoulders. I'd have to figure out a way to deliver them right where I needed them to keep them from bogging down in the foliage. We had twenty-two available, which would require at least two aircraft. The small number also probably wouldn't stop a concentrated wave, but we'd be okay if we kept it to a few hundred 'verts.

I also found the FL-207. Made by my old friends at Omicron, it was an old-model flying bot that had been used in a jungle environment to target a specific species of flying rodent. The rodent in question emitted a sonar-like signal, and the bot used that to home in on them. The same function would allow them to find sonic emitters, which made them perfect for what I wanted. They were small, with a 0.6-meter wingspan, and had limited ammunition, but what they did have was ideal for taking out transmitters. They fired an eleven-millimeter rocket that exploded into a shotgun pattern as it approached the source of the sound. Unfortunately, they were *too* perfect, so there was no way Zentas would let me have them. And it would tip off my plan if I asked. They had no viable use for the mission—they wouldn't do anything to a hominivert except piss it off.

If I could somehow get to the arsenal, though . . .

I didn't realize how long I'd been staring at the stuff until dinner arrived. It was Hanson again, the guy from breakfast. "You got promoted to dinner duty?"

"I was just going off shift and the person who was supposed to do it was busy, so I volunteered."

"Thanks for doing that," I said.

"It wasn't much of a sacrifice. Hope you enjoy."

I did enjoy it. There was grilled chicken and a salad with a creamy dressing that I couldn't quite place but had great flavor. I let my mind drift, and for whatever reason, Hanson's statement stuck in my head. *Wasn't much of a sacrifice.* And then I had it. I'd been looking at it all wrong. I was looking for a technological solution when I needed a human one.

I needed to talk to Zentas.

**I BROACHED THE** subject of meeting with him the next time I saw Eddleston, but she had no intention of letting me see her boss anymore. She had control of me, and she liked it that way. She probably didn't want me letting Zentas in on the fact that most of *her* ideas were in fact *mine*. I didn't intend to do that, but I couldn't come right out and tell her that without revealing what I was actually doing. She stood in front of my cell, hands on both hips, head up, jaw square, like something out of a book on how to take charge of a situation. I couldn't get over how young she looked. I'd always pictured the face of evil to be older.

"He's not available." She almost sneered as she said it.

"Ever?" I'd been fine with the situation, but I couldn't let her dictate everything. I wanted to change how we fought the mission, and only Zentas could do that. I also wanted to ask him a question about something unrelated. It had come to me, the night before, when I couldn't sleep. Why had he had someone plant the bomb to kill me outside the governor's? It didn't matter much now, but once it got in my head, I couldn't get it out.

"He's happy with the current arrangement." Her attitude was pissing me off.

I made the decision right there to destroy her.

"You mean the arrangement where you pass on my ideas, but you don't tell him where they came from? Is *that* the arrangement that makes him happy? You know he's not stupid, right?"

She didn't respond, but the power façade cracked for a second and her face reddened. The truth hurts. I'd put voice to what we'd previously left unspoken, and now she couldn't pretend that I didn't know. She tried to hide it, but when she spoke, it was with a touch less confidence. "And?"

And now it was time to make her pay for it. I let her stare me down, and finally broke off the eye contact. I let out a small breath—not quite a sigh, didn't want to be *too* melodramatic—and said, "Fine. If I can't talk to him, you pass on the idea."

"What have you got?" She didn't even sound suspicious. She thought she'd broken me. I almost felt bad for her. Almost.

"It's the FL-207s. They fly, so they're maneuverable through the jungle, and they have a low-yield weapon that won't cause a lot of collateral damage. We've got seventy of them in the inventory. Because they can fly, we can bring them in after the attack starts. I just need Zentas's engineers to work to modify the targeting system so that they focus specifically on the hominiverts. Maybe a size profile, or something, unless there's a big enough heat difference between the primates and a human." I threw that last bit in there to distract her.

"They're about a degree below human. I'm not sure if that's enough for targeting." She fell for it. As a xenobiologist, she probably had to.

"I don't think that will be enough for the bots to differentiate with the jungle clutter. That's why I need Zentas. I need to know what his engineers can modify within the specs of the bots. There's nothing in the inventory that serves our purposes as is. We're going to have to do some work."

"I'll pass it along and see what they can do."

I hoped she did.


**EDDLESTON STARED LASERS** at me when she and Zentas showed up the next morning during my breakfast. Apparently my plan worked. With her boss there, she couldn't yell at me about it, which made it funnier, and I had to hide a smile behind a bite of eggs.

"I'm disappointed, Carl. The FL-207? That's an amateur-level attempt. You want me to give them to you so that you can target them against the low-frequency broadcasts."

"Give me some credit. I knew you'd see through it. But Genocide Barbie over there wouldn't let me talk to you, so I had to do something to get your attention. You've probably figured out by now that she doesn't know what she's doing and that everything she's given you over the last few days came from me."

If a glare could get even more angry, Eddleston's did. I smiled openly this time. Screw her.

"It's not genocide. They're not human," said Zentas, missing the point.

"That's your takeaway from this?"

"You wanted to see me, Carl. What do you want?"

"I wanted to ask you a question. You wanted me here so you could use me to further your cause . . . so why try to assassinate me outside the governor's mansion?"

"*That's* why you wanted to see me?"

"No. But you're here, and it's been bothering me. I can't figure it out."

He considered it, probably wondering whether to tell me the truth. I figured he would. It fit his style. "We didn't try to kill you. You were never in danger from the bomb. You were *meant* to find it."

Interesting. So he'd wanted to use it to scare me . . . or no, not scare me. To get me looking toward EPV and simultaneously keep me from leaving. Like I'd done to him, he'd used my own stubborn nature against me.

He was good.

"What about the hominivert attack on my patrol? That seems risky."

"A calculated risk. You seem to have an innate ability to survive. And we could have driven off the animals at any time by turning off the broadcasters driving them toward you and turning on the one nearby to push them away."

"It was a good move. You really threw me off the trail with that one. I never suspected the setup." It was true, but it also didn't hurt to stroke his ego a little.

"It worked for a while, but ultimately fell short of the goal."

"Which was?" I asked.

"I wanted you to see EPV as the enemy."

Of course. If I thought EPV tried to kill me, I'd want to get back at them, which in another timeline could have led me into the arms of Caliber sooner. "I did— for a while, at least. I wonder how things would have worked out if I'd taken that bait fully."

"I wonder too. And while I'd love to stand around and chat all day, Carl, I'm a busy man. Can you get to the point?"

"I've got a solution that meets your needs and saves lives."

"And why should I trust you?"

*He shouldn't.* But I still had to make my play. "Send *me*."

"Send you where?"

"To the site where the hominiverts attack. Send me there. You need an optic . . . something that will make the news and bring public opinion to bear. Who would make more news than me on the ground trying to save the day?"

He thought about it. "Interesting. You'd sacrifice yourself like that?"

"You're going to kill me anyway."

"Not necessarily." That he didn't straight-up say he wouldn't made me respect him a little bit. It also meant he was cocky, which I was counting on. "But I'm intrigued. Why would you do it though? Are you trying to change your legacy? 'Hero dies trying to save lives as marauding animals terrorize human outpost'— something like that?"

"If I die, nobody else has to," I said.

"Perhaps," he said, but his tone said he didn't agree.

"And we don't need to kill the hominiverts, either. Once they've killed me and trashed a dome, you've got everything you need."

He stayed silent for several seconds. "No, I don't think that will work. We need their bodies on the scene. We can't have any doubt about what happened and that the animals were responsible." I started to protest, but he held up his hand. "*But* . . . we may be able to do it with significantly fewer animal deaths—not that I care either way in that regard." He thought about it some more. "If we did it, we could make sure they've destroyed a couple uninhabited domes before they got to your location."

He was close to saying yes, but I wasn't ready to quit. "How many fewer casualties?" I didn't have any leverage with which to negotiate, and we both knew it. Zentas was polite enough not to point it out.

"We'll see how it goes." I took that for agreement. I didn't blame him for not caving on the casualties. He didn't have to concede anything, and he didn't. "Why don't you start by telling me your plan?"

"I want the Mark XIs."

"Interesting choice. Do they have enough firepower to drive the apes away?"

"There are twenty-two of them. I guess it depends on how many hominiverts show up."

"Thousands. Nonnegotiable."

Well then. I was fucked. No way could I win that fight. "Sure. I can do it," I said. "I'll need some noisemakers, though. Missiles or bombs. It doesn't matter which, as long as I can deliver and target them precisely. Give me a helmet with an interface and I'll put them where I need them."

Zentas considered it, trying to read me, probably. This was the moment that mattered. He flinched but didn't give in. "What do you need the missiles for?"

I was ready for that question and answered without hesitation. Sounding confident mattered. "The Mark XIs can kill individual hominiverts, but with only twenty-two of them, depending on how the battle goes, we take out maybe a couple hundred 'verts before we get overrun. I don't expect that that will be enough to make them quit, and I don't know if you turning off the transmitters will cause them to leave or if they'll keep going in the same direction. It's hard to predict the results of a free-for-all. You can't have a set of transmitters near the dome to stop them, because there's too much chance that someone will discover them, which will expose your plan. So I need some explosions to add to the chaos and scare them away. Give them a better reason to turn around."

Zentas started to speak, but I cut him off.

"*And* if everything goes to shit—and everything *always* goes to shit—I can target the primates directly with the missiles and kill a bunch. Call it a backup plan."

He stayed silent for almost a minute, thinking. "So you're not going to use the missiles to try to attack the low-frequency broadcasters."

*Of course* I was. "No. There are too many of them, and I don't know their locations. It would be pointless—literal shots in the dark." It wasn't a total lie. It would be an almost impossible task. That didn't mean I didn't intend to try. "And while we're discussing things that you're not going to like, I actually do want four FL-207s. And before you say no, hear me out. You can send them up without ammunition. But they're faster and more maneuverable than drones; plus, they've got better AI, which I need since I'm working this solo. They're perfect for this mission. I need eyes in the air to help me target."

"No ammunition?"

"I just need the camera feeds so I can see where to target the missiles to drive off the bulk of the hominiverts."

"And if you try to change the deal midway through?" asked Zentas.

"I'm sure you'll take care of that part."

"That's pretty cynical."

That didn't make it wrong. He'd have a fail-safe to make sure I died valiantly. "I don't expect you'll leave things to chance," I said.

"No, I won't."

"Then we have a plan?"

"We have a plan. Two days. Make your final arrangements for what you need with Ms. Eddleston. I have business elsewhere."

I wanted to know where he'd be when the mission happened, but I couldn't ask. It might tip him off that I wasn't playing straight. He suspected that, of course. He'd expect me to try something, just as I expected that he'd try to kill me. But his ego would tell him that he was smarter than I am and that he'd be a step ahead. Maybe he would be. I guess we'd find out.

# CHAPTER TWENTY-NINE

**M**Y GUARDS SHOWED up for my walk, which I hadn't expected after screwing over Eddleston. Either she wasn't bitter or she forgot to tell somebody to turn it off. That was good, because I needed the opportunity to do something ridiculous. On the surface, the idea of doing something stupid is counterintuitive. But in this case, I needed it. Zentas thought he held the winning hand; however, he'd think a level beyond that. He'd know that I also knew he had the winning hand, and then he'd get suspicious of why I didn't fold, which would make him reevaluate. I couldn't have that.

I needed a diversion.

My plan relied on misdirection. I needed Zentas looking one way while I manipulated things somewhere else, and a single diversion wouldn't do, because he'd expect it. I needed him to think he'd found the diversion so he wouldn't expect the next one. Diversions within diversions. The more moving pieces I had, the harder it would be for him to tell the cover play from my real move.

Unfortunately, I had to manipulate some ground-level grunts to make it happen by taking advantage of the trust I'd built up with the guards. While I didn't take pleasure in it, I could live with myself. They'd chosen the wrong team.

The same two soldiers came to get me—the man and the woman. I still didn't know their names, and I didn't ask. Not knowing made it easier to screw them over. We walked for a bit, and I stayed quiet, waiting for them to make the first move. They would. I had no doubt. They'd been left in the dark, and soldiers in the dark would always seek out illuminating information.

The woman spoke first. "So . . . any more information on the big mission?"

"Looks like it might be all automated," I said.

"They've got us preparing weapons like we're part of it," said the man.

"Backup, maybe? I'm not sure. How fucked up is that? I'm planning this thing, and they don't even tell me." I left the *fucking civilians* unsaid, but they got the message. "Hey, what's up there?" I asked, as we walked by the ramp up to the airlock.

"Airlock," said the man.

"To the outside?" I asked.

"Yeah. Of course."

"Damn, I thought we were way underground. I haven't seen daylight in a week."

"You get used to it," said the woman.

"Not sure I ever will." I let it go for another two laps. I couldn't push it too hard. We made small talk, until I brought it back around. "You think I could look outside?"

They glanced at each other, uneasy. "We would, sir, but cameras."

"Who's going to care? There's a window there if there's an airlock. I just want to see the real world. Come on. What am I going to do? I don't have an enviro-suit. It's not like I can run away."

It took three more laps around the compound, but they finally gave in. The ramp up was wide—big enough to accommodate a large primate—and had a shallow grade. It leveled into a wide platform at the top, probably so they could receive goods, cycle the airlock, and then worry about distributing them down into the base proper. The inside door had a small round window, and through it I could see that there were no enviro-suits inside the airlock. That worked for me. I moved to cycle the door.

"What are you doing?"

"Having a look." I didn't stop, and they didn't physically move to intercept me, so I entered the airlock. It was large for an airlock, maybe four meters in diameter, to allow for large deliveries. It had two doors to the outside—a standard personnel door, and a lift door. I moved to the personnel door because it had a window, which fit the story I'd given them for being there. The door behind us *thunked* shut, and the pressure pushed against my ears.

"It's funny, how you miss this kind of thing," I said.

Neither responded, but the man tapped his foot and looked back through the other door, as if he expected someone to be there any second. Someone might, for all I knew. It wouldn't matter.

"Thanks. I needed that." I stepped away from the window after half a minute and stretched. As the woman moved toward the door to cycle us back in, and both of them lost focus on me for a second, I sprang toward the bay door, turned the handle to unlock it and hit the button to open it.

Klaxons blared and a red light flashed.

The three of us stared at each other, but nobody moved. The door rose slowly behind me with a rumble.

"What the fuck did you do?" yelled the woman over the hiss of the vents spewing air trying to keep overpressure.

I shrugged. "Sorry." I turned and ducked under the rising door.

I ran.

They hadn't expected it. How could they? No sane person would run into a contaminated environment without a suit. They couldn't know that I wanted to appear less than sane.

A hard-packed dirt road led away from the underground facility and I followed it. Jungle loomed on either side, and if I wanted to hide, I could have gone either way. Problem was, I couldn't hide. I didn't have a suit on, and exposed to the climate and fauna of the planet, I could measure my life span in hours. But so could my escorts. How they reacted would determine what happened next. If they chased me, they'd catch me, being half my age and in better shape. But their training conditioned them to fear the outside—correctly—so maybe they'd hesitate.

It didn't matter. If they caught me, it still served my purpose. I'd told Zentas that I'd sacrifice myself, so by trying to escape, it made *that* look like my plan. I acted beaten, then tried to bolt.

I slowed to a fast jog. I had no idea where I was going, but the road led *somewhere*, and anywhere would do. If I could find any government-controlled camera on this Mother-forsaken planet, someone might see me. That would be even better than getting caught, even though Zentas would probably kill me before any rescue arrived, to keep me from talking—

Something slammed into me from behind, and I went down hard. Not *something*. *Someone*. It was my male escort. "You *asshole*!" he said. My head rang and my eyes whited-out for a split second as he punched me in the back of the head. I rolled to my right, trying to throw him, but he held on with his legs and drove what felt like a forearm into my neck, driving my face into the dirt.

"Just zip tie him," said the woman from behind me. "Stop beating him up."

"This fucker just sent us all to quarantine," complained the man.

"That's the least of our worries. We've got an audience back in the airlock. We're in a shitload of trouble," she said.

"I really am sorry," I said. "Ow!" The zip tie dug into my wrists. I couldn't blame the guy.

"Shut up," said the man.

"They're going to kill me, you know. What was I supposed to do? Sit there and wait?"

"We all do what we gotta do," said the woman. "Get up, or I'll have McCombs drag you."

"Stay down," said the man. "Do it. Fucking try me."

*No, thank you.* I struggled to my feet, awkwardly, since he'd bound my hands behind my back and I was still a little woozy. They marched me back to the airlock where six or seven other people waited, all in full enviro-suits. I guess they had a plan to deal with runaways.

I spent the last full day of what might be the rest of my life in a makeshift isolation room. They wrapped my cell in plastic. Apparently, the facility didn't have a true quarantine. They probably took the two guards somewhere that had one. Either way, I never saw them again.

Eddleston came by to see me—probably to watch me suffer. They had rigged a speaker system so she could talk to me from outside. "Why'd you do it?"

"There's no way that Zentas lets me live through this mission. I figured I had better odds in the jungle."

She considered it. "Maybe. Or maybe you had another reason."

"Yeah? What reason would that be?"

"I don't know. I've got a team out there sweeping the area, making sure you didn't drop some sort of transmitter."

"I didn't." I hadn't even thought of it, and even if I had, I didn't have one. I didn't care that she didn't believe me. The search would make some soldiers miserable, which lowered the morale of my enemy. One more small thing that might help me win. "We'll see."

It impressed me that she didn't mention what I did to her in front of her boss—how I'd made her look bad. I'm not sure how she did that. It had to be eating her up on the inside. Or maybe that's just me. That would be another one for my shrink, I guess, if I ever talked to her again. It didn't seem likely. Perhaps that was why Eddleston could let it go. She knew I was going to die and could take comfort in that.


**BY THE TIME** I got out of quarantine, they'd finalized the plan. I got a lot of what I wanted, but not everything, which was to be expected. The first two domes—the sabotaged ones that we expected the 'verts to destroy—were unoccupied. There were more sabotaged domes along the way, but Zentas had finally agreed to let the 'verts bypass the one with the greatest number of people on duty. At least that's what they told me. I couldn't verify it, so I let it go. I had to fight the fight I could and not the one beyond my control.

My fight would come at what would hopefully be the end of the whole thing, in front of Dome 19B, a research center for a non-Caliber company. Records showed peak population for the dome at eighteen, but the main shift would have cycled out more than two hours prior, leaving seven people on duty. Maybe. I didn't exactly trust the source of the information. The number didn't matter. This was the dome I could save if I did things right, and whether seven or eighteen, I'd try to save everybody in it.

I understood that it might be a last stand for me, that Zentas intended it to be. I could live with that. Or die with that, as it was. I might have saved some lives, so if my time was up, at least I'd have used the last days doing something worthwhile. Make no mistake—I didn't intend to follow the plan. But even my version held a lot of risk. Thinking about all that the night before the mission should have had me keyed up, but I slept, peaceful and dreamless for the first time in forever.

# CHAPTER THIRTY

T RAINED ON the day I was scheduled to die. Because of course it did. An enviro-suit was waterproof, obviously, but the water running down my faceplate would screw with the way my heads-up display looked, forcing me to concentrate harder to do even simple tasks. And I had a lot of tasks. I'd sold the plan to Zentas as me on the ground directing the entire operation. It stretched the boundaries of what I could manage, especially when half of it was a deception. I also had to watch for the moment of Zentas's treachery. I could have used a good executive officer helping me manage the less important parts of my plan, but you fight with what you've got, not what you wish you had.

I asked to get to the site early so I'd be set when the 'verts arrived, but Zentas said no. He wanted to maintain the illusion that we reacted after the attacks started, and I couldn't blame him for that. I had to try, though.

I got reports of the first two domes falling via the comm in my helmet. I didn't have access to the camera feeds that someone had hacked from the two facilities, but I could monitor the Ops net. They hit the correct two domes, and both were, as planned, unoccupied. The compromise of the facilities would set off alarms when the 'verts breached it, but alarms went off all the time, and no dome had ever been breached. There would be no rush to check them, and when they eventually did, they probably wouldn't immediately alert the military. That would fit Zentas's plan and allow the 'verts to get deeper into settled territory before Oxendine's team tried to react. That was the good news.

The bad news: there were enough 'verts involved to draw audible "oh shits" from the Ops crew.

I got the unarmed FL-207s up in the air first, which gave me four video feeds that I set to cycle through in the top right corner of my display, shifting through the cameras at three-second intervals. I gave each bot a search sector, quartering the zone where I expected the first 'verts to appear. I needed early warning and needed to track their speed and direction so I could predict their arrival. It also projected what anyone watching would expect me to do with them, and I had no doubt someone was watching.

I had initial estimates on where to expect the 'verts from the work I'd done on the map, but no plan ever lasted long in the real world, and I couldn't afford to mistime my moves. At the moment, though, *how many* concerned me more. The more that came, the more destructive I'd have to get. The fewer of them that attacked, the fewer I'd have to kill to get them to leave. I hoped for the best but planned for the worst, because it usually went that way. I'd try to save them, but as always, if it was them or me . . . it was them.

I waited in the airlock, sitting in a cart that would take me to my first ship. I had two. One carried twelve Mark XI combat bots and three missile launchers, while the other carried the remaining ten bots. We waited a few more minutes after the attacks on the first domes. When someone played back the radar tracks after the fact—and someone would—they'd see me reacting to a crisis.

I couldn't say for sure what the military would do when they got their first report, but they wouldn't react in time. I didn't know much for sure, but that part . . . I'd have bet a lot on it. Oxendine would look for more information, especially after being burned with our covert mission on the hidden dome. Much like me, she'd employ sensors, but without drones, she'd be stuck trying to get a view from satellites, which wouldn't find enough information through the jungle cover. Time would tick by as she gathered intel, and by the time she acted, the battle at Dome 19B—my dome, twenty-four klicks away from Dome 1—would be over. She'd consider air assets, but the 'verts would be too close to the dome for her to use missiles without destroying it. After that, she'd finally dispatch ground troops, just in time to find the aftermath. I'd try to leave them a sign, but Zentas would expect me to do that, and he'd have a plan to stop it.

I had on a Caliber enviro-suit and helmet, and they could monitor everything I saw and heard. The second I even flipped to a wrong frequency, they'd push a button and turn my helmet into dead weight. A brick. At least I'd found his location. He'd be watching everything from the Ops center.

That was probably how they intended to kill me— with the suit. It wouldn't take much. A small explosive in the helmet somewhere near the temple, and I'd be dead. That's how I'd have done it, had the roles been reversed. Zentas had surely thought through all my possible moves. I'd certainly thought through his. I had no choice but to play it straight.

Or make it appear that way for as long as possible.

As if to accentuate the point, Zentas showed up at the

inner door. He had on a headset and spoke into my helmet on a private channel. "I'd like to think in another situation we'd have worked together willingly," he said.

"Maybe."

"We're a lot alike."

"Probably." I didn't like it, but I couldn't really deny it, given my history. I'm a hypocrite a lot of the time, but the odds in front of me made me introspective. It seemed pointless to lie to myself.

"Since I probably won't see you again, I guess this is farewell. I'd wish you luck, but I feel like your definition of that wouldn't end well for me," said Zentas.

"And I'd like to hope that we *do* see each other again. I'd enjoy that a lot." Say one thing for someone planning to kill you: you didn't have to be nice to him anymore.

I LAUNCHED MY mission twelve minutes after confirmation of the first 'vert attacks. After situating my three missile launchers in a clearing about five kilometers away from my planned battle area, I landed with my first twelve bots in a large clearing about three hundred meters from Dome 19B. The dense jungle obscured the dome from my location, but I'd looked at it from every angle during reconnaissance. It was considered a mid-sized facility, at about ninety meters in diameter and thirty-one meters high at its apex.

My line of sight ended about thirty meters away at the edge of the clearing, made worse by the water slicking off my faceplate. Sunset in the jungle meant low light, so I toggled my viewscreen to infrared assist, giving me a composite picture of the world that approximated dusk in an environment with less vegetation. I used infrared with my FL-207 scouts as well and relied on their AI to give

me a count of the 'verts they found. The composite estimate came in at right around two thousand. That clearly
pushed me past my decision criteria for how to engage. I'd
have to use the missiles to have any chance.

Since I'd lost the argument for more time, I had about
ninety seconds to get everything set. I sent orders to the
twelve Mark XIs, spreading them into a skirmish line
along the back of the clearing, pushing far enough to each
flank to cover the front area of the dome. I didn't intend
to stop the primates. I couldn't. The 'verts were coming
fast, and the bots could only shoot so many. Instead, I
wanted to put up a wall of bullets in front of the dome
and push the 'verts out to each side, let them flow past the
dome. Once past it, I didn't think Zentas could get them to
come back, and there weren't any other occupied facilities
within five kilometers. I assumed most of his transmitters
would focus on driving the pack toward us. Was *pack* the
right word? What did you call a group of alien primates?

No time for that.

One of the FL-207s tracked the main body of the 'verts,
feeding me real-time information. I peeled the other three
off to look deeper, to search for a second wave. I hoped
there wasn't one, but I had to be sure. It also gave me an
excuse to use the FL-207s for the secret part of my plan.
Nobody hit the kill switch on them, so I could assume they
hadn't picked up on my intentions yet. The rain stopped.
Thank the Mother for small blessings.

I held the second transport aircraft containing ten more
Mark XIs in a circular pattern about a minute out. I wanted
to assess the initial contact before I committed them. The
military would see it on radar, but it identified as a transport for one of Caliber's subcontractors, so they wouldn't
react. I had two options programmed: I could air-drop the
bots right in front of the dome to make a final stand, or I

could drop them behind the first wave of 'verts. Zentas had pushed back on that, but I won that argument. We didn't know how the primates would react when the shooting started. Perhaps they'd run, but just as likely they'd attack. If that happened, I wanted the option to attack them from the other direction. Confusion and chaos were my friends. If I got the animals disoriented and moving in a bunch of different directions, it bought me time. More important, it bought Oxendine time. If I could hold out long enough, she'd eventually get her troops into the fight. It might not save me, but it might save a lot of other people.

I pulled a set of preprogrammed targets out of a save file in my helmet and prepped them for the missile launchers. This was where it got tricky. I'd planned a lot of moving parts, making it almost impossible to track all of them at once, figuring if I struggled to track it, so would someone watching me. With things set, I started moving through the jungle, back toward the dome.

Zentas's voice sounded in my ear. "Carl. Where are you going?"

"I'm getting out of the line of fire. The only way this works is if I'm alive and controlling the battle. It wouldn't do for me to get killed in the first wave." As I suspected, he was watching me. Good. *Watch the shiny object and pay no attention to the sleight of hand.* While I spoke, I had one of the FL-207s use its sonar sensor to do a quick search through the low-frequency band. Risky, but I did it quickly—on and off in under three seconds. I hoped nobody noticed, or, if they did, they didn't understand what they saw. It fed me the hit I needed. A single set of coordinates, and then another. Two transmitters.

"You running away wasn't part of the plan."

"Did you think I was going to lead the charge? I'm getting behind the giant fucking robots."

Mercifully, Zentas shut up. I kept moving, pulling a second set of coordinates from a file as I walked. I readied them beside the first, doing a quick rotation of the lines of targets I'd preprogrammed to line them up with the two hits from the FL-207. I had two data points, and that made a line. A quick mental calculation showed the points as five-hundred meters apart, which confirmed what I'd learned about the range of the transmitters back at Caliber before I got captured. I assumed that the transmitters were deployed in straight lines. That was the most unimaginative, basic way to do it, and the easiest. They'd need line after line—a grid—turning them on as the primates passed to keep the 'verts moving.

I was about to see what happened when part of that grid failed.

If someone didn't stop me.

The coordinates showed right there on my heads-up, which others could see, but they were just columns of numbers. It would take work to translate them to a map, and only someone intimate with my thinking would immediately jump to the correct conclusion. I didn't intend to give them that much time.

The ground vibrated beneath me, providing warning before I even heard the 'verts. A few seconds after came violent crashing, the sound of branches breaking. I picked up my pace toward the dome and simultaneously sent both sets of coordinates to my missile launchers and fired them. Each weapon system had sixteen munitions, and I was burning half of that on the first volley. That done, I pulled up the video feed from the center bot. I didn't have to watch—their programming directed them to destroy a single type of target, and they'd do that automatically and as efficiently as they could—but I wanted information. I wanted to see. I had ten more bots to drop.

The first 'verts broke from the jungle into the clear, then went down in a volley of high-velocity, large-caliber bullets. Dying primates tumbled over one another, some blown backward, some staggering forward before falling. The distinctive sound of the heavy guns echoed until inhuman screams drowned it out.

Then the missiles hit.

Even from two hundred meters away, the impacts shook me. My helmet dampened the outside noise to protect my hearing, and the clearing disappeared from my video screen in a gout of dirt and dust and flying metal. I stumbled. Trying to watch video and run through a jungle at the same time wasn't easy.

Time stood still as I waited for the field of view to clear. More missile impacts in the distance announced my other purpose, which started a mental timer in my head. It wouldn't take long for someone to notice that I'd targeted twelve missiles—half of my volley—against suspected transmitter positions. I'd tried to hit three rows of them, four in each row. If successful, I'd have opened a huge gap that would allow the 'verts to retreat.

The dirt cleared, and the edge of the jungle came into view through the dust. Nothing moved. As my helmet returned my normal hearing . . . silence. I stood there for several seconds.

It had worked.

The closer missile barrage had arrested the momentum of the 'vert pack. If I'd gotten the transmitters, maybe they'd head back the other direction.

A screech—hundreds of screeches, joined together in one symphony of pissed-off primate—echoed through the jungle. They'd fallen back, but not far. The bots scanned for targets but didn't fire. Crashing in the jungle . . . it took me a moment to realize that it wasn't getting farther away. They weren't retreating.

The crashing came closer.

The bots turned as the 'verts swarmed in from the sides. Whether simple survival instinct or something else, the 'verts now avoided the clearing and ran and leaped in and around the bots on the flanks.

I ran too.

I tripped as I worked to toggle the video off so I could focus on the ground around me, catching myself just before my faceplate hit the dirt. I struggled back to my feet and kept going. My own survival instinct warned me my time was about up. Someone had their finger on a button that would pop an explosive in my helmet at any second. Zentas wouldn't tolerate my running away. I didn't have a choice. Running back toward the killer bots and the screaming, pissed-off primates would end me just as surely.

I needed more time. I had one last move to make, and I couldn't make it without my helmet. I forced myself to calm down. Hurrying would cause mistakes. Slow is smooth, and smooth is fast. I triggered the drop point for the second set of bots right at the edge of the dome. Hopefully I'd make it to them before the 'verts got me. I could make my last stand there.

Then I did the smartest and stupidest thing I could do: I flipped the safety switch on my helmet and popped it off in one move.

The acrid smell of smoke and burning flesh hit me, almost making me gag. I tossed my helmet and started running for the dome but spared a glance back when it popped and started smoking. *Too late, asshole.* As I expected, they'd implanted a micro-explosive in it. Just enough to kill me. In about three seconds I'd learn whether they had a backup in the suit. I didn't have time to remove it. The 'verts wouldn't wait.

Losing my helmet had two major drawbacks. One, I'd now exposed myself to the hostile environment again and had about twelve hours to live, most of which would be spent in agony as different microbes and bacteria destroyed my body from the inside out. The more immediate concern, however, was that I no longer had any control over the battle. Now it was just me, running through the jungle, trying not to die. And I couldn't see. The lights in my helmet had gorked my night vision and it was getting close to dark under the jungle canopy.

It started raining again.

It was oddly freeing. Not the rain . . . the lack of control. I *wanted* to be in control, but now that I couldn't do anything, it felt good. I put one foot in front of the other and picked my way through the undergrowth. Shots still rang out behind me—at least some of the bots were still fighting. Closer, though, came the sounds of branches breaking and vegetation crunching, punctuated by intermittent screeches. Cool water ran down my face and neck, starting to soak my undergarments from the inside.

I broke into the open, almost stumbling again, then catching myself. They'd cleared the vegetation around the dome, and a few lights inside lit it for me in the approaching twilight. Unfortunately, I had sixty meters to go and no entrance in sight, even if I got there. And no more jungle to provide cover from whatever came from behind me.

A ship whooshed overhead, and I glanced up. That would be my bots, coming to save me. I didn't have to get inside the dome. I just had to get behind the giant killing machines.

A golden-orange flash blinded me, followed about two seconds later by a bone-jarring explosion. I hit the ground by instinct, purple spots in my eyes. The loamy scent of wet dirt filled my nose, and it took me a second or so to process what happened.

My bot ship had exploded.

Shit.

*Of course* it exploded. When he lost contact with me, Zentas destroyed it. I hadn't even thought about self-destruct devices in the transport. *Stupid.* A second later a two-ship of military jets screamed overhead. Maybe Zentas hadn't killed his own ship after all. That fit my luck if Oxendine's assets showed up just in time to splash my only hope for survival.

I jumped to my feet and started running again. I didn't think the jets would have clearance to attack the primates, but they might. My dying as collateral damage would be sweet irony to some historian down the road. If the fast-movers *did* start unleashing ordnance, every meter I could put between myself and their targets would help.

I had about thirty meters to reach the dome when I sensed the 'verts behind me. I stopped and turned. The dome didn't matter. Being so close with no way to enter was like being on a saltwater ocean and needing a drink.

I could barely pick out the 'verts in the low light, their dark green skin and fur blending into the background. I detected them by motion, my eye drawn to movement. I spotted three, then a fourth. For some reason they hesitated at the edge of the cleared area. Maybe they'd learned their lesson from when the last clearing turned into a killing field. They didn't know that I couldn't repeat that here. I didn't have any bots, and I no longer had control of the missiles. Not that I could use them this close, even if I did.

A series of explosions rumbled behind them—bombs from the jets, if I had to guess—but much too far away to affect me.

One of the primates screeched, and they charged.

Shit.

What had been four became ten, then more. I couldn't count. I couldn't move. My brain told me to do something. Anything. Maybe curl into the fetal position and hope they ignored me. But I couldn't force my body to act. For all that I'd thought about death in the past, in that moment I didn't want to die. Maybe my therapist would call that a breakthrough. Guess I'd never know.

The first 'vert reached me and swung a massive hand in a looping arc. I dropped to the ground, almost fast enough to get under the blow, but not quite. The heavy punch glanced off my upper back, driving me down into the dirt. The pain didn't register, though it probably would once the adrenaline left my system. I curled into a ball, thinking in that split second that if I took a submissive posture, maybe it wouldn't hit me again.

A series of small explosions lit the night around me, leaving spots in my vision. The beast let out a horrific screech, then went silent, shaking the ground as it fell. More 'verts cried out around me. More explosions. It took me a moment to place the sound: the thin popping of explosive bullets delivered by Bitches. I tried to dig myself into the dirt. Someone—a group of someones—was firing from behind me, and I didn't want to get caught in the fire as they lit up the primates.

Something loomed over me, just a shadow, silhouetted by the faint light coming from the dome, and for a second I thought another 'vert had come for me.

"How's it going, sir?"

Mac.

I couldn't speak. My brain spun, trying to figure out how he got there. He was on a ship, long gone from the system. Except he wasn't. Or I was hallucinating. The speaker from his helmet might have altered the voice. Maybe it just sounded like him.

"Mac?" I asked, finally.

"Come on, sir. Let's get you to a medic." *Mac.* He reached a powerful hand down and I took it, allowing him to pull me to my feet.

"How?"

He led me back the way he'd come, toward the edge of the dome and away from the rapidly dwindling fight. "Those two women you have on the team? Ganos and the captain . . . turns out, they're pretty smart."

"They're still here too?" I asked.

"Of course. No way I'd be here without them. They did all the work. I just came along with a pile of grunts."

"But you left the planet."

"Ganos faked that. And before you ask, the captain convinced the general to send a mission out here. Told her exactly what to watch for. Now, can we get you to a medic?"

"We need to stop Zentas. He's at—"

"He's at a secret base, we know. The captain is on the team going to take down the facility and capture him. One of the drones we had from that kit of goodies you received picked you up outside."

"What are the fucking odds of that?"

"Pretty good. The captain had them looking."

"Wow. She did good."

"No lie, sir. You probably need to watch out for your job with that one around."

"I'm safe. I'm retired, remember?" I laughed, and it turned into a cough.

"Okay, sir. Medic. Now."

That was the best plan I'd heard all day.

# CHAPTER THIRTY-ONE

THE REHAB FROM environmental exposure didn't hurt any less the second time, though given the alternative, I didn't complain. Soldiers guarded the outer door of the containment rooms in the hospital—I chose to think of them as a protection detail, not jailers, but in reality, that wasn't settled yet. I'd been under duress, but I'd still killed a bunch of 'verts—one more entry on my résumé for the war-criminal hall of fame—and helped Zentas and his crew do a bunch of other illegal stuff. And I hadn't exactly been an angel even before he'd captured me. Add to it the conflicting jurisdictions of the government and the military, and a lot had to get sorted out before a decision came on my freedom. The guards did let people visit, though, as long as they came in one at a time. That worked for me. My conversations would be monitored, but I had things I wanted to discuss with people individually, and the situation at least gave the illusion of that.

Mac waited with me, of course. Mother help whoever thought they'd stop him from doing that. He'd brought in a chair and set up camp just outside my bubble. Nobody would get to me without going through him. Even when he had to step out when people visited, he didn't go far.

"What are you going to do now that the mission's over?" I asked him.

"Don't know, sir. I've got enough time in to retire. I'd never really considered hanging it up before, but now? Maybe. Not sure where I'd go, though."

"There's a lot of land available on Ridia."

"What would I do there? I'm not cut out to be a farmer."

"Work for me. I've pissed off some powerful people. I doubt they're going to leave me alone just because I call it quits and go home." Selfishly, I wanted somebody near me that I knew. Someone I could trust.

"You think someone will come after you?"

"Given how things tend to go for me, you think they won't?"

Mac laughed. "I'll give it some thought."

"Ganos is here," I said.

"I'll be right outside."

Ganos entered, grinning like an idiot, which warmed me inside. She must have found a hairstylist, because she sported her same short cut in a fresh shade of blue. "You look like shit, sir."

"Thanks. I only feel slightly worse than that. You look good. I like the hair."

"Thanks. I've heard that the meds for exposure are a bitch."

"How'd you do it?" I left the question open-ended. She'd tell me what she wanted to, and that was enough.

"I faked our departure, which was pretty easy, and then I went after Caliber hard. I found evidence in their system of multiple facilities out in the jungle, and the captain took it from there."

"You know that Zentas will probably go free. Even if he doesn't, the corporation will still be there. They might come looking for you." I worried that I'd ruined her life. Again.

She clenched one fist and smiled. "I won't be hard to find. I'll be in the new house Parker just bought for us with the money I got for this job. Let them come. I'll be ready."

I believed her. "Ganos . . ." She met my eyes, and we held the look. "Thanks. You're amazing."

She waved it off. "Come on, sir. Who are you talking to? Of course I am. By the way, I checked through your messages while you were detained to see if I could find any clues. There wasn't anything important other than a note from General Serata. I didn't read that one. You want me to forward them to you here?"

I thought about it. "Nah. Delete them all."


I EXPECTED FADER next, but Oxendine came in first. She probably pulled rank. Or maybe she didn't have to. Fader would have deferred and done what she thought was proper. Or maybe not. How well did I really know her? I'd expected her to honor her word and take the team off the planet, yet here we were.

Thank the Mother.

Oxendine had an unlit cigar in her mouth, which she removed before triggering the speaker.

"You bring a cigar into a hospital?" I asked.

"You're all of a sudden a stickler for rules?" She had a point. "There's a lot to figure out in this case." Straight to the point, as always. We disagreed on how a lot of things should work, but we both appreciated directness. "The level of illegal activity . . . it's unprecedented. I think there are seventeen charges against you right now, unless they've come up with more during my walk over here."

"I was trying to save lives. I have nothing else to say until I speak to my attorney. He's on another planet, by the way. It may take a while."

"Can you let me finish, Carl? Just once can you shut your mouth and let someone else talk?"

Well that hurt. It was a fair shot, though. I was feeling defensive, which made me chatty. "Sure."

"As I was saying, there are a bunch of charges against you, but I think we'll be able to cut a deal, assuming you'll give evidence against Zentas and Caliber."

"Gladly."

"I didn't think that would be an issue. No promises, but once you're done in quarantine, you are released on your own recognizance. Don't leave this dome, and don't leave the planet until I give you the go-ahead."

I gestured to the medical hookups in my arm. "If I have my way, I'm never leaving the dome again until I can leave forever. The planet . . . My job here is done."

"We'll get you out of here as soon as possible. I can assure you, nothing would make me happier than putting you on a ship to somewhere else."

I laughed. "Fair enough."

"One more thing . . . I'm letting you know as a courtesy. I've made inquiries about Captain Fader."

"She was doing her job. Anything that happened is my fault," I said.

"And she was doing it well, *despite* it being your fault. I'm asking to have her put on my staff here."

I hadn't expected that. "Ah. Well, that's certainly your prerogative. I'm not sure who will make that decision, but it won't be me."

"But you can certainly influence it."

"I'll talk to her and see what she wants. I think she's earned that."

"She has. But Carl . . . despite how she pulled this off, she's not like you. You know that. She and I see the world the same way. You know how valuable it is to have a boss like that. Talk to her, but keep that in mind as you do."

"I will," I promised. She had a point. They *were* a lot alike, and Fader could do worse than to model herself after Oxendine. She'd never be like me, and that was okay. There was more than one way to be an officer, even if I forgot that sometimes. "Do you think Zentas will be prosecuted?"

"Honestly?" she asked. "I doubt it. He'll take a public-relations hit when all this comes out—and it *will* come out. It always does. People have seen your report. Someone will leak it. But do I think he'll ever see even a day in a cell? No. He's rich. Who knows, though. Maybe we'll get him. Stroud jumped up quickly to volunteer to testify, which will help."

"She's not being charged?"

"She claims she was in the dark."

"You believe her?"

"Hard to say, but after talking to her, I think I do. Even if I didn't, I'd cut a deal to get the bigger fish."

I agreed with that, considering I'd used that very rationale a few times since I'd come colonyside. "Being rich shouldn't be a defense."

Oxendine gave me a sad smile. "But we both know it is. Still, we do our part, and we do it the best we can. It's all we can do."

I nodded. I wished I had her attitude. It was so much healthier than mine. But I wasn't wired that way. Then again, what could I do? Find Zentas and kick his ass? The idea did have some appeal, but it was a dream. "Where is he now?"

"Already on a ship."

"His own?" I asked.

"Nope. One of ours. I won that argument."

"Good. I hope he's uncomfortable." I could live with a little bit of pettiness.

Oxendine laughed. "Seriously, Carl. Thanks."

"For what?"

"For doing what I couldn't do. Finding the illegal out-posts. It was my job, but I didn't do it."

I understood her being hard on herself, but I cut her some slack. She'd done better than I could have if our roles were switched. "They hamstrung you from the out-set and it falls under the governor's purview. It's not your fault."

"I'm the commander. It's always my fault."

I couldn't argue against that, but her acknowledging it made it better. "Speaking of the governor, what came out of this with him?"

"He's in damage-control mode. He fired Davidson and blamed as much as he could on her, and he's ac-tively seeking maximum penalties for the violations we can prove."

I laughed. He'd taken my advice. "Is it working?"

"Hard to say. The real judgment on that will come from Talca. It might be a few weeks until we can assess the political fallout."

"Sure." I sat quiet for a moment, when something came to me. "Oh, one other thing. Your hacker, Trine. Eddleston told me that she got off planet. She probably used an alias and fake papers, but she hasn't had time to get anywhere, so you can probably put out a call to search anything that left here in the past few days when it arrives wherever it's going."

"I'll do that. Thanks."

"Take care, Ox." It still felt weird to call her that. "I wish I could say I was glad I came."

She laughed. "I wish I could say *I* was glad you came."

"Send Fader in, would you?" I asked.

"Sure. Take care, Carl."

Fader entered as she left.

"I heard you were on the mission to take down Zentas's facility. Did they put up a big fight? I know they had some soldiers there."

"A few shots, but we came in by air and took them by surprise. We also brought a ton of firepower. Surprisingly few people want to die for a paycheck."

"Eddleston—"

"We got her, sir. Karlsson too."

"Tell me Eddleston resisted and you had to shoot her."

"No, sir."

"That's too bad."

"How are you, sir? Everything okay?"

"I think so. General Oxendine and I have come to something of an agreement." I didn't explain it. As well as Fader had done, my understanding with Oxendine was above her pay grade.

"That's good. You were doing the right thing."

"Maybe. I took things upon myself that I probably shouldn't have. Don't get me wrong . . . I'd likely do it again. But that doesn't mean there wasn't a better way."

"You got the job done, sir, just like you said."

"I didn't. *You* got the job done. I charged in and got myself in trouble. You sat back, figured it out, and made it happen. Without you, I'm dead, and Zentas's plan works."

She fidgeted, clearly uncomfortable with the praise. She'd have to get used to it. "I'm glad you're okay, sir."

"Thanks. Of course, I thought I told you to get Mac and Ganos on a ship and leave."

"And I thought you showed me that you don't always follow the rules."

I laughed. She was still a step ahead of me. "Oxendine wants you to come work for her."

"She mentioned that. I don't know. I've got a good job."

"You've got a political job. Yes, it's a good one, with a lot of visibility. But if you work for Oxendine, you'll learn how things work at the level where things really happen. She's a good officer."

"You think I should take it, sir?"

"I do. You've got a big future. You need to prepare for it." I smiled. "Just don't let Oxendine get to you so much that you forget everything I taught you."

She laughed. "What are you going to do, sir? Are you hooked again?"

"Not me. I'm going back to Ridia. Nice and quiet. I like it there. That's assuming that the charges against me get dropped."

"Come on, sir. You don't expect me to believe that. You liked this. The military needs you."

"They don't need me," I said. "They've got you."

# ACKNOWLEDGMENTS

*Colonyside* was a much different experience for me as a writer than the previous two books. With *Spaceside,* I knew I was struggling at points, and the book didn't come together until right near the end of the process. With *Colonyside*, I thought I had it in good shape and really didn't figure out the issues until much later, at which point I rewrote about sixty percent of it. For this, I owe a debt to my editor, David Pomerico. David earned his money on this one, as he did some heavy lifting. His notes made this book what it is. As always, any faults that remain in the book are my own. To the rest of the Voyager team, thanks also, for always making things easy. Every time I deal with anyone at Voyager on anything it feels like they really want what I want, which is to put out the best book we can in every way. Special thanks go to Andrew Gibeley, who has moved on, but who I credit with getting *Planetside* and *Spaceside* in front of a lot of readers who wouldn't have otherwise found them. Ellen Leach is an excellent copy editor, without whom this book would have many more mistakes than it does. Any remaining errors are mine, not hers.

I'd like to thank my agent, Lisa Rodgers, without whom I wouldn't be here. She continues to make things easy for me—all I have to do is write. She's the best.

I'd also like to thank Joshua Bilmes, who is a tireless champion of his authors, and the foreign rights team of Susan Velazquez and Karen Bourne, who keep selling my books in other countries.

I'd like to thank Sebastien Hue for the outstanding cover art for both this and *Planetside*. I still believe a lot of people picked up the first book just because he made it look so good.

In my writing process I rely a lot on beta readers, and for *Colonyside*, I'd like to specifically thank Ernie Chiara, my brother Patrick, and my sister-in-law Melissa for their frank comments that helped shape the bones of the book. Rebecca Enzor is a great author who has read all my books early on in the process and continues to be one of my most important writer friends. Jason Nelson provided great input both on the writing and on some of the technical aspects of computing. I'm pretty sure Ganos wouldn't exist without him. I'd like to especially thank Dan Koboldt, who started out as my mentor and is now my staunchest ally in the author business.

Thanks go to R. C. Bray, who narrates my books for audio, and who is responsible for a lot of people finding my books because they listen to anything he records. R. C. Bray has always been the voice of Butler in my head, even as I wrote the first draft of *Planetside*. His narration brings so much to the series, and I couldn't ask for a better partner for audio.

Most important, I'd like to thank the readers. To anyone who ever picked up a copy of one of my books and then said to someone else, "Hey, you really should try this." Thank you. I really mean it. Without you— without people buying *Planetside*—*Colonyside* never happens.

Finally, I'd like to thank my wife. Publishing is an inconsistent beast, and there are times when you've got to do a lot of work. When you throw a day job on top of that, it can be tough. It gets easier when you have the love and support of a great life partner. I love you, honey.

# The
# PLANETSIDE
## series from
# MICHAEL MAMMAY

### PLANETSIDE

978-0-06-269466-9

When semi-retired Colonel Carl Butler answers the call from an old and powerful friend, it leads him to a distant base orbiting a battle-ravaged planet. His mission: find the MIA son of a high councilor. But witnesses go missing, evidence is erased, and the command is lying. To find answers, Butler has to go planetside, into the combat zone.

### SPACESIDE

978-0-06-269468-3

A breach of a competitor's computer network has Carl Butler's superiors feeling every bit as vulnerable. They need Butler to find who did it, how, and why no one's taken credit for the ingenious attack. This one screams something louder than a simple hack—as soon as he starts digging, his first contact is murdered . . .

### COLONYSIDE

978-0-06-298097-7

A CEO's daughter has gone missing and he thinks Carl Butler is the only one who can find her. Soon he's on a military ship heading for a newly formed colony where the dangerous jungle lurks just outside the domes where settlers live. It should be an open and shut case. Then someone tries to blow him up.

MAM 0121